POSSESSING VIOLET

CORRUPT OBSESSION, CORRUPT IDOL

DINAH HARPER

COPYRIGHT

This is a work of fiction. Names, characters, places, and incidents are either the product of the author's imagination or are used fictitiously, and any resemblance to actual persons, living or dead, business establishments, or locales is purely coincidental.

CORRUPT OBSESSION

CONTENT WARNING

This is an erotic novel that depicts a toxic relationship between step-siblings. This book has been banned from numerous retailers so read at your own discretion.

For a full list of triggers, you can visit my website:

https://www.dinahharper.com/corrupt-obsession-content-warning

CHAPTER 1
JESSE

"Please keep an open mind," Mom pleaded.

Jesse stared out the car window without taking in the scenery. This was the fourth guy Mom dated that she had introduced him to. The others hadn't lasted, and he didn't have high hopes for Isaac either. The men seemed nice enough, but no one could measure up to his dad. He knew it and so did Mom, but that didn't stop her from trying to find someone. She waited a year after Dad died before she started dating. He thought it was too soon, but late at night he heard her sobbing and knew she hated being alone. That didn't mean he had to like these guys, though.

"Isaac's a firefighter," Mom said.

He glanced at her, interested despite himself. Firefighters were bad asses. Not as cool as his dad being in the Air Force, but at least Isaac's job was more interesting than Tom, the store manager or Brian, who worked the front desk at a dentist's office. Mom briefly dated another teacher, Mr. Harding. He taught History, spoke in a monotone, and had awful coffee breath. They'd all been duds.

"Isaac can take you to the station and show you the firetrucks."

His lip curled, but Mom didn't see, since he'd turned back to the window. He wasn't a kid. He wasn't going to be bribed into liking this guy by a trip to the station... Though, it would be cool to sit in the driver's seat of a firetruck or slide down a pole.

"How did his wife die?" he asked.

Mom hesitated long enough for him to glance at her.

"Mom?"

"She walked out."

"Walked out?" he repeated, unsure what that meant.

"He woke up and she was gone. She packed a bag and left him with their two-year-old daughter. That was eleven years ago."

He jerked forward, making his seatbelt lock. *Daughter?*

Mom gave him an innocent look. "What's wrong, son?"

"You can't date a guy who has a daughter!"

Mom's lips twitched. "Why not?"

"Girls are annoying! They're always giggling, talking, crying..." He glared as Mom snickered. "Find a guy with boys or no kids at all."

"Sorry, honey, that's not how this works."

"A girl," he said in disgust. So far, none of the men Mom dated had kids, so it hadn't even occurred to him that he could have a step sibling.

"Her name's Violet."

"What kind of name is that?"

"Violet's a lovely name. It's a beautiful color, flower, and a candy I'm quite fond of."

"Have you met her?"

"No, we're going to meet her for the first time together," Mom said as she turned into the park. "I'm sure she's sweet. You two are just a year apart. You should have a lot in common."

"She's a girl," he growled. "We won't have anything in common."

Mom pulled into a stall and killed the engine before she turned to him, her expression unusually grave. She reached out and cupped his chin. "It's been hard since your dad died."

Her eyes watered, but she smiled anyway, pushing through as she always did.

"That's an understatement. Losing your father is the hardest thing that's ever happened to us, and it's been rough. Some days I wasn't sure I could get out of bed, but you helped me pull through. You're your father's son, all right. Strong, brave, wise beyond your years. I'm not sure I would be intact without you, but..." She stroked his cheek. "I don't want you to shoulder more adult responsibilities than you already have. You shouldn't worry over things I need to take on. I want you to have a childhood and enjoy life, even though the world seems a little less bright without your dad in it."

He swallowed hard as his eyes stung with tears.

"We need to let people in." She tipped her head to the side. "I think Isaac's a good man and if you give him a chance, I think you'll see that for yourself. Isaac and I enjoy each other, and we want to see how you and Violet get along. If it doesn't work..." She shrugged. "Then it isn't meant to be. But Violet may surprise you. From the stories Isaac's told me, his daughter isn't like the girls you're used to."

He frowned. "What does that mean?"

"You'll have to see for yourself." Mom scanned the park and then lit up. "There they are."

He followed her gaze and saw a tall, burly man kicking a soccer ball across the grass to a girl who looked tiny from this distance.

"Ready?" Mom asked.

"Sure," he said with a shrug, and pushed open his door.

He put his hands in his pockets as they approached the pair. The girl darted forward with a speed that made him blink. He was impressed with her control of the ball, but Isaac was no slouch and blocked her attempt to score a goal. Isaac was nimble for such a large man. When he darted toward Violet's abandoned goal, she let out a banshee scream before she launched herself at her father's legs in an illegal tackle attempt. Isaac's laughter rang out as his daughter fought like her life depended on it.

"Oh, my," Mom murmured, clearly taken aback by what they were witnessing.

Isaac grabbed his daughter who had both arms wrapped around his right leg to prevent him from kicking and tucked her under his arm as he scored. Violet's angry bellow made several people who had been watching their antics chuckle.

"You *cheated*!" Violet shouted.

"So did you."

"I'm allowed because you're ten times bigger than me!"

Isaac was about to reply when he spotted them. He strode over, casually toting his daughter under one arm like she weighed no more than a toddler.

"Lynne," Isaac acknowledged with a smile before he extended his hand. "And you must be Jesse."

He nodded and shook Isaac's massive leathery hand.

"Dad!"

Violet's impatient tone made Isaac grin before he set his daughter on her feet. She flung back a mane of tangled black hair. Her eyes were a striking hazel that sparkled with enthusiasm. She had pale skin, rosy cheeks, and her lips were a deep red he would have suspected was lipstick if she wasn't dressed like a boy in long khaki shorts and a striped, green shirt that was two sizes too big. The girls he knew wouldn't be caught dead in such an outfit, but Violet didn't seem to care about her appearance. He hadn't decided what to make of her when she smiled at him. His lips curved in response, his bad mood and the reason they were here in the first place, forgotten.

Violet switched her attention to his mom. "You're Lynne?"

"It's great to finally meet you."

Violet didn't shake hands. Instead, she gave Mom an exuberant hug and exclaimed, "I've never met one of Dad's girlfriends before!"

Jesse blanched at that label. He knew Mom dated, but he'd never thought about the men she dated as her boyfriend. He resisted the urge to stick out his tongue and looked at Isaac, who was staring up at the sky with an embarrassed expression that made Jesse feel better.

"Is that so?" Mom said, clearly pleased with this information. "He didn't tell me that I'm the first woman he's introduced you to."

Isaac removed his hat to run his fingers through his hair. "I didn't think there was any need to mention..."

"I've been trying to set him up with these women from church *forever*," Violet interjected. "But he's so..."

"That's enough." Isaac clapped a hand over his daughter's mouth and asked, "Are you two hungry? There's a food truck nearby."

"That sounds great." Mom nudged Jesse to get his attention. "Son? Would you like something to eat?"

"Sure."

He was disconcerted when Violet broke away from her father and grasped Mom's hand as if they'd known each other for years instead of two minutes.

"Dad says you're a teacher," Violet said.

"Yes," Mom murmured. "I alternate between kindergarten and second grade."

"Why?"

"I don't like to teach the same thing every year, so I bounce back and forth. Do you like school?"

"Yes, I love English and History the most."

"What do you love about those subjects?"

Walking behind them, he could see their profiles. The raptness with which they stared at one another told him more was happening beneath their surface level conversation. Mom and Violet were engrossed in one another, while he and Isaac hadn't exchanged a word. Violet was clearly of his mother's ilk, a free spirit, while he was more like his father— disciplined, rigid, and preferred routines.

He glanced at Isaac, who strolled beside him. He was watching his mom and Violet's exchange with great interest. He expected Isaac to butter him up like the others had, but Isaac didn't ask him what he wanted to be when he grew up or who his favorite sports team was. Isaac didn't attempt to make any small talk, which simultaneously annoyed and eased his nerves over this uncomfortable meet up.

They ordered tacos and settled on a picnic table. Violet was more interested in watching their parents than eating. She propped her chin on her hand and gazed at them with rapt attention. It was clear that as far as she was concerned, Isaac and his mother were meant for each other, but he wasn't so sure. He should be assessing Isaac, but his eyes kept returning to Violet's animated face. The way she looked at his mom with such longing made his stomach tighten.

"Jesse's a great soccer player," Mom shared.

Violet turned to him and sized him up. "You are?"

He shrugged, unsure why having her full attention made him feel funny. He talked to girls all the time. What made her different from all the rest?

"Let's play," Violet said, swinging her legs over the bench seat and leaping to her feet.

He glanced at Mom, who gave him an encouraging smile. By the time he started after her, Violet had crossed the field to retrieve the soccer ball and was making her way back to him. As she neared, he stopped and then braced when he realized she wasn't going to slow down. He grunted as she collided into him. He got a whiff of her hair, which smelled like strawberries.

"What do you think?" she whispered breathlessly, even though there was no one around.

"About what?"

She gave him an impatient look and jerked her chin in the direction of their parents. Was it his imagination, or had they moved closer to one another?

"Your mom's so nice."

Violet sounded awed.

"So ladylike and pretty." Violet cocked her head to the side as she watched them. "Dad's so happy. I've never seen him like this."

When he didn't comment, she looked up. Again, he felt that odd stirring in his stomach. Had he eaten something bad from the taco truck? No, it was the way she was looking at him. Something about her made him nervous, which didn't make sense. Girls flocked to him. They passed him notes in class, asked him to be their boyfriend, and did a lot of annoying things to get his attention. That didn't make him uneasy, but the way Violet looked at him, dead on, without the coy, flirtatious shyness he'd come to expect made him sweat. She treated him like they'd grown up together, instead of being introduced half an hour ago.

"How are your eyes green?" he muttered. "They were brown a minute ago."

"They do that," she said dismissively and dropped the ball at their feet as she said, "What do you think about my dad?"

"I don't know anything about him," he said truthfully.

"He's a good guy." She pursed her lips before she admitted, "Though he can be strict."

"My dad was in the military. I doubt your dad is as strict as mine was."

"Oh." Her expression softened before she reached out and rubbed his arm. "I heard your dad died. That must have been hard."

It was the worst that ever happened to him, but Violet's presence made the pain ebb for the first time since it happened. "I'm okay."

She nodded, taking him at his word, and stepped away. He let out the breath he'd been holding and watched her impressive dribble. When she tried to kick the ball past him, he instinctively stopped it and saw her eyes narrow.

"That was a practice shot," she said quietly.

"Sorry," he said, and stepped back to give her a clear shot. "You want to try again?"

"No. Let's get straight to it."

That had an ominous ring to it. He got a preview of how she played and believed she wouldn't use the same tactics on him that she had on her father. He was wrong. She had some skill, but she was a casual player, unlike him. He scored three times and was about to shoot his fourth goal when she kicked him in the shin.

As he dropped to his knee, Violet made her first goal and let out a triumphant shout. Across the field, Mom was on her feet with a hand over her mouth. He wasn't sure, but he thought Isaac was grinning. He gritted his teeth as he got to his feet. He couldn't fight dirty like her, but he was stronger and quicker. If he was unable to best a girl a year younger than him, then he didn't deserve a spot on the team this year.

He skillfully avoided Violet's fouls and scored goal after goal. He was having the time of his life, while she became steadily more aggravated. When she lost her temper and swore at him, he was so shocked, he stopped in his tracks. Violet seized the opportunity to take the ball, but she didn't get more than two paces before he stole it back. Violet lost her temper and tried to punch him. He bobbed and weaved, slipping every one of her wild swings.

"Okay, I'm sorry," he said with a laugh and held his hands up in surrender.

"You're such a jerk face!" she shouted.

"It's not my fault you suck," he said, and instantly regretted his taunt when she lunged at him.

They tussled, rolling on the grass before he landed on his back with her on top of him. She planted her tiny fists on either side of his head as she loomed over him.

"You take that back!" she roared in his face.

Her face, filled with wrath, was just inches from his. Her wild hair blocked out the rest of the world. Clumps of it brushed across his forehead and cheek. It was soft and smelled awesome. He should be trying to gain control of the situation before she slapped him, but he was too enthralled to defend himself. She was the wildest, most beautiful thing he had ever seen. Something inside of him stirred, roused by the girl warrior straddling him.

His life had been filled with so much death and loss. He had no other family aside from his mother. He thought it was them against the world, but he had a sudden image of Violet at his side. She was so vivid and filled with fire and fight. Life with her would be an adventure. The tight ball of dread in his stomach that had been there since he lost both grandfathers at the age of six suddenly disappeared.

Violet was shouting, but he couldn't hear anything over the sound of his heartbeat. When she was suddenly lifted off him, he reached out to pull her back before he came to his senses and realized Isaac had a hold of her.

"Damn it, Violet! That's too far," Isaac snapped before he strode away with her once again tucked under one arm.

Mom knelt beside him. "Are you all right?"

A little lightheaded, he stayed put and folded his hands on his stomach as he looked up at her. "Yeah."

She brushed back his sweaty hair. "You held your own against her for a time."

He heard the amusement in her tone. Under other circumstances, he would have been irritated, but he was too busy sifting through the odd feelings and ideas Violet had evoked.

"You did the right thing, taking the high road and not retaliating when she kicked you in the shin."

"It's not a big deal," he said and sat up.

Isaac had taken Violet far enough away that they couldn't hear what was being said. He cupped her chin as he spoke to her. His face was stern and very unhappy. Violet's bravado was gone, as if it had never been. As her father lectured her, she deflated and began to blink rapidly. He got to his feet, dusting grass off his clothes, and started toward them.

"Jesse," Mom said in warning, but that didn't stop him.

Isaac broke off as he approached and faced him, while Violet stayed as she was with her head bowed.

"I apologize for Violet's behavior. She has a hard time controlling her temper. We're working on it."

"She didn't hurt me."

"She tackled you."

"I play football."

Isaac's severe expression eased slightly, but he said, "Thank you for letting her off the hook, but she owes you an apology."

Before he could say that wasn't necessary, Violet pivoted to face him. The sight of her eyes filled with tears made his heart stutter. He'd seen many girls cry, but none of them made him want to drop to his knees and beg her not to.

"I'm sorry," Violet said, rubbing her eyes with the back of her hand. "I didn't mean to hurt you."

"You didn't," he said and reached for her without knowing what he wanted to do. Desperately uncomfortable and aware that Isaac and his mom were watching, he tugged on his shirt before he turned his hat backwards. "I'm sorry I said you sucked. You're better than some of the guys on my team."

Violet's mouth kicked up on one side, even as a tear slid down her cheek. "Thanks." Her eyes flicked to Lynne. "When I play, I lose my head."

"She's competitive," Isaac said apologetically as he put an arm around Violet's slumped shoulders. "Since she's usually going up against grown men, we let her take any advantage she can get. I didn't know she wouldn't hold back when she's playing with kids her age."

"It doesn't bother me," Jesse said.

Isaac didn't smile, but the flash of approval in his eyes made him straighten a little, even though he didn't know how he felt about him just yet. He hadn't embarrassed Violet, as his father used to when teaching him a lesson. That told him a lot about the man. Though they hadn't had a one-on-one conversation, he found himself leaning toward Mom's opinion that Isaac was a good guy.

"I'm really sorry," Violet said, breath hitching suspiciously.

Jesse stiffened as more tears poured down her face. "It's fine," he said and would have stepped forward, but Mom moved first.

"It's okay, honey. Everything's fine," Mom soothed as she gave Violet a hug.

"I wanted everything to be perfect and I..." Violet hiccupped. "I ruined..."

"You didn't ruin a thing," Mom admonished. "Being passionate is a gift, we just need to know how to channel it and accept defeat gracefully." When Violet began to sob, Mom patted her back. "There's no reason to be upset. You didn't give Jesse a bloody nose or a black eye, which he's gotten from playing sports."

Violet raised her face from his mother's chest and looked at him with puffy eyes. "You're not mad?"

He shook his head.

Violet looked up at Lynne. "You aren't going to break up with my dad?"

"No, I'm not going to break up with your father," Mom said with a broad smile. "In fact, after meeting you, I think I like him even more than I already did."

Violet's eyes widened. Jesse was disconcerted to see that she'd somehow cried the green out of her eyes, and they were now brown again.

"Do you love him?" Violet asked.

"Violet!" Isaac said sharply and reached for his daughter, but Mom's response made Isaac freeze.

"I do."

Jesse's heart slammed against his ribcage. Mom hadn't told him she loved Isaac and from the look on his face, this was his first time hearing it as well. Violet looked like Christmas had come early. All of them were in various states of shock, while his mother calmly stroked Violet's hair.

"Love is a strange thing. It creeps up on you when you least expect it," Mom murmured.

"Are y'all getting married?"

"Violet."

Isaac's voice had lost all power. It was more of a croak.

"I don't know if your dad's in the same place as I am," Lynne said before she put her arm around Violet's shoulders. "I think you and I have given Jesse and your dad enough shocks for the day."

And with that, Mom and Violet strolled away, leaving him with Isaac. He waited until they were out of earshot before he spoke.

"Do you love her?" Jesse asked bluntly.

Isaac closed his eyes, tipped his head back, and stared up at the cloudless sky. His Adam's apple bobbed as he said, "From the moment I laid eyes on her." He took a deep breath before he looked back at Jesse. "The only other woman I loved like this walked away."

"Mom won't walk. She's a military wife. She'll stick with you till death."

Isaac nodded, but he looked troubled rather than thrilled. They both knew their lives had been set on a different course. He matched Isaac's pace as they followed in Mom and Violet's wake.

"You did well with Violet. I think she scares most boys," Isaac said.

"I don't scare easy."

"I can see that." A pause and then, "I'm not trying to replace your dad or rush things with your mom. We can take this as slow as you need. You let me know if it's too much."

Though Isaac could be saying this to win brownie points, he suspected the man was as honest as his daughter. If he wasn't comfortable with the speed of everything, Isaac would give him time. Since his father died, it seemed that days inched along. There was nothing to look forward to. Nothing piqued his interest like before. Now, everything was moving at the speed of light. He'd come here to meet a guy his mom was dating, and within the hour, he was ninety-nine percent certain this guy would soon be his stepfather.

When they joined Violet and his mother in the parking lot, Mom gave him a searching look and touched his shoulder before she went to Isaac. When she lifted her face for a kiss, Jesse turned away and found Violet in front of him, her gaze fixed over his shoulder. He knew the moment they kissed, not because he heard anything, but because Violet jumped up and down and silently clapped.

He wasn't prepared for her to fling her arms around him. She hugged him the way Mom had when she got the news that Dad died. It was tight enough to hurt, but coming from her, he found he didn't mind.

"We have to keep them together," Violet said fervently.

When he didn't respond, she looked up. The tears were gone, and her warrior spirit was back, making her eyes shine.

"You want us to be together, don't you? A real family?" Violet asked, hands twisting in his shirt.

When he didn't answer, Violet's expression fell. When Isaac called her name, she stepped back. The loss of her body against his made that ball of dread come back. As she started toward her father, he couldn't help himself.

"Violet!"

She looked back.

"I do want that," he said.

She gave him a megawatt smile that made his chest flood with warmth. She ran to her dad, who tucked her against his side. Isaac climbed into a white pickup truck and held up his hand in farewell as they drove away.

"I'm sorry," Mom said as he dropped onto the passenger seat. "I wasn't planning to say that. It just came out. You must be overwhelmed. I know it's too soon, but—"

"It's okay."

"It is?"

"Yeah." He reclined his seat a little and tossed his arm over his eyes, which were burning. He wasn't sure why. "I get it."

Mom clutched his arm. "You do?"

"Isaac's exactly what you said he was, and Violet..."

"She's never had a mother," Mom said quickly. "She's been raised mostly by her father's friends and families from church, since Isaac has long work hours. She just needs some guidance—"

"She's perfect just the way she is."

"Aww, that's sweet of you to say." Mom lightly punched his arm.

"Especially when you said girls are annoying, and you didn't think you'd have anything in common."

"You're right. She isn't like the girls I know, though she did cry at the end." He grimaced. "I hope she doesn't do that often."

Mom laughed as she started the engine and rolled down the windows. "Tears aren't always a bad thing. Sometimes, there are no words to express how you feel. The only thing you can do is cry."

He heard her sniffling and extended his free hand while the other arm stayed draped over his eyes. Mom grasped his hand and squeezed.

"I never thought I would feel like this again," Mom whispered.

He knew exactly how she felt because he felt the same. For the first time since Dad died, he was looking forward to something, and that something was seeing Violet again. Something about the way she'd looked at them, as if they were the answer to prayer, and they possessed something she desperately wanted, made him want to be everything for her that she would ever need.

With his father in the military, being an only child, and constantly on the move, loneliness was something he was very familiar with, and it was stamped all over Violet as well. The way she talked to him like they were on a team made his mouth curve. That hug she'd given him, he wished it had lasted longer. He wasn't sure what it was about her that had captivated him, but he wasn't going to examine it too closely. He was grateful for the break from the monotony, for something unexpected and intriguing to turn his life right-side up and bring color back to his world. He'd been trudging through life, but today he'd been offered an opportunity to rejoin the living, and he was going to take it.

CHAPTER 2
JESSE

5 MONTHS LATER

ISAAC GRIPPED JESSE'S SHOULDER. "ARE YOU READY?"

He looked up at Isaac and noticed that he had beads of sweat at his temple. He grinned and raised a brow. "Are you?"

"Of course," Isaac said gruffly as he smoothed a hand down the front of his suit. "I just wish we could have gotten hitched at the courthouse and avoided all this."

Isaac gestured to the church where their guests were taking their seats.

"Mom already did that with my dad. She wanted an official wedding this time around," Jesse reminded him, even though they'd heard her say it countless since Isaac proposed.

Isaac scanned the road. "They're late."

"Mom says women are supposed to be."

Isaac gave him an appraising look. "No nerves?"

"About what?"

"You aren't worried things will change once we're married?"

"No."

"What about the adoption?"

Mom and Isaac introduced the idea several days ago. Since they had no other relatives, Mom wanted to ensure he had family if anything happened to her. He didn't need Isaac to adopt him to know his stepfather would be there for him. Isaac was a man of his word, but they both knew it would give Mom peace of mind.

"Once you marry Mom, you'll become my dad. The adoption is just a formality," he said.

Isaac visibly relaxed. "I'm glad to hear that."

"But I'd like to keep my dad's name."

He was his father's legacy, the only insurance that the Sampson family name would continue.

Isaac nodded. "I expected that. You don't have to change your name. You're family whether you carry the Carr name or not."

He'd suspected Isaac wouldn't mind, but he was relieved to hear it, nonetheless. In five short months, he and Isaac developed a bond that rivaled the one he'd had with his father. The fact that he'd been given another strong father figure to guide him through life was a blessing.

"The only one who may fight you about keeping your name is Violet. She was set on all of us being Carr's," Isaac said with a grin. "But I know you can handle her."

"I'll talk to her."

Isaac gave him a considering look. "This has been a whirlwind and you two have taken everything in stride."

If only Isaac knew how much he and Violet had schemed to hurry along their nuptials. Mom didn't need to be convinced. She was in love with Isaac and, after losing his father, didn't want to waste any time. It was Isaac who needed to be prodded and coaxed. With the three of them on board, Isaac had no choice but to surrender, which he did by proposing two months ago.

Mom and Violet had taken over after that, resulting in this hasty wedding. Mom was happier than he'd ever seen her. It was patently clear that his mother hadn't loved his father the same way she did

Isaac. Was it meant to be that his father passed so he and Mom could find Isaac and Violet? The four of them fit together like they were meant to be. Life, for the first time in a long time, felt right.

Isaac straightened. "There they are," he said as a minivan turned into the parking lot.

Isaac hurried forward. Jesse followed in his wake, adjusting his tie. The first suit he'd worn was for his dad's funeral. He was glad it was a happy occasion that made him don his second suit.

"Late enough to make an entrance, not late enough to be rude," Mom's friend Molly announced as she leapt out of the driver's seat and came around to the side door. Molly eyed Isaac. "Shouldn't you be inside? It's bad luck to see the bride before the wedding."

"I don't believe in that stuff," Isaac said impatiently and stepped forward to open the door himself.

"Okay, okay. Hold your horses."

Molly slid the door open and a second later, Isaac breathed, "Violet."

Jesse stepped to the side to get a look and felt his heart skip. Violet perched on the seat, a vision in a pale pink gown. Her wild hair had been drawn back from her face into some kind of fancy braid, aside from two spirals that framed her face. Mom had been teaching Violet girly stuff like how to dress and do her hair, but this was such a drastic transformation from the girl he'd come to know that he was momentarily dumbstruck.

Violet had an uncharacteristically bashful look on her face as she took Molly's hand and carefully stepped out of the van.

"You look..." Isaac cleared his throat. "You're growing up too fast, kiddo."

Violet flashed him a smile before she turned to help Mom out of the vehicle. Seeing his mom as a bride in a white gown and short veil made his chest tighten. Molly stood off to the side, capturing the moment with a camera as they took each other in.

"You two look so handsome," Mom gushed, grinning from ear to ear.

"And you..." Isaac shook his head, clearly at a loss for words.

Jesse understood completely. As Mom and Isaac leaned toward one another for a kiss, Violet made her way over to him.

"Do I look okay?" she whispered.

"Okay?" he echoed.

She tugged on her skirt. "No one's ever seen me in a dress before. I feel silly."

"You don't look silly," he reassured her. "You look..." Like Isaac, he struggled to come up with the words that would let her know she outshined every girl their age. "You're perfect."

Even as he inwardly castigated himself, Violet's face cleared. "Really?"

"Yes."

Violet gave him a giddy smile and patted his chest. "You look great."

He cleared his throat and eased away from her, worried she'd feel his heart racing. He thought he'd overcome those odd nerves he sometimes experienced around her, but for the first time in months, they were back.

"How's Dad?" she asked, glancing over her shoulder at their parents, who were having a moment.

"Nervous, but hanging in there," he said and then blurted, "You're wearing makeup?"

Violet jerked her head back around, eyes wide and startled. "You can tell?"

"Yes."

During their parent's whirlwind romance, they became best friends and were nearly inseparable. His favorite pastime was observing Violet, who wore her emotions on her sleeve. He'd come to know her face as well as his own and immediately picked up the subtle enhancements—her already long lashes were thicker, and her lips were a shiny, muted hue instead of her natural deep red.

"Don't tell Dad," Violet whispered.

"I think you'll get a pass today," he whispered back. "But if he does lecture you about it, blame Mom."

Violet's eyes danced with mischief. "Good thinking." Violet extended her foot so he could show off her fancy shoes. "Aren't they pretty?"

"Yes. And you painted your nails?"

"My first time ever! I got glitter nail polish." She wriggled her toes, so they sparkled in the sunshine.

"You two ready?"

Violet whirled and threw herself into her father's arms. "I'm so happy! I never thought this day would come."

Isaac kissed the top of her head. "Well, now that it's here, we don't want to waste a moment of it, do we?"

"No! Let's do this!"

Violet winked at Jesse before she grasped her father's hand and towed him up the stairs to the church, where everyone waited for them.

He went to Mom and grasped her hands. Thanks to a growth spurt, he was now taller than her.

"You were right to push for a wedding and not get married at the courthouse and rob us of seeing you like this."

Mom turned her face away. "I love you, son, but don't. I'm hanging on by a thread. Save it for after the ceremony, please. I'm going to bawl if you…"

He placed her hand on his arm and patted it. "Got it."

He heard the strains of a sweet melody as they climbed the steps. As they approached the open double doors, he saw Isaac and Violet reach the stage. She stepped to the left, while Isaac stepped to the right. When the music changed, everyone got to their feet. Mom's hand trembled on his arm as they made their way down the aisle.

It was a modest crowd who'd gathered to celebrate this day with them. After he placed Mom's hand in Isaac's, he stepped to his stepfather's side.

"We're gathered here today in celebration of Isaac Carr and Lynnette Sampson," Pastor Sonny began.

Jesse's gaze moved from Mom to Violet. She was so excited, the bouquet of flowers she held, shuddered. As the ceremony progressed, Violet's expressive face showed a kaleidoscope of emotions. When Isaac slid a ring on Mom's finger, Violet blinked back tears.

Violet had a hard, defiant shell that concealed the most fragile heart he had come across. Violet loved hard. Mom gave him the psychology behind it—that never having a mother and Isaac being physically and somewhat emotionally absent made Violet cling to him and Mom. She wanted them around all the time and fretted when they weren't together. That wouldn't be an issue anymore. Now, they would be together forever.

"I now pronounce you husband and wife. Isaac, you may now kiss the bride," Pastor Sonny announced.

The church exploded with whistles and cheers as Isaac dipped Mom for a dramatic kiss. Violet clapped so vigorously; petals littered the ground around her. When Isaac and Mom started down the aisle, he offered his arm to Violet. She took it and leaned into him.

"This is the best day of my life," she whispered.

As he looked down at her, he heard himself say, "Me too."

"ARE YOU *SURE* Y'ALL ARE GOING TO BE OKAY?" MOM ASKED.

"Yes," he and Violet stressed at the same time.

They'd debated about this for weeks. Mom and Isaac offered to make their honeymoon a family vacation, but he and Violet insisted they go on their own. Isaac had been surprised, but pleased, but Mom clearly didn't like the thought of leaving them behind.

"Mom, I just turned fifteen," he reminded her.

"So?"

He rolled his eyes. "You're just going for the weekend. The neighbors are watching out for us, and we can call 911."

"But…"

"Honey." Isaac wrapped his arm around her waist. "We have to go, or we'll miss the plane."

Mom gave in by throwing her arms around him and Violet and drawing them in for a tight hug. "You two are the best kids. I love you to pieces, you know that? Please be safe and if you need anything, call us. We can always come home and—"

Isaac covered Mom's mouth and carried her toward the door that led to the garage. "I'll try to keep her from calling you every hour. If you're going to throw a party, now's the time since the house is such a mess, we wouldn't know the difference—*ow*!"

He yanked his hand from Lynne's mouth.

"Don't listen to your father, kids!" Mom scolded. "Don't leave the stove on, and make sure the doors are locked before you go to sleep."

"Yes, Mom," he and Violet said dutifully as Isaac dragged her out the door.

"I love you!" Lynne cried.

"We love you more!"

"That's not possible!"

He and Violet watched from the doorway as Isaac placed Mom in the passenger seat. As the truck reversed out of the garage, their parents waved while Violet blew kisses until the door slowly came down.

"They actually left us," Violet said, stunned.

"Want to throw a party?"

She snickered as she closed the door to the garage and made a big show of locking it before she turned and surveyed their new house, filled with unwrapped furniture and stacked boxes. "Is this real life? Pinch me."

He tugged on that curl in front of her face that had been driving him crazy. "This is real, all right."

The last thing he expected was for her face to crumple.

"Vi? What's wrong?" he demanded.

When he drew her against him, she burst into tears.

"Did someone say something?" he demanded over the sound of her heart-wrenching sobs.

It had been a hectic day with their parents tying the knot, followed by a casual lunch reception, which finished just in time for Mom and Isaac to catch their flight. Violet hadn't seemed upset. On the contrary, she was so over the moon, she couldn't keep still. So, where was this coming from?

"Tell me what happened."

She shook her head.

He rubbed her back and was momentarily distracted by the soft, buttery material of her dress. "Come on. Talk to me. You know I hate when you cry."

"I just..." She twisted her hand in his shirt. "I'm..."

He ducked his head to hear her better and caught a whiff of something sweet and alluring. Violet had been experimenting with perfumes. This one was new and definitely his favorite.

"I'm scared."

Her confession brought his attention back to her weird breakdown. "Scared of what?"

She raised her tear-streaked face and tugged urgently on his shirt as she babbled, "I'm scared something's going to happen! I've never been so happy in my life. I kept thinking something was going to happen before they got married. They'd break up or someone would get into a car accident or..." She groaned and slumped against him. "I wake up every day, thinking this must be a dream. That I made you and Lynne up and—"

"Why can't this be real?"

"Because good things don't happen to me!"

He tugged on her braid, which was coming undone. "What do you mean, good things don't happen to you?"

Heartbroken green eyes searched his. "I wasn't enough for my mom to stay. Dad loves me, but he's never known what to do with me. He was relieved to drop me off with other families so he could go to work. I've never had a home or real friends, and then you and Lynne come along, and you're so great, and you actually like me and..." Fat tears slid down her cheeks. "I'm so scared something terrible's going to happen and this will all disappear."

He clasped her face between his hands. "Nothing is going to happen."

He saw the flash of anger on her face, so was prepared when she tried to jerk away.

"How do you know?" she snapped.

"Because I'm not going anywhere."

"But what if something happens between Mom and Dad?"

"Then we'll figure it out."

"It's not that simple."

"Yes, it is. You're just making it complicated."

She shoved at him. "I knew you wouldn't understand."

He clutched her shoulders and gripped so she would pay attention and stop fighting him. "I understand better than you think. You think you're the only one who's felt lost and lonely? Who thought you and Isaac were too good to be true?"

She went very still.

"Mom and I were miserable before you brought us back to life."

Her lower lip trembled. "Really?"

He gave her a little shake. *"Really."*

She sniffled and looked down. "I'm sorry. I'm having a hard time taking it all in. New mom, brother, *and* house?"

"We deserve it, Vi. Life hasn't been smooth sailing for any of us."

"I guess."

When she rubbed the back of her hand across her face, removing the last of her makeup, he slid an arm over her shoulders. "What time did you wake up this morning?"

"I couldn't sleep. I was too excited."

She didn't fight him as he led her down the hallway.

"And terrified something was going to happen?"

She hesitated before she shrugged. "Maybe."

"You're exhausted." Belatedly remembering her bedroom was still a disaster, he led her to his. "You should shower and get some rest."

Violet headed for his bed. "Sleep sounds good."

"You don't want...?" he began, but didn't bother to finish when she flopped on his bed in her fancy dress.

He eyed her for a moment before he picked up her foot to undo the strap of her heel. She struggled to sit up.

"Oh, I'm sorry," she began. "I can..."

"I got it," he said as her shoe clattered to the floor.

She propped herself on her elbows and watched as he took care of the other shoe as well.

He raised his brow when he saw the odd look on her face. "What?"

"Dad expects me to take care of myself. I'm not used to anyone treating me like a child."

"I'm not treating you like a child. I'm taking care of you. That's my job." When she frowned, he shared, "When my dad died, Mom was in shock. I had to feed her for a couple of days, even help her get dressed."

Violet's eyes widened.

"It's drummed into me to care for my family. I was brought up knowing when my dad wasn't around, I was the man of the house."

"I guess that's why Dad talks to you like you're an equal, even though you're only a year older than me," she mused and tipped her head to the side as she examined him. "Your dad must have been really special. I hear Mom say it all the time, that you're just like him."

Unconsciously, he mimicked his father's military stance and clasped his hands behind his back.

"You're the best brother a girl could ask for, Jesse Sampson."

Something about the way she said that made his throat thicken.

He looked around for something to do, but he'd unpacked and arranged his room to his liking as soon as they moved in.

"Always taking care of everyone," Violet murmured as she settled back against the pillows. "Who takes care of you?"

He stiffened. "I take care of myself."

"Not anymore. You take care of me; I take care of you."

"I don't need anyone to take care of me."

"Yes, you do." She patted the empty space beside her. "Come lie down."

"What?"

"You may have gotten more sleep than me, but you're tired too."

"I'm okay."

Her eyes narrowed before she pouted and batted her wet eyelashes. "You're just going to leave me after I bawled my eyes out and confided my worst fears to you?"

He glared at her before he rolled his eyes and rounded the bed. When he stretched out beside her, she rolled into him. Her voluminous skirt flopped over his black slacks. He grumbled, even though her weight against him felt nice.

"I love you," she whispered.

He stopped breathing.

"I've said it to Mom, and she's said it to me, but you and I haven't... I just wanted you to know."

He couldn't speak past the obstruction in his throat, so he didn't say anything. Minutes passed. He stared at the ceiling and fought the pull of sleep but was just starting to drift off when she slapped his chest.

He jolted. "What was that for?"

"Aren't you going to say it back?" she demanded.

His mouth curved as he murmured, "I love you, Violet."

CHAPTER 3

JESSE

2 YEARS LATER

Jesse snagged a soda from a cooler and retreated to the shade. As he took a swig from the icy can, he took in the view. It was a beautiful summer day at the lake. Kids cannonballed off the pier under the watchful eye of their parents and the older kids who waited for their turn to ride one of the jet skis that someone had brought. The air was filled with gleeful screams, someone playing a guitar, and shouts from a football game.

He spotted Mom sitting on Isaac's lap near the grill. Isaac hadn't wanted to request time off from work to camp with church friends, but his smile said he was enjoying himself. Mom was a good influence on him. In the two years they'd been married, they had their fair share of disagreements, but they were happy.

"My turn!"

He followed the sound of Violet's voice and saw her wading through the water toward a group playing chicken. She stopped in front of Malcolm, a boy a year older than him. Malcolm leaned down to whisper something in her ear. Violet wore a one-piece bathing suit with shorts, but her back was completely exposed. Jesse's eyes narrowed as Malcolm's fingers brushed the base of her spine.

A second later, Malcolm sank beneath the surface, so Violet could hop on his shoulders. When Malcolm straightened, he reached up to steady Violet and took advantage of her position to grip her hips and smooth his hands down her legs. He playfully staggered, making Violet shriek and clutch at his head, the only thing available for her to hang onto. Malcom's broad smile said he was enjoying this a little too much for Jesse's liking.

He started forward as Malcolm and Violet faced off with Marissa, who was on Benny's shoulders. The guys moved forward so the girls could battle. Marissa was older and outweighed Violet by a good thirty pounds, but if he had to bet on either girl, his odds were on Violet. He was proven right less than five seconds later when Marissa toppled off Benny's shoulders and hit the water with a splash.

Violet did a celebratory shimmy as Marissa got back on Benny's shoulders. By the time he reached them, Violet had dethroned Marissa a second time.

Marissa sputtered as she came up for air. "Your sister's ruthless."

When he started to pass, Marissa grabbed his arm.

"You're taller than Benny. Maybe I can beat her if I'm on your shoulders."

He didn't answer her. His eyes were on Malcom. Instead of sinking into the water to let Violet off his shoulders, Malcolm coaxed Violet to slide down his front. Jesse's blood ran hot as Malcolm held Violet close while his hand moved over her bare back.

"Jesse?" Marissa prompted.

"Maybe later," he said shortly, and broke free of her to close in on his target.

"You want to ride with me on the jet ski?" Malcolm asked Violet.

"She's going with me," Jesse interjected.

Malcolm raised his head. Some of what he was feeling must have shown on his face because Malcolm immediately dropped his hand and eased back. "Hey, Jesse."

He grabbed the back of Violet's shorts and tugged her away from Malcolm.

"Violet knocked Marissa down twice," Malcolm shared.

"I saw," he said in a flat tone.

Malcolm held his gaze for a few seconds before he looked away. "I think I'll join the football game."

"You do that," Jesse said quietly.

As Malcolm headed toward the shore, Violet shaded her eyes with her hand and looked up at him. "Everything okay?"

He searched puzzled hazel eyes and knew she was oblivious to the liberties Malcolm had taken. As his gaze moved lower, his blood, already hot, went molten. From this angle, he could see down the front of her swimsuit. It took all his self-control to focus on her face and not the gentle swell of her breasts. The urge to go after Malcolm and put his fist in his face made him grind his teeth.

Violet cocked her head to the side. "Are you mad because I beat your girlfriend?"

"Ex-girlfriend," he growled and tugged on her strap. "I think you need to pull this up."

Violet stared at him. "Are you serious? I'm the most covered up girl here. I'm in a one piece *and* shorts. Did you not see Marissa's tangerine bikini? I was worried she was going to come out of her top when I pushed her in the water."

"I don't care what Marissa's wearing, I care what you're wearing. So, can you please...?" He tugged on the strap again.

"You're just as bad as Dad," she grumbled, though she did pull up her top so it covered her more adequately. "If it was up to you two, I'd still be shopping in the boy's department."

"That's not a bad idea," he said and grunted when she put her elbow in his stomach.

The days of Violet dressing like a tomboy were a distant memory. Though she still shied away from dresses, her clothes were now distinctly feminine. She dressed modestly, mostly to please Isaac, who looked pained when she wore anything too revealing.

"Are you really taking me on the jet ski?" Violet asked.

"Yeah, I'm next." He moved deeper into the water to flag down Logan, who was heading toward them.

"All yours," Logan said as he and his brother hopped off the jet ski.

He helped Violet on before he settled in front of her.

"You have to hold on to me," he instructed.

"Oh." She scooted forward and wrapped her arms around him. "Like this?"

"Tighter."

She attempted to crack his ribs as she tightened around him like a boa constrictor. "Like this?"

"Yup," he said in an even tone, and felt her arms tremble before she gave up and loosened her hold. "Ready?"

"Hold on."

He tried not to tense as she shifted around behind him to get comfortable. Plastered to his back as she was, he could feel the tiny, hard points of her nipples. Her thighs gripped him snugly. His hands tightened on the handlebars. The thought of her wrapped around Malcolm like this made his simmering temper go up a few notches. Over his dead body.

"Ready," Violet chirped.

He let out a long breath as he applied gentle pressure on the throttle. He glanced toward the shore and wasn't surprised to see Mom standing with her hands on hips. Isaac was reclined against the table, but made no motion to tell him he didn't have permission to take Violet for a ride. He held his hand up to reassure them that he would be safe before he headed out.

As they glided over the water, just the two of them, he relaxed. It had been a great weekend on the lake with friends and family. Summer was coming to a close. They would be back at school in two weeks. He was going into his junior year. Just two more years in Texas and then he would join the military. He stopped bringing it up because Mom tried to talk him out of it. She couldn't. He promised Dad he would follow in his footsteps. It was a done deal.

Violet smacked his stomach, disrupting his peace.

"Why are you driving like a grandpa?" she grumbled.

"I'm being safe."

"Come on, Jesse. How often do we ride jet skis? What if we don't do this again? We have this lake to ourselves. Let it rip."

"Mom would kill me."

"Mom isn't around."

He couldn't see her face, but he knew she was pouting. She lowered her voice to a tone she knew he couldn't resist.

"Please?"

"Just enjoy the moment, Vi."

"Maybe I should have gone with Malcolm," she muttered.

He craned his head around to look at her. "What did you say?"

She jutted out her chin. "You heard me. Why have all this horsepower if you aren't going to use it?"

She barely got the last word out before he gunned the throttle. The jet ski bucked beneath them. Violet let out a startled shriek, which immediately turned into a delighted whoop as they soared across the water.

"You're the best brother ever!" Violet screamed.

He grinned despite himself. Mom had tempered Violet's savage nature, but occasionally, her old recklessness made an appearance. It had gotten them in trouble countless times. He indulged her when he could so she wouldn't seek out trouble with a partner in crime who wouldn't have her back if things went south. Out of sight of anyone who would report back to their parents, he gave Violet the thrill ride she was seeking. He'd be damned if she asked Malcolm or any other guy for a ride.

As they made their way back to the pier, Violet squeezed him around his middle. "Can I drive?"

He hesitated. "You'll go slow?"

"Yes."

He didn't see it, but he knew she was rolling her eyes. "Fine."

He stopped so they could switch places. Once she was settled in front of him, he showed her the button for the throttle.

"Just apply a little pressure," he cautioned and bit back a curse when the jet ski jerked. "Vi!"

"I'm sorry." She giggled as she adjusted her grip until they were gliding forward at an easy pace. "I'm sad we're leaving tomorrow. This has been so fun!"

"It has been," he said, as they approached their group of over forty people. "Dad's enjoying himself."

"He always does. I don't know why he puts up such a fight."

"He's a recovering workaholic. Old habits die hard."

"Marissa's waiting for you," Violet sang. "She's been changing her bikini twice a day. Have you noticed?"

"No."

Violet turned to give him an arch look. "Seriously? Each one she puts on is brighter than the last." Violet's voice dropped as she muttered, "And smaller. Her mom is so embarrassed."

He grunted. He dated Marissa for two weeks in sixth grade, and she had been trying to convince him to be her boyfriend again ever since. He liked her as a friend and did his best not to lead her on, but she made it clear to him and everyone else that she wanted more.

"Lara's also been trying to get your attention. Every time she sings, she looks right at you."

He'd noticed and started excusing himself or making sure he could duck behind someone until she was finished. Lara was pretty, sweet, and had the voice of an angel, but when she wasn't singing, she was painfully shy and had a stutter.

As he brushed Violet's wavy black hair out of his face, he smelled the soft floral scent of violets and rose. The already delicate fragrance was faint from her time in the water, but knowing Malcolm had probably caught a whiff of it reminded him what had pissed him off in the first place. He gripped her waist. "You want another ride, you come to me. I don't want you going with anyone else."

"Why?"

"Because I said so." As the image of her legs draped around Malcolm's face came back to him, he tacked on, "And no playing chicken again either, unless you're on my shoulders."

"You're so weird," she muttered.

"Promise me."

"Fine, *Dad*," she drawled as she killed the engine.

He flinched, not liking that label one bit, but before he could say anymore, she slipped off the jet ski into the water. He stayed put and helped two girls get on before he swam toward shore. Violet joined Mom and Isaac near the grill and made herself a plate of food. With his family occupied, he tracked down Malcolm, who was making his way back to camp. He waited until they had distanced themselves from everyone else before he called out to him.

"Malcolm!"

Malcolm stopped and looked over his shoulder. Jesse saw his brows come together in a frown before it was replaced with an easy smile.

"Hey, Jesse, what's up?"

"I just wanted to give you a friendly warning."

His pleasant tone belied the inferno in his chest. They were at a church event. He couldn't get in a fight with the worship leader's son, but he wasn't going to let what happened with Violet slide.

Malcolm blinked. "Warning?"

"Yeah." He kept a smile on his lips as he loosened his grip on his temper so the heat of it leaked into his eyes. "Touch Violet like that again, and we're going to have problems."

Malcom's mouth sagged before he said in affronted tones, "I'm sorry?"

"You think I didn't notice you slide her down your front or look down her bathing suit?"

He saw a flash of guilt before Malcolm puffed out his chest.

"I don't know what you're talking about."

"Yes, you do. If I see you do that with Violet or any other girl who doesn't know what you're up to, you won't like what happens. You got me?"

Malcolm stepped back with his hands up. "I'm sorry, man, if you thought I was being inappropriate. I never meant to—"

"See that you don't," he said shortly, and turned away before he ruined everyone's day by breaking every finger Malcom had dared lay on Violet's skin.

<hr>

THEY GATHERED AROUND THE CAMPFIRE TO EAT, PLAY GAMES, TELL SCARY stories, and sing their hearts out. Everyone seemed to be having the time of their lives. Normally, Jesse would be in the thick of things, but he hadn't been able to shrug off his bad mood, even though Malcolm had taken his warning seriously and steered clear of Violet.

He sat on the fringes, observing, rather than engaging. His aggravation steadily increased as he watched his peers approach her throughout the night. He had never noticed how many male gazes followed her. Josiah tried to teach her how to play the guitar and spent a ridiculous amount of time positioning her fingers on the strings. He could tell within five minutes, Violet was over it, though she let Josiah talk to her for another ten before she excused herself.

When she made her way to the fire where they were making s'mores, Rhett offered her a toasted marshmallow on a stick. Violet reached for it eagerly, but her eyes flared when Rhett pulled it back and shook his head. Rhett said something. Violet grinned before she used her mouth to pull the marshmallow off the stick, which was obviously Rhett's condition for her to have it. Jesse was prepared to push Rhett into the fire, but Violet's laughter as she tried to eat the large marshmallow made him pause. He glanced around to see if Isaac or any other male thought what was happening was inappropriate, but everyone was in his spirits and oblivious to what was happening in their midst.

He raked his fingers through his hair. What the hell was wrong with him? His friends weren't trying to lure her out into the woods to have their wicked way with her. They were being overly attentive and toeing the line, but nothing that warranted getting their noses broken. That didn't mean he had to like it. She was too naive to see their true motives, but he did.

He was glad when Violet joined the women, but it wasn't long before some of the guys wandered over. When she rubbed her arms, Miles took off his hoodie and offered it to her. Violet blinked, clearly taken aback. Jesse shot to his feet, blood rushing in his ears. There was no way in hell Violet was going to wear some other guy's jacket. But Violet took the matter out of his hands when she politely declined Miles' offer and said she was turning in for the night.

Jesse fumed. He was angrier than he had ever been in his life. He was so pissed, if any of his friends came over to him, he wouldn't hesitate to put them in a chokehold. What was happening to him? He slumped in his chair and tipped his head back as he tried to calm himself. He'd always prided himself on being collected, pragmatic, and mature. He was none of those things right now. He wanted to ram his fists into something to take away the fire in his blood. Why? Because Violet almost put on another guy's hoodie.

He stared through the maze of branches to the twinkling stars and tried to think past the red haze. He had always been protective of Violet, but these amplified, aggressive emotions were dangerous. Since when did the sight of another guy touching her drive him into a killing rage?

He heard the chair beside him creak as someone dropped onto it before he heard, "You've been in a foul mood."

"So, you should leave me to it," he growled.

"Want to talk about it?" Logan asked cheerfully.

He clenched his jaw against the compulsion to fling his friend into the trees. "No."

"Do you want me to pray for you?"

He raised his head and glared at him. *"No."*

Logan drummed his fingers on the arm of the chair as he said, "Malcolm told me you threatened him."

He tensed. "It was a warning."

"You really think he was out of line with Violet?" Logan asked with a frown. "He's a good guy. It may have looked bad, but—"

"Don't, Logan. I saw him."

"He did it with others around. No one else thought what he did was inappropriate."

"No one was paying attention."

"Is Violet upset?"

"She had no idea what he was doing, but *I* do. I'm a guy."

Logan sighed and stretched his legs out. "I'm not saying you're wrong, but Violet's more than capable of standing up for herself if she was uncomfortable." He eyed Jesse's dark expression and sighed. "You have your work cut out for you if you police every interaction she has. What are you going to do, hide in the bushes when she goes on dates?"

"Who said she's going to date?"

Logan stared at him. "Are you hearing yourself?"

"She's fifteen!"

"Sixteen next month." Logan held up his hands when Jesse straightened. "Don't kill me. I remember the date because I went to her party last year." When Jesse switched his hostile gaze to the fire, Logan shook his head. "Violet's just a year younger than us. Why do you care if she dates? You do."

"She's a girl. It's not the same," he muttered.

"How old does she have to be before you let her date, Dad?" Logan dodged the soda can Jesse hurled at him. "Now, now. No littering or we'll get fined."

He surged to his feet. "I'm going to bed."

"You do that. I'll sit here a while and pray for you. I think you need it."

Jesse muttered under his breath and blinked rapidly so his eyes could adjust to the darkness as he made his way through the maze of tents. He unzipped his and fumbled with his phone for light before he flopped on his back, hands folded behind his head as he lay on his sleeping bag.

Logan's words knocked around in his head. Violet had never shown interest in his friends or talked about any boy in school that she had a crush on. She wasn't like other girls who wanted boyfriends to hold their hand during recess or make out behind the gym after school. Just the thought of her doing so made his blood pressure spike. Why did the thought of anyone asking her out make him feel like there was a demon clawing his insides, trying to get free?

Someone tugged on the zipper. "Jesse?"

He raised his head. "Violet?"

"I think Tina's getting a cold. Is anyone in there with you?"

"No."

He sat up and unzipped the tent. Violet crawled in, the tiny flashlight on her necklace revealing what she was wearing.

He grabbed a handful of the shirt that was four sizes too big for her. "Isn't this mine?"

"Yup," she said, supremely unconcerned, as she secured the tent and turned to examine his sparse setup. "Why is your tent so small? Or is it just that you're so big?"

"Just be grateful I have room, and you aren't being eaten alive by mosquitoes," he said testily as he unfolded his sleeping bag for her.

"Tina's been coughing nonstop. I don't want to get sick."

As Violet crawled around on all fours to spread out the sleeping bag, her shorts shifted, showing a flash of bright blue underwear. He resumed his position, flat on his back with his hands behind his head. Violet moved his backpack and rearranged things to her liking before she flopped beside him.

"Ouch."

He snickered. "Sorry, I didn't bring another sleeping bag."

She shifted. "I feel a stick in my back."

He closed his eyes as she fussed around. The flashlight on her neck swung, lighting up his eyelids briefly before she landed heavily beside him. He heard a click as she turned off the light on her neck.

"I should have grabbed my sleeping bag before I left, but I didn't want Tina to feel worse than she already did. It's just for one night, right?"

When he didn't speak, she nudged him.

"Are you up?"

"Unfortunately."

"Why are you so crabby? Mom asked me if something happened. What's going on with you?"

"Nothing."

He could feel her eyes on him, though he knew she could see very little. The only illumination came from the distant fire, which penetrated the thin material of his tent.

"Did I do something?" she asked as she nestled against his side

"No," he said gruffly.

"Why are you so tense?" she complained, prodding his flexed arm.

He made a concentrated effort to relax.

"Tell me what's bothering you," she ordered, smacking his chest.

"Nothing's bothering me." He was very aware of her hand on his heart, which was picking up speed.

"Siblings aren't supposed to keep secrets from each other. They're supposed to tell each other everything."

He opened his mouth to say they weren't real siblings, but the words died on his tongue as the truth slammed into him. He didn't want her wearing some other guy's clothes, didn't want anyone arranging her fingers on guitar strings or trying to feed her because he saw her as his. She was his to touch and provide for, and these guys were encroaching on his territory, they just didn't know it.

"You know you can tell me anything, right?" Violet asked.

He jerked. "What?"

"About why you're angry." She peered at his face in the meager light. "Seriously, what's going on with you? You're acting so weird."

"It's nothing," he croaked.

"We used to be so close."

Violet sounded hurt.

"We're still close. You're practically on top of me," he muttered in a disgruntled tone, hoping and dreading that she would take the hint and give him some space. He was dying here. He stopped breathing when she propped her knee on his thigh.

"And we're staying like this until you confide in me," she declared.

"There's nothing to confide. I've just got a lot on my mind."

A pause and then, "You're thinking about school, aren't you?"

"I'm thinking about sports."

"Do you think about anything else?" she asked in a disgusted tone.

"No," he lied.

"What's there to worry about? You're always one of the best players on the team, no matter what you play."

"I don't want to take anything for granted."

Just as he anticipated, she immediately lost interest and yawned.

"You sure you aren't mad?" she asked sleepily.

"Yes."

She sighed. "If you weren't a guy, I'd think you were on your period. You're so moody."

He tunneled his fingers into her hair and massaged her scalp. "Go to sleep, brat."

"*You're* a brat," she countered fiercely before she went boneless. "That feels good."

He kept up the head massage until she drifted to sleep. He lay there, mind racing, as her familiar scent teased his senses. From the moment they met, he instinctively knew she was integral to his future. And he was right. Her existence grounded him, brought color back into his world, and gave him direction, purpose, and joy. He knew he loved her but had never acknowledged that his feelings extended beyond being brotherly until the sight of Malcolm's hands on her triggered violent, primitive instincts he hadn't even known he possessed.

He didn't want her legs draped over Malcolm's shoulders, he wanted them on his. And that look he had down her swimsuit... The image of her breasts kept flashing in his mind at the worst times— during prayer, while he was talking to Mom... It was wrong on every level, but the more he tried to suppress his fantasies, the more lecherous they became. Part of his anger was directed at himself for viewing her like Malcolm and the others. He tried to keep his thoughts pure—to see her as a sexless friend or stepsibling, but now that the blinders were off, his body reacted with a vengeance.

When his dick hardened in response to her nearness, horror speared his gut. He closed his eyes and tried to think of awful things to make it go away. He conjured up the day his dad died and the phone call that made Mom drop to her knees and scream in a way he would never forget. The normal sucker punch he received when he thought back to that day was a mere finger flick with Violet pressed against him. He thought of natural disasters, a car accident they passed on their way here, and his grandmother in her rocking chair, knitting.

It wasn't working. It was getting worse. He began to sweat, and it had nothing to do with the temperature. He tried to shift away but froze when she stirred. The last thing he needed was for her to notice his tented crotch. She would freak out, and rightly so. Here he was, pissed at his friends for shooting their shot, yet he lay beside her with a throbbing cock. Violet slept soundly because she trusted him. He wasn't going to break that trust by relieving himself while she lay beside him.

But his mind latched onto the idea and played out different scenarios in his head. His dick got so hard, it became painful. Gently, but firmly, he extracted himself from her. She made unhappy, annoyed sounds, but didn't wake. Slowly, he unzipped the tent so he wouldn't make too much noise and draw attention to himself. When he stepped outside, he took a deep breath of the cool night air before he strolled away from the congregation of tents, trucks, and RV's. He was relieved no one called out to him.

There was just enough light for him not to trip or twist his ankle as he navigated through the trees. He tried to banish the erotic fantasies by humming one of the worship songs they sang around the campfire not even an hour ago, but his mind fixated on what Violet would have done if she discovered his hard on. If her knee propped on his thigh brushed against it, would she have freaked out? He had no idea how much she actually knew about sex, but what if she shocked the hell out of him and grabbed it? Explored and pleasured him?

He stopped in his tracks and reached into his pants to grip his dick, which was leaking precum. He bit back a groan, braced his hand on a tree, and prayed he would hear if anyone approached before they saw what he was doing.

He bowed his head and let the forbidden floodgates open. Images of Violet doing things to him and him doing things to her made him shudder. God, this was wrong, but he couldn't stop. *She's not really my sister*, he reminded himself as he climaxed.

"Shit," he hissed as he sprayed his cum over the trunk of the tree.

As the awful tension drained away, he hastily tucked himself in his pants and caught his breath. Guilt dulled the pleasure coursing through him. If anyone knew what he'd done... He straightened and peered through the darkness. But no one did. And Violet was clueless. No harm done.

He started back to camp and was relieved not to cross paths with anyone. He unzipped the tent and waited for Violet to stir. When she didn't, he crawled in beside her and turned on his side, facing away from her.

He took a deep breath and caught a whiff of his cum mixing with her delicate scent. He should have washed his hands. He should have slept in the SUV. He shouldn't have come back here. He should... Before he could leave, she fit her body to his back, spooning him and draping her arm over his middle. He clenched his jaw and closed his eyes. He'd already come. He should be okay for the rest of the night.

<hr>

He woke on his back with Violet's hair tickling his nose and her knee once again inches from his aching cock, which was hard enough to use as a hammer. Groggy and horny, he wasn't as gentle moving her off him as he'd been last night.

"Wus going on?" she moaned.

Her raspy tone made his hard on worse. He tore out of the tent to discover the sun was just coming up. He wasn't pleased to see a handful of adults, including Isaac, standing around the dying fire. Isaac straightened like he wanted to talk to him. Jesse slashed his hand through the air and turned in the opposite direction. He hoped Isaac thought he had to take a leak. He did, but he also had to take care of his throbbing dick before he faced anyone.

Being half awake dulled the shame of jacking off to Violet again. It didn't take much for him to blow his load, not when he had the pleasure of moving her dead weight off him and her scent was imbedded in his clothes. Her skin was so soft. Why did it feel so different from his own? If he ever had the opportunity to put his mouth on her...

He tipped his head back and let out a moan that came out louder than he intended. The shock of it ruined what would have been one of the best orgasms he'd ever had. He had just enough time to piss and put himself away before someone called his name.

He hoped he didn't look like the pervert he felt he was as he faced Isaac. "Morning."

"Morning." Isaac cocked his head to the side and gave him a considering look. "Are you okay?"

"Yup."

"Mom said you weren't yourself yesterday."

"I'm fine."

That reassurance was enough for Isaac, who turned back to camp. "We could use your help loading up."

"Sure." They reached the clearing when he decided to disclose, "Violet's in my tent."

He watched Isaac out of the corner of his eye, curious if his stepfather would sense that something was amiss. He'd seen straight through Malcolm and his friends yesterday. Would Isaac sense his feelings toward Violet had changed?

Isaac's brows drew together. "I thought she was sharing a tent with Tina."

"Tina was coughing so Violet bailed and came to me."

Isaac nodded and clapped him on the shoulder. "Good. Let's get to work."

He blew out a breath before he fixed a smile on his face and greeted Pastor Sonny.

———

They were about fifteen minutes from home. The sun was setting, Isaac was behind the wheel, and the open windows let cool air circulate through the cab. Mom and Violet fell asleep about a half hour ago. The only sound in the SUV was the whistling wind and country tunes on the radio.

He spent the morning helping the men load trucks and trailers with camping equipment until he spotted Violet trying to take down his tent. When he rushed over, she gave him a sheepish smile as she gestured to the mess she'd made.

"I wanted to help, but I have no idea how…"

"No problem. I got it," he said, and knelt to pull out a stake anchoring the tent to the ground.

"Thanks for letting me invade your space."

When she groaned, he glanced back and saw her stretch. His shirt lifted to show her tiny gray shorts.

"Anytime," he rasped and turned back to his task.

"Did I dream it, or did you leave the tent several times?"

He fumbled with a pole. "I had to take a leak."

"Hmm."

His head jerked up. "What's *hmm* mean?"

The look she was giving him made him break out in a cold sweat. She couldn't know...

"I thought you might have rendezvoused with Lara or Marissa."

She was so far off base that he gawked at her before he shook his head. "No."

"They were hoping you would ask one of them out before we started school."

"I'm not interested in them."

"Aha! But you are interested in someone?" she asked with great interest.

When he realized he'd been staring at her mouth for a few seconds, he forced himself to look down at what he was doing. He cleared his throat. "I'm not interested in anyone."

"I'm going to find out at some point. You won't be able to hide it from me!" she called over her shoulder as she headed to the bathroom.

He worked until Mom forced him to take a break and eat something.

"You seem troubled, son."

He hadn't been able to meet her eyes as he reassured her that he was fine, just tired and ready to go home. If she only knew... He didn't bother telling Mom that Violet slept in his tent. It wouldn't occur to her that anything inappropriate would happen because she saw Violet as her blood daughter. But she wasn't. And he wasn't truly her brother.

He glanced at Violet who slumped against the door, fast asleep. He considered offering his hoodie for her to use as a pillow, but saw they were already in their neighborhood. As the SUV went over a bump, her breasts bounced. He quickly looked away, inwardly cursing. He was so screwed.

Now that the paper-thin platonic wall had disintegrated, it was impossible to switch his mind back to seeing her as a sibling. Thankfully, only he and God knew that he'd crossed a mental boundary. At least he hadn't done something monumentally stupid like jack off in the tent or cop a feel. He wasn't *that* far gone. He had to find a way to act normal around her because it wouldn't take long for her to notice he was acting different. They were extremely close, and he didn't want to risk ruining their relationship by exposing his feelings or introducing things she wasn't ready for or interested in if she truly saw him as a brother.

He straightened as Isaac pulled into the garage beside Mom's SUV. Neither Mom nor Violet stirred as the garage door came down.

"We can unload tomorrow," Isaac said as he hopped out of the SUV and eyed his sleeping wife. "You got Vi?"

His stomach clenched. "Yeah."

Mom and Violet were heavy sleepers. He had been carrying Violet to bed or cars or wherever she happened to fall asleep ever since their parents got together. This was nothing out of the ordinary. Or, it hadn't been until he realized staring at her too long could make him hard.

He got out of the SUV and came around to Violet's side. Dad draped Mom over his shoulder. He used the same hold on Violet and followed Dad into the house, detouring to Violet's bedroom while Dad continued down the hallway to the master bedroom.

He hit the light switch with his elbow, illuminating Violet's pastel bedroom. He flicked back her covers before he gently deposited her in bed. She smiled as she sank into the plethora of pillows.

"You're the best," she murmured with her eyes closed.

He mock scowled. "You made me carry you when you could have walked?"

"Umm hmm."

"Like I said, you're a brat," he said, trying to sound irritated as he brushed her tangled hair away from her face.

"But you love me, anyway, don't you?"

His hand stilled before he retracted it.

Her brows bunched together. "Jesse?"

"You know I do," he said gruffly.

She sighed as she turned on her side and burrowed into her pillows. "I love you, too."

"Sleep tight," he said before he turned off the light and went through their connecting Jack and Jill bathroom to get to his room. He flopped on the bed and stared at the shadowed ceiling as he came to terms with the fact that his life had just turned upside down.

CHAPTER 4

JESSE

4 MONTHS LATER

Jesse lay in bed with Violet's panties wrapped around his cock. He snagged it from her hamper before he joined the family for dinner.

A few months ago, he stumbled across Violet's underwear that she'd dropped after her shower. He didn't kick it under the counter or discreetly toss it into her hamper. No, he'd picked it up and proceeded to jack off in the sink.

Taking her underwear had become a habit. Every couple of days, he stole another. His unhealthy fetish went into overdrive when Mom took Violet shopping for her sixteenth birthday and bought her an array of underwear in different styles and patterns.

He stroked his cock but couldn't bring himself to climax. He brought her underwear to his mouth and gnawed on the crotch, whining like a dog, desperate for more of her taste, but he'd sucked it clean. He knew it was sick. He knew it was wrong, but he couldn't stop. Four months ago, he'd been a normal, happy, healthy teen, but that camping trip changed everything. He wished he'd remained ignorant of his feelings and the blinders had stayed on. Guys who thought it was shitty to be in the friend zone had no idea what utter hell it was to have the love of their life see them as their brother.

How was he supposed to regulate his emotions when his days started and ended with her? He woke to the sight of her brushing her teeth or doing her hair in their shared bathroom. Before she went to bed, she usually sought him out for a hug. He started giving her side hugs so she wouldn't know the effect she was having on his body. Her signature scent of violets and rose lingered in his room, car, and on the shirts and hoodies she borrowed. They drove to and from school together and hung out with the same people. The only time he wasn't with her was during class or practice. He had no respite from her and the worst part was, he didn't want one. He was a glutton for this exquisite torture.

His friends had been ribbing him for dismissing every girl who flirted with him. If only they knew the girl he wanted was the same one they did. None of his friends dared ask Violet out, but he knew it was coming. It was just a matter of time. And when it did, he had no idea how he was going to cope.

Violet had blossomed into a girl that would draw the eye of any straight male, even if she wasn't their type. Thankfully, his reputation of being an overprotective brother and Violet being known as a good, Christian girl kept most boys at bay. She was also studious and introverted and shied away from the spotlight. He was grateful she didn't try out for cheerleading. There was no way he would have been able to focus with hundreds of guys ogling her in that tiny uniform.

He tossed his arm over his face and blew out a frustrated breath. His body raged 24/7, his hormones whipped into a frenzy by her constant presence. Everything she did, however innocent, his mind interpreted as sexual. At dinner, Violet had a glass of eggnog. When some of it dribbled down her chin, it looked so much like cum that he'd lost touch with reality and reached under the table to grip his hardening cock before he remembered where he was.

When they were watching TV, she started doing these crazy yoga stretches in front of him. Thankfully, Mom called Violet to the dining table to help with crafts for her kindergarteners. He retreated to his room, only for Violet to ask him to get something out of storage. She barged in a second time because she needed help with her math homework. He tried to distract himself with a book and then a movie. He tried to seek refuge in sleep. Nothing worked. When everyone finally retried, he unearthed his most recent acquisition, but even her underwear couldn't get him off.

He jumped out of bed and pulled on sweats before he padded into the bathroom. He flicked on the light and splashed his face with cold water to snap himself out of this awful frenzy. He was beating his dick so often, he considered asking his friends how often they did it. Would they guess that his constant state of arousal was because of Violet? He couldn't risk anyone making that connection, so he kept it to himself.

He scanned the vanity for something of hers that would get him off, but there were just hair ties, bobby pins, and other things that did nothing for him. He winced as his dick pulsed, begging for release. He eyed her towel and leaned over to smell it. There was an earthy scent mixed with her sweet pea body wash. He wrapped the damp towel around him and began to thrust. A minute later, he let out a frustrated hiss. It wasn't enough!

As he began to open her drawers, desperately looking for something of hers that would aid him, he realized how much noise he was making. He eyed the door that led into Violet's room and pressed his ear to it. Silence.

A wicked idea formed that was so provocative, his cock wept in anticipation. His heart thudded in his ears. As he reached for the door handle, the magnitude of what he was about to do hit him full force. Fantasizing about Violet was one thing, stealing her underwear was another, but sneaking into her room in the middle of the night?

I'm just going to make sure I didn't wake her, he told himself. But even as he turned the doorknob, he knew that wasn't true.

Her door wasn't locked. There was no need to since they trusted one another and had a double knock policy that prevented any awkward situations.

He turned off the bathroom light and let the door swing open. He waited for a gasp or the sound of Violet sleepily asking if something was wrong, but nothing happened. He stood there for a full minute, warring internally, before he stepped out of the shadows.

He cursed the colorful Christmas lights that Mom and Violet had strung around her room for the holidays. If Violet opened her eyes, there was nowhere to hide. She tended to be a heavy sleeper, but there was always a chance that she could wake like she had when he left the tent to jerk off.

He approached the bed cautiously, blood rushing through his veins, making his skin itchy and hot. His ears were pulsing, and a trickle of sweat slid down his spine. This was dangerous—the riskiest thing he'd done thus far. If he was caught, the results could be catastrophic. That possibility should have made him leave, but his need was too great. He couldn't think straight.

He held his breath as he took her in. Violet lay on her side facing him. She wore a pink long sleeve shirt with her hands stacked beneath her cheek. His mouth quirked. She was adorable. He listened to the rhythm of her deep, even breaths and found himself matching her. Amazingly, his clamoring demons began to settle. Maybe being near her was enough, and he wouldn't need to compromise his morals by...

Violet let out a little moan before she flipped to her back. The colorful Christmas lights gilded her face, highlighting her full lips, which were slightly parted. He focused on her rising and falling chest. It was clear she wasn't wearing a bra. Her nipples were hard and pointed straight to the ceiling.

Even as he called himself every vile name he could think of, he sank his hand into his sweats and began to stroke himself. It didn't take long. Being in her room and seeing her face instead of conjuring it in his mind sent him soaring over the edge. *I'm going to hell,* he thought as his climax hit. He bit his lip to stop his moan and staggered at the sheer intensity of it. He put his hand out to brace himself before he realized he would jostle the bed and wake her. Terror made him light on his feet. Swiftly, he righted himself and backed into the bathroom without taking his eyes from her. He closed the door and waited several seconds to make sure he was in the clear before he flipped on the light.

Chest heaving, he stared at the closed door, unable to believe what he'd just done. He'd just crossed another line, one that could put him behind bars. Cursing, he stripped off his shirt, sweats, and ruined underwear and stepped into the tub. He tipped his face up to the hot spray. His behavior was escalating at an alarming rate. He was scaring himself.

Should he get help? The thought of broaching such a topic with Isaac or his mom made him ill. They wouldn't understand. What if they told Violet? That sent a bolt of panic through him. He didn't want to destroy what they had. He would rather have her platonic love and affection than have her look at him with pity or, worse, have her distance herself because she didn't feel the same.

Sometimes when she looked at him, he thought he saw something more, but he wouldn't act unless he was one hundred percent sure, and he wasn't. Unrequited love had to be one of the most excruciating human experiences. In church, they discussed love like it was this gentle, peaceful emotion that aligned your life and made you whole. Love was driving him demented. It was a cruel, ruthless master that drove him to do all sorts of twisted, depraved things. Love was an incessant hunger, a thorn burrowing ever deeper in his heart. His love had no bounds—no line he wouldn't cross, nothing he wouldn't dare for a few hours of peace from the all-consuming pain. Several months ago, his behavior would have been abhorrent. Now, he was creeping into her room and jacking off like a pervert. What next?

But you didn't get caught. She didn't wake, and now you can finally sleep, he reasoned with himself. At least he hadn't touched her... The thought of putting his hand on her pert breast made his cock twitch. His inner sicko urged him to go back to her room for one more hit. *It's late. The chances of her waking are slim. One more look and you'll never do it again.*

He cut off the water with a vicious twist and wished he could shut off the despicable thoughts running through his mind as easily. His father had drummed into him the importance of discipline, integrity, and honor. All of that had fallen to the wayside. He didn't know who he was anymore. All he could think about was her. Being in constant proximity to someone he was in love with and who was completely oblivious was like being in purgatory. He was forever burning, in agony, and he was starting to lose it.

He wrapped a towel around his waist and slicked back his hair. Now that his mind wasn't clouded by lust, the answer was obvious. If he couldn't have the girl he wanted, he had to find another. Even though the thought was distasteful, what would be even worse is if desperation caused him to do something unforgivable that ruined their relationship. He had to redirect his fixation for both their sakes. It was the only sane solution.

When he got into bed, he closed his eyes and tried to ignore the quiet, insidious voice that fanned the flame of dark desires he was desperately trying to keep at bay.

CHAPTER 5
VIOLET

2 MONTHS LATER

VIOLET SUNG ALONG TO THE UPBEAT PLAYLIST SHE CREATED TO KEEP HER motivated when she had to cook, clean, or do laundry. Her clean clothes pile that she'd ignored for almost two weeks was driving Lynne crazy, so she'd finally given in and was folding and sorting.

She paused frequently to check her group texts. Her nerdy friends were asking if anyone had finished a project that was due next month, while her girlfriends gossiped about crushes and boyfriends. The group chat she was in with Jesse and their mutual friends asked if they wanted to go to the movies on Friday. Jesse hadn't responded. She could hear the TV going in the living room and the low rumble of Jesse and Dad's voices. Since it was Wednesday, there was no rush for him to answer, but she suspected he would say yes.

She hung her tops and jackets in the closet before she carried neat stacks of clothes to her drawers. As she surveyed her underwear, she frowned. She walked around the bed and looked under it to make sure she hadn't missed any stray clothing before she went to her hamper and dug around.

It was the strangest thing... Certain panties had an uncanny habit of disappearing during a wash cycle and reappearing during the next. It was hard to be certain since she didn't do laundry consistently, but sometimes she'd wash a specific pair for an outfit and when the day came, she couldn't find them. The panties always magically reappeared at some point, but sometimes she felt like someone was pranking her. But why would anyone take her underwear? Even stranger, why would they fold and put them back after using them?

A series of chimes on her phone distracted her from her bizarre underwear problem. *Vi, what's going on with you and Tobias? Allison said she saw him pass you a note in class?!*

You and Tobias? *Since* when?

I've never even heard him talk.

OMG, what did the note say?

Tobias was a quiet guy she had History with and who haunted the school library. They crossed paths often, since she hung out after school when Jesse had practice. Tobias was always scribbling in a notebook. One day, she asked him what he was writing and was dumbfounded when he showed her pages of poetry that sounded like Shakespeare. Tobias was awkward and terribly shy, but when he was talking about poetry, he became animated and incredibly passionate.

Tobias and I are just friends. He's a poet, she shared. *He's been asking for my opinion on some of his work.*

There was a long pause as the girls digested this. She hadn't known how to react when Tobias started asking her for feedback. She'd been flattered but had no idea what the poems meant. Knowing how much his art meant to him, she didn't want to hurt him, so she said things like, "powerful," "moving," or "I really like the direction you're going in." That seemed to be enough for Tobias.

Are the poems about you? Marie asked.

That had occurred to her, especially when a few mentioned a girl with hair that mimicked the ripples on the surface of the ocean and eyes the color of amber. But he'd also handed her poems that spoke of ravens, dragonflies, and roses, so... *I don't think so. I think he's just happy to share them with someone.*

He's in love with you, Georgia gushed and added a row of heart emojis.

"Lights out, honey," Mom called through her closed bedroom door.

"Okay!" she called and rolled out of bed to brush her teeth.

Although she was getting a little too old for Mom to give her a bedtime, she didn't fight it. No matter how much sleep she got, mornings were always a struggle for her. Somehow, Jesse managed sports, school, and homework effortlessly on only four or five hours of sleep. Everything came so easy to him. If she didn't love him so much, she'd hate him for being so perfect.

She hopped into bed and turned out the light, but continued texting. When most of the girls signed off for the night, she rolled her eyes when Georgia started messaging her directly. Her friend was convinced that Tobias had a crush on her and that she was in denial. When she insisted they were just friends, Georgia demanded to see his poems to determine for herself whether they were about her or not.

She hadn't realized how much time had passed until she heard Jesse and Dad making their way to their rooms. She heard Jesse's door close and, ten seconds later, her parent's door at the end of the hall.

She yawned and placed the phone face down on the nightstand, unable to continue debating with Georgia. She'd tell her friend she'd fallen asleep, which they both should be doing right now. Why had Allison brought that up? Now, the girls would be watching her and Tobias like hawks in class and Georgia, being the bold, curious soul that she was, may ask Tobias outright if he was in love with her. She sighed. She'd make sure to talk to Georgia tomorrow before she pounced on poor Tobias.

She pulled the covers up to her chin, turned on her side, and tucked her arm under her pillow just as the bathroom door swung open. She blinked, sure her eyes were playing tricks on her. Did the door open on its own? Just as she was about to raise her head to get a better look, Jesse stepped into her room. She opened her mouth, but whatever she meant to say was forgotten when she registered that he wasn't wearing any bottoms.

Her eyes snapped shut, but the image of his penis jutting out beneath his t-shirt was burned in her brain. What was happening? Did he forget to put on pants before he came to talk to her? Was he sleepwalking? His footsteps were muffled by the carpet, but she felt a soft whoosh of air as he stopped beside the bed.

She waited with bated breath for him to reach out and shake her awake, but he just stood there, hovering. Did he know she was awake and wanted her to acknowledge him? But why would she when he was half naked?

She heard a long, deep inhale. Was he *sniffing* her? No, he couldn't be. Why would he...? Jesse's muffled groan scrambled her thoughts before she heard an odd noise, something she couldn't place. A minute that felt like an eternity passed before curiosity got the better of her. A nightlight placed near the foot of the bed allowed her to see what was happening when she cracked one eye open.

Shock reverberated through her. Jesse was touching himself. No, not just touching, but stroking rapidly.

This had to be a freaky hallucination, or maybe she'd fallen asleep and this was a nightmare. This couldn't be happening in real life. Jesse couldn't be standing beside her bed, masturbating. She closed her eyes, unable to comprehend what was happening. She willed herself to wake up, but the dream continued. She lay there, paralyzed in her body, as the sounds of Jesse pleasuring himself assaulted her ears. It went on and on. She didn't know what to do, so she played dead. She didn't realize she was holding her breath until her lungs protested. She panicked when she had to take a gulp of air, but thankfully, she wasn't the only one who gasped.

Jesse made a noise, almost like he was in pain. Unable to bear the suspense, she peeked again and saw him grip the head of his penis. When his breath hitched, her gaze rose. The primitive elation on his face made her insides squirm. A grunt was her only warning before something spurted on her sheets. She was too stunned to flinch when some of it hit her cheek.

Jesse panted as he spread what he'd spilled over her bed. When his hand came toward her face, she stopped breathing. His hand stopped inches from her face, fingertips twitching before it retracted.

A flash of light scared the bejesus out of her. She clamped her eyes shut, terrified he'd seen them open. She would just die if he... She heard a soft scrape and then nothing. *What the hell was happening?* She opened her eye just a sliver. Jesse's face was illuminated by her cell phone in his hand. A message must have come in, which is why it lit up and caught his attention. He scrolled on her phone. She frowned, surprised he knew her password. He grunted and set the phone facedown as she'd had it before he turned on his heel. Her stomach flipped at the sight of his muscular butt as he disappeared into the bathroom and closed the door soundlessly behind him.

The bathroom light came on. The water ran. She heard the normal sounds of him brushing his teeth and using the bathroom before she heard his door close as he exited into his bedroom.

Violet stared at the closed door, unable to process what just occurred. She pinched herself. The tiny bite of pain assured her she was very much awake, unless her mind could mimic pain in a dream. But there was evidence... She reached out to touch her sheets, but before she made contact, she stopped. The foreign substance on her cheek suddenly burned white-hot. Stomach tight as a fist, she wiped away the tiny droplets with her sleeve and turned her back on her damp sheets and scooted to the far side of the bed.

She closed her eyes and let out a shaky breath. Even though she'd witnessed it with her own eyes, she didn't want to believe it. Jesse was her brother. He wouldn't... She pulled the covers over her head. Maybe she was coming down with something. She had to be to imagine something so deplorable. Jesse was a saint, the poster boy of their high school and church. He had never shown an ounce of depravity or perversion. This wasn't him.

She clasped her stuffed longhorn to her chest and buried her face in its fur. This didn't happen. It couldn't have. She drew her knees up to her chest and willed her mind to erase the past fifteen minutes from her memory banks.

***

VIOLET STARED BLEARILY AT HER REFLECTION AS SHE BRUSHED HER TEETH. She had no idea if she'd gotten any sleep. It didn't feel like it.

Jesse's double knock startled her. She hesitated, before she said, "Come in."

She tapped her toothbrush on the edge of the sink to remove excess water as Jesse entered.

"Morning," he said.

"Morning," she returned and set her toothbrush in its holder and reached for her hairbrush.

"Mom made breakfast if you're hungry," he said.

"Okay."

He reached for his comb. She kept her eyes trained on herself as he styled his hair with just a few passes. He was already dressed in jeans and a dark gray sweater. She frowned when he put on a hat. Why brush his hair if he was just going to cover it?

"Are you okay?" he asked.

"Yup," she said without looking at him.

"You sure?"

"Mm hmm."

There was a long pause. She felt the intensity of his gaze before he said, "I'm ready when you are."

When he left, closing his door behind him, she stared at the place he'd been standing. She hadn't inspected her bedsheets this morning to confirm her fever dream. She couldn't handle that, so she ignored it, just as she had Jesse. She was worried that looking at him would revive those graphic memories she was trying to repress.

"I'm out, kids! Have a great day! Stay safe!" Mom called as she headed out the door.

"Love you!" Jesse shouted.

"I love you more!" Lynne hollered back.

Despite herself, Violet's mouth curved. She and Dad never used to say the L word, but thanks to Jesse and Lynne, it had become a daily declaration she never tired of hearing. The familiar ritual eased some of her tension. It was just another day. Everything was the way it should be. And she had to get going.

She gave up on her hair and pulled it back with a clip. She rushed into her bedroom and dressed in jeans and a sweater like Jesse to combat the chilly February morning.

When she made her way to the kitchen, she spotted Jesse outside, wheeling their elderly neighbor's trash can to the street. On his way back to the house, he was hailed by two women power walking. Violet couldn't hear what they were saying, but she didn't need to. The women's broad smiles and the way they patted his arm told her they were impressed with his thoughtfulness.

She'd heard it for years—adults praising Jesse for being so helpful, kind, and responsible. It wasn't an act. Jesse was the same at home as he was at school and church. He was a natural leader. People gravitated to him, unconsciously sensing his grounded nature. He was everything everyone believed he was and more. She knew for a fact that he was a genuinely helpful, sweet guy. He had made her life immeasurably better. She had been so insecure, so terrified of things going wrong. His steadfast patience, love, and support healed wounds she didn't know she had. It took years for her to accept that this was her real life, and it wouldn't dissolve when Mom and Dad had a fight. She didn't want anything to change. Not now, when she finally had everything she'd ever wanted and more.

As Jesse started up the driveway, she hastily made herself a breakfast sandwich. By the time he opened the door, she had the leftovers in the fridge with a note for Dad when he came home from work.

"Ready?" Jesse asked.

"Yup."

She braced one hand on the wall as she shoved her feet into her boots.

"That's the second time you've said that this morning," Jesse observed.

"What?"

"Since when do you say yup?"

She shrugged as she made her way to the SUV. Mom bought a small, fuel-efficient car once Jesse got his license and let him take the SUV since he usually needed the extra room for his sports equipment.

She settled her backpack on the floorboard and belted herself in as Jesse got behind the steering wheel. He fiddled with the radio as they made their way out of the neighborhood. She unwrapped her breakfast sandwich and stared out the window as she tried to think of the day ahead and not about anything that could ruin her picture-perfect life.

"Did you see that text about Brody and the others going to the movies on Friday?" Jesse asked.

"Yes."

Several seconds passed before he asked, "You want to go?"

"I don't know," she heard herself say.

"You told me a couple of days ago, you wanted to see that movie."

"I know, but..." She waved her half-eaten sandwich. "I can always see it later."

"There's no reason for you to see it later unless you have other plans this weekend?"

"Maybe. My friends were talking Dand..." She shrugged.

"You need me to drive you anywhere?"

She shook her head. "No, I can catch a ride."

"I don't have to go to the movies. I can take you wherever you need to go."

She relaxed a little. He sounded like himself. Helpful, supportive, sweet. "No, you should go to the movies. I'm sure it'll be fun. You can tell me if it's good."

"I'd rather you come with us. When you know what you're doing with your friends, I'll decide what I'll do."

She didn't know what to say, so she finished her sandwich in silence and crumpled the foil into a ball. Lost in thought, she didn't realize she hadn't said a word until he parked the car, and she undid her seatbelt.

"You okay?" Jesse asked.

"Of course." She scanned the crowd for her friends. She was relieved to be at school, where she had classes and numerous things to distract her. She reached for her backpack and froze when Jesse touched her arm.

"You don't seem like yourself this morning."

"I didn't get the best sleep," she said and pushed her door open, eager to escape.

"Hey."

"Yeah?" she asked, tugging on her backpack zipper, even though everything was secure.

"Look at me."

She mentally braced before she turned her head. She wasn't sure what she was expecting. Of course, he hadn't changed overnight. His face was the same—chiseled jaw and what some of her friends called perfect lips. When they met, he'd been four inches taller than her, but now he towered over her and most of their peers at six foot three. Sunlight hit striking sky-blue eyes that stood out even more because of his dark brows and hair. She searched his face for an explanation for the disturbing images in her mind, but all she could see was baffled concern.

"Are you sure you're feeling okay? You're pale."

She didn't have time to stiffen as he cupped her cheek.

"Are you coming down with something?"

She gave him a bracing smile. "I'm feeling a little better now."

He cocked his head to the side and dropped his hand. "You should have stayed home."

"I have a test today."

"You could always make it up."

"No need," she said and waved as a girl approached the SUV. "Your girlfriend's coming."

He didn't turn to look. "Who?"

"Sasha."

"We're not official," he said shortly. "If you need me to take you home..."

"Yes, I'll call you, but I'm sure I'll be fine, Dad."

She grimaced at the last word she'd tacked on, but Jesse didn't notice because Sasha was knocking on his window. Violet slipped out of the car and slung her backpack over one shoulder as Sasha drawled, "Hey, handsome."

She walked away before she heard Jesse's response. She wasn't sure what had come over him, but in the past few weeks, he'd gone into a dating frenzy. When he didn't have practice or a game on the weekends, he usually spent it with the girl of the week. Sasha was the first to pass the two-week mark. When she asked him why he was suddenly playing the field, he'd said it was necessary. She wasn't sure what that meant and hadn't been interested enough to push for clarification since she was sick of hearing about his love life from her friends who were dying to be included, even if it was just for a day. Unfortunately for them, Jesse was dating only juniors or seniors. She was grateful. She didn't want to have to console her friends when Jesse moved onto someone else.

"Vi!"

Georgia stood beside her yellow Fiat, waving frantically. One glance at her friend was all it took to know what was on her mind.

Her life had taken an outlandish turn while Georgia was still stuck on Tobias and his nonexistent crush.

"You left me hanging last night!" Georgia exclaimed as she hooked her arm through Violet's.

"I passed out," she said apologetically.

"I'll forgive you if you let me see one of Toby's poems." When Violet gave her a level stare, Georgia sucked her teeth. "What if he's carefully crafting these poems to express how he feels, but you're too stubborn to see it?"

"And if they are just poems and not secret love letters?"

"That's why you have me!" Georgia said cheerfully.

Her brow arched. "Because you're a whiz at poetry?"

"No, but I *am* a whiz when it comes to love."

Violet frowned. "You've never had a boyfriend."

"Exactly! Those who can't fall in love are fated to spot it miles away for everyone else."

Before she could respond to that, someone pressed against her other side.

"I see Jesse's still with Sasha," Marie whispered.

Georgia held up her finger like she was trying to figure out which way the wind was blowing. "My senses say they'll call it quits before the end of the week."

"I think they make a cute couple," Marie said.

"You say that about every girl he's with."

"And I'm right!"

"He's hot. He could choose someone butt ugly and his looks would bring her up three levels."

"Georgia!" Violet and Marie exclaimed, appalled.

"You know I'm right." Georgia glanced around to make sure no one was listening before she murmured, "Is it just me or does Jesse look bored out of his mind, no matter who he's with?"

Violet stiffened. "What do you mean?"

"I *mean*," Georgia emphasized, showing off her pink braces. "He's going through these girls like hotcakes because they aren't who he really wants."

"That's crazy. Why pick them in the first place if he's not interested?" Marie asked.

"I don't know." Georgia bumped Violet with her hip. "Why don't you ask him who he's really stuck on and go for her instead of breaking all these girls' hearts?"

Violet made a face. "Can we not talk about my brother's love life and speaking of, please don't go up to Tobias and ask him if he's in love with me."

"But," Georgia began, but the bell rang, saving Violet from having to hear any more of Georgia's insane theories.

VIOLET DECIDED NOT TO GO TO THE CAFETERIA FOR LUNCH. HER SLEEPLESS night was catching up to her. She wasn't in the mood to run into Jesse or be harassed by Georgia. She detoured to the library, which she could always count on for peace and quiet. She nodded to the librarian and got a nod in return before she walked on the outskirts, looking for a cozy chair to curl up in for twenty minutes.

As she neared the back, she spotted Tobias in his normal spot. Her mood perked up a bit. Tobias may be a little eccentric, but he was kind and didn't mind sitting in silence. She didn't technically want to be alone, so finding him here was great. As she approached, she realized he was talking to someone out of her line of sight, and he looked upset. She slid into an aisle and peered over the books to see who he was talking to. Her mouth dropped when she spotted Jesse. What the *heck*? She didn't think Jesse knew Tobias. What could they possibly be talking about?

Jesse must have asked Tobias a question because he nodded adamantly. Satisfied, Jesse turned on his heel and walked down the main aisle. Violet made sure to exit the row and hide at the end of the bookshelf so he wouldn't see her. When the coast was clear, she hurried toward Tobias, who was on his feet and gathering his notebooks.

"Tobias."

He visibly stiffened and didn't turn to look at her as he tossed his bag over his shoulder.

"Tobias?"

He started for an exit door that led outside.

"Hey!"

She rushed after him, aware that several heads shot up from the cluster of work tables.

"Tobias, wait!"

She jogged to catch up to him. He didn't look at her, but kept his gaze fixed straight ahead.

"What happened?" she demanded.

"I never meant to make you uncomfortable," he said stiffly. "I apologize. It won't happen again."

"Uncomfortable?" she echoed. "What are you talking about?"

"Your brother said I was making you uncomfortable with my poems. I won't bother you with them anymore."

She was so taken aback, she stopped in her tracks. Tobias continued across the field, putting as much distance between them as possible. Why would Jesse lie about Tobias' poems making her uncomfortable? How did he even *know*...? An image of him scrolling through her phone after he orgasmed flashed in her mind. The confirmation she hadn't wanted smacked her in the face. This was proof positive that he'd read her messages with Georgia, which he would have been unaware of if he hadn't come into her room last night.

She stood there, staring into space as her phone chimed. Mind awhirl, she reached for it and wasn't pleased to see a message from the person who was responsible for her current distress.

Where are you? I bought you soup.

She pocketed her phone and made her way back to the library. She got several sidelong glances that she ignored them as she staggered to a one-person desk. She placed her backpack on top of it and used it like a pillow, burying her face against the cool nylon. What was happening to her life? Yesterday, everything was fine. Everything was *right,* and now everything was going topsy-turvy. Her brother, who she thought she knew better than herself, had gone rogue.

The bell rang. Immediately, those around her began zipping up backpacks. She forced herself to get up and follow the crowd into the hallway. She made her way to her next class and took a seat at the back instead of the front where she usually sat. Her friends spotted her and made their way over with puzzled expressions.

"Why are we sitting back here?"

"I didn't get much sleep last night. I'm worried I'm going to fall asleep in front of Mrs. Gindler," Violet said in a monotone.

She frowned as she spotted Marissa weaving through the desks.

"You don't have this class," she said.

"I'm at the lab down the hall. Jesse told me to give this to you," Marissa set a paper bowl on the desk before she left, giving the teacher an apologetic smile.

Violet wrapped her cold hands around the bowl, knowing without sniffing it that it would be her favorite lentil soup. When Mrs. Gindler called their attention to the board, she obeyed, but didn't hear one word the teacher said.

"Violet."

She jolted awake at the sound of Jesse's voice. She raised her head to see him coming around the couch where she had been napping.

"What time is it? You're done with practice?" she mumbled, fumbling for her phone.

"You shouldn't have asked Georgia to give you a ride home. I would have skipped practice if you didn't feel well." He brushed her hair aside to feel her forehead. "What is it? Do you have a fever?"

"Migraine," she muttered, pushing his hand away.

"Migraine? Do you have your...? No, not for another week," he muttered.

She peered up at him through one puffy eye. "What are you talking about?"

"Nothing," he said gruffly. "Did you take something?"

"Yes, I just need to rest. Stop fussing."

There was a short pause, and then he asked, "Are you washing something?"

Her heart skipped. "I tossed my bedsheets in the wash. Can you hang it when it's done?"

"Sure. Do you want anything to eat?"

"No. I just need to sleep."

He stood over her for a moment before he pulled her into a sitting position.

"What are you doing?" she grumbled.

"Taking care of you."

He sat and pulled her down, so she lay with her head on his lap.

"I'm not really sick."

"If you weren't sick, you wouldn't be so pale. You should have stayed home today." He absently stroked her hair. "Did Marissa drop off the soup?"

"Yes."

"Why couldn't I find you at lunch?"

She closed her eyes. "I got held up talking to my teacher. I decided to go to class early and get some studying in."

"Hm."

"Hm, what?" she said testily.

"I went by both classrooms. I didn't see you."

"That's odd," she said, words slurring a little as she unwillingly relaxed under his soothing touch.

"Must have missed you," he said in a low voice.

"Must have."

"Next time you don't feel good, you tell me. You don't tell your friends to take care of you. That's my job, remember?"

"But…"

"Next time I'm sick, you can baby me."

She peered up at him. "But you're never sick."

"I'll pretend so you can pay me back."

She snickered. It was impossible to stay angry at him. He was so ridiculously caring and protective. Before she realized she needed something, he provided. That had to be why he said what he had to Tobias. He'd misinterpreted her texts with Georgia and thought Tobias was bothering her. She would seek out Tobias and apologize for what Jesse said and reassure him that she hadn't been uncomfortable.

As Jesse's fingers tunneled into her hair, the confusion and turmoil she carried throughout the day slipped away. This was the Jesse she knew. The Jesse she loved. The brother she'd come to depend on. For three years, they'd been deliriously happy. For the first time in her life, she felt safe and stable. She needed everything to stay the way it was.

Last night was an aberration. Whatever had possessed Jesse to enter her room and do what he had, wasn't him. Everyone made mistakes. She couldn't let one action ruin their relationship. She wouldn't. She chose to forgive and forget and erase it from her memory.

Decision made, she relaxed completely and allowed herself to enjoy Jesse's comforting touch. She needed everything to go back to normal. She couldn't accept the alternative.

CHAPTER 6
VIOLET

3 MONTHS LATER

"So, honey, have any boys caught your eye?"

Violet whipped her head around to make sure Dad wasn't within earshot. She spotted him in the backyard, tossing a football with Jesse as they kept an eye on the grill.

"Mom!"

Lynne threw back her head and laughed. "Your father knows you're going to date someday."

"He literally told me a week ago, I can't date until I'm thirty."

"He's kidding."

"He isn't," Violet said flatly.

Lynne flicked a hand covered in flour. "I'll take care of that for you." She bobbed her brows. "So? Is there anyone you want to tell me about?"

"Not really."

Lynne looked disappointed. "Really? When I was your age, I had a crush on a dozen boys."

"I..." She carefully measured out the ingredients for one of three buttermilk pies they were making. "I'm just focused on school."

"Huh."

"What?" Violet said defensively.

"Not that I want this to happen," Lynne drawled as she arranged her dough in the dish and began to pinch the edges. "But I was your age once. I keep expecting you and Jesse to rebel at some point, but you two are the most well-adjusted, strait-laced, responsible teenagers I've ever met. My friends are convinced we've either drugged you two or we're hiding some dark family secret." Lynne shrugged. "I tell them we're just blessed to have such levelheaded kids."

Violet fixed a smile on her face that she hoped concealed the way her stomach curdled. "We still have time to disappoint you. I have two more years of high school and Jesse... he might go nuts his senior year."

Lynne glanced into the backyard with a proud smile on her face. "I doubt that."

Violet turned on the mixer to stop any further conversation on the topic.

They'd just put their pies in the oven when Jesse and Dad came in with the meat they cooked on the grill. As she set the table, Dad spun Lynne and gave her a loud kiss. Once they were seated, she took Jesse's hand on her left and Lynne's on her right as they bowed their heads to pray. She tried to ignore the distracting brush of Jesse's thumb stroking her skin as Dad blessed the meal.

"Lord, thank you for everything you've given us. Thank you for providing for us and blessing our family. Protect us as we begin a new week. Give us wisdom and strength to see us through. Amen," Dad said.

"Amen," they said in unison.

It was a lazy Sunday evening with delicious food and stimulating conversation. They discussed Pastor Sonny's message at church that day in length before they moved onto what was going on in the community and their schedules for the week. Dad and Jesse were too impatient to let the buttermilk pies cool properly. They each dug into their own, while she and Lynne were satisfied with a slice. Dad had to turn in since he had such an early shift.

When Lynne yawned, Violet offered to clean up. Lynne gave her a grateful smile as she and Dad headed down the hall with their arms around each other.

Violet eyed Jesse's pie, which was more than half gone. "You aren't going to eat it all in one sitting, are you?"

"I could."

"Don't," she warned. "Because Mom will come after you with a knife if you scarf down our pie, too."

"You wouldn't tell her it was me, would you?"

"I would," she said, tipping her nose in the air as she carried dishes to the sink.

"You're heartless. You know this is my favorite," Jesse said as he gathered the rest of the plates and piled them in the sink.

"Maybe you should have pie instead of a cake for your birthday this year."

He froze. "Give up German chocolate cake?"

She crossed her arms over her chest. "What's it gonna be?"

"Can't I have both?"

She tilted her head to the side as she considered. "I could bake for your birthday instead of buying you stuff you never use."

"I use what you give me."

"You used that nice shirt *once*."

"Because I outgrew it within six months."

"And the cologne?"

He shrugged. "I sweat too much. It doesn't last."

She took in the sweat stains on his shirt that clung to his athletic physique and wrinkled her nose. "I can finish up here. You should shower."

He spread his arms wide. "Can I get a hug first?"

She held her hands up as she backed away. "No! Stay back!"

"I just want to thank you for making my favorite pie."

"You just did," she pointed out. "There's no need to touch me."

He moved swiftly, but so did she. She ran to the living room and put the couch between them.

"Jesse." She tried to sound stern, but a nervous laugh escaped. *"Don't."*

His speed never failed to shock her. When he darted around the couch, she let out a panicked yelp. He picked her up and pinned her on the couch.

"I'm going to tell Dad!" she yelled into his chest.

"Promise me you'll make me cake and pie for my birthday, then I'll let you go."

"No!"

He put more of his weight on her, sinking her into the cushions.

"Fine, I promise!" she croaked.

He sat up and grinned down at her. "You're so easy."

She glowered and made a show of smelling herself, even though his scent wasn't as repulsive as it should be. "I'm going to get you back for that."

He climbed off her, stripped off his shirt, and draped it over his shoulder. "Looking forward to it."

As he strolled away, she lay there for a second, before she gave herself a shake. She'd seen Jesse shirtless countless times during practice, while camping, exercising, or at the beach. There was no reason for the sight of his naked torso to make her stomach jitter.

She stored the leftovers in the fridge, cleaned the kitchen, and washed the dishes. By the time she entered her bedroom, Jesse was out of the shower. She grabbed her pajamas and did the double knock on the bathroom door to make sure the coast was clear. When she didn't get an answer, she entered and eyed Jesse's door as she stripped.

After her shower, she put on lotion before she brushed her teeth and re-entered her bedroom. She sat at her desk and worked on an essay that was due on Friday, before she double-checked her backpack to make sure she had all her homework assignments for tomorrow.

With just one month of school left, projects were coming to a close. There was a flurry of tests and then they would be on summer break. The year had passed in a blur. Next year she would be a junior. She couldn't wait! This year she'd been Student Body Secretary. Maybe next year she could be Student Body President? Would her peers vote her in? There was only one way to find out. Dad hadn't let her attend prom this year. Maybe Mom could talk him into letting her go next year?

My friends are convinced we've either drugged you two or we're hiding some dark family secret.

Lynne's voice echoed in her mind as she climbed in bed and pulled the covers up to her chin. From the outside looking in, she knew that they looked like the perfect blended family. They attended church every Sunday, Mom and Dad were happy and in love, and she and Jesse were as close as blood siblings. Jesse got a lot of attention for being a star athlete and was a great student on top of that. They both were. Everything was perfect. Or, it had been before she discovered Jesse's nighttime habit.

By day, Jesse was an honorable Boy Scout. He never touched her inappropriately. He never even looked at her in a way that made her uncomfortable. He seemed as open and loving as he'd always been. When she looked into his eyes, there was nothing deceptive, lecherous, or evil. She couldn't make sense of it.

The visits were sporadic. Sometimes days would pass without incident, allowing her to believe it was a thing of the past, only to be roused in the middle of the night by the sound of him jerking off.

She tried to go to bed early, hoping she would be too deeply asleep to hear him come in. But the stress of wondering if tonight would be one of those nights kept her wide awake. She considered locking the bathroom door to bar him from her room, but then he'd know she knew. And, for some reason she couldn't fathom, that was worse than enduring the deed.

The sounds of him masturbating were burned into her brain. She knew from the rhythm of his strokes and breathing patterns when he was close to climax. She catalogued every sigh, moan, or grunt. Some nights, he came immediately. During others, he struggled. Those were the worst because ten minutes felt like an hour when she was playing dead.

He was becoming bolder. He went from spilling on her sheets to now coming on her face. It took every ounce of control she possessed not to react. She was terrified that one day, she would flinch, open her eyes, or say something.

Initially, it seemed Jesse regulated himself to once or twice a week. Now, that amount had doubled. He was also becoming more impatient. One night, she'd barely been in bed for fifteen minutes before he came in. And he wasn't as quiet as he used to be. She had always been a sound sleeper, but not *that* sound. He couldn't be trying to wake her, could he?

Even if she was truly ignorant to his nighttime shenanigans, at some point she would have questioned why she woke with stuff caked in her hair or had sticky, flaky patches on her skin. What if she'd naively asked Lynne about the stains on her bedsheets? She moaned into her pillow.

If only he would stop, then everything could go back to normal, and she wouldn't feel... Her legs clamped together as her core pulsed. It was humiliating and revolting, but somewhere along the way, her body began to react to the nightly ritual. Most nights, after he left, she had to...

She balled her hands into fists as self-loathing swamped her. It was all his fault. Before this, she rarely thought about sex. She never explored her body or tried to figure out how things worked. Because of him, she now knew what a man's penis looked like and what cum tasted like. One night, she'd gotten so aroused that she humped her stuffed longhorn. The next day, she washed him, but she didn't look at him the same and suspected the feeling was mutual.

It was so confusing to feel one way and have her body react in another. To overcome the excruciating shame and guilt, she rationalized that what happened during these interludes didn't count. That went for Jesse as well. The creeper who slipped into her room and did perverted, wicked things was a totally different person from her beloved brother. Once the sun rose, the dark, degenerate entity that possessed him at night evaporated and wiped the slate clean.

An hour passed. She lay on her stomach, a little rebellion on her part. When another hour crawled by, relief mixed with irritation. She wished he had a predictable schedule, but the times and days varied, so there was no way to predict anything. As another twenty minutes inched by, she concluded that Jesse had conquered his demons for the night, which left hers to deal with.

She flipped onto her back and slid her hand down her primed body. She rubbed herself through her pajama shorts and underwear. An image of his body that he'd casually revealed in the living room appeared in her mind, along with the memory of his weight pinning her to the couch. She bit back a moan as she arched her hips into her hand.

As pangs of conscience smothered her sexual desire, she tried to replace Jesse's face with another boy, as if that would make it less sinful. But it was impossible to picture anyone else when Jesse had awakened her libido. Her passions now revolved around him.

All the things her friends found attractive about him, she found herself inspecting for herself. The lips they thought were perfect, she'd seen him bite during orgasm. His athletic build gave him a body that didn't need to be covered up. She didn't know why he insisted on wearing a shirt during his visits. She wanted to see his body in its entirety and hated how often she harped on that detail.

She was terrified her friends could read her dirty mind and sense that she'd changed. But, like their parents, her friends seemed oblivious to any undercurrents between them. But why should they pick up on anything when she couldn't? Jesse treated her the same as he always had. There was no trace of the desperate hunger that brought him to her night after night. It was unsettling and made her question her sanity. She wished she could confide in someone about what was happening to her, but she didn't dare.

As she approached the finish line, her toes curled. As she prepared for take-off, movement off to her left made her freeze. The bathroom door swung open, and Jesse's familiar shadow appeared before she could retract her hand. She closed her eyes and hoped the comforter looked like it was merely bunched over her crotch so he wouldn't realize what she'd been doing.

He stood over her for a moment before he leaned down and inhaled. This was another part of the ritual, but tonight it sent a streak of panic through her. He couldn't smell her arousal, could he? She died a thousand deaths as he took another, longer inhale. *Just get on with it*, she silently screamed.

"Shit," he whispered.

Her eyelids flickered. She was shocked by his curse and the fact he'd actually spoken. Normally, all she heard were muffled, involuntary sounds, but hearing his voice tore the seams between this alternate reality and real life.

The wet sound of him stroking himself made her clench her teeth. It was the worst punishment to act like a lifeless doll when she was so close. Why had she wasted so much time wrestling with herself? She could have come and been asleep hours ago. Then, she wouldn't have to listen to the sounds he was making that made the space between her legs so slippery she may need to change her bedding.

Jesse's stifled moan unraveled her shaky control. She pressed on her clit, but it wasn't enough. She needed that back-and-forth motion. Jesse wouldn't notice, would he? He was focused on his own needs, and he was making enough noise that she knew he was close too. Moving as little as possible, she began to rub and was rewarded with a delicious wave of prickling heat. She sucked in a breath and heard Jesse do the same. She found herself matching Jesse's strokes. This was wrong on so many levels, but she was past the point of caring. Her heart soared. This was going to be the best orgasm she'd ever had.

"Violet."

She obeyed without thinking. Her eyes popped open and collided with Jesse's, which were dark, glittering pools. As always, he wore his shirt, and his cock jutted beneath it. He was close. She could tell from the way he was jerking on the head of his penis.

As she realized they were staring at one another, and they'd broken their unspoken pact, a bolt of heat lanced through her. Her climax bubbled up. She gasped for breath as her eyes began to roll.

"Shit," she heard again.

When the head of his cock touched her lips, they instinctively parted, allowing him to spill into her mouth, while remnants dribbled down her chin and cheek. Even in the midst of her orgasm, his gut-wrenching groan freaked her out. Their parents were going to hear!

As the hot euphoria of her climax faded, cold horror came charging in. She lay there, trying to control her breathing as her heart hammered so hard in her chest that she trembled from the force of it. Not wanting to face the consequences of her actions, she went motionless again, like a stupid animal who'd made a foolish move and hoped they would blend back in with their surroundings before the hunter took its shot.

Jesse didn't move for several minutes. Neither did she. She didn't even swallow, she was so determined for him to believe her looking at him had been a figment of his imagination. She willed him to walk away and continue the pretense.

She was so attuned to him, she sensed the moment he moved, even though he didn't make a sound. There was a light snick of the bathroom door closing. Jesse didn't wash his hands or use the toilet but went straight through to his bedroom and closed that door too. Everything went still and quiet and tranquil, as if what just took place between them never happened.

She finally swallowed. Was it her imagination, or was his cum sweeter? Was it because of the buttermilk pie? Dismayed over her thoughts, she sat up and feverishly scrubbed her face to remove all traces of him. The urge to shower and gargle with mouthwash was overwhelming, but the bathroom was neutral territory. Why did she have a feeling, if she went in there, he would try to talk to her? She would die if he did.

She rushed over to her drawer and got a new set of underwear and pajamas and tossed her ruined ones into the hamper. When she climbed back into bed, she huddled under the covers and writhed in anguish.

Her worst fears came true. Jesse's secret—now, *their* secret—was out in the open. She allowed herself to be enticed into participating in his twisted fantasy, which had abruptly transitioned into something else. Something terrifying. Something that could never be. This is what happened when she let her body make stupid decisions! This wasn't her and it wasn't him. They were good kids, *Christian* kids. This went against everything they believed in. What were they doing?

Tomorrow, she would put a stop to this. What was done in the dark had to stay there. She wouldn't allow it to see the light of day and change their relationship.

CHAPTER 7
JESSE

Look at me, baby. Open your eyes so we can finally talk, he silently begged, but Violet's eyes remained closed.

He wanted to sweep her up in his arms and shout for joy, but the fact that she'd gone back to feigning sleep didn't bode well. He sensed her distress but couldn't make sense of it. They didn't have to hide this anymore!

Over the past weeks, there had been times when he swore he saw her eyelids flutter or random body movements that led him to believe she was awake. He'd been pushing it lately, willing to risk it all to discover whether he was losing his mind.

Tonight, when he came into her room and tried to catch her scent, he detected something that shouldn't have been, something that reminded him of what he'd found smeared on several of her used underwear. Arousal. It sent his body into overdrive. He'd noticed the odd bunching of the covers over her crotch, but thought nothing of it, until it shifted. It took him only a second to figure out what she'd been doing before he entered. When her hand began to move in telltale circles, his heart stopped.

It had been a calculated risk to say her name. He said it loudly enough to rouse her if she'd been asleep, but when her eyes flew open, they were alert and glazed with lust. And then she started to climax. He hadn't been able to resist her open mouth. It was the most satisfying orgasm he'd ever had.

Please, baby. I'm dying here, he thought. He reached out to touch her but stopped when he noticed she was trembling. The urge to comfort her was overwhelming, but his need to put her at ease was stronger. Reluctantly, he retreated.

He walked through the bathroom to his bedroom and leaned against the door. His initial blast of elation had morphed into disquiet, but he wouldn't let that get him down. He would give her the space she needed this evening and talk it out tomorrow. He worried that she may always see him as a brother but tonight proved otherwise. She declared her feelings in the best way possible—by masturbating right alongside him.

He wanted to roar in triumph. He wanted to hold her on his lap and confess how much he loved her. How much he had been holding back. Nine months he'd kept all of this bottled up inside of him. He worried constantly that she or someone else would deduce how he felt about her, but that was at an end. God had mercy on him and made her want him in return. He no longer needed to date other girls in a futile attempt to dilute his obsession or use religion as an excuse for why he didn't go all the way with them.

He flopped on his bed and folded his hands behind his head and replayed her orgasm—eyes rolling, legs jerking beneath the covers in involuntary response, and her beautiful face covered in him. His heart swelled, felt like it was about to burst. Violet wanted him. He wasn't sure what their next step was, but it didn't matter because they were finally on the same page.

***

HIS HAND FLEXED ON THE STEERING WHEEL. HE WASN'T SURE WHAT TO expect from Violet this morning, but the bright smile and upbeat, inane chatter wasn't it. From the moment she bounded out of her bedroom and for most of the ride to school, she talked about a range of topics—everything but the one thing he wanted to discuss. He couldn't get anything in edgewise. He decided to let her take the lead, but he had no idea where she was going with this.

"You have games on Tuesday and Friday, right?" she asked distractedly as she typed on her phone.

"Yeah."

"All righty."

He waited a second before he asked, "You're coming, right?"

"I'm not sure. My friends asked me to do something Friday night."

On cue, her phone chimed.

"Who's texting you?"

"Georgia and Allison and…"

Another chime sounded.

"And?" he prompted as he turned into the school parking lot.

"Huh?" Violet looked around and waved when she spotted her friends. "There they are!"

He parked and tried to tamp down the flurry of emotions in his chest as she prepared to leave. "Violet."

"Yeah?"

"Hang on a minute."

Her body visibly stiffened. The unease he dismissed last night came back full force. He assumed they could finally talk openly, but Vi clearly wasn't ready.

"Look at me."

She made eye contact with him several times this morning, her eyes filled with rabid good cheer. Not now, though. They were more green than hazel, a sure sign that her temper was on the rise.

"What, Jesse?" she asked impatiently as her cheeks bloomed with color.

He wished he could touch her, but in the mood she was in, he had no idea how that would be received. She was skittish and on edge and couldn't make it plainer that she wanted to get away from him. What the hell was happening?

"Is everything okay?"

His voice was gruff with panic. He had the crazy urge to keep her in the car and drive to some secluded place where they wouldn't be interrupted so they could sort this out.

"I'm fine. I'll see you later," she said and slid out of the vehicle.

He didn't move as she hurried over to her friends. He sat there for a full minute, his mind racing. She'd been with him every step of the way last night, so what was the issue? Had she just become aware of his feelings and her own? Did she need more time to wrap her mind around this? He wished she would tell him, so he wasn't left feeling like everything he wanted was slipping through his fingers before he had a chance to grab hold of it.

Her feelings had changed somewhere along the way, she just didn't want to admit it. For weeks now, he'd sensed a subtle change in her gaze. She thought he wouldn't notice, but he was so aware of her, he felt the weight of her intrigued consideration during his games, on their commute to school, and when they watched TV. He thought he might have imagined it, but after last night, he was certain. To help her along, he stripped in front of her whenever possible, like yesterday after pinning her on the couch. Was she worried about what people would say? Their parents? He didn't care what they faced if he had her, but Violet didn't feel the same. So, where did that leave them?

He hissed through his teeth as he stepped out of the SUV and resisted the urge to slam the door. He wouldn't push it for now. Pressuring her would only cancel the progress he'd made. He'd lasted this long. He could wait a little longer, especially with last night's victory under his belt.

Good things come to those who wait, he reminded himself.

He turned to see Brody enter the gym.

"Hiding?" he echoed before he turned back to the hoop and took his shot.

Brody let out a disgusted sound as he made his way across the court. "Are you practicing for the NBA?"

"You know I'm going into the military."

"I was hoping you changed your mind," Brody muttered.

"I haven't."

He retrieved the ball and dribbled back to his spot to make another three-pointer. Brody placed himself beneath the hoop and passed him the ball. Several minutes passed before he noticed the odd look Brody was giving him.

"What?"

"You're taking this well."

He frowned. "Taking what well?"

Brody did a hook shot before passing the ball to him once more. "Violet."

He tensed. "What about her?"

He texted her to see if she wanted to go off campus for lunch. He hoped if she wasn't ready to talk, she'd still want to spend time together. She hadn't responded, which put him in a foul mood. He had no idea where he stood with her, and it was driving him crazy. He'd taken refuge in the gym during lunch to clear his head.

"I thought it was a rumor, so I didn't bother asking you about it, but I saw them with my own eyes." Brody shook his head. "Out of all the guys she could pick, she chose *him*? That loner who hides in the library?"

He tucked the basketball under his arm. "Tobias?"

Brody made a face. "Is that his name? He can't even make eye contact with anyone, and your sister looks at him and thinks, 'Hey, this guy should be my first boyfriend?'"

His heart slammed against his ribs. "Who says Violet's dating him?"

Brody stared at him. "I saw them."

He took a threatening step toward his friend. "Saw them *what*?"

Brody held up his hands. "Chill, bro."

"Tell me what you saw!"

"They were holding hands in the cafeteria." Brody searched his face. "I thought you knew."

He threw the ball at his friend before he snatched his backpack and stalked out of the gym. *She wouldn't do this to him*, he thought as pain and fury seared his chest. The bell rang, flooding the hallways with students. He went against the crowd to reach the cafeteria, but by the time he got there, it was empty. He broke into a run to get to Violet's next class. Several people called out to him and a teacher told him to slow down, but for once in his life, he ignored everyone. Brody had to be mistaken. There had to be another explanation for Violet holding Tobias' hand. Like, the kid had suddenly gone blind, and she was leading him around because no one else would, or something. She wouldn't date. Not now and not *him*.

He turned the corner as the second bell rang and stopped in his tracks. Tobias and Violet stood outside of her class. Violet was smiling at Tobias like... Like she should be smiling at him. Tobias grasped Violet's hand and pecked it before he scuttled down the hallway. Violet had a bemused look on her face before it morphed into a delighted giggle.

As if she sensed his presence, she looked down the hall to where he stood. Her eyes widened and her amusement vanished. He started toward her to get some answers, but she took a step back and raised her hand in a stopping motion before she disappeared inside her class.

What the fuck?

The third and final bell rang. Teachers came out to close their doors. One of them noticed him standing there and frowned.

"Mr. Sampson? Is something wrong?"

"No," he said and pivoted on his heel.

His temper, something that hadn't been provoked since last

summer, threatened to break free. Why would she suddenly decide to date after what happened last night? And why choose a creep like Tobias? The guy spent his days in the library or in empty classrooms, scribbling in a notebook and talking to himself. He told Tobias to steer clear of Violet, but apparently Tobias hadn't taken him seriously. Or, had Violet sought him out? The thought incensed him so much that he smashed his fist into the building, bruising his knuckles, but he didn't notice.

He was in no mood to sit in class. He walked toward the parking lot, nodding to the security guards who knew him by name. His reputation as a good student and athlete allowed him to walk off property without being asked if he had permission.

It took extreme discipline not to give into his demons as he navigated out of the parking lot and rode gently over the speed bumps. It wasn't until he was on a deserted country road that he slammed on the accelerator and let the engine release a roar that he silently echoed. He drove to a park. The sound of his phone chiming made him dig through the zippers to find it.

Madyson: *I couldn't find you at lunch. I have a surprise for you.*

Madyson: *Do you want to go to a concert in San Antonio this weekend?*

He tossed his phone on the seat, slammed the door, and paused. He'd been dating Madyson for a couple of weeks. He planned to break it off with her, but there'd been no need to rush. Is that why Violet decided to date? Because he was? Did she think last night meant nothing to him?

He scowled as he headed for the trail. Running always cleared his head and right now, he needed all the help he could get with his emotions clamoring. He should have pushed the issue this morning during their ride to school. He should have just laid it out and found out what was going on in her head instead of being blindsided like this.

To expel the black rage threatening to consume him, he ran full out. Was it a coincidence that Tobias asked her out today, or was this something Violet had orchestrated? His chest burned, and it wasn't from his pace. Tobias didn't have the balls to ask her out, which meant Violet had done this deliberately. Why? To punish him for dating other girls? But that look Violet gave him in the hallway wasn't smug or defiant. She'd been alarmed to see him and ran from him for the second time today instead of talking to him. That fucking burned him.

He slowed and continued along the trail at a jog instead of the breakneck sprint he'd started with. The run had taken the edge off his anger, though it still heated his brain. But he was thinking a little more rationally.

So, she was hellbent on ignoring what happened between them and decided to date Tobias. If Violet wanted to date, he didn't have the right to protest or be upset when he'd dated... and done other things while pining for her.

How would Isaac react to Violet's sudden decision to date? He secretly wanted Isaac to forbid it, but that was hypocritical and selfish on his part and when they came out to their parents in the future, that would apply to him as well.

He grimaced. Why the anti-social poet, though? What did she see in him? Abruptly, his bad mood lightened a bit. Better Tobias than one of his friends. Tobias had no game. He was awkward and weird, and it wouldn't last. Violet was just testing the waters. She wasn't truly attracted to Tobias. He was a filler, just like his girlfriends had been. But he used other girls to temper his fixation on Violet while she was deliberately bringing other guys between them. Why? Because she didn't trust what was between them? Was she too self-conscious of what others would say?

He gritted his teeth at the realization that his suffering wasn't at an end, but another beginning. Violet wasn't as deeply enmeshed as he was. If she was, she wouldn't care what others would say or think. She wouldn't care about the consequences. But she did. He still had a long way to go to convince her they were meant to be together.

He slicked back his sweaty hair as he made his way back to the parking lot. Her stunt still grated, but throwing a fit over her dating or forcing her to acknowledge their sexual attraction to each other would only make her dig her heels in and reinforce whatever reservations made her do this in the first place. He had to stand back and let her explore and experiment. Violet was a good girl. She wouldn't go too far. She wanted the freedom to choose. He could understand that, even if he didn't like it. If part of this was revenge for the girls he dated, he would let her have it.

He was confident it wouldn't take her long to realize that their connection was special. No one suited her like he did. He knew her better than she knew herself. He adored everything about her and would do anything for her, even let her date other guys, though it would drive him crazy to see anyone touch what was his. She would come to him when she was ready. And once he claimed her, that would be it for both of them.

CHAPTER 8
VIOLET

4 MONTHS LATER

VIOLET FROWNED AT THE COMPUTER SCREEN, WHERE HER UNFINISHED article for the school newspaper was laid out in incomplete paragraphs. She'd been sitting here for at least twenty minutes and hadn't changed one word. She stared at the screen, her mind a million miles away. The steady clicking of her pen gave away her agitation.

Someone stuck their head into the empty classroom, capturing Violet's attention. She sat up, a smile breaking across her face as the boy entered and came toward her.

"What are you doing here?" she asked her boyfriend as he stopped beside her.

"Looking for you." Tucker leaned down to give her a swift kiss. "Let's get out of here."

She didn't hesitate. She saved her work, shouldered her backpack, and felt her stomach flutter when he wrapped an arm around her waist.

"Jesse has practice, so I knew you'd be around here somewhere,"

Tucker said. "It took me a while to find you. Since when do you hide out in Mr. Halstead's classroom?"

"How'd you know I was hiding?"

He cocked his head as he looked down at her. "I was kidding."

"I wasn't," she said sourly. "Is there something on my face?"

Her boyfriend's brows arched. "I'm sorry?"

"I swear, people have been staring at me funny all day."

She blew out a breath as they left the building and headed toward the deserted parking lot. When she began her junior year with Tucker as her boyfriend, it caused a sensation. Tucker was a senior and lead singer of his band with a notorious reputation. Tucker may be known as a bad boy, but around her, he was sweet and attentive. After several weeks, people were finally getting used to seeing them together but today felt like day one all over again. She didn't understand it.

"I haven't done anything out of the ordinary, and I'm not wearing anything scandalous," she said, gesturing to her blouse and shorts.

Yes, the blouse was a little more fitted than what she'd gone for in the past, but compared to her classmates, her clothes were still modest and conservative. She'd been stared at so intently, she excused herself to go to the bathroom to make sure she didn't have a stain or rip in her clothes. She told herself it was all in her head until she heard her name said three times in her last class. The temptation to confront her classmates was strong, but what could they possibly be gossiping about? Her conscience was clear... for the most part.

As Tucker's eyes moved slowly and deliberately over her body, she gave him a little push as her cheeks flushed.

"Stop looking at me like that!"

"Like what?"

"Like..." She flapped her hands, unable to bring herself to say it out loud. "You know!"

"Like you're gorgeous? Like I want to strip you naked?"

"*Tucker!* You can't say that!"

"Why? It's true. You have nothing to be self-conscious about. They're just jealous because you're a knockout."

Her heart leapt when he patted her butt. She glanced around self-consciously, but there was no one around to witness Tucker's inappropriate PDA. Tucker felt like her first "real" boyfriend. Tobias and the others she briefly dated had been more friend than boyfriend, but Tucker made it clear from the start that he wanted much more. He kissed her on their first date and wasn't embarrassed to touch her in public. It was exciting and thrilling. She allowed him to go further than anyone else, though she hadn't gone *all* the way. The fact that she considered allowing him to be her first was shocking when she'd vowed to save herself for marriage. But with her sexual frustration mounting, Tucker was a much-needed, healthy outlet she could indulge in without feeling guilty.

Tucker led her toward his Bronco parked in the back corner of the mostly empty lot and opened the passenger door for her. When she made no move to get in, his eyes narrowed.

"You know what my dad said."

Tucker made a terrible first impression when he sped through their neighborhood after picking her up. Dad hadn't ordered her to break up with him, but she wasn't allowed to get in a car with Tucker. If they wanted to meet up, someone had to pick her up or drop her off.

Tucker rolled his eyes. "I swear, I won't speed again."

"If my dad finds out I got in a car with you, I'll be grounded for life."

"He won't find out."

"Jesse will tell him."

Tucker glanced at his watch. "He won't finish practice for another hour. I can bring you back before he's finished. He won't even know you left campus. You can say you were in the library the whole time."

Her insides twisted. This was just the sort of thing Dad had lectured her about—her boyfriend encouraging her to lie and break the rules. All the males in her life unanimously disliked Tucker. Her father, Jesse, and her guy friends had protested the moment they started dating, but they didn't see what she did.

Tucker's band played a set at a concert she and her friends attended this summer. They hung out after, and the rest was history. Tucker was so different from everyone she knew. He had big dreams of becoming a rock star. She loved listening to him talk about music and his plans to travel the globe. Being around someone who had such large aspirations made her reexamine her own future. He was free, liberated. Not bound by the constraints of religion or the weight of family expectations. Being near him made her feel like she could be a different person... But she wasn't willing to break all the rules just yet.

"I'm sorry, but I don't want to lie to Jesse or my dad," she said.

Tucker didn't do a good job of hiding his irritation.

"You're lucky you're hot," he growled and tugged her toward him and boxed her in the open doorway of his car. "You're driving me crazy."

"I don't," she began, but was cut off when his mouth covered hers.

He kissed her deeply. She was dimly aware of her backpack falling to the ground as he pressed himself against her, so she couldn't fail to feel his erection. She gripped his shirt as the space between her legs pulsed.

"Don't you want me?" Tucker panted as he brushed kisses over her cheek and gripped her ass.

"Of course I do," she whispered and tipped her head back to give him better access. God, she needed to be touched like this. She was starving, burning up. There were so many desires trapped inside her. So much she wanted to set free, so much she wanted to experience.

Guilt cut through her carnal desires. Good Christian girls didn't let their boyfriends put their tongues in their mouth or let them touch their butt. A good Christian girl would stop this and walk away. She stayed where she was. She hadn't been a good Christian girl for a while now. On the surface, not much had changed. She attended church, had the same friends, and continued to be a dedicated student. But no one knew the dark secret she shared with her stepbrother.

Jesse's visits continued. He hadn't been put off by her dating, as she'd hoped. They presented a wholesome image to the world while he crept into her room at night, and she pretended to be asleep. She hated that no matter who she dated, Jesse was still in the forefront of her mind. But she finally had a boyfriend who didn't treat her like a princess or a good girl. Tucker treated her like a woman, giving her the opportunity to act on her pent-up desires.

"You feel so good," Tucker rasped as he gripped her breast.

She arched into his touch.

"God, you're so hot for me. Let's get out of here."

"I can't," she said breathlessly and glanced around, reason asserting itself now that he wasn't kissing her. "We can't do this. Somebody might see! I have to…"

In a sudden move that took her by surprise, he picked her up and carried her to the back of his Bronco and pinned her against the cool metal.

"Now, no one can see us," he said huskily.

She stared at the surrounding trees, which gave them a false sense of privacy, before she looked back at Tucker, who was staring at her with a determination that made her tense. "Tucker, I can't…"

"You're not ready to give me your cherry yet," he said impatiently. "But I can give you a preview of what you're missing."

She braced her hands on his shoulders. "What are you talking about?"

"Let me show you," he cooed as he undid the button of her shorts.

She grasped his wrist, eyes wide. "What are you doing?"

"Making you feel good," he said against her lips. "Come on, give me this at least. Let me touch you."

"Y-you want to touch me *there*?" she whispered, scandalized.

He stared at her for a moment before he shook his head. "You're such an innocent. It's a miracle no one's got to you before now. I guess I have Jesse to thank for that."

He tested her grip on him before he pulled down her zipper. This was dangerous. She knew that, but she couldn't find the will to stop him as he lifted her shirt to examine her underwear.

"Of course you're wearing pink," he said with masculine approval. "So pretty and perfect."

"Tucker?"

She wasn't sure if he kissed her because he heard the uncertainty in her tone. If that was so, it was a good strategy. It was wiped any thought of resistance from her mind. She sensed his excitement and urgency as his hand brushed over the front of her. She gasped and was thankful for his bumper, which gave her something to sit on when her legs gave out.

"I'm going to make you feel so good," he panted as he adjusted his hand. "I want you to come on my fingers. God, you feel..."

One minute he was pressed against her and the next, he was gone. She opened her eyes and stared at the empty space where Tucker had been without comprehension before she heard a shout and then a strange scuffling sound. She rose on shaky legs, rounded the vehicle, and stopped in her tracks.

Jesse straddled Tucker, who was splayed out on the pavement. Even as she watched, Jesse drew back his fist and rammed it into Tucker's face. Tucker's head snapped back and collided with the pavement with a sickening crack. Jesse landed two more forceful blows before she came out of her horrified stupor.

"Jesse, stop!" she screamed.

Blood spurted as he landed another punch before she caught his swinging arm.

"*Stop!*"

Her desperate shriek finally seemed to penetrate the haze. Jesse stilled. Tucker's face was covered in blood from a split lip, a broken nose, and what might be a shattered cheekbone.

"What the hell, Jesse?" she whispered, shaken to the core.

As Jesse rose, she collapsed beside Tucker to make sure he was all right, but before she could touch him, Jesse roughly hauled her to her feet. She hauled in a breath to yell at him, but the chilling look on Jesse's face wiped her mind clean.

"Touch her again, I'll kill you," Jesse said with chilling softness.

Her mouth dropped. "Jesse, he—"

He ignored her and began to tow her across the parking lot. She dug in her heels.

"I'm not," she began before Jesse turned, crouched, and tossed her over his shoulder. She braced her hands on his back so she could see Tucker. "He isn't moving!"

"He's alive," Jesse said curtly as he set her beside the SUV and yanked the door open. "Get in."

She gawked at him, unable to believe what he'd done. She had no idea he knew how to throw a punch, much less how to systematically beat someone to a pulp. Tucker had been in his fair share of fights, but Jesse had incapacitated him with shocking ease. She didn't know Jesse had that level of violence in him, but the splatter of red on his shirt, arm, and hand said different.

"Why did you do that?" she demanded.

It was an unfortunate moment for her gaping shorts to drop to her knees. In the time it took her to haul them up and fasten them, Jesse had crossed quite a distance on his way back to Tucker to finish what he started. She wrapped her arms around his waist and pulled back with all her might.

"Jesse, *don't!*"

He stopped, but didn't turn back to the car. She was very aware that if he wanted to, he could continue to beat the crap out of Tucker and there was nothing she could do about it. His chest pumped as he tried to rein in his temper. He was angrier than she had ever seen him.

"Jesse?"

"Get in the car."

His voice trembled with rage. She hesitated before she loosened her hold on him. She felt a modicum of relief when he turned from Tucker's prone form to follow her back to the car. She warily eyed his blank expression as she climbed in. He held the door open for her out of habit. She flinched, even though he didn't slam the door. She almost wished he had.

As he stalked around to the driver's side, she turned in her seat and was relieved to see Tucker sitting up and clutching his head with both hands. She hoped he was okay. If she had her phone, she would have texted one of his friends to check on him, but it was in her backpack on the other side of Tucker's Bronco. Considering what just happened, her backpack didn't seem all that important at the moment. As Jesse got in, she faced forward.

"Did he force you?" Jesse spat as they left the parking lot.

Her head whipped toward him. "F-force?"

"Did you want him to touch you?" he clarified impatiently.

For a second, she considered lying before the telltale wetness between her legs and honesty made her confess, "Yes."

Jesse didn't say a word, but his temper filled the cab, making her heart skip erratically. She ran a shaking hand through her hair. "I'm sorry. I don't know what I was thinking."

"Don't talk," he said harshly. "Before I crash the car."

Sick to her stomach, she looked out the window, and bit down on her lower lip until she tasted blood. Jesse thought Tucker was forcing her? His reaction was understandable if that's what he believed, but she wished Jesse asked questions before he got physical with her boyfriend. She buried her face in her hands. This was all her fault. Anyone could have come by. It just so happened that it was Jesse who interrupted them. Everything happened so fast that her mind was still spinning.

They didn't exchange a word the whole ride home. When Jesse pulled into their driveway, he braked hard enough to make her rock forward, so her seatbelt locked. She cast him a wide-eyed look he didn't notice since he got out of the car and, this time, slammed the door behind him.

She sat there for a moment, unsure what to do. It wasn't until he disappeared inside that she realized Dad could be home. The bolt of fear that struck her caused her to undo her seatbelt and sprint after Jesse.

She burst through the front door and took in the empty living room and kitchen before she raced down the hallway. She got a glimpse of Jesse in his bedroom as she made her way to the end of the hall. She was relieved to see her parent's room was empty, and her father wasn't sleeping after a long shift.

She made her way back to Jesse's room, nervously plucking at her top as she stopped in the open doorway. He paced manically, a far cry from his controlled, athletic grace. She was at a complete loss on how to fix this, especially when she and Jesse weren't on the best terms.

They'd grown apart this summer. Jesse attended sports camps, helped renovate the church and went dirt biking, hunting, and fishing while she spent her time with whoever she was dating and her friends. Mom and Dad had remarked on her suddenly full social calendar, but they'd been happy for her rather than disappointed. Little did they know, she was doing it to avoid Jesse and exhaust herself so she could sleep through his visits.

It had been a sound strategy, but it hadn't had the desired effect. Her body still responded to Jesse despite the emotional distance and distractions she'd placed between them. The shame of being sexually attracted to her stepbrother caused her to give Tucker privileges she otherwise wouldn't have if her hormones weren't running amok.

She glanced at the clock. Mom would be home in an hour and a half. She had never been more grateful that Lynne helped with after school programs. She wasn't sure when Dad would be home, but she would do anything to gain Jesse's promise not to tell him what she'd done with Tucker.

Her father would lose his mind. Would he take matters into his own hands and go after Tucker with a gun for daring to touch her? When she decided to date Tobias, she went to Lynne first, who made good on her promise to handle Dad. Though it clearly pained him, Dad allowed her to date on one condition—that she wouldn't allow any boy to pressure her to do anything she wasn't comfortable with. That was Dad's way of telling her she wasn't allowed to have sex. She hadn't gone all the way with Tucker, but that wouldn't matter to Dad. Imagining his reaction made her sweat. The thrill of breaking the rules and treading into forbidden territory had long since faded. Now, all she could think of was the consequences.

"What the hell were you thinking?"

Jesse's words, dripping with disgust, made her hang her head.

"I'm sorry."

"Sorry?"

Out of the corner of her eye, she saw him feverishly rake his fingers through his hair.

"If I hadn't seen it with my own eyes, no one could have convinced me that you would let him touch you like that."

A ripple of defiance stole through her. "Why not? He's my boyfriend! I'm *seventeen*. Other girls..."

He pivoted to face her.

"You aren't like other girls! You're better than that."

She swallowed hard and averted her gaze.

"Or I thought you were."

The verbal blow stole her breath. Jesse had never been intentionally hurtful, but that stabbed her straight through the heart and momentarily distracted her from their parents' impending arrival. Before she could think of a response, Jesse whirled and sank his fist into the wall. She gasped, hands over her mouth, as he retracted a hand now covered in not just Tucker's blood but his own. She thought that would be the end of it, but when he pulled back his fist again, clearly about to pummel the wall to bits, she rushed forward. She hauled back on his arm, stopping the force of his punch so he merely cracked the wall instead of creating another gaping hole.

"Please stop," she begged.

He shrugged her off as if he couldn't stand her touch, as if she was contaminated. He skirted around her, looking anywhere but directly at her. Once again, he ran his fingers through his hair, not registering the dust, plaster, and blood that was getting all over him.

"You're hurt," she said quietly.

He began to pace again, head bent, hands flexing at his sides.

"Let me clean your hand."

No response. No reaction to her voice. Cautiously, she started toward him. She had to snap out of this agitated state. This wasn't the Jesse she knew. For nine months, she'd known there was more to him than what he presented to the world, but somehow, this side of him was more shocking than the late-night visits. Anger wasn't a part of his makeup. Neither was violence. Seeing both made her feel like she was talking to a stranger.

"What can I do?" she whispered, willing to do anything to make this right.

"You should leave," he said in a flat monotone as he stared at the floor.

"Jesse."

"I thought I knew you better than I knew myself. I never thought you would let anyone..."

His leg flashed out, sneakers colliding with an old dresser that shuddered, but otherwise didn't move. Encouraged by this, Jesse kicked it again and then kneed it in a move that she knew would hurt tomorrow. Knowing even in the depths of his rage that he would never hurt her, she inserted herself between him and his target. Just as she expected, he immediately backed away from the dresser, which was apparently indestructible.

Despite the wild look in his eye, she reached for him and clasped his face.

"Stop hurting yourself," she pleaded.

He tried to jerk away, but she wouldn't let him, tightening her hold and matching the steps he took to put distance between them.

"Look at me," she ordered.

He looked over her head, jaw set. Her eyes filled with tears as she stroked his cheeks.

"Please."

He tugged her hands from his face. Knowing he was about to push her away, she plastered her body against his. He went rigid.

"I'm sorry that I put you in that position. I'm sorry you had to see... I wasn't thinking." A tear slipped down her cheek. "Please don't be angry at me."

"Step back," he said coldly.

The compulsion to obey was strong, but she stayed put. The moment she backed away, he would continue taking his anger out on the room, which would make it impossible to keep anything from their parents. She needed him cool and rational. She didn't know what to do with the Jesse before her, who was trembling with the need to wreak havoc. All she knew was he wouldn't hurt her, and although he wanted space, her presence was the only thing stopping him from going nuclear.

"Please don't tell Dad," she said.

He glared at the wall and didn't respond.

"I swear, I won't do it again."

Again, nothing.

"Jesse." She went on tiptoes to force him to look at her, and when that didn't work, she yanked his head down. Stubbornly, his gaze remained averted. Anxious, frustrated, and exasperated, she did the only thing she could think of and brushed her mouth against his. Stormy blue eyes immediately snapped to hers. She jerked back, hands dropping away, stunned by her own impulsivity. What the hell was she *doing*? First Tucker and now she was kissing her stepbrother. What was happening to her? She backed away, twisting her hands together, cheeks hot.

"Is that how you get your way these days? With kisses?" Jesse asked in a cynical tone.

Her mouth dropped before she glared at him. "No!"

"Then what was that?"

She flung her hands in the air. "I just wanted you to calm down!"

"So, you kissed me."

Her stomach writhed. "I-I don't know why I did that." When he continued to stare at her, she snapped, "We've kissed on the lips before."

"By accident."

"Yes, well, so was this."

His eyes narrowed. "You really think I'm not going to tell Dad what happened today?"

"I don't know why you would." She was relieved to return to their real problem. "You'd be in just as much trouble as me! You beat the crap out of him! Dad won't—"

"Dad's going to pat me on the back, and you know it. Dad warned you about boys like Tucker. Boys who will take advantage of your inexperience to pressure you into something you aren't ready for."

She crossed her arms over her chest and jutted out her hip. "Who says I'm not ready? I know what I want!"

His eyes darkened. "Do you?"

"Yes!" she said defiantly. "I'm not a little girl. I'm going to be a senior next year. I'm allowed to experiment if I want to! If I want him to..."

He closed the distance between them in two strides. She fell silent as he towered over her.

"You want him to what?"

Something about his tone caused the fine hairs on her nape to rise. The only sound in the room was her rapid breathing. As he stared at her, not speaking, her nipples hardened into points so sharp, they hurt. Embarrassed and confused, she stepped back and collided with the massive dresser.

"You want to experiment?" he asked softly as he crowded her.

She swallowed hard, heart thudding in her ears as she tried to think. His hand moved between them. She went cold when she felt a tug on her shorts. When he began to pull down her zipper, she clutched his wrist and shook her head. He held her gaze as he nudged her shorts down. Her breath halted when he cupped her like Tucker had. His fingers pressed against the gusset of her underwear. Not penetrating, but firm enough to push the material between her lips.

"How much have you experimented?"

His voice, rough with anger, caused her insides to clench. Warmth pooled low. To her horror, she felt herself secrete. She held her breath, hoping he wouldn't feel her underwear dampen, but a second later, his fingers shifted, rubbed, and then his expression hardened.

He brushed her underwear aside and slipped a finger inside her. She let out a strangled yelp and banged into the dresser in a desperate bid to get away, but Jesse was relentless. His finger sank so deep, her mouth opened on a silent gasp.

"You're soaked," he growled against her temple and hissed when her pussy bathed him in more honey. "Christ."

"I..." She closed her eyes as another finger joined the first. "Jesse."

"How many times?" he growled.

She grabbed fistfuls of his shirt and tugged, unable to utter a single word. Her mind was whirling, emotions spiraling, back arching as he caused her womb to weep. She went on tiptoes as he sank deeper than her hairbrush ever had.

"How many times?" he bit out.

"I... I don't know," she babbled as her shorts dropped to her ankles, allowing her to spread her legs, which he immediately took advantage of.

"You've done it so many times, you didn't keep count?"

His voice was so guttural she could barely understand him, but what he was saying didn't matter when he was fingering her. Was this really happening? It couldn't be. It was broad daylight. Jesse never did anything sexual during the day, but there was no denying he was definitely touching her.

Shock made her lightheaded. Jesse caught her as she began to sway. Her head swam as he picked her up and settled her on his bed. Her legs hung over the side as she lay on her back, chest pumping as she tried to wrap her mind around what was happening. She jerked as her underwear was dragged down her legs. When she heard a zipper being undone, she stopped breathing. She felt the coarse brush of his jeans against her shin as he stepped out of them.

"Jesse?" she whispered.

A large hand cupped the back of her knee and began to lift it, spreading her wide. Her hands dove between her legs to cover the heart of her that had been touched for the first time today by two different boys within the same hour. She should stop this. She should talk some sense into him, but one look into blue eyes that still glittered with banked rage made her body pliant in instinctive submission.

"I was so patient. I thought we had an understanding, but you gave yourself to him," he growled as he dragged her ass to the edge of the bed.

"I..." she began, but her mind went blank as something began to enter her. She looked down the length of her body as Jesse gripped her hip, holding her still as he fed his dick into her with his bruised, bloody hand. Belatedly, she tried to scoot away to stop him, but his hold tightened, keeping her in place.

The tendons in his neck stood out as he bared his teeth and eased his way in. He still wore his white t-shirt, splattered with specks of red. His nipples stood out starkly as he stared down at where they were joined. He braced himself over her, the gold cross on the chain around his neck dangling over her face as he buried himself inside her. His groan drowned out her own.

"Jesse?"

"How could you?" he panted as he withdrew and gently began to drive in again. "How could you do this to me?"

As her unused channel spasmed in pain, she grasped his shirt, feet kicking for purchase as her body tried to adjust to his invasion. Panicked tears leaked out of the corner of her eyes.

"I don't know what you're..." Her voice died as he speared her core, tearing through her hymen.

Jesse went rigid, and then his head came up. He stared down at her, eyes wide with astonishment. Every ounce of anger drained away to be replaced with anguish. He cupped her wet cheek with a shaking hand.

"You're a virgin?" he whispered.

She nodded jerkily.

He rested his forehead against hers. "God, I'm sorry. I'm so sorry, baby."

He chanted his apology while she lay rigid as a board beneath him. She was dimly aware of the sound of kids playing basketball in the street. His blinds were up. There was a bush obscuring part of his window, but if anyone looked in, they'd see...

"Look at me."

Her skittering thoughts halted. She met his gaze as he stroked back her hair. He looked like her brother again. Composed, gentle, affectionate. But he was inside of her, and he hadn't pulled out yet. She could feel his dick pulsing inside of her like a piece of heated steel. Now that the pain was receding, it felt... okay.

"You never..." he began unsteadily and then hissed and closed his eyes as his dick twitched inside of her.

"That was the first time he ever touched me."

His eyes shot open and bored into hers. "And that's the last time. No one's ever going to touch you but me." His gaze moved over her face and landed on her lips. "You don't know how long I've been waiting for this." His hips moved and when she didn't flinch, his breath hitched in excitement. "I'm sorry. I need this."

She didn't make a sound as he began to move. She knew he was larger than other boys his age and had witnessed his strength, but she had never experienced both until now. He was going too deep, too fast.

"Jesse, you're hurting me," she whispered.

He didn't slow down. He was deaf to anything but the urges of his body and ruthlessly sought relief.

"Jesse!"

She pushed and when that got no reaction from him, her hands slipped under his tee and raked over his back. That only seemed to spur him on. She fought him in earnest, scared and in agony, but Jesse was oblivious to both. When he finally climaxed and slumped on top of her, she was covered in cold sweat.

He eased to the side so she could take a full breath. Pinned partially beneath him, she stared at the ceiling, battered, shaken, and numb. This wasn't supposed to happen. It couldn't happen. But it had. Now, what?

Jesse lay on his side facing her. She tensed as he splayed his hand on her quivering abdomen.

"I'm sorry."

She wasn't sure whether he was sorry for what he'd just done, how rough he'd been, or believing she hadn't been a virgin. It didn't matter. Nothing did anymore.

He gripped her face and tipped it toward him. Sated, heavy lidded eyes searched her blank, tear-streaked face.

"I'll make this up to you," he vowed as his thumb passed over her bottom lip.

The only way he could make this up to her was if they pretended that it never happened. As if he'd heard her thought, he grimaced.

"I'll never forgive myself." He stroked her cheek. "I promised myself I'd never hurt you, that I'd always protect you. I failed on both counts today, and I can't take it back. Can you forgive me?"

She nodded without thinking it through. Accepting his apology was a reflex, something that had been drilled into her by going to church her whole life. Nothing was so egregious that it couldn't be forgiven, even this… She gulped back tears as she began to shake.

Jesse drew her against him. Even though he was the cause of her pain, she wrapped one arm around him and sobbed against his throat as everything that had happened over the past hour overwhelmed her. He stroked her hair and apologized over and over.

"I swear, Violet," he breathed fervently. "I'll never—"

She turned her head and latched onto his mouth. She wasn't sure whether she did it because she didn't want him to make rash promises, or because she wanted a different type of comfort. Either way, it did the job. The talking stopped, and the physical reassurance she desperately needed after he'd used her body so brutally came in the form of a gentle, almost reverent kiss.

She had kissed a few boys, but most of her experience came from Tucker. He was a playboy and had great technique, but there was something about the way Jesse kissed her, as if she was made of fragile glass, that soothed the trauma of her first time. That hadn't been him. That was his dark alter ego that paid her midnight visits. This was Jesse, the one who clasped her face as he kissed her, as if she was the most precious thing in the world to him.

Kissing other boys caused her tummy to flutter, but with Jesse, she felt like her world was spinning. He kissed her with an absorption that blocked out everything else. He didn't stop, even to let her catch her breath.

When his fingers probed between her legs, she stiffened and tried to push his hand away.

"Let me do this for you," he breathed against her lips.

She was prepared for more pain when his finger slid inside her. To her surprise, it evoked a pleasant, familiar throb of desire.

"Does that feel good?"

She bit her lip.

"Violet."

Her eyes opened and stared into his.

"Tell me how it feels."

He wasn't angry, but his intensity was back. She flushed under his dissecting gaze as her awareness flared out, reminding her where they were and that soon Mom and Dad would be…

Jesse's thumb rubbed her clitoris. She let out a stifled shriek and bucked.

He kissed her cheek. "Yes, let me know what you like. I want to make you fly."

He asked her for guidance on how he was making her feel, but words were beyond her. Her moans, gasps, and shudders led him instead. When she finally came, she bit her own forearm to stifle her scream.

"Good girl."

She heard Jesse's satisfied tone from a long way off. She felt his hand smoothing what was dripping out of her onto her belly. Her eyes fluttered shut against her will.

"Jesse," she slurred.

He kissed her temple. "Everything's fine. Go to sleep."

"But I…"

He covered her mouth with his. Their tongues dueled before her mouth went slack. He broke the kiss, chuckling, and kissed her forehead. "Sleep, baby."

She swam up from the depths. Her body ached like she had the flu. Was she ill? She opened her eyes and took in her surroundings. The room was dark, but a nightlight oriented her in her bedroom.

She listened, but no voices drifted down the hall. Had she missed dinner? She braced her hand on the bed to sit up and felt an unfamiliar, dragging pain between her legs. Her breath caught in her throat as graphic visions whizzed through her mind. Her hand slid over her body and stilled. She was no longer wearing a top or shorts. She was in one of her nightgowns. Her brows drew together. *Was* it a dream? Her fingers pressed between her legs, but there was no sticky residue. She was clean, but tender and achy. Why couldn't she remember?

She threw back the covers and went into the bathroom. She didn't turn on the light but went to Jesse's door and put her ear to it before she stepped through. Jesse's room was dark, but the door leading into the hallway was open, allowing her to see that the room was empty. Frowning, she peered at the made bed, which had sheets tucked so tight, she could bounce a quarter off it.

Worried that she was losing her mind, she entered the hallway. The door to her parents' domain was closed, indicating one or both of her parents had turned in. What time was it? The living and dining room were empty, but there was a lone lamp on. She peered at the numbers on the microwave but was distracted by an unfamiliar flickering light in the backyard. Jesse stood by the fire pit. She stared at him through the glass, heart thudding in her ears, palms damp with anxiety.

As if he sensed her, he half turned. With the fire behind him, she couldn't see his face, but he beckoned her outside with his hand.

She hesitated before her need for answers and confirmation pushed away her uncertainty. She slipped on sandals as she crossed to him. He held out his arm as she neared. She didn't hesitate to tuck herself against his side.

"Feeling better?" he asked.

She stiffened. "I'm fine."

He stroked her arm. "That's good to hear."

She hovered on the precipice, wanting to know if what her mind was shrieking at her was true, but she didn't voice it. Instead, she huddled beneath the umbrella of denial and let the flames of the small fire hypnotize her. She absorbed Jesse's strength and warmth. She didn't want things to change between them. This was familiar, comfortable, meant to be. That other stuff was titillating, but wrong on every level.

Her eyes narrowed as she spotted something in the fire. She took a step forward. "There's a..." She fell silent as she got a better look. Her heart lodged in her throat. "Is that my top and shorts?"

"And underwear," Jesse confirmed.

She whirled to face him. "Why are you burning it?"

His eyes were a mix of blue and orange flame.

"You know why."

She crossed her arms. "No, I don't."

"Every time I'd see those shorts or top, I'd think of Tucker."

Her breath stalled. Her face drained of all color, and she swayed.

"Hey." Jesse drew her trembling form against him. "You aren't okay. You should be lying down."

Before she could speak, he picked her up and started toward the house.

"I told Mom and Dad you weren't feeling well. Dad's shift went long, so he went straight to bed. Mom made soup and then turned in. Are you just sore or do you need—"

"What did you tell them?" she hissed.

"About what?"

"About what?" she echoed shrilly. "About your bruised knuckles, the hole in your wall, Tucker and..." Her throat constricted as she thought about what happened between them.

"They didn't see the hole. I moved something in front of it until I can patch it up. They didn't notice my hand, and there's no reason for them to hear about Tucker. As far as they know, I brought you home from school, and you went to bed because you weren't feeling well."

He carried her into the house and settled her at the table before he made his way to the kitchen, where he busied himself at the stove. He sounded so matter of fact, so controlled and blasé, as if losing his temper and taking her virginity was nothing out of the ordinary. She didn't know how to feel or behave. He was acting as if nothing had changed, so maybe it hadn't?

He brought her chicken tortellini soup and bread rolls and made a bowl for himself.

"Do you want tea?" he asked.

"Water's fine," she said awkwardly and stared at the pills he set on the table. "What's this?"

"Ibuprofen."

Her cheeks heated as she swallowed the pills. As he began to eat, she took in her familiar surroundings. Everything looked as it should, but she felt different, like she'd gone to Narnia for a year and came back to find she hadn't missed a second. But that's what she wanted, right? For everything to be as it should?

She glanced at Jesse. His blood splattered shirt had been replaced with a pristine white tee and sweatpants. His gold cross was on display. The memory of it swinging back and forth as he thrust inside her made her womb clench. She clamped her thighs together and blew on her spoonful of soup before she took a bite. It was delicious. She hadn't eaten since lunch, and it was now... She glanced at the clock. Almost eight.

"Do you want anything else?"

She focused on Jesse to discover he had inhaled his soup. Her mouth twitched. "No, thank you. I'm still working on it."

He grinned at her. "Sorry, I was starving."

She went solid as he kissed her forehead and got to his feet. Her eyes followed him to the kitchen as he rummaged in the fridge. If she hadn't been an active participant in what happened today, she wouldn't be able to sense that anything had happened. There were no strange undercurrents or awkwardness. Jesse was back to being the affectionate big brother and she... She looked down at her soup. She was going to resume playing her part of younger sister. That was best for everyone.

"You don't like it?"

She jolted as Jesse's question broke through her hazy musings. "No, it's great. I guess I'm still tired."

He gave her a sympathetic look as he brushed back her hair. "You want me to run you a bath?"

Even this question wasn't out of the ordinary, since she and

Lynne talked openly about their periods. Jesse didn't mind pampering them or being sent to the store for pads or tampons, while her father flat out refused.

"No, I'm okay. I'll just finish what I can and turn in," she said lightly.

"Okay." He glanced outside. "I have to watch the fire."

"Yes, you do that." When he turned away, she hesitated before she asked, "Did you burn anything else besides...?" Again, she blushed like a virgin. She wasn't anymore, so she would have to get past her embarrassment.

Jesse raised a brow. "Should I have?"

"I don't know." She broke eye contact and wrapped her foot around the leg of her chair. "Your sheets? Were they stained?"

"No."

She didn't hear him move, so wasn't prepared for the hand that grasped her chin. She felt her face turn beet red as he stared down at her.

"I got the blood out of them," he said in a low rumble that made her nipples hard. "You don't need to worry."

"You dressed me," she whispered.

"I knew Mom would want to check on you. She couldn't find you naked."

Very practical on his part, but, "You cleaned me."

His gaze fixed on her mouth. "Seemed like the proper thing to do."

His eyes rose to hers. Her heartbeat accelerated.

"Is there anything else you want to ask me before I tend to the fire?" he asked gently.

She shook her head. His finger slid along her jaw before he turned away. She turned back to her soup and ate mechanically before she put her bowl in the sink. Habit made her clean up the kitchen and wash the dishes. She glanced outside and saw Jesse staring contemplatively into the fire. What was he thinking? Did he feel like his life turned upside down, or was deflowering his stepsister something they would forget ever happened? That they would never speak of, like his late-night visits?

While she brushed her teeth, she scanned the bathroom for any sign of their hookup, but everything looked boringly mundane. She wished she had her phone to see if there was any word from Tucker. Had word already gotten out of Jesse fighting Tucker?

It wasn't until she swallowed her birth control pill that her eyes flew to the mirror, wide as saucers. Holy shit. She had been put on birth control a year ago to regulate her heavy, painful period. It never occurred to her that she would need it for its main purpose. She went cold with terror at the thought of getting pregnant. She was a Christian. It had been drummed into her that life was sacred and to be protected and preserved at all costs. She didn't believe in abortion, but if she was accidentally impregnated by her stepbrother, she would have no choice but to... Bile rose. She swished mouthwash to banish the taste from her mouth before she staggered to bed.

She tunneled under the covers and clasped her stuffed longhorn to her aching chest. She made a lot of stupid decisions today. The repercussions were steep, but they could have been much worse. Unfortunately, Tucker got the worst of it. Was he pissed at her? She hoped he hadn't been hurt too badly. And her consequence had been to lose her virginity. Not to the man she thought, but the most unlikely person imaginable. Even as pangs of anxiety washed over her, memories of Jesse in the throes distracted and made her body tingle.

She banished such sinful thoughts and thanked God that Mom and Dad were unaware of what happened this afternoon. Although she was worried about how she and Jesse would deal with each other moving forward, she was too tired to fight the tug of replenishing sleep. She gave in to oblivion with a soft sigh.

CHAPTER 9
JESSE

Jesse stood beside Violet's bed. Thick lashes rested against her cheeks and her mouth was parted slightly, letting him know she was deeply asleep.

She was his. Finally.

He brushed her hair back as he marveled at the strange string of events that led to the consummation of their relationship. In the middle of practice, one of his teammates told him that Tucker had bragged about taking Violet's virginity and sharing her with his bandmates. The way the rest of the team avoided his gaze told him everyone had heard the lies Tucker was spreading, but no one had the balls to tell him except Reggie.

He hadn't thought twice about stalking off the field, changing out of his uniform, and tossing his gear in the car. It was sheer coincidence that he spotted Tucker's Bronco and saw two people on the side of it. Even as he started toward them, they'd moved to the back of the car. The last thing he expected to find was Tucker with his hand in Violet's pants.

He'd taken great pleasure in smashing his fist into Tucker's pretty face. He would have killed him with his bare hands if Violet

115

hadn't stopped him. He knew about Tucker's playboy reputation and had wrongly assumed Violet would break it off if Tucker pressured her sexually. It never occurred to him that Violet would welcome his advances.

As the rage flooded back, he slid his thumb into Violet's mouth to calm him. She jerked back, but he followed, unwilling to give her space. He rubbed his thumb over her tongue, encouraging her to suck. When she reflexively obeyed, he bit back a groan and buried his face in her hair spread over the pillow.

He fooled around with his fair share of girls but never slept with any of them. He hadn't wanted to. He'd been saving himself for her. He thought they had an unspoken understanding. The betrayal and pain that consumed him was something he never wanted to experience again. He drew in a steadying breath and was comforted by her bewitching scent he couldn't get enough of. It didn't matter that Tucker had his hand in her pants first. He was the only man who had been inside her. That's all that mattered.

Today, Violet finally made her move. She kissed him. From the mortified expression on her face, she hadn't meant to, but he was damn glad she had. That impulsive kiss funneled his anger into lust. If only he'd known she was acting on instinct or desire rather than bribing him to keep quiet. Thinking she was using wiles she learned from Tucker to manipulate him, he'd been coarse, rough, out of line.

Violet let out a pitiful whimper. He nuzzled her, wondering if she was having a bad dream or if she was in pain despite the pills he'd given her. He felt a flash of regret that her first time hadn't been the gentle, loving experience she deserved. If only he'd known she was a virgin... But catching her and Tucker red-handed, he wouldn't have believed her if she'd said so.

Assuming she'd given herself to Tucker first and considering how slick she was, slow and tender had been the furthest thing from his mind. And even when he realized she was a virgin, he'd denied himself for so long that he hadn't been able to hold back the force of his need. With all that rage still pumping through his system from dealing with Tucker, he'd been primitive and savage. Violet didn't accept his claim meekly. She fought him. It had been an exhilarating, eye-opening experience. It wasn't romantic, but it was perfect because it was them, stripped of all civilization. Violet rose to the challenge and after, still trusted him with her body and allowed him to bring her to orgasm. He'd never been more grateful that he'd practiced on other girls beforehand. Violet came so hard; she passed out cold.

Knowing their parents would be home soon, he cleaned and dressed her. He didn't have time to inspect her the way he wanted. Instead, he put her in bed before he stripped off his sheets and rearranged his room to cover the hole that would prompt questions he couldn't answer. Once his bedding was in the wash, he checked on Violet, which led to him jacking off on her. He'd just cleaned her face with a cloth when Mom arrived.

"What's wrong?"

"Vi isn't feeling good," he said in low tones, and hoped Violet wouldn't wake at this inopportune moment.

He felt like he was coming out of his skin as Mom approached the bed and brushed back Violet's tangled hair. He prayed to God he got every drop of his cum as Mom pressed the back of her hand against Violet's damp forehead and cheek.

"She feels feverish," Mom said with a frown. "Has she taken anything?"

"No, she was hoping to sleep it off."

"I'll make soup," Mom said.

As Mom walked to the door, he couldn't resist doing one more pass over Violet's face with the washcloth. When he looked up, he saw Mom in the doorway, watching him with a fond smile.

"You're such a good brother," she'd said before she walked away.

He was never meant to be her brother. He'd known from the moment he laid eyes on her that he was destined to be more. It was everyone else who had it wrong, not him.

Jesse straightened and withdrew his thumb from Violet's mouth.

He vowed to give her time to recover, but he was hard as a rock. He pushed his pants down and grabbed Violet's hand and curled her fingers around him. He moved her hand along his length and shuddered in absolute bliss. Her tiny, silky fingers felt amazing and with the memory of what it felt like to be inside her heating his blood, it didn't take long.

He tipped his head back, gasping, as he climaxed. He spread his cum over her skin and held her face still as he sank his tongue into her mouth. She mewled and tried to get away, but he held her captive until she surrendered.

He eyed the closed door. There was still a chance that their parents would check on her. It was risky as hell for him to come into her room, but he couldn't resist.

He tucked himself away and gave her a swift kiss. She frowned, face scrunching up in what looked like disgust, before she turned her back to him. He grinned as he stepped back.

When she joined him by the fire pit, pale, dazed, and confused, he sensed her questions, but she didn't voice them. He had to tread carefully. They had gone astray before. He wouldn't allow that a second time. He would begin his campaign tomorrow and show her how their relationship was always meant to be.

CHAPTER 10
VIOLET

Violet woke before daylight. She tiptoed into the bathroom and washed her face and teeth before she left her bedroom. She was surprised to see a glow from the dining room and found Dad sitting at the table, reading his Bible.

"Hey, kiddo. How are you feeling?"

"Okay." Her heart was in her throat as she came forward and gripped the back of the chair. "What are you doing up so early?"

"God woke me up, told me I needed to read the Word." He tapped the open Bible. "Mom told me you weren't feeling good yesterday. I checked on you before I turned in, but you were out. I prayed over you."

She gave him a tremulous smile. "It worked. I feel much better."

He pulled out Lynne's chair. "Coffee?"

She made a face. "No!"

He chuckled. "Cocoa it is."

She sat as he went to the kitchen. She tucked her hands between her thighs as Dad made her a comfort drink. She thought that just by looking at her, people would be able to tell some monumental change had happened, but even her sharp-eyed father didn't seem to think anything was amiss. That was a relief.

"There you go."

She grinned when Dad set a mug heaping with marshmallows in front of her. "Thank you."

She popped a few in her mouth before she realized Dad was watching her closely. She froze.

"What?"

"When Lynne told me you weren't feeling good, I thought something else may have happened."

Her pulse skipped. "Like what?"

"I don't know." He took a long draw on his coffee. "I thought, maybe, boy troubles?"

She wrapped her hands around the mug and stared at the quivering marshmallows.

"Vi?"

She met his serious gaze.

"You rarely get sick. Is there something you want to tell me?"

"Tucker and I broke up," she heard herself say.

She hadn't realized she'd made a conscious decision until the words left her mouth. She'd been trying not to think past getting something to eat—the primary reason she'd gotten up at this hour. Apparently, her mind had made some decisions while she slept.

Even if Tucker didn't hate her for Jesse beating the hell out of him, she wasn't the same person she'd been yesterday. She couldn't act as if nothing had happened. Jesse was partially right. Tucker had been pressuring her sexually and eventually, she would have given into him, and it wouldn't be because she had any deep feelings for him. It would be to assuage her body's needs. Now that Jesse had done that for her, there was no need for her to use these boys as a distraction or outlet. All these months of emotional turmoil had been washed away by yesterday's events. She was a new person and had officially stepped into womanhood.

"I thought that may be the case," Dad said.

She narrowed her eyes. "You're smiling."

"Can you blame me?" He held up a hand before she could say a word. "I'm sure Tucker's a good kid, but I don't like the way he treated you. He always had an arm around your neck like you were his property..." He shook his head. "You want a guy who looks after you and respects you. Tucker only cared about himself. You can do better."

She pushed her marshmallows down into the hot cocoa.

"You want to tell me why you broke up with him?"

"No."

"Maybe you should take a break from dating." When she gave him a level look, he tacked on, "Or date one of the guys from church, so I don't have to worry so much."

"Morning."

They turned their heads as Jesse entered the dining room with messy hair and a wrinkled shirt. Jesse came straight to her. Her stomach clenched as he clasped her face between his hands.

"You feel okay?" he asked.

She gripped his hand, very aware of Dad watching them. "I'm fine. Just hungry."

Jesse nodded and kissed her forehead. "I'll make you something." He moved to Dad and clapped him on the back. "What about you?"

"I can eat."

She cut into her melted marshmallows with her spoon, dunked them in cocoa and shoveled them in her mouth.

"Vi said she had boy problems. You know anything about it?" Dad asked.

She choked as Jesse turned away from the open fridge with an egg carton in his hand.

"Boy problems?" he echoed.

"She said her and Tucker are done."

"Dad!" she exclaimed and swatted his arm.

"What? I'm spreading the good news. We've all been worried, especially Jesse. He didn't tell us about Tucker's background, but I didn't need him to. All you had to do was look at the kid to know he was bad news."

"I get it!" she said loudly. "It's over."

He looked up at the ceiling and murmured, "Thank you, Jesus."

She was considering kicking him when Lynne appeared, tying the sash of her robe over her nightgown.

"Everything okay?"

"Yeah, we're just thanking God for answering prayer," Dad said.

Before she could make a retort, Lynne clasped her face, just as Jesse had.

"How are you feeling, honey? Do you need to stay home from school?"

"No, I'm back to normal. I'm just hungry."

"I'm on it, Mom," Jesse called out.

Mom patted her cheek before she gave Dad a kiss and made her way to the kitchen. She gave Jesse a hug before she grabbed a cup of coffee and settled at the table.

"Do you have a scripture for us, Isaac?" Lynne asked.

"I opened my Bible to this." Dad bent over the page and tapped a passage. "Ecclesiastes 3: 1-8. There is a time for everything, and a season for every activity under the heavens: a time to be born and a time to die, a time to plant and a time to uproot, a time to kill and a time to heal, a time to tear down and a time to build..."

Lynne nodded as Dad read the passage that described the ever-changing seasons of life.

"There's a time to tear and a time to mend, a time to love and a time to hate, a time for war and a time for peace," Dad finished and cocked his head to the side as he contemplated the highlighted passage. "I've had my fair share of worries and internal battles lately. I'm always trying to control every outcome and prepare for what I think will happen."

Violet was caught off guard when Dad suddenly grinned at her.

"But there's no need to worry. God heard my prayers and answered them. What isn't meant to be, God won't allow."

Her mouth dropped. "Dad!"

"Did I miss something?" Lynne asked with raised brows.

"Vi broke up with her wannabe rock star," Dad shared with unashamed delight.

"Oh, honey, is that why you weren't feeling well yesterday?" Lynne asked with great sympathy as she reached across the table to pat her hand.

Jesse plopped a plate of pancakes in front of her and Mom. "Better eat them while they're hot."

***

She was putting the finishing touches on her makeup when Jesse double knocked on the bathroom door. Before she could say he could come in, he did so, startling her.

"You sure you want to go to school?" he asked. "You don't have to if you'd rather stay home and rest."

She lifted her chin. "I'm fine."

He held her gaze. "You don't have to pretend with me. I know I hurt you yesterday." His eyes moved over her face as he reached out and gently stroked her side. "In more ways than one. I want to make sure you're okay."

She swallowed hard, eyes watering slightly at his tenderness. "I really am okay."

Whatever he saw in her eyes must have reassured him because he nodded.

"I'm ready when you are," he said and left without another word.

She stared after him, heart thudding in her ears, every nerve ending buzzing. Everything was the same and yet... not. He wasn't ignoring what happened, but he also wasn't discussing it in detail. She was grateful and confused.

Once she was in her bedroom, she automatically looked around for her backpack before remembered where she left it. She wished she knew what to expect at school today. She suspected Tucker wouldn't show his bruised face... Unless he decided to report Jesse's unprovoked attack to the school? Had anyone witnessed what happened? Were any rumors circulating? Had Tucker tried to contact her?

With countless questions crowding her mind, she headed down the hall. Mom was already gone and after a quick scan of the kitchen and living room, she headed outside where Jesse was already in the SUV. She walked toward him, feeling naked and awkward without her backpack.

She slipped into the passenger seat and buckled herself in. Jesse had the country station on. She tried to get lost in the music, but her mind was overwrought as she anticipated what the day would bring.

"Where's your backpack?"

"It was on the side of Tucker's Bronco. I hope it's still in the parking lot," she said, rapping her fingernails on the door.

"Hopefully, someone turned it in."

"Yeah."

There was a long pause before he asked, "You're breaking up with Tucker?"

The toe of her right shoe tapped restlessly. "Yes."

"That's good."

She waited for him to elaborate, but when he didn't, she didn't pursue it. Instead, she asked, "You aren't worried you'll get in trouble?"

"For what?"

She finally looked at him. He wore a white shirt with jeans and a navy hat pulled low over his eyes. The gold cross on his chain gleamed on his chest.

"For assaulting someone," she said sharply. "You could get kicked off the team for fighting. What you did to Tucker could get you banned from sports completely."

"I had cause."

She tensed and balled her hand into a fist as she reminded him quietly, "He didn't force me."

A hint of the rage he displayed yesterday crossed his face as he shot her a hard, glittering look. "Don't, Vi."

"I'm just being honest! If you get pulled into the office…"

"I won't."

"How do you know that?"

"Because Tucker had it coming and he knew it. Why do you think I walked out of practice yesterday?"

She straightened, this new piece of information catching her totally by surprise. Jesse should have been occupied with football practice. That's why she took leave of her senses and allowed Tucker to take such liberties. She was so rattled, it never crossed her mind why Jesse had stumbled across them in the first place.

"Why'd you leave practice?" she asked.

The muscles in his forearms flexed as he tightened his hold on the steering wheel. "I had a bone to pick with Tucker, but once I found you two, why I was looking for him no longer mattered."

"So, you weren't looking for me, you were looking for him," she clarified.

"Yes."

"And you weren't expecting to find me with him."

He shifted restlessly in his seat, yesterday's aggression permeating the air.

"No."

So, the events that unfolded yesterday wasn't because of her, as she thought. Jesse was already angry enough with Tucker to leave practice. Catching Tucker fingering her set off Jesse's temper, which was the driving force behind his behavior. If she hadn't been in that compromising position when Jesse found them, she would still be a virgin today.

Feeling suddenly ill, she looked out the window and was relieved to see they had reached school. She scanned the parking lot, but there was no sign of Tucker's Bronco.

When she pushed open her door, Jesse said, "I'll come with you to lost and found."

Apparently, he didn't see her backpack either. As they made their way toward the cluster of buildings, she eyed the other students. No one pointed or came running up to them to confirm any juicy gossip. When their friends called out to them, she and Jesse raised their hands in acknowledgment, but they didn't stop to chat. Again, everything seemed normal. Freakishly so.

She didn't have high hopes that her backpack had been turned in, but to her immense relief, some angel had done the right thing. She immediately plunged her hand into the front pocket and said a silent prayer of thanks when she found her phone. As they walked out of the office, she scrolled through her messages and was relieved not to see anything out of the ordinary. By some miracle, the atomic bomb that went off in her life yesterday had gone unnoticed by anyone else.

"Vi."

She looked up with a frown. Jesse was looking down at her with a strange look on his face. "What?"

"Any word from Tucker?"

"No."

Jesse nodded. "That's good."

When the bell rang, he squeezed her arm.

"I'll see you later."

She watched him walk away. Faithful Marissa materialized at his side. Jesse hadn't dated after he broke up with Madyson four months ago. He'd been single for some time, which had caused quite a lot of speculation and gossip. Girls fawned over him, desperate to win his favor, but he seemed immune to their charm.

She turned in the opposite direction to go to her first class. She wasn't sure why her chest was tight or why her eyes began to water. She dabbed at the corner of her eye and fixed a smile on her face. All was well. Yesterday happened. She couldn't take it back and if she could, would she? She crossed the threshold into womanhood. Today, she was wiser and more mature.

So why did she feel so lost and lonely?

WANT TO GET LUNCH SOMEWHERE?

She didn't respond to Jesse's text for two periods. She wasn't sure whether she should keep her distance from him or not. He had taken everything in stride, but that feeling of calm acceptance she woke with was beginning to wane.

Her friends were talking and laughing around her, but she felt disconnected, like her normal frequency was off. It was clear that they hadn't heard anything about what happened between Jesse and Tucker. They would have bombarded her otherwise. Georgia asked about Tucker during recess. She said they'd had a fight and were on a break. Her friends rubbed her back and gave her sympathetic hugs. The urge to confide in them was so strong, she had to excuse herself from their huddle.

In her next class, she noticed she was still getting odd looks like she had the day before. She kept her attention on her assignment and tried to ignore the paranoia that everyone could see right through her. If anyone knew that she, Violet Carr, had lost her virginity yesterday, *no one* would be giving her intense stares. They would be gawking. And if they knew who she'd lost it to...

"Are you sure?" someone whispered. "No. *Violet?*"

Her back stiffened as someone a row back gossiped about her. She reached for her phone and accepted Jesse's invitation to get lunch off campus. She had to get out of here.

The moment the bell rang, she dashed out the door and jogged to the parking lot. Jesse was already behind the wheel. She wasn't hungry, but the strain of appearing normal when she felt anything but was taking its toll. She was terrified she would accidentally blurt out something to her friends and once that happened, there was no taking it back. Better to be with Jesse. At least she didn't have to pretend with him.

"Hey," he said as she tossed her backpack on the floor and hopped into the passenger seat.

"Hey," she replied and rolled down the window for some fresh air.

"What do you want to eat?"

"Anything."

"Mexican?"

"Sure," she sighed.

"Are you okay?"

"Yup."

Jesse stopped by a well-known taco place. She surveyed the menu and jolted when Jesse touched her back.

"Know what you want?" he asked.

"Uh, can I get chicken tacos, and I'm going to grab an iced tea from the fridge."

He nodded and jerked his head, indicating for her to sit. She nabbed her drink before she sat at a glossy round table. Jesse stood behind two stocky construction workers. She found herself comparing Jesse's build to the grown men. Jesse's broad shoulders and military stance made him appear much older than his eighteen years. He had also put on some muscle while helping to rebuild the church this summer. He had a knack for it and had been working with a general contractor as an apprentice on the weekends.

Her eyes moved over him, taking in the well-fitted jeans and trim waist. As her eyes moved up, she spotted something above his collar. She half rose from her seat before she sat, hands over her mouth, as she stared at the scratches she'd left on the back of his neck. The urge to lift his shirt and inspect his back was overwhelming.

As Jesse stepped up to the counter, the cashier adjusted her black hat and blushed. Jesse smiled kindly at her and gestured at the board as he ordered. Jesse was back to being the nice guy. The helpful guy who held doors open for people and was always willing to lend a helping hand. No one would believe that he had an explosive temper, one that could ignite without warning. Thinking of the hunger in his gaze as he pinned her to the bed made her clamp her legs together and slant them to the side as her core pulsed. He'd been ruthless yesterday. Determined. She was still having trouble believing it happened. There was no visible mark on her to prove it hadn't been a bizarre figment of her imagination, but her mark on him was irrefutable proof of the intense battle they'd waged.

Jesse set his drink on the table and cocked his head to the side. "What?"

She bit her lip and gestured for him to sit before she reached out and gingerly touched his neck. She traced the mark, knowing he'd bled for it to still be there today.

"Did anyone say anything about your neck?"

"No."

"There's," she swallowed nervously, "marks."

He held her gaze as he rolled his shoulders. "That's not the only one."

"I'm sorry."

"I deserved it."

She flicked water droplets from her sweating can of iced tea. "It must hurt."

"It was worth it."

She looked away as her heart lurched into her throat.

"Vi."

Reluctantly, she looked back at him.

"Have you heard from Tucker?"

She shook her head.

He nodded, apparently satisfied.

"I was thinking of texting him we're over, but I'd rather talk to him in person."

"He knows."

"Still."

Jesse opened his mouth to argue, but the cashier called his name. Violet shook her head as the girl fussed over him before handing over a bag with their food. As Jesse turned, he headed toward the door. Surprised, Violet got up and followed him.

"I thought we were going to eat here."

"I know a better place," he said.

She thought he was going to stay in the school's vicinity. To her surprise, he drove quite a way before pulling into a deserted park.

"Where are we?"

"I come here to run on the trail."

She frowned. "When do you come here?"

"During lunch or after school if you catch a ride home with someone. It's out of the way, so it's rarely crowded."

"It's nice," she said as she handed over his massive burrito.

They ate in companionable silence, taking in the squirrels, birds, and a lone jogger that passed. When she finished her food, she tossed her trash in the plastic bag, sat back, and closed her eyes. She raised her face to the cool breeze that came through both of their open windows and let out a long sigh.

She thought her life had turned upside down, but what had really changed? She and Jesse were okay. She assessed the vibes in the car and detected nothing bad. There had been tension between them when she started dating, but now it was gone.

She had enjoyed Tucker, but wasn't upset about breaking up with him, which reaffirmed that she had been scratching an itch that no longer existed. The only thing she'd lost was her innocence, and girls lost that every day. Not to their stepbrother, but there was no erasing that fact. It would never happen again, so there was no sense in bemoaning the series of unfortunate events that resulted in her and Jesse having sex. In retrospect, insisting that she knew what she wanted and that she was old enough to experiment had contributed to Jesse losing control. He hadn't meant to go that far. Maybe he meant to teach her a lesson that had spiraled out of control?

"Vi."

She turned toward his voice with her eyes still closed. The last thing she expected was to feel his lips on hers. Her eyes flew open, and she straightened in her seat.

"Jesse, what...?"

He brushed his mouth against hers lightly, teasingly. She

blinked, befuddled and alarmed by the spurt of heat that shot through her body.

"Don't think," he said against her lips. "Just feel."

"But..."

He cut her off as he covered her mouth with his. She didn't have a chance to think. His lips on hers short-circuited her brain. The tingling numbness that came upon her during his midnight visits engulfed her. Jesse's response to her paralysis was to deepen the kiss and replace the chill with scorching heat. She tried to mentally detach from what was happening, but the feelings he evoked wouldn't allow it. They lured her in and bathed her in sensation. When she whimpered, he broke the kiss to nuzzle her affectionately.

"It's okay, baby," he cooed. "I'm not going to hurt you."

She gripped his wrist as she tried to catch her breath. "I know that, but we can't—"

He brushed his thumb along the apple of her cheek. "There's a time for denial and a time for acceptance."

His spin on the scripture Dad had shared this morning made her heart skip.

"A time for restraint and a time to indulge." Jesse kissed the corner of her mouth. "It's our time, Violet. Stop thinking and *feel*." He brushed his lips against hers. "Open your mouth."

She parted her lips before she thought better of it. Jesse didn't give her time to change her mind. He took advantage of her obedience and sank his tongue into her mouth before he clasped her nape and drew her over the console, ignoring the fluttering hand she placed on his chest.

He kissed her with an absorption that made everything else cease to exist. She was lost in a maelstrom of feeling. She had never experienced anything like it. There was tenderness, desire, and a desperate urgency that seeped from him to her.

There was no thought of consequences or right and wrong. There was only mounting desire and the overwhelming need to do something about it.

When Jesse finally drew away, she clutched at him because she felt like she was teetering on the edge of a precipice. It took her a second to remember where they were, since she'd completely lost touch with her surroundings.

Jesse searched her eyes and cupped her flushed cheek. "You feel it, don't you?"

She swallowed hard, nodded. She thought she saw a flash of relief before he rested his forehead against hers.

"After school, I'll take care of us, okay?"

When she didn't respond, he tensed. He cupped her chin and searched her glazed eyes.

"After school," he repeated, voice dropping as his temper ignited. "You with me?"

"Yes."

He gave her a hard kiss before he pulled back. "Don't think."

As he turned the key in the ignition, she faced forward and dazedly fastened her seat belt. Thinking was beyond her at the moment.

Neither of them said a word as Jesse raced back to campus. They pulled into the parking lot as the second bell that signaled they should already be in class rang. As she bailed out and prepared to run to class, Jesse called, "Vi!"

She pivoted to face him.

"You with me?"

He had an odd look on his face she couldn't interpret and didn't have time to decipher because she was late.

"Yes," she shouted, exasperated, before she took off.

CHAPTER 11
JESSE

"Is it true?"

Jesse looked up from his notebook to find Blaine, Anton, and Brody in front of his desk. They were staring at him avidly as if... He straightened and crossed his arms over his chest as he leaned back in his chair. "Is what true?"

"That you beat up Tucker?" Blaine blurted and got elbowed by Anton.

Jesse narrowed his eyes. "Where'd you hear that?"

"One of the guys in Tucker's band said you jumped him in the parking lot after school yesterday. Did you?"

Brody eyed Jesse's bruised, swollen knuckles and drawled, "That's what I would have done if I heard the nasty rumors he was spreading about my sister. Me and some of the boys were thinking of kicking Tucker's ass, regardless of whether it's true or not."

"It's not true," Jesse snapped.

"It isn't?" Blaine asked and took a step back as Jesse shot to his seat.

"Violet never slept with him." The memory of him claiming her virginity made his dick twitch. He sat before any of them noticed he was getting an erection. "She's breaking up with him."

"Because she heard what he said about her?"

"No," he growled and fixed them with a level look. "She came to the conclusion that he's a dick all on her own. I don't want her to hear what Tucker said about her. It'll just upset her."

"How are you going to stop her from hearing about it? It's all over school."

"By countering it with the truth. She wouldn't sleep with him, so Tucker started that rumor to ruin her reputation. It's as simple as that."

Anton and Blaine glanced at one another before they left to spread the word, leaving Brody behind.

"I would have had your back if you asked me to come with you," Brody said.

"I know."

"Coach Rick was pissed you took off like that."

"I apologized to him this morning."

"How much damage did you do?"

Jesse flexed his sore hand. "Enough. I wanted to do more, but it's probably best I didn't. He'd be in the hospital, otherwise. He'll think twice before he pulls a stupid stunt like that with Violet or any other girl."

Brody shook his head. "I hope Violet learned her lesson, but I have a feeling she didn't. What does she see in these losers?"

He had no idea, but if he had any say in it, Tucker would be the last guy she ever dated.

Brody filled him in on what he missed at practice yesterday and their upcoming game before he was cut off by their teacher, who called their attention to the board. As Brody took his seat, Jesse slouched in his chair and stared at the clock.

Why the hell had he brought them back to school? He should have taken Violet home. Giving her two class periods to think was dangerous. The last time he thought they were on the same page, she started dating Tobias. He wouldn't stand aside this time. He couldn't. Not after having her. Not after being inside her. Not when he was so close to having all of her.

He felt like he was walking a tightrope. He was afraid of coming on too strong and scaring her or giving her too much space, allowing her to come up with more obstacles to throw in his path.

For four months, he'd been forced to watch her date the most bewildering lineup of guys imaginable. They were the bottom of the barrel, the invisible one's other girls dismissed without question. Even his friends grumbled about her bad taste and asked him why he allowed it, but Violet was deaf to anyone's advice. He knew it would be difficult to see her with Tobias. Little did he know, he was just the first, with each guy getting progressively worse until Tucker came along.

Tucker was the only one bold enough to kiss and pet Violet in front of him. The sight made him physically ill. He suspected Tucker did it deliberately to see if he would do anything. He wanted to, but he didn't want to give Violet any more reason to avoid him as she'd done all summer, and she'd seemed genuinely happy. The only thing that kept him sane was believing she wouldn't go beyond chaste kisses.

His aggression in sports had increased. He did his best to fill his days with as much activity as possible. At night, he staked his claim in the only way he could. They never had a replay of Violet touching herself or waking up when he was in her room, though he'd done his best to make that happen.

The need to check on her was hammering at him. She said she was with him, but what if she changed her mind again? He dragged his sneakers restlessly across the floor as his heartbeat accelerated. Then he would find a way to change it back again.

The fact that she joined him for lunch was a good sign. It had been a calculated risk to kiss her at the park. She'd been shocked and resistant at first. He kept his kisses light, almost teasing to draw her in. It didn't take long for her to respond and then came that sweet acquiescence that frayed his control. He had to stop, or he would have taken her right there in the car. Her look of dazed pleasure was one he intended to see often.

Violet wanted him, but she didn't want to want him. She'd done her best to keep their relationship platonic, but yesterday he broke through. He wasn't going to let her withdraw. She was just as susceptible to their chemistry as he was. He'd chain her to him with bonds of the flesh and fulfill sexual desires she tried to keep hidden. She so badly wanted to be a good girl, but she wasn't, just like there was another side to his wholesome facade. He had to destroy Violet's image of him as her brother and make her see him as a man. He would make her love *him*, regardless of the title he carried.

Eight minutes left.

Mom finished work in an hour and a half, maybe two hours. Dad had the day off, but mentioned he was helping someone from church and wouldn't be back until dinner. They would have the house to themselves. Would Violet let him touch her? If she allowed him another chance between her thighs, he wouldn't waste it.

He lifted his hat to comb his fingers through his hair and touched the back of his neck where she'd left her mark. He took a picture of his back in the mirror last night, mesmerized by the chaotic pattern she'd created, which would fade all too soon. Under other circumstances, he would have loved showing off her brands in the locker room, but he couldn't afford rumors to spread when he was supposedly single, so he would have to be mindful of such things in the future.

The teacher eyed him but made no comment as he rose and slung his backpack over one shoulder. He was halfway to the door before the bell rang, signaling school was over. Blaine called his name, but he didn't stop. He briefly debated whether he should go to Violet's class or wait by the car, but he didn't want to risk missing her. In the end, he headed to the parking lot.

He leaned against the SUV and searched the crowd for Violet or her friends from her last class. Minutes passed. He was about to go hunting when he saw Violet crossing the parking lot with Lettie. His fears evaporated when Violet made eye contact and gave him a smile. His heart thundered in his ears as she said goodbye to her friend and made her way over.

He waited until she had hopped into the SUV before he climbed behind the steering wheel. Violet stared straight ahead with her hands clasped in her lap. *Nervous*, he deduced, but he could work with that. She hadn't run or gone into another bout of denial. She came to him. That's all that mattered.

The adrenaline rush made it difficult to concentrate. *Please may Mom and Dad not be home*, he silently chanted. When he pulled into the driveway, he opened the garage to make sure their parent's cars were missing and said a prayer of thanks when he saw they were gone. He turned toward Violet with a silly grin, but she was already closing the passenger door and heading to the house. He'd spent the drive running all sorts of scenarios through his head and hadn't said one word to her.

He jogged after Violet and caught a glimpse of her heading down the hallway. He checked to make sure they were truly alone before he stood in the open doorway to her bedroom. She took out her binder and set it on the desk. The sight of her trembling hands reminded him that he needed to tread carefully.

"Vi."

"Hmm?"

"Look at me."

She went motionless. The long silence and sudden awkwardness that filled the air made him move quickly. He let his backpack drop to the ground and strode toward her. He clasped her face and gently lifted it.

"Violet."

Her lashes lifted, revealing her eyes had turned green, a sure sign that she felt conflicted. He leaned down and rested his forehead on hers.

"It's me, Violet."

"I know," she rasped. "But this is so…" Her eyes glistened with tears.

Declarations she wasn't ready to hear clogged his throat. He swallowed them and murmured, "Do you trust me?"

She blinked, the question clearly taking her by surprise before she nodded. A tear hovered on her lower lashes. He brushed it away before it could fall. Tears had no place here unless it was tears of joy.

"I won't hurt you," he promised.

"I know."

He covered her mouth with his and felt her jolt, but she didn't try to break away. Encouraged, he tilted his head to deepen the kiss. When her mouth tentatively parted, he immediately accepted the invitation. She tasted of bubble gum and iced tea. She was more addicting than German chocolate cake.

He backed her against the wall, hands sliding from her face into her hair. He angled her head the way he wanted and claimed her mouth.

"Kiss me back," he breathed.

She was passively allowing him to do what he wanted, but he wanted her active participation. Demanded it, in fact. Violet had matured from the impulsive wild child he met at fourteen, but her true nature still lurked beneath the surface. He didn't want just the sweet parts of her. He wanted the competitive savage who would do anything to win and the warrior who marked up his back. He wanted the vulnerable, lonely girl who had unabashedly claimed him as her friend the moment they met. And he wanted the dirty girl who had touched herself and masturbated right along with him. She was holding back, and he wasn't going to allow it.

He brushed kisses along her jaw. "How does this feel?"

She swayed as he sucked on her earlobe.

"Tell me," he growled and squeezed her hip to beckon her out of her head.

"It feels good," she said so quietly, he wouldn't have been able to hear her if he wasn't pressed against her.

"And this?"

When he put his hand on her breast, she went very still.

"How does this feel?" he pushed.

"Um..."

When his thumb brushed over her nipple, her stifled gasp was music to his ears.

"How does this make you feel, Vi?"

"Hot," she said in a strangled tone.

"And this?"

He placed a wet kiss on her neck and felt her body vibrating under his hands.

"Makes me weak," she whispered.

That's all he needed to know. He stepped back. Immediately, her nerves came back, but he didn't give her time to get her defenses in place. He crouched and hoisted her over his shoulder.

"Jesse?"

He didn't answer her because it was taking all his discipline not to toss her on the floor and sink himself inside her.

He closed her door to the bathroom. If their parents came home and saw his bedroom door closed, they wouldn't think anything of it. If they went to Violet's room and saw the bathroom door closed, they would assume she was in there. It would buy them a few minutes to get themselves situated if they needed it. Also, he wanted her in his bed. Tonight, he would go to sleep not just with the memories of what they were about to do, but the physical proof soaked in his sheets. He couldn't wait.

He set her on the edge of his bed. She looked up at him, clearly unsure, but battling it back for him. Humbled, he leaned down and kissed her forehead. When she closed her eyes and kept her face turned up to him like a flower seeking the sun, his heart melted. He ignored the demands of his body as he stroked her rigid back and kissed every inch of her face until she was completely relaxed.

"Arms up," he said quietly.

Her eyelids lifted. Green eyes surveyed him for a moment before she obeyed. The blast of triumph that ripped through him caused his hands to shake. He grasped the bottom of her shirt and lifted it, uncovering every exquisite inch of her. She held his gaze for a moment before she blushed and raised her hands to cover her breasts, encased in baby blue satin.

"No, don't do that," he admonished, twining their fingers together and holding her arms wide so he could take her in.

"Jesse!" she protested, twisting and hunching in an attempt to hide her bare upper half.

He couldn't believe she was self-conscious about her body. She was gorgeous.

"I don't think," she began.

To squash her nerves and rising panic, he flattened her on the bed and took her mouth to stop the words he didn't want to hear. To his surprise, she kissed him back with a fervor that made his dick throb. She was channeling her anxiety into sexual aggression, which was just fine with him. But he underestimated the effect her enthusiasm had on him. She was setting him alight! He detached their mouths and moved down her body so he could retain some semblance of control. He wanted this to last, and he was determined to examine her body.

He kissed his way down her neck, inhaling her heavenly scent. As his tongue traced her collarbone, she quivered and then went lax beneath him. Her breasts were so sensitive, even lightly nuzzling them made her squirm and gasp. When he slid even further down, hands smoothing along her sides, he suddenly stopped and buried his face against her quivering stomach, unable to believe this was really happening.

Her fingers sank into his hair. "Jesse?"

Emotion swelled in his chest, making his eyes sting. He lifted his head and looked up the length of her body. As their eyes met, hers flared before her expression softened. She didn't say a word as she stroked his cheek. Time stalled as their spirits realigned with one another. This was meant to be. Did she feel the rightness of it? There was just him and her. It wasn't just sex, though desire plagued him night and day. Their connection was magnetic, an unstoppable force. She was the moon, and he was the ocean, obeying her push and pull —forcing him to withdraw or flood the shore. He was defenseless against her, a slave to the bond that snapped into place at fourteen. She was everything to him, but did she feel the same? He turned his head and kissed her palm. He would show her how much she meant to him; how much he adored her. No one would ever love her more than he did. It was time to prove it.

He continued his reverent exploration. He gripped her tiny waist as his lips dragged over the silky skin of her stomach before tracing her hipbones with his tongue. When he undid the button of her jeans and pulled down the zipper, she stopped breathing. Discovering she wore matching underwear made his mouth water. He took off her shoes and socks and when he tugged on her pants, Violet hesitated before she lifted her ass, allowing him to drag them off.

He knelt at the foot of the bed with Violet splayed out before him, clad in just a bra and panties. He saw her naked yesterday, but he hadn't been able to admire her. Now, he did.

God took his time with her. Her face alone was portrait-worthy, but her body surpassed those he'd seen in movies, magazines, or TV. Nothing compared to flesh and blood. She had breasts that he now knew fit perfectly in his hand, a small waist, wide hips, and thighs that some guys would have labeled as too thick, but he loved them. They were feminine, muscular, and strong. Her skin was still tan from the summer.

As his hand brushed over her satin covered mound, she clamped her thighs together. His lips quirked as he kissed the tops of her thighs to coax them to part while he massaged her calves.

He'd been fantasizing about this for over a year. After jacking off with her underwear and trying to lap up what she left behind, he could now partake directly from the source. He intended to go slow. To savor and seduce, but the smell of her arousal made him salivate.

"Come on, baby. Spread your legs for me. I need to taste you," he said hoarsely.

"Taste *what*?" Violet demanded, bracing herself on her elbows to gawk at him.

"You liked my fingers in you?"

She bit her lip when his thumb dipped between her thighs.

"Did you?" he demanded

"Yes."

"You're going to like my mouth on you even more."

"*What?* No way!"

He gripped her waist to stop her from scooting up in bed. "It'll be good, I promise."

"That's gross! Why would you even want to...? My answer's no!"

When she started to struggle, his shaky control snapped. He yanked the drenched underwear down and off. When he pried her legs apart, she sat up, her cheeks flushed with mortification and anger.

"Jesse, don't you dare—"

Her voice cut out as he put his mouth on her. The vibrant taste of her burst on his tongue. Stealing her underwear versus being between her thighs was like someone describing what a dish tasted like rather than sampling it himself. There was no comparison, and he was starved. He ignored her panicked voice and fluttering hands that pushed at his head and smacked his shoulders. He wasn't going anywhere.

He'd never done this before, so it took him a while to figure out what he was doing, but he figured he was on the right track when she let out a strangled shriek and fell back on the bed.

"Oh my God, please stop," she begged.

He had no intention of stopping, not when he was finally drinking nectar straight from her, as God had intended. He was mesmerized by the rolling movements of her body and loved the tortured, helpless sounds she made. He drowned himself in her and rode her restless hips.

Violet threatened, begged, then sobbed as she yanked at his sheets, lost in the throes. He watched her fight her orgasm and him, but in the end, had no choice but to surrender. When she climaxed, her piercing scream hurt his eardrums. When her slick walls contracted, he slid his finger in to give her pussy something to grip onto.

When her orgasm passed, she tried to turn on her side to get away from his mouth and pushed at him with weak, shaky hands.

"Please, Jesse. I can't take anymore."

"I'm almost done," he soothed.

He finally stopped not because he was satisfied, but because he was ready to burst. He shot to his feet, shucked his shirt and shoved down his underwear and jeans. He didn't have the patience to kick off his shoes or step out of his pants but leaned forward and slid inside her. Violet moaned as he penetrated her tight channel. Her eyes flashed open as he kissed her, forcing her to taste herself. She tried to turn away, but he wouldn't let her.

"You're perfect," he panted. "The best thing I've ever tasted. I'll never get enough."

She bared her teeth as he sheathed himself.

"How does it feel to have me inside you?" he said harshly.

"Incredible," she breathed, wrapping her arms and legs around him, taking him even deeper and running her hands over him.

He jerked as if she'd put her mouth on his cock. "Vi, don't..."

Eyelashes wet from tears she'd wept in ecstasy, lifted as she glared at him. "So, you can touch me, but I can't touch you?"

"I'm going to come."

She licked his lip. "So, come."

That's all it took. He spilled at her command, just from the wonder of being inside her. He slumped on top of her and buried his face in his sheets, groaning that he hadn't lasted. But it was difficult to be truly disappointed with Violet beneath him and her fingertips caressing his skin.

"I didn't know," she whispered.

"Know what?" he muttered.

"That people put their mouths..."

As her inner muscles fluttered around his dick, he raised his head to look down at her. Her eyes were glassy from her orgasm and despite all they'd done, she still looked a little embarrassed.

"You didn't know about oral sex?"

She shook her head, eyes wide.

"We're gonna do it often," he stated, brushing his lips over hers.

"We are?"

Detecting the eagerness she tried to conceal, his mouth curved. "Yeah." When she squirmed, he raised a brow. "Want me to do it again?"

Her cheeks bloomed with color. "No!" she said adamantly, but her body said otherwise.

Violet wasn't a good girl, thank God. His dick twitched with renewed life.

"Jesse."

Her tone warned him before he saw the uncertainty creeping back.

"I don't know if we should..."

"Do you like what I do to you?" he interrupted.

She blinked. "I..."

"It's a yes or no answer."

When her eyes slid away, his heart stopped.

"Violet." He cupped her cheek to get her attention. "Tell me you like what I do to you."

"I do, but..."

He thought they were of one mind, but she was slipping away while he was still inside her. How could she not realize what was between them was a gift, not a curse? He instinctively knew it would never be like this with anyone else. She was it for him. Why didn't she realize that? Terror that he would lose her stoked the ashes of his temper.

"We don't have to make any decisions right now or share what's happening between us. We have time to explore each other and just be." He searched her eyes. "Have you felt this way with anyone else?"

She shook her head. The relief that passed through him made him drop his forehead on hers. He wasn't alone in this. She may not be ready to commit to forever, but she was willing to let him in. For now, that's all that mattered. Everything would fall into place. He would reel her in so gently, she wouldn't realize she'd been caught until it was too late.

"What we have is special, once in a lifetime. It would be a crime to ignore it."

Her vulnerable expression altered, became impish. "Crime?"

He tugged on her bra, so her breast popped out. "A *serious* crime."

He was done talking about this. There were far more important things to do, like pay homage to her neglected breasts. Her expressive face was such a turn on. She couldn't conceal her reaction to what he was doing to her. He hardened inside of her and soon, was grinding against her.

"Kiss me," he ordered.

She pressed her mouth to his. At his gruff encouragement, she grew bolder and more confident. When her tongue darted into his mouth, he groaned.

"Yes, that's what I want. Give it to me."

This time, she was with him every step of the way. The air was permeated with the smell of sweat, sex, and her unique blend of violets and rose. She quickly picked up his rhythm. He raised his head to look down at her. Her hair was spread over his sheets, she was clutching at him with both hands, and her breasts were bouncing with each thrust. Her eyes were bleeding back to hazel. She was flushed with passion. She held on to him as if she were afraid of being tossed into the abyss. She stared at him with a mixture of fear, wonder, and need. He got off on all of it.

When he felt himself getting close, he rubbed her clitoris, wanting her to come with him.

"Tell me how this feels," he said against her lips.

Her eyes fluttered shut. "It feels..." She flinched and clutched at his biceps as her hips bucked against his hand. "Like I'll die if I don't... Oh, God. *Jesse*."

Saying his name in that thready tone made him giddy. "Say it again."

"Oh my God."

"My name," he growled and stopped his ministrations so she would give him what he wanted.

Her eyes opened, stormy green chasing away the hazel. "Jesse."

"Jesse, what?" He couldn't resist teasing her when he was between her legs and his fingers were slipping through honey that was all for him.

"I want..."

She didn't bother finishing her sentence but brushed his hand aside and took over the motion he'd been doing.

He was stunned for a moment as one of his fantasies materialized right before his eyes. "That's my girl. Make yourself come."

"Jesse," she breathed before she convulsed.

He ground against that bundle of nerves, prolonging her climax as she wrapped her arms around him and shuddered like a survivor being rescued from a shipwreck. This time, it took him longer to come. He set a decent pace and when he finally orgasmed, he was out of breath and immensely pleased. He collapsed on top of her, but made sure to move his top half to the side so he wouldn't smother her.

He was sated to his bones, and a had a feeling that Violet was finally on the same wavelength. She was completely relaxed beneath him, the physical exertion calming her overactive mind.

A few minutes passed before he reluctantly peered at the clock. Damn it. He wished they could stay like this for days, but life was still chugging along, propelling them forward.

When he forced himself up and knelt on the bed, Violet gave him a quizzical look, which turned indignant when he unceremoniously spread her legs.

"Jesse!"

Her mortified tone made him grin, but his eyes were on his semen that spilled from her. Prompted by some primitive instinct, he pushed it back in and, when it poured out again, spread it over her skin. He wanted her covered in him. Thankfully, she didn't fight it. She watched him from beneath half lowered lids until he regretfully noticed the time again.

"If we're lucky, we have about ten minutes before Mom comes home," he announced.

"What?"

He wasn't surprised when she jackknifed up and ran to the bathroom. He finally kicked off his clothes and stretched out on the bed. He considered joining Violet in the shower, but had a feeling she wouldn't like that. He closed his eyes and drifted with a smile on his face. His dreams were finally coming true.

CHAPTER 12
VIOLET

3 DAYS LATER

VIOLET PUT THE FINISHING TOUCHES ON HER MAKEUP BEFORE SHE BACKED UP
to take in her appearance in the bathroom mirror. For church, she
donned a dress she normally reserved for special occasions. The
dress ended at mid-thigh, which Dad wouldn't like, but the length
was counterbalanced by the long sleeves and modest neckline. She
gave the tiered skirt a swish, admiring the ruffle detail that in the
past made her feel silly. But her mindset had shifted over the past
few days. She had never been more aware of her femininity and for
the first time in her life, she was fully embracing it.

She slid the heart pendant that Mom and Dad had gifted her on
her sixteenth birthday back and forth along the fine gold chain as
she eyed her reflection. Last week she attended church as a virgin
and this week, she returned with more sexual experience than
anyone who had been initiated four days ago should. But Jesse
wasn't just an overachiever in sports and academics. She'd known
from his nightly visits that he had a high sex drive, but the physical
reality was another thing entirely.

When they attended school on Friday, she did her best to act normal. She thought she was doing a good job until she caught the odd look Marissa was giving Jesse. She glanced at him and found that he wasn't listening to the conversation but focused completely on her. The make out session on the way to school had been brief and unfulfilling, and Jesse was clearly still feeling the effects of it. One look at his heated gaze was all it took for her to get embarrassingly damp. He was going to give them away! She promptly excused herself from the group and managed to avoid him until lunch, when he yanked her into an empty classroom.

"Why aren't you answering my messages?" he demanded.

"I think we should steer clear of each another until things calm down."

He cocked his head to the side. "Calm down?"

She was too embarrassed to bring up the way he'd been looking at her earlier, so she gestured to her hard nipples, which were aching for the attention he paid them the previous day. The connection between them had always been strong, but now it was tuned to a frequency so raw and sensitive, it was difficult to be around each other without touching. Last night at dinner, they studiously avoided eye contact. Watching TV together was out of the question. Jesse expended energy by shooting hoops on the driveway with Dad, while she went to her bedroom to give her overstimulated senses a break.

"I need some time to adjust. This is a lot." That was a vast understatement, but it was the best she could come up with when Jesse was looking at her like he wanted to eat her alive. Her unfettered response would have been embarrassing if it wasn't obvious that Jesse wanted her just as much.

"I'll give you space after," Jesse said.

She frowned. "After what?"

He'd shoved her into a janitor's closet for some heavy petting. At some point, he put her hand on him. She got the hang of it quickly. It wasn't long before he begged her to put him in her mouth.

Remembering how much pleasure she got from him going down on her yesterday, she was eager to make him feel the same.

He whispered what he wanted her to do, and she accomplished her goal as the bell sounded, signaling lunch was over. Despite her worries about being caught, Jesse turned on the light to watch her swallow and lapped up what spilled over. When she tried to leave, he pinned her against the wall and French kissed her until she was dizzy before allowing her to go to class.

Jesse had a football game that evening. She rode to and from the game with Mom and Dad, while Jesse caught a ride home with a teammate. When he came into her bedroom, high on his win, and tried to kiss her, she freaked out.

"You can't do that when Mom and Dad are home!" she said, scandalized.

"Fine. Tomorrow."

She didn't know what he meant by that until he told Mom over breakfast that they were going for a drive and then meeting up with friends to see a movie. Mom smiled and told them to have fun.

"Who are we meeting up with?" Violet asked when she climbed into the passenger seat.

"No one. I lied."

"You did? Why?"

"I can't tell Mom what we're really going to do."

Her heart thudded in her ears. "What are we going to do?"

His eyes glittered under heavy eyelids. "I guess you'll find out, won't you?"

Part of Jesse's lie was true. They went for a drive. To her surprise, he drove out of the city limits. When Jesse got his license, they had practically lived in the car, high on their newfound freedom. They thoroughly explored the Texas Hill Country and neighboring quaint towns. This was a throwback to a simpler time. She didn't say so, but she was relieved to get away from home and the constant fear of being discovered. She hadn't realized she needed a time-out from the rest of the world, but Jesse delivered without being asked.

She spoke very little during the nearly two-hour drive. Her mind still struggled to process everything that had happened in the past few days and the potent sexual chemistry that strummed her nerve endings. She was pleasantly surprised when Jesse pulled up to a beautiful lake and delighted when he pulled a thick blanket and cooler from the trunk. Beneath the shade of some trees, they had a picnic. They lounged on the blanket, chatting about everything and nothing as they ate and gazed at the water.

It seemed inevitable that Jesse would touch her and that she would lift her face for the kiss she'd denied him the night before. He lowered her to the blanket and drowned her in sensuality. There was no thought of denying him or herself. He told her not to think, and she wasn't. That was beyond her. Her principles and sense of propriety were lost in the undertow of a passion that overpowered all else.

Jesse was irresistible. Playful, indulgent, generous, persistent. He seemed intent on giving her as much pleasure as possible and was painfully fascinated with her body. She felt the same, though Jesse had to come twice before he allowed her to explore him as thoroughly as he had her. The day passed by too quickly, and before she knew it, they were heading home.

Dinner passed in a lust-hazed fog, but she came to when Mom cupped her flushed cheek and said, "It looks like you got some sun. Did you have fun today?"

"Lots," Jesse answered for her.

She didn't have to look at him to know he wore a broad grin. She resisted the urge to kick him under the table and avoided looking at Dad.

"What movie did you see?" Mom asked.

She felt a burst of alarm that was immediately canceled out by Jesse, who said, "We ended up driving further than we anticipated. The spot on the lake was so nice, we thought it would be a shame to leave after only an hour, so we stayed and canceled our other plans."

She was grateful yet taken aback by his glib tongue. When had Jesse become such a proficient liar?

The door to her left opened, bringing Violet out of her reverie. Jesse stepped into the bathroom, dressed in gray slacks and a black button-up shirt for church. He went motionless when he spotted her. As his eyes moved over her, she grinned and did a spin so he could get the full effect. When she stopped, she saw Jesse had closed his door and was undoing his belt.

Her heart leapt in treacherous anticipation, even as she blanched. "What are you doing?"

"What does it look like?"

She took a step toward the safety of her bedroom. "I told you; I'm not doing anything while Mom and Dad are around!"

"They're eating breakfast."

"I don't care!" she hissed.

She tried to escape into the safety of her bedroom, but he wrapped an arm around her middle, pulling her back while firmly closing her door.

"Jesse," she groaned as he turned her to face him and backed her up to the vanity. "We can't."

"Don't you want me?" he asked huskily.

She wanted him so badly, it scared her. "We're going to church!"

"That's not what I asked you."

He cupped her jaw, his piercing blue eyes making her stomach jitter. The way he focused on her as if there were no one else in the world was thrilling and unnerving. Did he start out this intense with every girl he was with? The stab of jealousy gave her the strength to yank her chin out of his hold. He frowned, but didn't back off.

"Tell me you want me."

"I do, but—"

He gave her a hard kiss. "That's all I need to hear, baby."

She was distracted by the endearment, which he'd uttered a handful of times. The first time she heard it was when he apologized for ruthlessly taking her virginity. She loved the soft, tender way he said it. Had he called all his girlfriends, baby? Even as she pondered this, Jesse knelt at her feet, pulled her dress up, and kissed her over her underwear. Her toes curled, and her blood thickened as desire snaked through her veins.

"You can't," she croaked.

"I can," he said simply, and with one tug had her underwear dropping to her ankle boots. "Hold this."

She obeyed automatically, holding her skirt out of his way before she belatedly tried to sidestep. "Mom and Dad…"

"Are occupied," he said as he draped one of her legs on his shoulder. "Like we're about to be."

Even as she braced herself against the vanity, she made one last token resistance. "Jesse, I don't think we should…"

"Shh, baby, we don't have much time."

Her lungs seized as his tongue slid through her folds. Two days ago, she wouldn't let him kiss her, and now she was letting him go down on her with their parents just a few rooms away. This wasn't right. It was disrespectful and immoral and wicked and… Her legs quivered as his tongue feathered over her clitoris. It was also mind-numbingly pleasurable and felt too good to stop.

"Ungh."

The garbled sound escaped as she rocked against his mouth. There was no self-consciousness. Not after what they'd done yesterday. Jesse made it clear that he loved her response and didn't want her to hold back. She couldn't if she wanted to. He fanned an inferno inside of her. Needs she didn't know she possessed and a soul deep hunger she worried would never be satisfied.

She looked down and saw Jesse watching her. The way he catalogued every hitch in her breath, every muscle twitch, unsettled her. Already, he knew so much more about her body than she did. What made her cave, what made her crazy, what made her sob. It still made her stomach dip when she locked eyes with him. Part of her still couldn't believe they were doing this. The other half wept with joy.

She ran her fingers through his hair and saw his eyelids droop in ecstasy. It amazed her how little it took for him. He was a natural sensualist. Uninhibited, unashamed, eager to please, and be pleased. It was a wonder he'd been single for four months. He was famished and she was reaping the rewards.

She clutched his hair and tipped her face up to the bright lights as she prepared to have her world blasted apart.

"Jesse!"

The sound of Dad's angry voice coming from Jesse's bedroom startled her so badly, she would have fallen if Jesse hadn't steadied her.

"Isaac, for God's sake," Lynne protested. "You're going to wake the whole neighborhood. Calm down. We don't know all the facts. Let's just see what they say."

"They haven't said anything," Dad retorted. "And I'm getting to the bottom of this right now."

She swung her leg off Jesse's shoulder and backed away, eyes wide with horror. Their parents couldn't know, could they? As Jesse got to his feet, wiping his mouth with the back of his sleeve, they heard her bedroom door being flung open.

"Violet!"

She jumped and hastily locked the bathroom door in case Dad tried to come in. He sounded pissed. What the hell happened?

"I'm in here, Dad." She looked around frantically for her underwear, snatched it off the floor, and pulled them on. "I'm getting dressed. What's going on?"

"Where's Jesse?"

She stared at him as she lied. "I think he went outside for something."

"I want to see you in the dining room. We need to talk."

She and Jesse stared at one another as the sound of their parent's voices faded.

"They know," Violet whispered and touched her throat, which felt like it was beginning to swell.

Jesse looked thoughtful. "I don't think so," he said, as he buckled his belt.

She couldn't believe his blasé attitude. "What else could they be talking about? I've never heard Dad yell like that in my life!"

Jesse clasped her face. "Whatever it is, we'll deal with it together. We're going to be okay, I promise."

His calm demeanor stopped her emotions from spiraling out of control. She hauled in a deep, steadying breath and tried to think rationally. If Dad had suspected they were intimate, he could have forced his way into the bathroom and caught them red-handed. He hadn't. Maybe Jesse was right, and it was something else. Clinging to that slim hope, she asked, "What do we do?"

"I'll go out your window and come around to the front door."

She pressed her ear to the door leading into her bedroom and walked in to make sure the coast was clear. Her heart was in her throat as Jesse quietly opened her window and climbed out. This was what their life had come to? She shook her head and started for the hallway when she heard Jesse say, "Morning, Mr. Davidson."

She wheeled around as their neighbor replied, "Jesse, what are you doing tending to the plants in your Sunday's best?"

What else could go wrong? She was tempted to linger to hear Jesse's reply, but the distant murmur of her parent's voices reminded her they were waiting for her. Hands trembling, she started down the hallway and prayed Jesse would hurry so whatever she was walking into, she wouldn't have to face alone.

The moment she entered the dining room; her parents fell silent. Dad's forbidding expression made her palms sweat. Mom looked troubled.

"What's going on?" Violet asked.

"That what I want to know. Is there something you want to tell us?" Dad asked.

It took everything she had not to wring her hands. Guilt and panic clouded her mind, making it hard to think. She couldn't hold

Dad's intimidating stare, so she looked to Lynne for guidance. "I have no idea, what...?"

"We just received a call," Lynne said quietly. "Tucker's in the hospital, being treated for serious injuries we're told were caused by Jesse. Do you know anything about that?"

She mentally reeled. "Tucker's in the hospital?"

"Yes," Dad said tersely. "And I want to know why. The only reason Jesse would have given Tucker such a beating is because of you. So, Vi, what happened?"

Her rash behavior was coming back to haunt her. This was proof that no one got away with anything. Would she have to admit that she let Tucker touch her inappropriately and that's how Jesse found them? Knowing how upset and disappointed her parents would be made her eyes fill with tears.

"Oh, honey," Lynne said sympathetically and started toward Violet, but Dad held up a hand, stopping Lynne in her tracks.

"I need answers," Dad said curtly. "We've been lenient with you two because you've never given us any reason not to trust you, but I never thought I'd get a call saying Jesse put someone in the hospital. Do you know how serious this is? Tucker could press charges for assault!"

The blood drained from her face.

"Why did you break up with him?" Dad demanded. "Did he do something to you? Is that why Jesse attacked him?"

She opened her mouth, but nothing came out. She had no idea what to say. She willed Jesse to walk through the front door and jolted when Dad slammed his fist on the table, rattling their empty plates and cups.

"I knew I shouldn't have let you date that kid. He had trouble written all over him. I thought you had enough discernment to break it off. Now, I hear Jesse had to intervene on your behalf and beat him senseless. Do you have any idea how serious this is? What the hell happened that would make Jesse...?"

The front door opened. Jesse strolled in with his hands in

pockets. She had no doubt he'd gotten out of that sticky situation with Mr. Davidson just fine. No one would suspect Jesse of doing anything immoral or unlawful, especially when he was dressed so impeccably. Jesse scanned the room with a benign expression, which vanished when his gaze landed on her distraught face.

"What's wrong?" he demanded.

"A lot at the moment," Dad said, crossing his arms over his chest. "You have a lot of explaining to do."

"Okay, about what?" Jesse asked, showing no sign of discomfort or guilt.

"About the call I just got saying you're responsible for putting Tucker in the hospital."

Jesse stared at him for a moment before he asked, "When did he go to the hospital?"

"Today."

"For what?"

"A skull fracture, a nasty concussion, and a few other presents you gave him."

"But that happened on Wednesday. If Tucker was hurt so badly, why wait so long to go to the hospital?"

"He thought the pain and dizziness would pass, but his parents finally forced him to get checked out."

"I-Is he going to be all right?" Violet asked, twisting her hands together.

"That hasn't been decided yet," Dad said testily. "And what I want to know from both of you is *why* he isn't all right." Dad focused on Jesse. "You want to explain yourself?"

There was a long silence before Jesse said, "I want to talk to you alone."

Violet took a step toward him, hand extended to stop him from saying anything.

"Stop right there," Dad ordered and shot her a hard look. "Start talking or go to your room." He raised a brow. "What's it going to be?"

She willed Jesse to look at her, to give her some clue about what he was about to tell them, but his gaze didn't waver from Dad. Why did he want to talk to their parents alone? He wouldn't make matters worse by talking about *them*, would he? It was bad enough that her recklessness led to Tucker being in the hospital. She didn't need Dad to know she'd also kissed Jesse, which led to her losing her virginity.

"Violet, go," Dad said.

She lingered a moment longer but had no choice but to retreat. She couldn't say anything without possibly contradicting whatever story, or truth, Jesse decided to tell. She walked to her bedroom, closed the door, and eyed the window. For the first time in her life, she considered running away, but that would be short-lived, embarrassing, and even more incriminating if Jesse didn't tell their parents everything.

She sank onto her bed and buried her face in her hands. Ten minutes ago, she felt worldly, mature, and powerful. Now, she was terrified of what repercussions lay in wait for her, Jesse, and Tucker.

What if Tucker sustained permanent brain damage? She had a flashback of his head slamming into concrete. Even though she witnessed firsthand the damage Jesse had inflicted, she hadn't even texted Tucker to make sure he was okay. Her only concern had been to break up with him once he returned to school. What was wrong with her? Technically, she was still his girlfriend, yet she hadn't checked on him and had moved on with another guy while he was recovering from his injuries.

Her only defense was that what happened between her and Jesse had been such a shocking turn of events that it eclipsed what happened with Tucker. So much so, she had completely dismissed him from her mind. From Tucker's point of view, Jesse had attacked him without provocation. She had been willing, and then her overprotective brother beat the crap out of him. If Tucker told his side of the story, Mom and Dad would hear about the compromising position Jesse found her in.

Her stomach lurched. She shot to her feet and put her ear to the bedroom door, but she couldn't hear anything. What was Jesse telling them? Why was it taking so long? Why was silence more ominous than shouting and glass breaking? Were their parents in shock? Is that why she couldn't hear their reaction?

Consumed by the need to do something, she started organizing her backpack and was so deep in her head, she didn't hear the door open.

"Violet?"

She whirled to find Lynne peeking her head around the door.

"Are you ready for church?"

Lynne wasn't smiling, but there was no sign that she'd been crying. Lynne didn't look horrified, disappointed, or revolted, just weary. That was a good sign, wasn't it?

"Yes, I'm ready."

As Mom slipped back into the hallway, she dashed through the bathroom to Jesse's room, but he wasn't there. She hurried down the hallway only to find the living and dining room also empty. What the *heck*?

"They're waiting for us in the car," Mom said.

She opened her mouth to ask questions but thought better of it and stayed quiet. She had to talk to Jesse first. She flew down the steps and saw Dad behind the wheel of Mom's car. She slipped into the back seat and glanced at Jesse, but he was looking out the window, giving her no clue as to what just happened. She buckled her seat belt and twisted her hand in the folds of her dress as she waited for someone to announce her sentence.

They were several minutes away from church when Dad finally spoke.

"We got in touch with Tucker's parents, and thankfully it seems like there won't be any long-term damage. Jesse offered to go to the hospital to apologize, but they didn't want him there. They've decided not to press charges." Dad's hand cut through the air. "None of this is okay. Violence is never the answer and with something this serious, we should have been told instead of being blindsided with a call like that. I expected better from both of you. As punishment for his actions, Jesse's dropping out of football."

She audibly gasped. Football was Jesse's favorite sport, and he was one of the best players on the team. Last year, they made it to the national championship, and they were counting on Jesse to take them there again. Football was sacred in Texas and ranked just a few notches below church. She looked at Jesse for his reaction, but his face was still averted.

"Jesse claims that you weren't involved."

She looked in the rearview mirror. Although Dad wore sunglasses, she felt the impact of his stare.

"I don't believe that for a second. You're the common denominator here, and you break up with Tucker the day Jesse fights him?" Dad shook his head. "I'm revoking your dating privileges. You aren't allowed to date for the rest of the school year. You also aren't going out after school or on weekends for the foreseeable future."

Lynne reached across the console and gripped Dad's arm. "Isaac."

Dad smacked the steering wheel, clearly still aggravated. "No! I'm not going to be lenient with her. I've done that far too much already and look where that's got us. If Tucker's parents chose to press charges, Jesse could have destroyed his future, all because he felt the need to defend his sister from a guy I knew she shouldn't have been with! I'll be damned if Violet turns out like *her*."

Violet went rigid. He didn't say her name. In fact, he never had, but she knew exactly who he was referring to—the mother who left in the middle of the night when she was two. To suggest that she was anything like the selfish woman who had abandoned them hurt so badly, it stole her breath. She turned her face toward the window so Dad wouldn't see her face crumple.

"Violet made a mistake," Lynne said into the loaded silence. "And Jesse made a mistake. They'll be punished for keeping secrets, bad judgment, and they'll have to earn back our trust. It's a blessing that Tucker and his parents were so understanding. Let's leave it at that."

No one said another word as they pulled up to the church. Violet stepped out of the car and fussed with her dress to give herself time to get a hold on her volatile emotions. Lynne stood beside her and waited patiently. When she started toward the church, Lynne stroked her back. She didn't meet anyone's eyes as she walked up the steps and paused on the threshold, unsure if she should be allowed in the chapel after what she'd done this week. Several hundred years ago, she would have been stoned to death.

"Don't take what your dad said to heart," Lynne murmured as she put an arm around her waist. "He's upset, but he'll get past it. We all will."

She swallowed the lump in her throat. She didn't deserve Lynne's sympathy or faith in her. Tucker was just the tip of the iceberg. If Mom knew what she and Jesse had done... She raised her head and saw Dad standing beside a pew, watching her hover on the threshold, almost as if he knew... Abruptly, he turned away and took a seat, staring straight ahead at the empty stage.

"Have faith," Lynne encouraged as she started down the aisle to join Dad.

Someone came up behind her. Her heightened senses told her who it was, even though Jesse didn't speak. She had so many questions, but this was neither the time nor place. And did it really matter what tale Jesse told? Dad knew she was to blame, even though Jesse tried to keep her out of it. The worst part was, Dad was right. It was her fault. They would discuss this later. First, they had to smile and maintain their image as a loving, Christian family.

She moved through the crowd and entered the pew her parents were sitting in from the opposite end. Jesse settled beside her. She nodded to those who greeted her and couldn't avoid several hugs that made her feel even worse. They thought she was one of them. That she was still pure and good, and she wasn't. Not by a long shot. She felt sick to her stomach.

"This message has been on my mind all week," Pastor Sonny began, gravely eyeing the congregation. "How one sin can change the trajectory of your life. We assume one tiny sin won't hurt, that no one will find out about it, but no sin escapes God's notice."

Violet resisted the urge to slouch in her seat as Pastor Sonny made eye contact with her.

"We're going to examine the life of the great King David. He went from shepherd boy to king and was hailed as a mighty warrior, but one transgression robbed him of the blessing God had for him and caused the rest of his life to be plagued with pain and betrayal." Pastor Sonny paused for effect before he continued, "Of course, I'm referring to his affair with Bathsheba."

Violet knew the story of King David's infamous affair—how he spotted a beautiful woman bathing from the rooftop of his palace and summoned her to him. When Bathsheba became pregnant, King David had her husband killed in battle to claim her for himself.

"One sin," Pastor Sonny said thoughtfully as he strolled across the stage. "Adultery doesn't seem like such a big deal, but when a child is conceived, King David tries to pass the child off as the husband's and when that didn't work, he murdered his loyal soldier." Pastor Sonny shook his head. "People don't understand that one sin will always lead to another. Once you start on that path, you can't stop. Before you know it, you're trapped in a web of your own making. King David thought he got away with it, but God sees all, and the punishment was severe."

Pastor Sonny listed the many consequences of King David's sin, beginning with the death of the child that had been conceived during the affair. But it was the tragic story of the incestuous relationship between David's children, Amnon and his half-sister, Tamar, that made Violet's blood run cold. Amnon was so obsessed with his sister that he faked being ill to have his sister feed him and then raped her.

"It says here in verse fifteen that after Amnon had Tamar, he hated her more than he once loved her." Pastor Sonny paused so the congregation could take that in. "Can you imagine wanting someone so much that you risked everything to possess her, only to discover your all-consuming love was just fleeting lust? Amnon wanted her purely because he couldn't have her, and he paid for that sin with his life when his brother, Absalom, struck him down to avenge her."

Pastor Sonny held up a finger.

"King David passed his sins onto his sons, who mirrored and amplified them. We think one misstep won't hurt anyone and that if we're found out, we can handle the fallout, but we forget that it's not just us that's affected. It's our family, those we love most, who suffer the most for our choices. In King David's case, that generational curse was passed on. And it doesn't stop there. It trickles out to our friends and community. Everything you do matters. I think, if we keep that in mind, we could save ourselves and those we care about a lot of grief."

Convicted to her core, Violet closed her eyes. Discovering that she and Jesse engaged in a sexual relationship would devastate their parents on multiple levels. She and Jesse weren't blood siblings, but they had been raised as such and that's how their parents wanted them to view each other. Sex complicated things, which is why blended families discouraged it from happening in the first place. To make matters worse, their parents didn't believe in premarital sex.

If Dad grounded her for suspecting she had influenced the fight between Jesse and Tucker, what would he do if he found out she initiated a sexual relationship between her and Jesse? Jesse paid her midnight visits, but he'd never gone beyond that. She kissed him and then unwittingly taunted him by giving him the impression she was experienced, which made him lose control. She hadn't stopped Tucker or Jesse from putting their hands in her pants. She hadn't fought Jesse off when he put her on his bed. A part of her wanted to know and experience, and she had, without considering the aftermath or future complications. What if her carnal recklessness destroyed their family, as it had King David's? When she was younger, she'd been terrified Lynne and her dad would break up. What if she caused her worst fear to come true?

"In Luke 8:17, it says that all secrets will be brought to light and made known to all. If you think you're going to get away with your sin, believe me, you won't. It may take years, even decades, but your misdeeds will be exposed, and you will pay in one form or another. It's inevitable," Pastor Sonny said with such conviction that Violet wanted to drop to her knees and repent.

She didn't realize her hands were balled into fists until Jesse placed his on top of hers. She pulled away and would have scooted closer to Lynne, but she didn't want to bring unwanted attention to them. Jesse couldn't touch her like that anymore. They could never repeat what they'd done this week. For as long as she could remember, she longed for a family. God had answered her prayers and given her a mother and brother who gave her the love and affection she longed for. She couldn't lose them.

Right then and there, she began to pray. *Lord, punish me in whatever way You see fit, but please keep my family intact. My parents don't deserve to be hurt because of my choices. I swear I'll right my wrongs. I'll fix my relationship with Jesse. We'll never do anything immoral ever again. Please don't expose my weaknesses and faults. I'll do better. I'll do anything to make this right. Please have mercy on me.*

As if Jesse sensed her distress, he brushed the back of his hand against her thigh. This time, she moved away. Just as she predicted, Lynne glanced at her. Violet rested her head on her shoulder. Lynne didn't admonish her, but cupped her cheek, comforting her like she was a child. At that moment, she felt like one. Overwhelmed, ashamed, and wishing someone would clean up her mess.

"What some people try to do is turn their sin into something good, but nothing that begins in sin will be blessed by God. It will always fail," Pastor Sonny boomed.

She hadn't considered the long-term ramifications of sleeping with her stepbrother. She'd been caught up in sexual discovery, in fulfilling dark desires, and pleasure. How could she be so stupid?

Was it her imagination, or had Pastor Sonny looked directly at her several times? Did God give him the ability to single out which church members this message was for? She'd been lambasted so severely, she could barely sit upright. Each point cut deep like a whip. Between finding out that Tucker was in the hospital and this message, it couldn't be clearer that God was giving her one last warning before she ruined her life.

Amnon's reaction after finally having his half-sister played over and over in her mind. *He hated her more than he once loved her.* It would kill her if one day Jesse despised her or looked through her as he did the other girls he'd dated. Before, she'd been his sister, which made her special, but by sleeping with him, she became like all the others. Easy, forgettable. There'd been no need to date and woo her —he went straight to sex. And she let him. What if, like Amnon, Jesse desired her because it was taboo and titillating and once he got his fill...?

Ice spread through her belly. It was better to end it now before anyone got hurt. Already, her feelings were engaged, while it could be just about sex for him. He was jacking off in her room even when he had girlfriends. They hadn't been enough for him. He was oversexed. Maybe any girl would do, and she was just... available?

"Let's pray," Pastor Sonny said.

Heart heavy, she closed her eyes. The tears that dropped to her lap went unnoticed as the pastor prayed over the congregation, hoping they could learn from King David's mistakes and do better in their own lives.

***

"Violet."

She swiveled on her chair to see Dad standing in her bedroom. They hadn't exchanged a word all day. During dinner, Lynne tried to lighten the mood by entertaining them with tales of her students. Violet hadn't been able to enjoy the food, company, or stories and had excused herself to take refuge in her room. Guilt lay on her shoulders like a heavy, suffocating winter coat. She hadn't been able to look Dad or Jesse in the eye. She wished she could reverse time and walk away from Tucker when he tried to pressure her to get in his car. So many red flags and missed opportunities to do the right thing. She could have saved them all a lot of grief is she'd stopped it from the beginning.

She spent her time cleaning the heck out of her room and purged all signs of debauchery. She washed her clothes and bedsheets, vacuumed, organized, and erased incriminating text messages. She also messaged Tucker, apologizing for what happened with Jesse, and asked if there was anything she could do. Her fervent, long-winded message received a one-word reply: *No*. Apparently, she didn't need to break up with him. It seemed the sentiment was mutual.

Dad advanced into her room and sat on the edge of her bed. "I was harsh with you today."

She lowered her gaze. "I deserved it."

"That phone call was a nasty shock. I'm glad Tucker's going to be all right and that Jesse got off with a tap on the wrist. It could have been a lot worse."

She nodded.

"I know Jesse didn't tell us everything and honestly, I don't think I could handle the truth. But I know one thing. Nothing could have caused such an extreme reaction from him except you. He'd do anything for you, even if it cost him everything. Do you understand that, Vi? Jesse came this close to having something on his record today that would never go away. Your actions have consequences now. Consequences that can mar your future."

"I know," she said shakily as her eyes filled with tears.

Dad let out a gusty sigh. "Just... be more mindful. Think before you leap. That's all I'm asking. Can you do that for me?"

She nodded and tried to give him a smile but failed.

Dad got to his feet and squeezed her shoulder. "Go to bed. It's been a long day."

Once he left her room, she walked into the bathroom and, for the first time ever, made sure to lock the door that led into Jesse's room.

Jesse had approached her twice, but she shot him down. She didn't want to risk Mom or Dad hearing them talk and honestly, there was nothing to say. He'd been so sure no one would find out about Tucker, but like Pastor Sonny said, the truth would always reveal itself.

No one could ever find out about her and Jesse. If it got out, she knew beyond a shadow of a doubt that nothing would ever be the same. If Dad discovered they slept with one another, he wouldn't kill Jesse, but it could turn Dad and Lynne against one another if they defended their own child. Or maybe they would all realize she was the problem. Her nails sank into her palm. They had to end it now before anyone suspected. Perhaps they could work their way back to seeing each other as friends instead of lovers.

Tears slipped down her face as she brushed her teeth and readied herself for bed. When she walked back into her room, she paused. She had no doubt Jesse would come to her after their parents went to bed. She couldn't let that happen, even if it was just to talk.

Sniffling, she locked both doors that led into her room. Dad instructed them to leave their doors unlocked in case of an emergency. This was an emergency of a different sort. Boundaries that needed to be set.

She climbed into bed and willed herself to sleep, but Pastor Sonny's warnings made her toss and turn. It was just after eleven when the bathroom light came on. From the gap beneath the door, she saw a shadow approach and then the sharp snick of the doorknob as Jesse turned it back and forth. There was a pause and then a louder rattle as he used more force. She pulled the covers over her head as Jesse cursed.

"Vi!" he hissed.

She didn't move. Several minutes later, she lowered the comforter and saw the bathroom light was off. She blew out a breath, turned on her side, and prayed for wisdom and strength in getting them on the right path tomorrow.

CHAPTER 13
VIOLET

She was brushing her teeth the following morning when Jesse tentatively knocked on the bathroom door. When she didn't answer, he tried the locked door.

"Violet?"

When she didn't answer, she heard a thump. She wasn't sure whether it was his hand or forehead that hit the door.

"Violet."

The frustrated longing in his tone made her eyes water. She rinsed her mouth and quickly finished up her tasks in the bathroom. She unlocked his door before she double timed it to her bedroom and locked hers.

All night, she rehearsed what she would say to him. She had no idea how he would respond. He heard the same sermon at church yesterday. He had to see the parallels and recognize the risks they were taking—not just with their own relationship, but their family. After sleeping on it, she hoped he'd come to the same conclusion. Bottom line, he meant too much to her to risk losing him. He couldn't argue with that.

As she dated, she'd been pushing the limits with her wardrobe, but today she wasn't trying to attract or please anyone. Not Jesse, Tucker, or any other guy. She pulled on jeans and a loose fitted top, put her hair in a ponytail, and put in gold heart earrings. Comfortable, simple, not sexy at all. She just wanted everything to go back to the way it had been before sex got in the way.

When she made her way into the dining room, she found Mom and Dad at the dining table doing devotions. This was usually something that happened on the weekend, not a weekday. Mom was typically in a hurry to get to school and on his days off, Dad was often working on a house project, fishing, or helping the church with something. Apparently, they were planning on being more present, which worked in her favor.

"Hey, honey," Mom greeted.

She was comforted by Dad's half smile. All was forgiven. Today was a new day and an opportunity to make good choices. She went into the kitchen to make herself oatmeal and stiffened when Jesse materialized at her side.

"Morning."

Her eyes flicked up, clashed with his stormy blue ones, and quickly looked away. "Morning. Do you want oatmeal for breakfast?"

"You left something on the bathroom counter."

"Sorry about that," she said lightly. "I'll grab it later."

"Jesse," Dad called. "You're going to talk to Coach Rick today about leaving the team?"

"Yeah," Jesse said curtly.

There was a startled pause and then Mom asked, "Do we need to talk more about this, son?"

"No," Jesse said and shocked them all by turning on his heel and walking out the front door.

Mom and Dad glanced at each other and then Violet as she turned to watch his exit. Jesse had never talked back to their parents or showed any disrespect before. His terse tone and display of temper wasn't like him at all.

"Should I talk to him?" Dad murmured.

Lynne let out a long sigh and sat back in her seat. "Are we doing the right thing? This is his senior year. Making him quit football is a huge punishment."

Dad rapped his fingers on the table. "We can't let him get away with thinking what he did is okay."

"Of course not, but his team could make the national championships, and he's worked so hard."

"The only way for him to learn his lesson is to have him give up something he cares about. Anything else won't be a real punishment," Dad countered.

Through the living room window, Violet watched Jesse pick up the basketball and start dribbling on the driveway. She assumed he was upset about them when he probably wanted to talk to her about dropping out of football. It was a big deal. He was letting his whole team down. Everyone would want to know why he was quitting. What was he going to say? Her shoulders slumped. Another thing to add to the never-ending list of things that were her fault.

Glumly, she turned when the kettle screamed and poured hot water over the oats and added brown sugar and milk. She sat at the table, only half listening as her parents debated what was an appropriate punishment for Jesse. She secretly hoped they would come up with something else and couldn't conceal her dismay when Dad put his foot down.

"I didn't ban him from playing sports completely, which I could do. Giving up football will make him think twice before he acts in the future."

As Dad left the table, Mom focused on her. "Are you okay?"

"This is all my fault," Violet said and dropped her spoon, unable to take another bite.

Mom didn't deny it. "It's better for both of you to learn these lessons now rather than later." Mom chucked her under the chin. "This seems like a big deal now. It may seem like your world is ending, but one day you'll laugh over this." When Violet gave her an incredulous look, Lynne's lips quirked. "I swear you will. And as for your punishment, no going out with friends after school. Once Jesse talks to Coach Rick, you two come straight home."

"Yes, ma'am."

Violet lingered over her oatmeal until it was time to leave. When she walked out the front door, she saw Lynne talking to Jesse on the driveway. He had his head bent as he listened to his mother and nodded. As Violet approached, he unlocked the SUV so she could get in and went into the house to get his backpack while she fidgeted in the passenger seat. Lynne backed out of the driveway as Jesse got behind the wheel.

"We have to talk," he said as he fired up the engine.

Violet clasped her hands between her thighs. "I'm sorry that they're making you quit football. I know how much you love it. Maybe if you talk to Dad, you can convince him to—"

"I don't care about football. I care about us," he snapped.

Her heart skipped a beat. "We're fine."

"Are we?"

"Of course."

He braked a little too hard at a stop sign as he navigated through the neighborhood.

"Is that why you're locking me out of your room? Because we're fine?"

A hint of the aggression he displayed the day he beat Tucker's ass was coming back, making her anxiety skyrocket.

"I think," she began stiltedly as she plucked imaginary lint off her jeans, "considering what happened yesterday that you would agree that..." Why was she so nervous? This was Jesse. She could tell him anything. "That what we did..." she fumbled and burst out, "We can't do that anymore!"

The veins on his arms stood out as his hands flexed on the steering wheel. "No."

She forgot about her rehearsed speech. "What do you mean, *no*?"

He shot her a searing look out of narrow, glowing blue eyes. "You don't get to end us because you're scared or have a guilty conscience."

"I don't have a guilty conscience," she lied. "I just realized…" She dragged her hands down her face. "What were we thinking? You're my *brother*."

"We aren't blood related."

"But we were raised as siblings. I never saw you as anything else until…" She shook her head wildly and held both hands up like a traffic cop. "No. *No!* This ends now. We never should have let it get this far."

He reached over the console and gripped her thigh. "I'm not going to let you do this."

"Did you see Mom and Dad's faces when they found out about Tucker? Can you imagine how they'd react if they found out about us?" Her voice quavered as her mind conjured up all sorts of traumatic scenarios. "They don't even believe in sex before marriage and we…"

He squeezed her knee. "It's okay, Vi."

"No, it isn't! Nothing about this is okay. It's wrong and sinful, and we did it anyway! Mom and Dad would *die* if they knew!"

"We can't make decisions based on how Mom and Dad will feel," he said harshly. "We're old enough to make our own choices and accept the consequences, whatever they are."

"I-I'm not willing to accept the consequences for this," she stammered as she tried to brush his hand off her leg. "I'm not going to be the reason our family breaks apart. I've made a lot of stupid decisions, but I can fix this."

His grip tightened. "There's nothing to fix. You and I are supposed to be together."

"We will be! As siblings, as family, nothing more!" She smacked his hand. "You can't touch me like this! It's inappropriate!"

Her voice was rising. She was getting hysterical. Her emotions were a wild, feral thing clawing at her, making her lash out. She wanted this done, buried, over. Why was he arguing with her? Deep down, he knew this was the right thing to do, he just didn't want it to end *right now*. But it would have at some point, most likely when he'd gotten his fill. This was a novel experience for him—a girl ending things. He was just being stubborn.

"Stop pushing me away," he rapped out.

"I'm not pushing you away. I just don't want you to touch me."

"Yesterday I was licking your pussy, and today I can't touch you?"

His vulgar language was as shocking as a slap. She felt the blood drain from her face. "Don't talk to me like that."

"You really think we can go back to acting like siblings after I've been inside you? After everything we've done?"

"Yes!"

He shot her a look filled with incredulous fury. "Didn't the last few days mean anything to you?"

An invisible needle pierced her heart. Their day at the lake had been so special, almost dreamlike in its perfection. She would cherish that memory, especially since she knew they could never repeat it.

He squeezed her leg. "Vi."

She swallowed hard. "The past few days have been nice, but—"

"*Nice?*"

She flinched, partly because of his deafening shout and partly because, "You're hurting me."

He snatched his hand from her leg and ran his fingers through his hair. "I don't believe this."

"Isn't it bad enough that you have to give up football? That Tucker ended up in the hospital? How many signs do you need to convince you this isn't meant to be? Didn't you listen to Pastor Sonny's message yesterday?"

"I heard it."

"And?"

A muscle ticked in his jaw. "That has nothing to do with us."

Her mouth sagged. He was being deliberately obtuse. Pastor Sonny's message was a warning of how a seemingly harmless transgression could cause so much destruction. She wasn't willing to risk their family. Nothing was worth courting such an outcome. Couldn't he see that?

Was this proof that regularly indulging in sin changed a person, so they cared only about satisfying their cravings, regardless of anyone else's feelings? Was Jesse that far gone? Her resolve hardened. She vowed she would get them on the right path and that's what she would do, regardless of his bullheadedness.

"I want our relationship to go back to what it was," she said into the fraught silence.

"And if I don't agree?"

"You don't have a choice."

Out of the corner of her eye, she saw his head turn in her direction. He didn't say a word. He didn't have to. His gaze, sharp as the tip of a knife, slid over her. When she was on the verge of begging him to look back at the road, he did so.

"This wouldn't have happened if you hadn't caught me with Tucker. It started this domino effect that's led us here. I don't want anyone else to get hurt, and that's what would happen if we continued on this path. I don't want to disappoint Mom and Dad any more than I already have." She blinked rapidly as her eyes filled with tears. "And you mean too much to me to risk our friendship."

He said nothing.

"We won't talk about it. It'll be like it never happened," she said.

He didn't move a muscle, but the force of his anger was an invisible force that hammered at her, making it hard to breathe. She braced for an explosion that didn't come. Several minutes later, she slumped in her seat. His volatile temper unnerved her. He'd changed so much in so little time. She wanted her patient, considerate, affable brother back. This wasn't him.

She wanted everything to go back to the way it had been when she had nothing to hide, and she felt safe and clean and there was no threat of being exposed. He had to know this was destined to end badly. It was taboo, scandalous and if discovered, would haunt them for the rest of their lives. No one would support them exploring such a path. Even their friends would be horrified. Once Jesse had time to consider the long-term effects, he would agree with her. But until then, things between them would be strained. She hated being at odds with him, but it was necessary. He wasn't thinking clearly. It would take time to reprogram their minds, so they didn't see each other sexually. It was best to end it now before they hit the point of no return.

Although she knew she should leave him alone, she couldn't resist asking, "What did you tell Mom and Dad about the day you beat Tucker?"

"A complete fabrication."

She twisted her hands together in her lap. "Thank you for not telling them the truth." The silence that followed made her cringe. "I'm sorry. For everything."

"I'm not."

She wasn't sure what he meant by that, but didn't ask him to elaborate. It was a relief to reach school. Before he parked, she had her seat belt undone, and her backpack on her lap. When she hopped out, she expected him to say something in parting, but he didn't.

A group of their friends were several cars over. She approached Marissa, Brody, Anton and a few others with a big smile, determined for everything to go back to normal.

"Hey," she greeted.

"Where's Jesse going?" Anton asked.

She turned. She thought he'd be right behind her, but he was striding in the opposite direction, across the empty field. "No idea."

"See you tomorrow," she told Marie before she headed toward the SUV. Jesse was already behind the wheel. She opened the passenger door and asked, "Did you talk to Coach Rick?"

"Yeah. Get in."

Apparently, his mood hadn't improved. The need to apologize rose again, but she knew it wouldn't do any good. She got in and fastened her seatbelt. "That didn't take long. I thought he'd try to talk you out of it."

"I talked to him at lunch."

Which explained why they were now creeping through traffic mere minutes after school ended. "Are you okay?"

"Does it matter?" he asked testily.

"Yes. If I hadn't let Tucker—"

"You saved his life. I wouldn't have stopped if you hadn't interfered."

That made her feel marginally better. "Have you told anyone besides Coach Rick that you're quitting?"

"No. Coach is going to break the news at practice."

"What reason did you give?"

He shrugged. "The truth. I made a mistake that made my parents pull me from the team. I deserve it."

She sat back and closed her eyes. Although Jesse didn't blame her, it didn't remove the crushing weight on her shoulders. She was grateful Jesse was speaking to her. She hadn't seen him all day and suspected he was avoiding her. Although she was secretly grateful he was making himself scarce, it made her feel even worse.

Although she did her best to act like everything was okay, she wasn't pulling it off well. Three of her friends asked if something was wrong. Georgia hadn't accepted her weak excuse and started interrogating her about the status of her relationship with Tucker. When she admitted that she and Tucker had broken up, her friends gave her hugs when she started to tear up. If they only knew the real reason she was crying.

Without conscious thought, she reached out to Jesse, seeking comfort, before she caught herself. She told him this morning that he couldn't touch her. That was a two-way street. Things were still too raw between them, even to hold his hand.

Her hand passed over her burning eyes. How had things gone off track so quickly? In a matter of days, it felt like she lost so much. Tucker, Jesse, her innocence, her parent's respect and trust. It had been a rollercoaster of highs and lows, and now she was at rock bottom with no idea where to go from here.

She hadn't expected this to be so excruciating. Why did doing the right thing feel like she was killing a part of herself? She felt drained, sad, and lonely.

She and Jesse were in the awkward, angry phase of a breakup. Even with her eyes closed, she sensed the battle going on inside of him. Whether that was because of her or the fact that his teammates and a good portion of the school would soon be speculating why he was quitting football, she wasn't sure.

When the SUV slowed, she opened her eyes and frowned as he turned into the same deserted park where he first kissed her.

"What are you doing? Mom wanted us to go straight home."

"She thought I'd talk to Coach after school, so we have time." He parked, undid his seatbelt, and turned toward her. "We need to talk."

Her heart skipped. "About what?"

His eyes narrowed. "About you and me."

"There's nothing to talk about."

He leaned forward, sky-blue eyes glittering as he stated, "You can't give me what you gave me and take it back, Vi."

"That was a mistake," she whispered.

"No, it wasn't," he clipped. "This..." He gestured between them. "Isn't a mistake. Can't you feel it?"

"Feel what?" she asked, feigning confusion.

He tensed. "Don't do that."

"Do what?"

"Act like you don't feel anything for me."

"I never said that. I love you. You're my brother."

He leaned in and growled, "We both know you haven't seen me as your brother for a while now."

It was the closest he'd come to acknowledging his late-night visits. The eruption of butterflies and heat in her belly horrified her.

She thought declaring that their relationship was wrong would be enough to suppress her body's reaction to him. Not so. Her weak, susceptible flesh was eager to jump back into the fire, heedless of the consequences.

When she tried to turn away, Jesse clasped her face, forcing her to look at him.

"I've been in hell for so fucking long. I can't go back to that." He rested his forehead against hers. "You love me, and not just as a brother. Admit it."

Her heart slammed into her ribcage as her eyes flooded with the tears she'd been keeping at bay all day. "We can't."

"We can." His voice vibrated with implacable determination.

She wanted to leap into the deep end. To let him lead and take care of everything, but she knew he wasn't thinking it through. Indulging for the moment would only lead to more heartache. "Jesse."

"Do you honestly think how we feel about each other is going to go away? We didn't just kiss. I claimed every inch of you. You wanted it just as much as I did. You still do."

She flushed and braced her hand against his chest, pushing for breathing space. "It doesn't matter! This is wrong."

"Stop saying that. There's nothing wrong with this."

"If this is so *right,* then are you willing to tell Mom and Dad?" she challenged.

If he truly wanted her, he would be willing to tell their parents this wasn't a fling, but a genuine, loving relationship he wanted to pursue. No such words emerged from him. The long silence cut deep and confirmed everything she'd been thinking. He didn't care how conflicted she felt or that, if discovered, it would devastate their parents. Like Amnon, he was focused purely on sex and wouldn't stop until he quenched his needs. He also seemed fine with keeping their relationship a dirty secret. Why? So there would be minimal damage in the long run?

She wrenched away from him and ran her fingers through her

hair as she tried to stuff down her feelings of being sullied and used. That's what she got for engaging in such a relationship. Regardless of how much her body enjoyed what Jesse did to her, it wouldn't last. She cattle prodded her hormones into submission and took a deep, calming breath. She promised God she would stop them from continuing down this slippery slope. Jesse was already too far gone, so she had to take a stand for both their sakes.

She stared through the windshield at the empty park as she said, "I've made so many mistakes. Mistakes with Tucker. Mistakes with you that have made things..." She swallowed hard. "Difficult. I'm sorry for that. I can't take it back, but I can do what's right, starting now. I just want to forget it ever happened."

Out of the corner of her eye, she saw he sat facing her, completely motionless.

"Please take me home," she said quietly.

"You think you can end it, just like that?"

Despite the way her heart banged around in her chest like a trapped bird, she turned her head to meet and hold his gaze. "Yes. Just like that."

Although his face remained blank, something shifted in his eyes that made the fine hairs on her nape stand up. Everything in her went on high alert. Obeying a gut instinct, she undid her seatbelt, yanked on the door handle, and tumbled out of the SUV all in one motion. She staggered before she caught her balance and stared at Jesse, who hadn't moved. Feeling frightened, foolish, and embarrassed at her overreaction, she glared at him.

"Get in the car, Vi," he said coldly.

She'd always trusted Jesse implicitly, but for the first time in her life, she hesitated. He seemed to be in control, but something told her if she got back in the car, he would cross every boundary she just set. She was ashamed that a part of her wanted him to. It would be so easy to get lost in him, but her fear of ending up alone was stronger than her sexual desires.

She slammed the door in his face and headed for the trail. They both needed to cool off. She'd go for a walk while he sat in the car and... She stiffened when she heard a door closing, the familiar beep of the SUV's alarm, and the sound of someone running toward her.

A hand wrapped around her upper arm. "Violet."

She pivoted to face him, squinting into the sun as she went on tiptoes and enunciated through her teeth, "We're done talking. Nothing you say is going to make a difference. I've made up my mind. You have to accept it."

He searched her eyes. "That's your final word?"

"Yes!"

He nodded and glanced around. "You want to see the park?"

She blinked, taken aback by how quickly his mood had shifted. "I... I think I'll take a walk."

He gestured for her to precede him. She eyed him for a moment before she turned on her heel and strode off. She expected him to continue the argument, but he gave her space, staying a few paces behind her so she didn't feel crowded. After minutes passed without a word exchanged between them, her hunched shoulders dropped.

His forceful pushback unnerved her. He had grounds to be disgruntled, even angry, but she expected him to accept her decision with grace. He'd always been so easygoing, respectful, and willing to cede to her wishes and now... Now, she had no idea what was coming next.

She was seeing him in a new light. His broody edginess thrilled and alarmed her. She shouldn't be aroused by it, but there was no denying that she was. There was something wrong with her. There was no other explanation for why she'd gotten wet when he ordered her to get back in the car. This was *Jesse*, the brother who braided her hair, comforted her when Mom and Dad fought, and helped her with her homework. Why hadn't she ever picked up on the steel beneath his guileless smile? Why was she simultaneously attracted and repelled by it? This wouldn't do. She was supposed to be purifying her thoughts, but her mind was overwhelmed with graphic, inappropriate fantasies that she tried to smother without success.

Why had no one ever mentioned how addictive sin was? It was a drug one could get hooked on by partaking of the forbidden just once. Jesse was so consumed by it that he wasn't himself. He hadn't been for some time, though. Jesse had been sipping from the pool of debauchery far longer than she had. Who knew what he'd been doing with his exes, who were so eager to get back together with him? He hadn't been caught, which had emboldened him to this point. Being outed by Tucker should have been a wakeup call that he wasn't going to get away with everything. Why didn't Jesse get what he needed from another girl? Why put so much in jeopardy to sleep with his stepsister?

Her calves cramped as she went uphill. She slowed to catch her breath and made a mental note that she needed to exercise more. She was grateful when the path curved beneath some trees. As she paused to enjoy the shade, she cocked her head when she heard running water.

"There's a stream that runs parallel to the path. Want to see it?" Jesse asked.

When she nodded, he led the way through the trees. She perked up as she got a glimpse of blue up ahead. When they came to a small clearing, she put her hands on hips and surveyed the tranquil scene. Sunlight danced on the surface of the fast-moving water.

"I can see why you like coming here. It's beautiful," she said.

She closed her eyes for a moment, letting nature soothe her troubled thoughts. If only she could rewind the clock. She longed for a time when things were simple and innocent, but a part of her knew those days were gone. Like Eve, she'd taken a bite of the apple and now there was no going back to seeing the world in cute, pastel shades. Now, she could see every vivid shade of the rainbow and had firsthand knowledge of the temptations in the shadows. With adult decisions came severe punishments, complications, and impossible choices. But she was doing her part and keeping her promise to God. That's all that mattered.

A soft gust of air was her only warning. She opened her eyes to find Jesse in front of her. Her hand flew up in a protective gesture as she stumbled back.

"What are you...?"

"I can't go back to what we were."

His flat delivery made her freeze, but it was the strange, unholy gleam in his eyes that made her heart begin to beat like a drum.

"I-I want to go back to the trail."

Even she could hear the anxiety in her tone. Jesse's only response to this was to match her retreating steps. His eyes were fixed on her like she was prey. He wasn't even blinking.

In a distant part of her mind, she noted that he had pretended to accept her decision so she would let down her guard and bring her somewhere secluded where no one would interfere. They were a significant distance from the path without a soul in sight.

"Last week was a dream for me. Taking your virginity and then having you surrender so completely, giving me everything..." One hand balled into a fist at his side. "Now, you say you want to forget it ever happened, and I'm supposed to go back to treating you like a sister." He shook his head. "It doesn't work that way, baby."

"We have to get home. Mom and Dad..."

"Things were perfect until that call came in," Jesse cut in, ignoring her nervous chatter. "I don't care that I have to quit football. That's a small price to pay for giving him the beating he deserved."

"Tucker—"

He closed the distance between them with a speed that made her let out a startled yelp. He pinned her against a tree and gripped her face as he ducked down, so they were eye to eye.

"That's the last time you say his name," he said through clenched teeth. "I'm sick of hearing about him. I don't regret what I did. I'd do it all over again, except I wouldn't stop until I was sure the damage was permanent."

"You can't mean that!"

"I do." He trailed his knuckles down the sensitive line of her throat. "He had no right to touch you."

His pupils were so dilated, there was only a thin ring of blue. She should run, fight, or scream her head off, but she was locked in a strange paralysis that kept her pinned between Jesse and the massive tree at her back.

"You can't tell me you don't feel anything for me. I won't believe you."

His knuckles trailed down to her breasts. When he strummed her nipple, she jolted.

"You love what I do to you," he rasped as he cupped her breast and tightened his hold on her face, giving her no way to hide her reaction from him. "You want this so bad, you're shaking."

She was shaking. Whether it was from desire or terror, she wasn't sure. She wrapped both hands around his wrist and tugged. "Please don't do this."

"I've never felt like this about anyone," Jesse said almost to himself. "I thought I would be satisfied once I had you, once you gave yourself to me, but you're always trying to slip away." His expression hardened, and his fingers dug into her cheeks as he pressed his lips to hers. "But I have you now, Violet. And I'm not letting go."

He held her gaze as his hand left her breast and went to the button of her jeans. Her paralysis broke. She erupted into motion, but he was anticipating that and swept her legs out from under her.

She landed on her back without any idea how she'd gotten there. Winded and stunned, she lay there, staring at the underside of the tree's canopy until Jesse blotted out her view. He undid her jeans, yanked them to her knees, and slipped his fingers inside her. She sat up with an outraged shriek as he retracted his hand. Before she could defend herself, he shoved those same fingers into her mouth so deep that she gagged.

"Tell me again you don't want me," Jesse mocked.

Along with bile, she tasted her own honey. She wrenched her head to the side and coughed.

"We're not going backwards," Jesse declared with frightening calm as he positioned her on her hands and knees and knelt behind her. "Nothing's coming between us. No other guys, Mom and Dad, even God."

She reached back and pushed at him. "You can't do this!"

"I have to do this. For both of us." When she tried to scramble away, he pulled her back and smacked her butt hard enough to stun her into immobility. "You're scared of what people think and too ashamed to admit what you really want."

His fingers slipped inside her.

"Soaked, just like I knew you would be. Are you wet for your brother, Violet?"

"Stop!" she sobbed as she tore at the grass to get away.

He gripped her hips, hauling her backwards, and slammed in to the hilt. She screamed. The horrible sound bounced off the trees and ricocheted back to them. As she hung her head, panting, she waited for the distant shout of some Good Samaritan coming to the rescue, but there was nothing but the pleasant sound of the stream, which she now realized would drown out any call for help.

"I come here often because of how isolated it is," Jesse said as he blanketed her much smaller form. "Scream all you want. Nobody's going to hear you."

"This isn't you," she said, her voice thick with tears. "Something's wrong. Can't you see that?"

"You're what's wrong with me," he groaned into her hair. "I haven't been sane for over a year. You love toying with me and throwing obstacles in my path. I'd let you do whatever you want to me, but the moment things get rough, you want to run. I'm not going to let you do that anymore. You're sticking with me."

He began to move in shallow, hard thrusts that stabbed something inside her that made her keen and uproot the ground around her.

"How can anything that feels so fucking good be a sin, Violet?" he panted as his hand slipped under her blouse and stroked her stomach. "We were made for each other. Can't you feel it?"

She let out a choked sob as he planted himself deep. She couldn't believe this was happening—that he was so far gone that he would take her in a public place. He was ruthless, shameless, completely out of control. As he began to move more forcefully, her knees sank into the soft earth.

"We're supposed to be together. Everything in me says so. I know you feel it, too. I'd do anything for you, baby, anything."

She shook her head.

He slowed his pace and pressed his cheek against her clammy one. "What, baby?"

"You wouldn't do anything for me," she said raggedly.

"Of course I would," he whispered as he rocked his hips. "Tell me what you want, and I'll give it to you."

"I want you to stop."

He abruptly pushed on her shoulders, so her face was mashed in the grass and her butt was up in the air.

"You don't want me to stop, and I'm going to prove it."

CHAPTER 14

JESSE

Violet's upper body arched as she released a beautiful, muted scream before she went limp. As he lapped up what poured from her, she shuddered and tried to scoot away, but her body was weak and uncoordinated, and she was no match for him. Eventually, she gave up and let him have his way.

When he was content, he rested his cheek on her sticky inner thigh. He'd never been drunk or high, but he suspected it was similar to how he felt right now.

For a few hellish hours, he thought he may have lost her, but she was back where she belonged. He sated his demons and made sure he fed hers, too. He fucked her on her hands and knees before he went 69, straddling her face, forcing her to get him hard again while he made her come with his mouth. After that, he took her missionary with her ankles resting on his shoulders. That's when she began babbling about sin, Amnon and Tamar, and some deal she'd made with God. He didn't care about a fucked up, incestuous relationship that happened three thousand years ago or what she promised God. He had his own deal with God—her. He lost his father so that God could bring Violet into his life. She was his destiny, his salvation, *his*.

She belonged to him and he to her. Why couldn't she see that? What she labeled as sin felt like a spiritual cleansing to him. She was home to him, and he wouldn't let her destroy the ties he'd so carefully nurtured.

She climaxed when he did her missionary and then burst into tears. He'd never heard her cry like that before. She was distraught, inconsolable. Nothing he said would calm her, so he did the only thing he could think of—turn those pitiful cries into gasps of pleasure by burying his face in his favorite place. She fought him and called for help until she was hoarse, but God was on his side. No one interfered. He made her beg for release and wrung out two more orgasms from her before he was satisfied.

He kissed her mound before he got to his feet and sorted himself out. He absently brushed debris from his legs before pulling his jeans up. He was grateful he'd worn a black shirt instead of white. If not, it would have been covered in dirt and grass stains from all the rolling around on the ground they'd just done.

He surveyed Violet, who made a delectable picture. She was splayed on her back, blouse hiked up to expose her abdomen and bra, jeans caught on one ankle while her other leg was completely bare. Her pussy glistened from his ministrations, inner thighs red and swollen from the love bites he'd left behind. The urge to wring more affirmations from her was tempting, but they didn't have time.

He retrieved her torn underwear and pocketed them before he crouched beside her. "Vi."

Her only reaction to his voice was a tear that slipped from the corner of her closed eyelids.

"We have to go, baby," he said before he gripped her limp hands and pulled her up.

He wasn't surprised when she swayed on her feet. He'd been rough. Brutal, actually, but hearing her chalk up the best days of his life as "nice" and her dismissal of their relationship put him into a mindless state that didn't leave room for tenderness.

He steadied her before he unfolded her crumpled blouse and

brushed grass, dirt, and leaves from her before he fed her leg into her pants and pulled them up. Both of their jeans were suspiciously dirty, but thankfully his dark shirt and her colorful top hid the worst of the stains.

"Can you walk?" he asked.

When she didn't acknowledge him, he inwardly shrugged and put her over his shoulder. She didn't fight or utter a sound. They were a ways from the parking lot, but now that he'd had her, he felt like he could climb Mount Everest.

He was grateful he didn't pass anyone on the path. He opened the SUV and settled her in the passenger seat. She finally opened her eyes, but didn't look at him. She stared straight ahead, expression blank.

He climbed in to fasten her seatbelt. She didn't react when he caressed her breasts or kissed her temple. She was acting like a lifeless doll. She was punishing herself for what they'd done, but he knew how to bring her back to life. When his mouth was between her legs, when he sucked on her nipples and played with her asshole, she went wild. Whatever was going on in her mind, he would overcome. He wouldn't allow her to withdraw, not when she was finally his. He would do whatever was necessary to keep her.

He retrieved his phone from his backpack before getting into the driver's seat. He wasn't surprised to see thirty text messages and over a dozen calls from his teammates. He would deal with that later. The only missed call he cared about was Mom's. He called her back as he turned the key in the ignition.

"Are you home?" Mom asked.

"No, we're on our way. Violet wanted to take a walk at the park. We're leaving now."

He glanced at Violet as he reversed. She was doing a good job of imitating a mannequin.

"Coach Rick called Dad and I," Mom said.

"I'm not surprised."

"I'm sorry, Jesse, but Isaac feels that—"

"It's okay, Mom."

She sighed. "I'll see you two at home. Can you start dinner?"

"Sure."

"Thanks, son."

"No problem."

He hung up, tossed his phone in the cupholder, and rested his hand on Violet's thigh. She didn't push him away, which pleased him. What he felt when he pummeled Tucker was nothing compared to the red haze that engulfed him this morning when she tried to end them. The only reason he hadn't pulled over to deal with Violet was because he knew his parents would be expecting a call from Coach Rick after he quit the team. Once that was out of the way, he would deal with Violet. They wouldn't go home until things were set right between them.

He stroked her thigh. What he'd done was wrong, but it was hard to feel guilty when he'd come inside her, had her taste on his tongue, and she was sitting docilely beside him, letting him touch her. Right and wrong ceased to matter where she was concerned. His need to possess her trumped all else.

The days leading up to Sunday had been a dream. Violet surpassed every fantasy. He worried he would scare her with his intensity and need, but she not only matched him, at times it seemed her desires surpassed his. She eagerly jumped into every scenario he created. He couldn't believe she was finally his. Their bodies were made for each other. They were so in tune, words weren't necessary. Everything was perfect until that fucking phone call, which tore down the walls of the alternate reality he constructed around Violet to insulate her from the outside world.

The stark terror on her face when Isaac nearly discovered them in the bathroom told him she wasn't ready to come out to their parents. Between finding out that worthless bastard was in the hospital and Pastor Sonny's sermon, he knew the progress he made had taken a major hit. Sensing her mental anguish in church, he tried to comfort her, but she rejected him.

With their parents present, he'd been forced to give her space. Discovering she had barred him from her bedroom was a nasty shock. He hadn't slept and had no choice but to draw his own conclusions about what that meant, which she confirmed this morning on the ride to school.

A part of her was still that lonely girl, afraid of being abandoned if she let people down. Yesterday, she crumbled under the weight of their parent's disappointment. He had never viewed her need for love and acceptance as a defect until he realized she would never choose him over their parents. That wouldn't do.

If Mom and Dad found out, they wouldn't excuse such blatant immorality or allow it to flourish under their roof. He suspected their parents would go so far as to separate them. He was willing to face whatever consequences came from his actions, but he had to make sure Violet would stick by him, and she wasn't there. Not even close. She would rather break up than defy their parents.

He ignored the fire that heated his blood. They would get there. One day, Violet would love him with the same fervor that he did her. Until then, he intended to keep her as close to him as possible. He wasn't going to let Pastor's Sonny's lesson about King David's mistakes or their parent's disapproval keep him from her. He loved her. His life revolved around her. He wouldn't let anyone come between them.

When they pulled up to the house, he was relieved to see Dad's truck was gone. He slipped on his backpack before going around to Violet's door. She displayed no awareness of their surroundings or him. Her face was smudged with dirt, hair a tangled mess, and if either of their parents caught a glimpse of her, no explanation would get him out of this.

"We're home, baby," he said as he undid her seatbelt, shouldered her bag and tugged her into his arms.

He carried her to the house and hoped the neighbors were otherwise occupied. He headed straight for their bathroom and kicked both doors closed before he set her in the tub. He dropped their bags and caught her before she collapsed.

"We have to clean up." He flicked a ladybug out of her hair. "Do you want me to bathe you?"

She looked right through him with eyes the color of rich moss.

He cupped her cheek. "Violet?"

No response.

"I'll take care of you," he said and began to strip her.

Once her clothes were in a pile, he got naked and climbed in with her. He expected her to balk when he started positioning her so he could clean her thoroughly, but she remained strangely compliant throughout. He was grateful, since he didn't know how much time they had.

"I'm sorry I was so rough," he said as he ran the soapy washcloth over her skin. "Are you hurt?"

She didn't answer.

He had to shampoo her hair twice. He scrubbed every inch of her, including the bottom of her feet and between every toe. He wished he could linger. The fact that she was allowing him to care for her so intimately without shame pacified the entity inside him that had compelled him to take her so savagely. The need to reinforce their physical bonds consumed him. He planned to possess her as frequently as possible to maintain their connection, especially when her mind and body were at war with one another. Eventually, they would align once she stopped fighting what was between them.

Even though he'd had her multiple times, his body reacted to her nearness. He couldn't be around her and not want her. He thought once she belonged to him that his obsession would ease, but it was worse than ever.

She stood in the back of the shower, as animated as a statue, as he quickly cleaned himself. She didn't react to the water that dripped down her face or when he came to her. He couldn't resist giving her a gentle kiss she didn't return before he wrung out her hair, wrapped it in a towel, and hastily dried her.

His senses were on high alert as he dressed her in sweats. The only sign of the rough sex they had at the park was her swollen lips, but that could be excused in a dozen ways. He carried her into the living room, settled her on the couch, and put on her favorite show.

"I'm going to start dinner. Do you need anything?"

She didn't look at him or acknowledge his question. He kissed her forehead before he went into the kitchen. From the tortillas, beans, and vegetables Mom had on the counter, he deduced dinner was supposed to be tacos. Once the vegetables were cut and the hamburger was simmering on the stove, he fetched Violet's hairbrush.

He settled her on the floor between his legs and combed her hair. He'd always loved playing with her hair. So much so, Mom taught him how to braid it. He did so now before he placed her back on the couch and switched positions, so he was on his knees facing her.

Her eyes were more hazel than that startling green. His coddling was having the desired effect. Before Mom and Dad arrived, he needed her coherent. Violet had always worn her emotions on her sleeve. A lack of them would be more noticeable than anything else she could do.

"Violet."

No reaction.

He stroked the apple of her cheek. "What's between us isn't sinful."

Her eyes focused on him.

"People search all their lives for the connection we have between us. It's rare and special. It's worth fighting for."

Her gaze flicked away. The entity inside of him snarled at the rejection, but he had to be patient. He couldn't force her to catch up to his level of adoration and worship.

"Do you remember what you said after Mom and Dad left for their honeymoon?"

She didn't move, but he sensed her withdraw even further. He ran his hands up and down her arms to stop her from tuning out and escaping in her mind.

"You said good things don't happen to you. You were terrified something would happen that would ruin everything."

When he clasped her face to force her to look at him, she closed her eyes in defense. She was trembling, which he took as a good sign. The ice was cracking. He nuzzled her, encouraging the breakdown.

"Those fears never went away. They're still here now, controlling you, trying to control me. This is a blessing, a fucking gift, and you're treating it like a curse." His lips captured the first tear that fell. "I'm not going to let you do it. I'm not going to let you destroy us. If you want to lie to Mom and Dad, to your friends, to God, I don't care, but you can't lie to me. I know you better than you know yourself." He kissed the shell of her ear and sighed in relief when she shivered. "Tell me you didn't like what I did to you. That you didn't feel painfully alive. You begged me for more."

She let out a choked sound.

"You want me, too," he whispered harshly. "I had to force you to suck me, but in the end, you wanted me to come down your throat."

When she punched his shoulder, he sat back and saw she was glaring at him through dripping eyes.

He softened and cupped her face. "Do you really think God is cruel enough to make us want each other if we weren't meant to be?"

"It's a test to resist temptation." Her voice was raspy from screaming.

"Or a test of our devotion to one another," he countered.

She shook her head.

"Don't compare what's happening between us to King David's affair with Bathsheba or those half siblings," he growled.

She pushed at his chest. "You're my brother."

"Not genetically."

"Legally, we have the same parents."

"Do the labels matter so much? What if I wasn't your stepbrother?"

"But you are! And anyway, it's still not okay! We're not supposed to have sex!"

"But getting married would make it right?"

Violet went ghost white.

"You..." she began in a strangled tone but was interrupted by the sound of the garage door opening.

Violet shoved him hard enough to make him rock back on his heels. She frantically wiped away her tears and then touched her hair and frowned as if she'd slept through him braiding it for her. He got to his feet but stole a kiss to put some color back in her face. He was on his way to the kitchen when Mom came through the door.

"Hey, kids."

"Hey, Mom."

When Jesse kissed her cheek, he caught the relief that passed through her eyes.

Mom clasped his face. "Are you okay?"

"Never better."

Mom blinked. "Really?"

"Going to the park put things into perspective and helped me clear my head."

He heard Violet's stifled gasp from the living room, but Mom didn't catch it. Mom followed him to the kitchen and perked up when she saw that everything was done.

"You're in pajamas already?" Mom asked, plucking at his sweatpants.

"We were sweaty and filthy, so we came home and washed up. Dinner should be ready in a few minutes. You can shower if you want. I got this."

Mom patted his chest. "Thanks, son. I think I will. Dad should be home soon."

That evening turned out to be busier than any of them anticipated. Coach Rick didn't give up. He called the landline to speak to his parents again, and several teammates stopped by to confirm what they'd heard and pleaded with Mom and Dad to change their minds. Jesse could see Isaac teetering on his punishment, but he didn't ask to be let off the hook.

When Isaac said he had to quit football, he'd been taken aback and initially pissed before he realized the time he would have spent at practice or at games could now be dedicated to Violet. If it came down to football or Violet, he would choose her in a heartbeat. Ultimately, he saw this as another reward for beating Tucker's ass.

It took two hours for his friends and teammates to accept defeat. He stood on the driveway as they let out dejected honks and drove away. Violet was beside him. She'd been drawn out of the house by the girls who'd come with their boyfriends or brothers. She was pale and subdued but functioning well enough that the only question her friends asked had been whether she was coming down with a cold.

Thanks to his behavior that morning and the parade of visitors, Mom and Dad were mainly focused on him at dinner. He thought no one noticed Violet's listlessness and the fact that she took just a few bites of the taco he made her until Mom rested her hand on Violet's arm.

"Honey, are you all right?"

As Violet visibly struggled to come up with a response, he asked, "I went too hard on you on the trail today, didn't I?"

Violet gave a little jerk and gaped at him.

"You're sore, aren't you?"

He was pleased by the flicker of rebellion in her eyes and charmed by the blush that hit her cheeks as she shook her head.

He sighed loudly. "Stubborn."

Violet yelped when he picked her up and snapped, "I'm *fine*! Put me down!"

"Don't be proud," he chided. "I'll go easier on you next time."

"You two," Mom chuckled as he carried Violet to her bedroom.

He closed the door behind him and made his way to her bed. He flicked back the covers before he set her down.

"Do you need Ibuprofen?"

"I said, I'm fine," she said sullenly and stared at the ceiling.

He glanced at the closed door before he decided to climb in beside her. Violet's eyes nearly bugged out of her head.

"Are you crazy?" she hissed.

As he stretched out, she rolled to the other side and would have escaped if he hadn't dragged her back where she belonged.

"Let me go!"

"Hush," he said as he gathered her against him and pressed her face against his throat.

"What are you doing?" she demanded, voice muffled.

"Giving both of us what we need."

"I don't want this," she said, wriggling, until he tightened his arms around her.

She let out an angry huff and muttered under her breath. The feel of her lips brushing against his skin made his blood sing. He ignored his body's reaction and focused on giving her the comfort that he hadn't been able to earlier in the day. He stroked her back, shoulders, and sides as he tried to soothe the physical trauma he wrought. For long minutes, she was completely rigid. Nearly fifteen minutes passed before she quivered and unwillingly collapsed against him.

"I didn't mean to hurt you," he murmured.

"But you did."

Her voice, thick with tears and tainted with fear, made him place kisses along her hairline.

"I'm sorry, baby."

"I've never seen that side of you before."

"Me either."

"You've changed."

"So have you."

She didn't deny it. More time passed before the last of her tension dissolved, leaving her boneless in his arms, just as he intended. He heard the distant clink of silverware and plates as Mom and Dad cleared the table, accurately deducing he wasn't coming back. He cuddled Violet against him, imagining a future where he could hold her like this without fear of being reprimanded for doing what felt like the most natural thing in the world to him. He thought she'd fallen asleep until her hand twisted in his shirt.

"I know this is special," she whispered.

His heart leapt at her acknowledgement.

She eased back so she could see his face. Her wide, beseeching gaze made his stomach twist.

"I don't want to ruin what we have with sex," she said in a rush.

He bit back a groan. "It won't," he began.

"*Please*, Jesse. Can we try to keep sex out of it and just see if...?"

Despite all he'd said, she was still in denial and trying to reverse the clock to a time they could never return to. She wanted to keep him at arm's length and was instinctively trying to loosen the bonds that sex fortified and strengthened every time he took her. He wouldn't allow it. He had every intention of exploiting their connection until they were so interlocked that she was a part of him.

As he tried to think of the easiest way to let her down, she cupped his cheek with a trembling hand.

Eyes sparkling with earnest tears, she said, "I don't want to lose you."

Nothing he said would reassure her that they were on the right path. She believed God would punish her for continuing their relationship by breaking them and the family apart. He had no intention of allowing either of those things to happen, but only time would prove him right.

"You'll never lose me," he promised.

"You'll try?" she pushed.

When he hesitated, her eyes welled with tears.

Pity made him say, "Yes."

Even as her face lit with relief, he knew he wouldn't keep his promise.

CHAPTER 15
VIOLET

2 MONTHS LATER

VIOLET LAY ON THE COUCH IN THE LIVING ROOM WITH MOM AND DAD, WHO sat in their individual recliners. Mom graded papers while Dad watched TV and switched from the news to sports and then an old, black and white sitcom.

"Isaac!" Mom said, exasperated. "Stop changing the channel. What about Violet?"

"It's okay. I'm used to it," Violet murmured.

And she wasn't watching anyway. When she was a child and had bad dreams or wasn't feeling good, she would sneak into Dad's bedroom and sleep on the floor. Just being near him banished the boogie man and made her feel better. At seventeen, she was hoping their presence would have the same magical effect, but the feeling of safety and comfort she was seeking eluded her.

She tensed when she heard a key turn in the front door.

"Hey," Jesse said as he entered with his backpack, gym bag, and a sweater slung over one shoulder.

"There he is!" Mom said fondly. "How was basketball practice, son?"

"Long." Jesse placed a kiss on top of Mom's head. "I'm starved."

"You should get cleaned up first. If you hurry, the food on the stove will still be hot."

Mom laughed as Jesse ran down the hallway to his room to shower.

"That saying about the way to a man's heart is through his stomach is true, isn't it, Isaac?"

"Yup," Dad said distractedly.

"What meal did I make that made you fall in love with me?" Mom asked.

"Hot honey chicken cutlets."

Mom grinned when she saw Violet watching her. "You're set, honey. You already know that recipe by heart."

"She isn't dating this year," Dad said as he changed the channel.

"I know, but that doesn't mean she can't keep an eye out for the one," Mom said with a wink.

Violet gave Lynne a weak smile before she returned her attention to the TV. She wasn't looking for the one and if she stumbled upon him, and he turned out to be as perfect as she'd always imagined, she'd tell him to find someone else. Someone who could give him what he was looking for. She had nothing to offer. The good qualities she'd once possessed had been wrecked beyond repair.

Her hand fisted under the pillow. Jesse hadn't kept his promise to keep sex out of their relationship. He hadn't even tried. Dad made her easy prey by not allowing her to attend after school programs, go out on weekends, and made Jesse her only option to commute to and from school. She was basically a prisoner, and Jesse took full advantage.

He was relentless in his demands, yet nauseatingly gentle as he pillaged and plundered. He took every opportunity to wring unwanted orgasms from her and comforted her when self-loathing got the best of her, and she burst into tears. Sometimes, when he felt a lick of remorse, he made promises that he couldn't keep for more than a few days. It was a hellish cycle of hope and then crushing disappointment.

His sheer brazenness astounded her. He ambushed her in the most unlikely places. School wasn't a safe zone. At any moment, she could be propelled into an empty computer lab or hustled under the bleachers so he could have his way with her. The only time she was truly out of his reach was in class, where she'd dozed off a few times. The stress was taking a toll on her. Her grades were starting a downward trajectory that she needed to get hold of before her parents saw her report card.

Jesse had easily worked his way back into their parents' good graces by utilizing the skills he picked up from the general contractor to fix things around the house. Little did Mom and Dad know, he was repairing the holes he'd made in his bedroom and covered everything up with a fresh coat of paint. Violet couldn't deny she'd been relieved when he got rid of the last reminder from the day he took her virginity.

She was so on hypervigilant, she sensed Jesse enter the room seconds before he spoke.

"Hey, Mom, how's Raiden doing?" Jesse called.

Violet tracked Jesse's voice into the kitchen, listened to the sound of him opening the cabinet to get a bowl, and heard the clink of the lid being set on the counter as he dug into the pot on the stove.

"He's doing a little better, but you can see how exhausted and confused he is," Mom said sadly.

Mom gave them frequent updates on Raiden, a student whose parents were in the midst of a nasty divorce, with the little boy caught in the middle. Raiden was so miserable, he begged to stay at school instead of going home.

"That's too bad," Jesse said. "I hoped after you talked to the mother, things would improve."

"No, she's too self-involved to see what she's doing to her son. Poor Raiden. He hugs me at least ten times a day. It breaks my heart."

"Maybe I can stop by and play basketball with him after school next week," Jesse offered.

Mom's face lit up. "That would mean the world to him."

Ambivalent emotions warred in Violet's chest. How could Jesse be the monster who had shoved her into the garage when she'd been stupid enough to get a drink of water after their parents had gone to bed to have his way with her, *and* the nice guy willing to take time out of his busy schedule to play basketball with a child going through a hard time?

Jesse appeared with a bowl cradled in his large hand. She stared at the TV, not acknowledging him or attempting to make space on the three-seater couch she sprawled on. She'd hoped he would eat at the table, go to his bedroom, or sit on the floor where he belonged. Instead, he stood there, waiting.

As the awkward moment stretched, Mom started to rise from her recliner.

"You can sit here, son."

"No need," Jesse said easily, and lifted Violet's legs before he sat and placed her feet on his lap.

Dad frowned at Violet, but she pretended not to notice. She hated that Jesse had so easily outmaneuvered her. His poise under pressure astounded her. Jesse had put them in some risky, compromising situations, but his unruffled composure and well-mannered, caring facade immediately disarmed authority figures who would have otherwise known he was up to no good. Could she blame them for buying into his golden boy act? Even she, who had seen him at his worst, still wanted to believe that the sweet, supportive older brother she'd known and trusted was still in there somewhere, despite dozens of incidents that proved otherwise.

She crawled to the other end of the couch and braced her pillow against the couch arm before she resettled, tucking her legs up so she was no longer touching him. She didn't want to be near him, but she also didn't want to be alone with her gloomy thoughts. Since their parents were present, Jesse would be on his best behavior.

"Allison brought you home?" Jesse asked her, ignoring the fact that she had blatantly ignored him since he walked through the front door.

She inwardly bristled. It was none of his business who gave her a ride home, but knowing their parents were listening, she had no choice but to answer. "Yes."

Jesse hadn't been happy when Mom and Dad lifted the ban on after school activities and going out on weekends last week. She leapt on her reinstated freedom, hitching rides and hanging out with friends whenever possible. Jesse was further foiled by the start of the basketball season. He'd been strangely disinterested and reluctant to join, but Mom and Dad insisted, probably out of guilt for the horrible football season his team had.

When Jesse finished his food, he set his empty bowl aside and shuffled along the cushions. She tensed as he slipped beneath her oversized blanket. Debating whether she could tolerate him or bail and go to her room, it was a horrible shock when he grasped her foot and pulled it onto his lap. She raised her head to snap at him, but he and Dad were deep in discussion about the stats the sports announcer rattled off.

She tugged, but his iron grip wouldn't let her go. She couldn't believe his gall. He knew she didn't want him to touch her and did it anyway. He was constantly pushing her and took as many liberties as possible with others present because he knew she wouldn't cause a scene. He was such an asshole! She should jam her heel in his balls or crush his fingers with her toes, but it wasn't worth ruining the relaxed atmosphere.

She bared her teeth as his calloused thumbs ran along the bottom of her foot. She bit her lip to stop herself from moaning when he hit a tender spot. She hated how observant he was. When she stiffened, he lightened the pressure and when she wriggled her toes, sensing she liked what he was doing, he lingered. It was ironic that their silent communication was better than their non-existent verbal communication. She had nothing to say to him. He didn't care how she felt or what she wanted. She learned what he said meant nothing. How could he be so in tune with her in one area and completely deaf and dumb to her wants and needs in others?

"This is nice," Mom said, surveying them with a smile.

It was rare for all of them to be together on a Friday evening. The only reason she hadn't gone to the mall with Marie and Allison was because she thought Jesse was going out with Brody and Blaine after practice.

"We should start this weekend off right," Mom said excitedly. "Anyone up for a movie?"

Knowing Jesse had to be up bright and early to work with the general contractor, Violet assumed he would decline. She was annoyed when he said, "Sure. What should we watch?"

She didn't offer a suggestion, since she wouldn't be paying attention. They debated for a couple of minutes before settling on some action movie. As Mom turned off the lights and closed the blinds tight, so the only light came from the screen, Violet tried to remember the last movie night they had. She used to love huddling under the covers, eating popcorn mixed with assorted candies. The memories were tattered and slightly out of focus, like they belonged to someone else.

It was the same four people sitting in the same room in front of the TV, but the contentment and sense of security she used to feel when surrounded by family had been replaced with a feeling of stark alienation even though Mom and Dad were mere feet away. It was like sitting in front of a fire, but not feeling the warmth of the blaze...

A soft snore made Violet shift her head. She wasn't surprised to see Lynne had fallen asleep before the movie finished its opening credits.

"She always does that," Violet said with a shake of her head.

"She works hard. The moment she lets herself relax, she's dead to the world," Dad said. "Let her sleep."

Despite herself, Violet found herself drawn into the movie, which was non-stop action from the opening chase scene. She was so engrossed in the story that it took a while for her to realize that the massage had stopped, and she was lying there, relaxed and comfortable, with her feet propped on her tormentor's lap.

The moment she tried to pull away, Jesse gripped her shin. He squeezed, telling her to stay as she was. How dare he? She tipped onto her back to kick him with her free foot and went rigid when his hand brushed over her bare thigh.

The TV screen went black as the main character dropped into a tunnel, plunging the living room into darkness at the same time that Jesse's hand slid into the leg of her pajama shorts and cupped her between her legs. She jerked as if she'd been electrocuted. Her confidence that he wouldn't make a move in front of their parents shattered into a million pieces. The sound of the character cursing and pounding the wall in frustration concealed Violet's uncoordinated, frantic bid to get away. She did an awkward backstroke like a swimmer as panic seared her insides.

An explosion on screen briefly illuminated the room. Her head snapped between both parents. Their recliners flanked the couch but were slightly in front of them and angled toward the TV. Mom's head was sharply tilted, indicating she was still asleep, while Dad perched on the edge of his seat, riveted by what was happening on screen. If Dad looked at them, the plush, oversized blanket draped over her body and Jesse's lap would conceal what he was doing, but... How could Jesse be touching her while they were in the room? Was he insane?

Jesse brought her attention back to him when his thumb slid inside her satin underwear. In the poor light, she saw Jesse's head turned toward her. He wasn't even trying to pretend he was interested in the movie. She strained to get away, but when he began to fondle her clit, she started fighting in earnest. When she savagely yanked on her captive leg, he flicked her underwear aside and sheathed his middle finger inside of her.

Her gasp was lost in a hail of deafening gunfire on screen. Out of the corner of her eye, she saw Lynne sit up. Dad snagged the remote to turn down the volume.

"Too loud?" Dad asked.

"A bit, but that's why we have those speakers, right? To get the full effect?" Lynne yawned as she rose and stretched.

Violet clawed the back of Jesse's hand jammed between her legs. He made no move to withdraw, even as Lynne started toward them. Lightheaded with horror, Violet closed her eyes as Lynne kissed Jesse's cheek. As her body tightened in reaction to Mom's nearness, the tip of Jesse's finger curled, making her break out in goosebumps.

"Vi's asleep?" Mom murmured.

"Mm hmm," Jesse said distractedly, as if he was engrossed in the movie. "She fell asleep not long after you."

It took everything she had not to react as Mom leaned over her, so close to where her son's fingers were buried inside her. Biting panic engulfed her as Mom tenderly brushed back her hair.

"Sweet dreams, my sweet girl," Mom murmured before she moved away.

"My bed is calling me," Mom said around a jaw cracking yawn as she kissed Dad's cheek.

As Mom shuffled down the hallway, Jesse called, "Sleep tight," even as he withdrew his finger and smeared what it was coated with on her clit and rubbed.

A silent battle commenced with Jesse trying to conquer her body while she desperately tried to retreat. When his grip slipped on the leg keeping her captive, she lunged for the lamp on the side table and snapped it on. As light flooded the room, Dad turned his head and squinted at her.

"Is it okay if I leave the light on?" she panted as she dragged herself to the opposite end of the couch, safely out of Jesse's reach.

Even though he clearly wished otherwise, Dad nodded and turned back to the movie. She buried her face on the arm rest for a moment, grappling for control over her body, before her eyes cut to

Jesse. Her stomach flipped when he put his middle finger in his mouth. Damn him!

She shot to her feet and froze when Jesse began to rise as well. She had no doubt that he would follow her. He wouldn't have touched her with Mom and Dad present unless he was already past the point of no return. Knowing the movie would conceal the sounds of whatever he planned to do to her, she retook her seat. A muscle ticked in his jaw.

She adjusted her pants before she sat as far from him as possible and huddled in the circle of light to keep the wolf at bay. She ran shaking fingers through her hair and tried to ignore the telling movements under the blanket bunched on Jesse's lap. Was he actually going to...?

When Jesse shot to his feet, Dad's head whipped around.

"I have to be up early for work," Jesse stated.

Dad nodded. "I'm surprised you stayed up this long," he said with a glance at his watch.

Jesse grunted as Dad turned back to the screen. He stood there, staring at her for so long, that Dad turned around again.

"You need something, son?"

"No," Jesse said and stalked down the hallway to his bedroom.

She tucked her legs to the side and dragged the blanket around her once more, trembling. She couldn't believe he just did that. He pushed the boundaries, but he'd never gone *this* far. Did he have no shame or scruples? She clamped her thighs together and ignored the low throb between her legs. She hated the way he'd conditioned her body to respond to him, to yearn for him. A glance at Dad quelled the desire Jesse tried to ignite.

Would Dad believe her if she told him that the son he was so proud of was doing the unthinkable to her? Her chest tightened. Although Dad hadn't brought it up since it happened, she knew he still blamed her for Jesse putting Tucker in the hospital. Dad had absolved Jesse, but not her. There was something in his eyes when he looked at her that told her he suspected she was no longer innocent.

If she got up the courage to tell him what Jesse was doing, and he didn't believe her or worse, accused her of being the problem, it would kill her. She turned off the light as her face crumpled.

"You turning in too, Vi?" Dad asked without turning to look at her.

"No. I'm staying."

Her shaky tone went unnoticed as the main character made an impossible, stylish leap from a helicopter.

How many times had she considered confiding in a friend, school counselor, youth pastor, or therapist who was sworn to secrecy? But who would believe her? Even she couldn't believe what was happening. The only person who would probably take her word for it was the one person who avoided her like the plague. Tucker had been on the receiving end of a temper that no one even knew Jesse possessed. Tucker had returned to school and explained his absence by spinning some tale about being approached by a record label. His return had briefly stirred up everyone's interest in her again, but this time, she didn't care. She had bigger problems to deal with—namely, her stepbrother, who everyone idolized and admired and thought wouldn't hurt a fly.

By the time the movie ended, she was once more stretched out on the couch with her head on the arm rest. Dad glanced at her and, when he saw she was still awake, flicked through a few channels before he settled on reruns of, *I Love Lucy*. When she was a kid, Dad only allowed her to watch old movies and shows so he wouldn't have to worry about anything explicit being shown.

They chuckled together as they watched Lucy's antics. When the episode ended, Dad got to his feet.

"You're going to stay up?" he asked.

"Yeah."

He came over and set the remote by the lamp so she could easily reach it.

"Night, kiddo."

"Night, Dad," she echoed.

She listened to him shuffle down the hallway as another episode began. She was tired but couldn't bring herself to go to her room. She turned off the lamp because the bright light was making her eyes water. She cocked her head when she heard footsteps making their way to the living room. Assuming Dad wanted a drink of water or had forgotten something, she looked up when a dark figure rounded the couch. When she realized it wasn't Dad, she opened her mouth to scream. Jesse lunged at her, clapping a hand over her lips before she could utter a sound.

He leaned down and rested his forehead against hers as he murmured, "I can't go another night without you."

Even as she prepared to bite his palm, he dragged her to the middle of the couch and flipped her onto her stomach. The blanket was tossed to the floor before her bottoms were yanked to her knees. Even as she turned her head to the side to catch her breath, Jesse was already sinking inside her. She clawed the cushions and kicked her feet as her body struggled to adjust.

"Shh," he soothed as he came down on top of her.

With her legs clamped together, he felt impossibly large, and though she was wet, it wasn't enough. The couch absorbed her groan as he withdrew and then pushed for more territory.

"Good girl. Almost there," he praised and ignored her furious hiss. "God, you feel so good, Vi. So perfect."

"What the hell are you *doing*? They could walk in any minute."

"I jacked off twice and still tossed and turned. My hand won't do. I need you. I need this. I'm going crazy. I can't escape even in sleep because I dream of you."

His hands skated down her arms until he reached her hands. Before she could pull away, he twined their fingers together.

"Do you know what it's like, never having a moment's peace? To want something so badly, you'll do anything to possess it?"

He shuddered and buried his face in her hair as he sheathed himself completely.

"Thank you," he said fervently.

"You're sick."

His tongue dipped into her ear before he breathed, "So are you. The difference between us is, I accept it."

She screwed her eyes shut as he began to thrust, stabbing deep, making her toes curl.

"This doesn't have to be sick. This doesn't have to be twisted. It can be beautiful if you'd let it. If you stopped fighting and let us be." His fingers tightened around hers. "I can feel you milking me and getting wetter. You love this."

She buried her face in the cushions as she tried to deny what he was saying, but her body wasn't under her command. It was under his, and it responded to him, bathing him in honey, welcoming him, while her mind did everything in its power to block out what was happening.

"You've been dodging me all week, denying me, denying yourself. Why do you do that? You want me to prove how much I want you? How I'm lost without you?"

Her stomach flipped as he released her hands and dropped off the side of the couch and pulled her bottom half with him. He positioned her so she was on her knees on the carpet with him behind her. Unfortunately, her face landed in the damp spot she'd just made on the cushions.

With a grimace, she straightened. Jesse immediately took advantage of the position to slide his hands beneath her top. He stroked her stomach and gripped her breasts as he gave her body time to adjust to him, to prepare for what was coming. One hand plucked her clit. To her disgust, she rested her head on his shoulder and spread her legs, giving him more access. He obliged while he sucked on her neck.

"Tell me you want this," he said darkly.

That cut through the sexual haze. Awareness crept back in. She yanked on his arm to get his hand off her breast, but all it got her was a nipple pinch that suffused her with more unwanted heat.

"Admit it. Just this once," he begged.

When she remained silent, his teeth sank into her shoulder.

"So stubborn," he growled and shoved her face into cushions that smelled of her weakness before his control disintegrated.

He blanketed her body with his as he began to move with hard, sure strokes. The only sound she could hear aside from Jesse's uneven breaths was Lucy wailing on the television. Between the hard, rhythmic smacking of their flesh and the TV, it was impossible to hear anyone approach. She prayed Mom and Dad were sound asleep as Jesse straightened and hauled her back with every thrust, so she took every inch, growling like an animal, desperately trying to meld them together.

Sensing he was close, she compounded her sins by touching herself to reach her own orgasm.

"Yeah, baby. Come with me," he said harshly as he picked up his pace.

When he climaxed, he folded over her, gasping her name. She ignored him as she chased her own orgasm, which was just out of reach. Jesse brushed her hand aside, strumming her clit, and encouraged her to impale herself on him until she shattered. He held her as she trembled, first with elation and, less than a minute later, with the familiar slap of shame and guilt. No matter what she did to foil him, they always ended here.

Jesse withdrew slowly. She pressed her thighs together and wasn't surprised when his hand slipped through his semen, pushing it back in before spreading it over her ass and lower back.

When he got to his feet, her mind urged her to get up, dress, and clean herself, but she couldn't move. She sensed Jesse leave the room and heard his bedroom door close seconds later. Even as the studio audience laughed, Violet wept.

CHAPTER 16
VIOLET

FOUR MONTHS LATER

THUMBS HOOKED UNDER HER BACKPACK STRAPS; VIOLET STOOD AT THE END of the driveway. Luck was on her side. Mom left early this morning to decorate her classroom for spring, allowing Violet to change up her commute without Mom asking questions.

As her neighbor passed with his dog, he nodded to Violet while also giving her a slightly puzzled look that made her blush. Embarrassed, but determined to follow through with her plan, she stared at the end of the street, willing her ride to appear and save her from going with...

"What are you doing?"

She stiffened, but didn't turn around to address the bane of her existence.

"I'm waiting," she said, stating the obvious.

"I see that. Waiting for what?"

"I'm catching the bus to school."

She was grateful they were in plain view of their neighbors who were heading to work or taking out the trash. It meant that she had countless witnesses if Jesse did something foul. He wouldn't, of course. He saved his reprehensible behavior for when they were behind closed doors. In public, his manners were impeccable.

"You're not catching the bus."

She tightened her grip on her straps. "Mom already left for work. She won't know we didn't ride together."

"But Dad will. He asked me what you're doing out here."

She whirled and spotted her father standing in the window with his coffee mug in hand. Damn. She hadn't thought to look in the garage to see if his truck was there. She assumed he was at work.

"You want to tell him what's going on or are you going to get in the car?"

Jesse's taunt made her vision bleed to red. He asked that question like he had nothing to hide, as if his future didn't depend on her keeping their secret. He should be kissing her ass, not provoking her. The fact that he was so certain she wouldn't tell anyone made her so angry, she couldn't speak. She wanted to. She *should*! But, as miserable as she was, she couldn't bring herself to get help.

On days like today, when Jesse pushed her to her breaking point, her mind played out every possible outcome. None of them ended well. If she released her pain, it would spread like a disease, infecting her family, rocking their church, and sending shockwaves through their tight-knit community. Nothing would ever be the same. Better to compartmentalize. To suppress her inner turmoil and believe that Jesse would come to his senses and stop. Also, confiding in someone meant explaining what was happening to her and... she just couldn't. That would make it all too real.

"Come on, Vi."

Jesse had the audacity to look exasperated with her, as if she had no grounds to be upset about what he did to her fifteen minutes ago.

"Violet?"

She broke eye contact with Jesse to see Dad standing on the front steps.

"Is something wrong?"

Bottled up emotions tore up her insides, making her eyes water.

Dad's expression darkened. "What is it?"

Her mouth worked before she finally got out, "Jesse pissed me off. I want to catch the bus instead of riding with him."

Dad blinked, clearly surprised. She and Jesse rarely quarreled. There had been no need to in the past.

"Jesse?" Dad prompted with a frown.

"I'll make it up to her."

Her skin prickled as Jesse gave that ominous promise.

"Avoiding your problems isn't going to solve anything," Dad admonished, shaking his head. "I taught you better than that. Settle it on the way to school. I'm sure Jesse didn't mean to upset you."

The pressure in her chest increased. A scream vibrated at the base of her throat.

Dad tossed Jesse a set of keys. "Take the truck. I need the SUV today." Dad gave her a level look. "Be good."

The subtle rebuke made it clear that he thought she was overreacting and being childish. Dad walked into the house. Several seconds later, the garage rolled up to reveal the truck that was almost as old as she was. It took a minute for her to have enough control to stalk to the truck instead of having a meltdown. Jessie didn't fetch his bag until she was settled in the passenger seat.

She buckled up and twisted her hand in the dark blue seat belt as the yellow school bus she'd been waiting for cruised past. All she wanted was a moment's respite from him, but it seemed like the world was conspiring against her.

Jesse didn't say a word as he started the truck and reversed out of the garage. Silence reined between them as they left their neighborhood. Her stomach was tight as a fist.

"Did I hurt you?"

He meant physically, but he didn't have to leave a bruise on her skin to hurt her. Marks made in passion would fade. It was the hundreds of invisible, razor-thin emotional cuts he inflicted that she knew would scar and haunt her for the rest of her life.

"Does it matter?"

He ran a hand through his hair. "I didn't mean to hurt you. That wasn't my intention."

"What *was* your intention?"

A muscle ticked in his jaw. "You know."

To scratch his itch before he started his day? She didn't fight back when he cornered her in the bathroom, ushered her into the tub, and pinned her against the tiles to ravage her. She didn't resist when he pushed her to her knees and fucked her mouth. It was only after he'd left her kneeling in the tub with her face dripping, and she heard Mom singing in the kitchen, that she snapped out of her daze and retched.

She wasn't sure why this morning was different from the others. He'd done far more demeaning things, but today it struck her how truly warped their relationship had become. The fact that they hadn't exchanged a word during that whole encounter, and he left the moment he achieved his goal, made her realize he'd truly turned into Amnon. He didn't loathe her, but he was addicted to using her to slake his lust and didn't care how that impacted her. Their relationship has turned into a sour, tangled, depraved mess.

Jesse had changed. He no longer cajoled. He no longer petted and stroked to prepare her for him. The affection she'd come to expect from him had vanished. She was just a body to him. No one seemed to notice that his smile wasn't the same, that he rarely laughed, and there was a hardness to him that hadn't been there before. When they were alone, and he wasn't wearing a mask, she was chilled by what she saw in his eyes. Her brother was gone and in his place was a stranger, one capable of anything.

When Jesse took the wrong exit, she gave him a sharp glance. "Where are we going?"

"For a drive."

Her blood turned to ice. "No!"

"We need to talk."

Talk? That was something they no longer did. Their commutes to and from school were done in complete silence. The only time they casually conversed was while hanging out with mutual friends or around their parents. If they were alone, Jesse was too focused on getting her on her back to ask about her day or hopes and dreams.

"We have nothing to talk about."

His hand flexed on the wheel. "We do."

She flung her hand in front of her. "So, talk! Why are we leaving Austin?"

"I don't want us to be interrupted, and I need to clear my head."

"We're going to be late for school."

"We'll make it back in time. We aren't going far."

She twisted her hand in the folds of her light sweater as they traded the congested, six lane freeways for a two-lane highway. At this hour, everyone was headed into the city for work and school, while she and Jesse sped in the opposite direction.

Despite Jesse's reassurance that they weren't going far, they were going further than she was comfortable with. She considered calling Mom and Dad to tell them Jesse had lost his mind, when he finally slowed and turned off the main highway onto an unmarked dirt road.

"Where are we?"

"We're almost there," he yelled as they rattled down the pitted road.

"Almost *where*?" she demanded, clutching the door handle.

"Here," he said as they rounded a bend.

Trees gave way to rolling flatlands covered in a blanket of bluebonnets that stretched as far as the eye could see. Taking photos amidst the wildflowers was a rite of passage for locals who flocked to every park, field, and even along the highway in hopes of getting the perfect shot.

As Jesse pulled off the road, she rolled down her window to admire the cerulean beauties. Until that moment, she hadn't realized what a gorgeous day it was. The morning chill was giving way to what promised to be a warm spring day. Birds chirped to one another. There was no sound of cars or people, just a lone farmhouse in the distance. The scene was so idyllic, it looked like a painting.

"Logan's aunt lives at the end of this lane," Jesse said. "I thought you'd enjoy seeing this."

"It's stunning," she murmured as she closed her eyes and tipped her face to the sun.

Her worries about getting to school on time and why they were here dissolved. Minutes passed in blessed silence. When she opened her eyes, she blinked back tears. She wasn't sure why. She braced her chin on her arms and stared at a sea of blue so dense, she imagined she could swim in it.

"Violet."

Her bubble of tranquility popped. Tension crept back in. Anxiety stole the sun's warmth from her face.

"What?" she said woodenly.

"I'm sorry if I went too far this morning."

The clean taste of toothpaste was canceled out by the aftertaste of betrayal, which tasted like bitter grapefruit. "But that isn't going to stop you from doing it again, is it?"

A pause and then, "No."

She swung around to face him as her chest quaked. "You have to stop! You can't do this anymore! Don't you see what it's doing to us?"

His expression was pained as he held his hands out to her in supplication. "I've tried, Vi. I—"

"Try harder!" she bellowed.

His Adam's apple bobbed as he swallowed. "I swear I am. But the more I resist, the more I try to push it down..." His hand balled into a fist. "The worse it is when I lose control."

"This isn't normal, Jesse. It's *wrong*!"

His expression hardened. "It could be right if you'd..." He looked away from her, down the empty road.

"If I what? Gave into you? Did whatever you wanted? Isn't that what I've been doing? What more do you want?"

"I want you to want me back!"

His bellow made her heart stop.

"You think it's enough to have your body?" he asked harshly. "To have you give into me?" He shook his head. "I thought that would be enough, too, but it isn't. I hate the way you look at me. The way you stiffen up when I touch you when I know a part of you wants it." His hand slashed through the air. "Needs it just as much as I do. I want you to let yourself want me back, Vi, and stop punishing us."

"I don't want you." Her voice wasn't as adamant as she intended.

His eyes narrowed. "Don't lie. It isn't always force. Most of the time, you're wet before I even touch you. Three days ago, you were rocking back so hard on my dick, I had to brace myself. What—"

"That's my *body*, not *me*!" she shrieked.

"Your body," he repeated in a flat tone.

"Yes!"

He stared at her for a full minute before he said, "You're not going to give in, are you?"

"Did I fight you this morning?" she asked waspishly.

He dismissed that with a wave of his hand, as if it was of no consequence. Rage licked the walls of her mind.

"I mean, you're not going to admit what's between us," he clarified.

"What's between us is *gone*! *You* destroyed it!"

His hand, still on the steering wheel, went white as he gripped it, making the veins on the back of his hand stand out.

"I didn't destroy it," he said roughly. "I embraced it, surrendered to it. Your fear of change, of Mom and Dad and *God* made this into something bad, but it isn't. This is a goddamn gift."

His eyes gleamed with zeal, sending a trickle of alarm through her.

"Dad said what isn't meant to be, God won't allow. God isn't stopping us from being together. He would have intervened in some fashion by now, don't you think? No matter what you do, God keeps pushing you toward me. He wouldn't even let you catch the bus! He brought us here so we could talk. Why can't you see that you're the only thing stopping us from being everything we're meant to be? Of being happy?"

"Don't you dare use God to justify your behavior. The only reason you've gotten away with it is because you're so good at fooling people, and I'm too weak to…" Her throat constricted as despair and rage warred within her. "You…" Eyes burning, she bowed her head as she desperately tried to regain control.

"It's not because you're weak. You haven't told anyone because you love me."

Her head jerked up. *"Love?"* She could barely get the word out. How dare he say that to her?

"You love me," he stated with such unshakeable confidence that she wanted to scratch his eyes out. "Deep down, you know we're supposed to be together. You wouldn't respond to anyone else the way you do to me."

"That's not true." The moment the words left her mouth, she regretted it.

"What's not true?"

His voice was calm, but she knew he was anything but.

She licked dry lips and couldn't resist casting a nervous glance around, but there wasn't a soul in sight. "I think we should go."

"What's not true?" he repeated.

When she didn't speak, he leaned toward her.

"It's not true that you only respond to me?"

She plucked at her jeans. He reached across the bench seat and gripped her chin, eyes glittering with the threat of violence.

"If I find out you allowed anyone to touch you, I'd kill them."

"No one has!" She swatted at his hand, which only held her tighter. "I'm not allowed to date, and I don't want anyone, including you! In fact, I think *you* should start dating again."

"Date."

His voice was flat and emotionless.

"Yes, date. Have sex with other girls." She lifted her chin in challenge. "If I loved you, if I believed we were supposed to be together, would I push you toward someone—*anyone* else?"

The hand on her chin fell away. She was about to reach for her backpack to retrieve her phone when she saw his eyes glistening with tears. Her stomach flipped. She couldn't remember the last time she'd seen him cry. She was horrified by the overwhelming need to apologize and comfort him. What the hell was wrong with her? He'd hurt her immeasurably and broken promise after promise. Why the hell should she care that something she said had finally gotten through to him? She shouldn't care.

But she did.

"You hate me," he said quietly.

She swallowed hard.

"If you hate me, say it."

She opened her mouth, but nothing came out. Her voice deserted her when she needed it most.

His expression softened. "You want to hate me, but you can't."

"Stay back," she ordered as he reached for her.

"I'm not going to hurt you," he crooned and gripped her leg and tugged, stretching her out on the bench seat with him hovering over her.

He ignored the hands that braced against his chest and rested his forehead against hers.

"You don't want me with someone else."

"Y-yes, I do!" she choked.

"Okay, baby," he said, clearly humoring her.

"I really do!" she insisted as he stroked her hair. "I'm serious. Get what you need from someone else. I'll interview them! I know what kinky shit you're into. I can find a skanky—"

His mouth covered hers. The kiss was hard and punishing, but when she stopped struggling, it immediately gentled. He began to kiss her tenderly, reverently, as he hadn't done for weeks. It was a shock, considering how he'd used her less than an hour ago. Her body quivered in delight, starved for affection and connection.

She tried to escape mentally, but Jesse wasn't rushing. He wasn't rushing to get off or worried about being discovered. His tongue tangled lazily with hers and enticed her to engage. She was drawn in by the taste of something sweet. What was that? Eager to erase the bitterness in her mouth, she allowed her tongue to dance with his and ignored his pleased hum. He'd eaten an apple for breakfast. Curiosity appeased, she tried to disengage, but Jesse didn't allow it.

He kept her mouth busy as he kissed her ten different ways—indulgent, deep, teasing, arousing. She couldn't keep up and was further distracted when his hand slipped beneath her sweater and covered her breast. By the time he raised his head and allowed her to catch her breath, her mind was spinning.

"You want me to kiss other girls like this?" he murmured as his lips drifted over her face.

She tried to gather her wits as he bunched her sweater under her chin. Even as she registered the cool chill on her bare skin, Jesse tucked the cup of her bra beneath her left breast. When he flicked her nipple with his tongue, she jerked like she'd been lashed with a whip.

"I love when your breasts get sensitive close to your period," he said before he latched onto her nipple.

He pinned her arms to the seat as she hissed and arched and bit back the urge to beg for mercy. It wouldn't make a difference to him. It never did. Despite his claims that God was on his side, she refused to believe it and prayed for divine intervention. Maybe the people in the farmhouse would get curious about why they were parked here and come investigate. Or perhaps a passerby would peek in, thinking they had car trouble or something had gone wrong. She strained to hear the rumble of a car, but all she could hear was the wet sounds of Jesse suckling and her own pathetic whimpering.

"You love this," he said raggedly, and turned his head from side to side, so her nipple dragged along his lips. "I could do this to you all day. You're so beautiful. A meadow of bluebonnets is nothing compared to you." He nuzzled her breast as he muttered, "I had girls offer me everything. I couldn't bring myself to take, even though I was desperate for relief. I'd rather be tortured in your presence and have you see me as a brother, then sink my dick into someone and try to picture your face while I'm with her. I need the real thing. I need you, Violet. No one else will do."

She tipped her head back to look out the open window and tried to follow the progress of slow-moving clouds as Jesse moved to her other breast. When she couldn't take anymore, she kicked her legs in frustration.

"*Jesse!*"

He eased the pressure and finally released her breast. He admired how puckered and swollen it was and peppered it with kisses before he buried his face between them.

"This has been hell."

His voice was muffled against her skin as he stroked her sides.

"I don't want it to be like this between us."

But it was, and there was no going back to the way it had been. Maybe in the beginning, they could have restored their relationship, but they'd gone too far. Their bond was so mangled, she couldn't imagine them having a relationship that was even remotely normal or healthy.

"I didn't intend to do this," he said, kissing the side of her breast. "I brought you here so we could talk about the future."

She stiffened. "What future?"

Jesse lifted his head and searched her face. "Ours."

She gaped at him.

"I'm going to graduate soon. I wanted to talk about what we should—"

"*We?*"

She shoved him hard enough to make him blink.

"Get off me!" she snapped.

He sighed. "Calm down."

"*You* calm down! Get the hell off me before I scream my head off."

It wasn't a huge threat, considering the isolated setting, but Jesse rose and sat behind the wheel as she shot up and hastily fixed her bra and yanked her sweater down.

"There's nothing to discuss with me. You're going to graduate and go off to college in another city or, better yet, out of state. I'll finish school and go my own way. Our futures aren't the same."

He stared at her, expression unreadable.

"There is no *we* or *our* or *us*. What we had, what we were, is gone. You…" She swallowed hard, eyes stinging with tears. "You hurt me more than anyone else. I trusted you. I never thought you of all people would ever…"

When he reached for her, she recoiled and wrapped her arms around herself.

"I want this to be over. I *need* it to be over." A tear slid down her cheek. "I need you gone."

"You don't mean that," he whispered.

He was clearly gutted. She ruthlessly stomped out the flurry of weak emotions that told her she'd gone far enough, that it wasn't the Christian way to repay evil with evil. She was supposed to overcome evil with good, but she didn't have that in her. All she had was anger. Lots of it. Months of suppressed rage and shame and helplessness erupted, spewing like hot lava. She had to get it out, to let him know how she saw him, and that there was no future where they were together.

"What's between us isn't a gift, it's poison," she said hoarsely. "It's corrupt and rotten, and nothing good has come from it. You think if it felt so good, if we were meant to be, that I would spend an hour scrubbing my body every time you touch me and still never feel clean?"

He went very still. She hardened her heart against the anguish creeping into his expression. This was her moment to end this once and for all, and she was going to see it through, even if it destroyed them both in the process.

"I hate that I can't look Dad in the eye. I hate that I have to watch every word I say because I'm terrified I'll let something slip. I hate that you were my first and that you conditioned my body to respond to you."

She trembled under the tremendous, crushing weight on her shoulders.

"You think what's stopping me from telling someone is love, but it isn't love for you. It's love for Lynne. Knowing what you are would destroy her."

"What am I?"

A tear slipped down her cheek as she said, "You're a monster."

His expression went blank, his vulnerability and agony vanishing so quickly, she wasn't sure it had been there at all. Silence reined. A bird swooped in front of the truck before it flapped away, chirping gaily. A breeze caused fine tendrils of hair to slide across her face.

"Say it, Vi."

She knew what he wanted to hear and finally had the strength to.

"You're right. I don't hate you." For just a moment, she saw hope flash in his eyes before she finished, "I feel nothing for you at all."

He didn't move a muscle, but the hairs on her arms stood up as something evil and inhuman stared out of Jesse's eyes. She got her first glimpse of the demon that lurked within him the day Jesse took her by the river. Recently, she'd begun to see him more frequently, as Jesse was ruled by his lustful appetites. The demon that used to possess him at night was now visible in broad daylight. He and Jesse were now one.

"I really tried, Violet," Jesse said ruefully, lips curved in a mocking smile as his eyes burned with wrath. "I tried for you, but I guess it wasn't good enough."

She clutched the door handle, heart pumping, as he cocked his head, examining her clinically.

"Telling a monster you feel nothing for him isn't very smart," he pointed out.

She stopped breathing.

"It gives him no incentive not to act like one."

Even as he reached for her, she shoved the door open and fell out of the truck. This was all horrifically familiar, but this time, she knew what he was capable of. Even as she scrambled to her feet and reached for her backpack to grab her cell phone, he slid across the seat after her.

For a split second, she considered trying to reason with him, but a glimpse of the bloodlust carved into his face convinced her fleeing was her only option. She plunged into the field of bluebonnets, her aim the lone farmhouse in the distance. She waved her hands, hoping someone was looking out of the window and would realize something was terribly wrong. She would have screamed in hopes that anyone within earshot would come to the rescue, but she didn't have time to haul in a breath when she could hear him gaining ground behind her. He was an athlete. Strong, fast. She would never make it.

Even as the thought crossed through her mind, Jesse tackled her from behind. The impact sent her sprawling in a patch of fluffy bluebonnets that cushioned her fall. She scrambled on her hands and feet, trying to get away. When Jesse hauled her back, Dad's training kicked in. She balled her fist and swung with all her might. Jesse dropped like a stone when she punched him in the ear.

Breath ragged, she continued on. As she stumbled through the wildflowers, she glanced back at the road. Her stomach lurched when she realized how far away she was. The farmhouse was her only hope. Out of the corner of her eye, she saw Jesse straighten. Panic gave her extra strength. She ran full out, faster than she ever had. It was life or death. She could do this.

She was close enough now to make out more details of the house. The porch had a swing and pots of pink and yellow flowers. Whoever lived there was a good person. They would help her if they were home. *God, please help me*, she begged. *Prove Jesse wrong. Save me. If You do, I swear I'll...* she was struck down again before she could strike a bargain with God.

Jesse took the brunt of the fall and this time, kept his arms around her instead of knocking her off balance. They rolled. He pinned her clawed hand to the ground and leaned over her, gold cross swinging. His eyes were alight. She would never forget the strange formation of clouds dotting the sky, being hemmed in by cheery bluebonnets, and the look on Jesse's face as he looked down at her.

Time stopped.

"Jesse?" she panted.

He leaned down, kissed her forehead, and murmured, "Lord, forgive me for what I'm about to do."

Violet lay on a bed of crushed wildflowers. She was naked. She knew that should bother her, but she couldn't find the will to care. Nothing mattered. Not anymore.

A figure appeared in her line of sight. She didn't bother focusing on Jesse. Instead, she admired a cloud that resembled an elephant head. That was more interesting than anything Jesse had to say. She hadn't been honest when she said she didn't feel anything for him, but it had been a self-fulfilling prophecy because now she really didn't. He'd given her glimpses of the monster within, but he proved beyond a shadow of a doubt that her brother was truly gone. They could never go back to what they'd been. Ever.

Jesse pulled her into a sitting position so he could slip a shirt over her head. Gently, he pulled her to her feet. The shirt was so large, it covered her to mid-thigh. When he crouched to pick her up, she hung lifelessly over his shoulder and spotted her torn peach-colored sweater and stained jeans clutched in his hand. She closed her eyes as her stomach rocked.

Her head spun as he settled her in the passenger seat of the truck. Automatically, she pulled the seatbelt across her chest and clicked it in. She pressed her feet together, noting that she was missing a sock. She stared down the dirt road that hadn't brought one car across their path.

Jesse opened the glove box in front of her and pulled out one of Dad's red paisley bandanas. He splashed it with water before he began to clean her face. His hands were trembling, and although he was talking, it sounded like gibberish to her. She couldn't hear anything over the echoes of her piercing screams ricocheting around in her head, interspersed with static. If she had the will to speak, she would have asked him for water to rinse out the taste of blood, semen, and dirt in her mouth. Instead, she let him scrub her face until he gave up and rounded the truck to climb into the driver's seat.

The moment the truck began to move, she deflated, closing her eyes and slumping against the door. It seemed that she closed her eyes for a minute. When she opened them, Jesse was tugging her out of the truck, into a pit. She flailed before her eyes adjusted and she recognized their surroundings. They were in their garage with the door already down, which is why it was so dark. Her sluggish heart leapt.

"Dad's not home," Jesse murmured as he toted her into the house.

She had a feeling of déjà vu as he placed her in the tub. This time, she wasn't shellshocked and heartbroken. She was coherent and functional, but her emotions had been switched off. She was grateful.

In contrast, Jesse fluttered around her, his unshakeable poise, gone. His face was drawn and the glassy horror in his blue eyes warmed her because this time it was he who was rattled. He manically scrubbed her down and seemed obsessed with cleaning every nook and cranny, even cleaning inside her ears like she was a child.

When he tried to dress her in a nightgown, she reached for jeans and a top.

"Violet."

"I'm going to school."

He said nothing, just stood there in jeans and nothing else.

"You don't have to take me," she said.

He spun on his heel and disappeared into the bathroom. She hummed as she stared at her array of underwear. What color did she want to wear? She was still trying to decide when Jesse reappeared, clean and fully dressed. She frowned.

"It's been fifteen minutes," he said.

"Oh."

He swallowed. "I think you should stay here."

"No." She had to go to school where her friends were. Where she felt safe, even if it was just for a little while. She couldn't stay at home, in her bedroom. She would lose it.

Jesse didn't argue. He selected white underwear and held it out for her to step into. He pulled them up without copping a feel or doing anything else lecherous and dressed her in jeans and a gray hoodie.

She led the way back to the garage and climbed into the truck. Jesse stared at her through the windshield for what seemed to be forever before he got in. The garage door opened, flooding the space with light.

She had no idea what time it was, but traffic hour had passed. Even though there was a clock on the dashboard, she couldn't bring herself to look at it. Her surroundings seemed sharper, brighter, more vibrant.

"I'm sorry."

Jesse's croak made no impact on her.

"I swear, I—"

"Shut up."

Her voice sounded as empty and hollow as she felt.

"I don't know what's happening to me. Something in my head just snapped."

"You should seek help," she advised coolly.

Jesse turned into the school parking lot. There was no one around since everyone was in class. She reached for her backpack and ignored her filthy clothes on the floorboard.

"Violet."

She glanced at him. The monster was gone. In his place was a tormented teenager. If she didn't know any better, she would have thought he was the one who'd been attacked. He was pale, sweating, and looked devastated. He'd aged five years in a matter of hours.

"Report me," he ordered.

His words sliced through the blessed numbness and zapped some of her dead emotions back to life.

Jesse blinked rapidly as his eyes filled with tears. "You should get help. I've gone too far. I'll accept the consequences, whatever they are."

He leaned over, gripped her face between both hands, and kissed her. It was an apology, a goodbye.

He pulled back, whispered, "I love you," and gave her one last, hungry kiss before he hopped out of the truck and slammed the door behind him.

He stalked toward school without a backpack, hands in his pockets. She sat there for several seconds before she slipped out, shouldered her backpack, and headed in the opposite direction.

As she opened the door of a building, the bell rang. Students flooded the hallways. Everyone walked around her like she wasn't even there. No one called out her name or tried to stop her from reaching her destination. Her feet felt like they were in blocks of cement. The closer she got to the office, the more she felt like she couldn't breathe.

"Honey, can I help you?"

Violet stared at the smiling office clerk behind the desk. The woman had short, curly hair, and pink hibiscus earrings. The woman looked so cheerful and warm, like nothing bad had ever happened to her, while Violet felt like she had been hacked to pieces with a machete and was about to fall apart.

The woman's smile faded. "Honey, are you okay?"

Violet nodded, even as tears began to slip down her face. The woman rushed around the counter and rubbed her hands up and down Violet's arms.

"What's going on, dear? What's happened?"

"I..."

Violet gulped back tears. This was it. This was her moment. All she had to do was tell the nice lady what had happened to her— what had been happening to her for six months, and it would be over. She had proof—semen in her mouth, pussy, ass. She was raw, bruised, and had his DNA under her fingernails. Her scratches would be all over his body, and his tongue was still swollen from her biting it. This was the right thing to do—what he'd urged her to do for both their sakes.

But she couldn't do it.

"I think I have my period and stained my pants," she wailed.

The woman's face cleared. "Oh, honey, we've all been there. It's going to be okay. Come, let me help you."

VIOLET WAS CURLED UP ON THE FRONT SEAT OF THE TRUCK WHEN THE driver's door opened. Jesse stared at her for a minute before he slid in and rested his hand on her head. She whimpered like a wounded animal as tears slipped out of raw, swollen eyes.

Once the sweet lady in the office gave her a tampon and reassured her that her pants weren't stained, she trudged back to the truck and collapsed on the seat. She lay there for hours, trying to gather the strength to go in and tell her story, but she couldn't move. She listened to the bells ring, knowing she was running out of time, and now it was over.

Jesse didn't tell her to sit up and put on her seatbelt as he started up the truck. As he drove, his hand sifted through her hair, stroked her cheek, and rubbed her quivering back while she sobbed.

Once Jesse parked the truck in the garage, he cradled her in his arms. She was too distraught to care if their parents were home but figured neither of them were when Jesse slid into bed with her.

He held her as she cried and beat her fists against his chest and screamed that she hated him. He didn't say a word. He let her rage and when it was over, he undressed her and tended to every mark he'd left behind.

It didn't surprise her when he eased himself inside of her. He didn't move, he just petted and nuzzled her. But she didn't want to be placated. She needed a release, an outlet for all the horrible things going on inside of her that were tearing her apart.

When she shoved him onto his back, he didn't resist. She rode him, setting a brutal pace that went on and on because her mind was too fucked up to let her climax. In the end, Jesse helped push her over the edge. When she collapsed on top of him, he held her until her breathing had evened out, and she was still and quiet. He didn't seek an orgasm for himself, but kissed her forehead, tucked the blankets around her, and left.

Violet turned on her side, stared at the far wall, and felt absolutely nothing.

CHAPTER 17

JESSE

3 WEEKS LATER

"I can't take it anymore. What's going on between you two?"

Jesse stopped in his tracks and turned to face Mom, who stood in the entrance of the kitchen, hands on hips.

"Vi," Mom said sharply as Violet tried to escape into the hallway.

Violet halted but kept her back to them.

Mom looked back and forth between them before she demanded, "What happened?"

Out of the corner of his eye, he saw Dad's head turn from the TV. Unease tripped down Jesse's spine, but he kept his face blank as Mom continued.

"From the moment you two came home from school until you went to sleep, you used to spend every moment together. I could hear you talking and laughing for hours, and now..." Mom swept her hands in the empty expanse between them. "You barely exchange a word. Isaac mentioned that disagreement you had a few weeks ago that made Violet so upset that she wanted to ride the bus?"

Mom shot Jesse a quizzical look, clearly expecting him to explain, but he remained silent.

"I thought you two worked it out, and we were all just busy—you, Jesse, with baseball, and Vi spending most of her time with Georgia and Allison because of that science project. But now, I *know* something's wrong."

Mom stopped, giving them the opportunity to confirm or deny her charge. Jesse slipped his hands into his pockets and gave Violet time to answer for both of them. He'd known this moment would come. It was only a matter of time before someone confronted Violet about her ghostlike appearance and the fact that she'd gone mute. Her fire, which had always been so much a part of her, had been extinguished.

Come on, baby. You can do it, he silently urged. He couldn't stand the suspense. Every day he wondered if it was going to be his last of freedom. Every time a stranger appeared in his classroom doorway or at practice, he wondered if Violet finally plucked up the courage to do the right thing, only for each instance to be a false alarm that left him drenched in cold sweat. The emotional roller coaster was exhausting. He wanted his fate decided. Waiting for the axe to fall was intolerable.

"Jesse?"

The uncertainty in Mom's tone sliced through his gut. Mom had always trusted him implicitly, but he glimpsed her bewilderment and a hint of apprehension. Had the incident with Tucker made Mom realize that she didn't know him as well as she thought, which meant he could be responsible for Violet's drastic personality change?

"Violet."

At Isaac's stern tone, Violet stirred. She turned, revealing a bloodless face and eyes so glassy and empty that Jesse looked away.

"Tell me this has nothing to do with Tucker," Dad ordered.

"This has nothing to do with Tucker," Violet parroted in a flat monotone.

Dad relaxed and glanced at Jesse. "You said you'd make it up to her."

He cleared his dry throat. "I tried."

Dad switched his gaze back to Violet. "That wasn't good enough?"

Jesse tensed. "It's not her fault. It's mine," he interjected swiftly.

Isaac's focus didn't waver from Violet. "I can't recall the last time I heard you two argue, much less fight. What could Jesse have done to make you hold such a grudge?"

Jesse felt like his heart was being squeezed in a vice. It took every ounce of self-control he possessed not to fidget as he waited for Violet to respond, but she said nothing.

"Ephesians 4:26 says not to let the sun go down on your anger. You've let this go on for weeks," Isaac said quietly. "The devil is always looking for an opportunity to come into a family and cause discord, to divide and conquer. There's nothing Jesse could have done that can't be forgiven."

"*Dad,*" Jesse stressed, but Isaac ignored him and continued his lecture.

"Matthew 6:14 says if you forgive others, God will also forgive you. No one is perfect. Give Jesse grace, Vi, so one day someone will do the same for you." Isaac paused a moment to let that sink in before he continued, "Jesse's running to the church to pick up supplies for the work we're doing on the McMillan's house tomorrow. Go with him. Talk. Bury this once and for all. If you can't resolve your issues, Mom and I will get involved, and we shouldn't have to. You two are adults now. Act like it." Isaac jerked his chin. "Go change, Vi. Jesse's leaving in five minutes."

When Violet didn't move to obey Isaac's order, the tension in the room thickened. Jesse sensed Violet wrestling with herself. His heart thudded in his ears as he waited for her to break her silence and condemn him. Isaac scooted to the edge of his seat, clearly ready to deal with this on his feet, but before he could, Violet abruptly turned on her heel and disappeared down the hallway.

As Mom watched her go with a concerned expression, Isaac's hard gaze cut to Jesse.

"You're always trying to protect her." Isaac held up a hand to stop his protest. "I know my daughter better than anyone. She's strong-willed, impulsive, and has a nose for trouble. Ever since Tucker, she's changed, and not for the better. She needs accountability. What's going to happen when you're not around to save her?"

He opened his mouth to crush Isaac's illusions about him and instead heard himself say, "I love her."

"I know you do." Isaac sighed as he leaned back in his recliner. "You'd do anything for her. She knows it and takes advantage."

Isaac was an honorable, hard-working, practical man, but when it came to matters of the heart, he was blind. Because he embodied everything Isaac had always wanted in a son, Isaac couldn't see his faults. On the flip side, when it came to Violet, Isaac discounted her good qualities and instead focused on the bad ones that reminded him of his first love that he'd never forgiven. How many times over the years had he defended Violet against a father, who was too hard on her and had never given her the grace he expected of her?

What would Isaac say if he confessed what he'd done? Isaac assumed because he loved Violet that he was incapable of truly harming her. He believed the same until she scorned his love and destroyed his illusions of a future together. He could set the record straight and clear her name. He steeled himself, but before he could speak, Violet reappeared.

She was dressed in black pants, a t-shirt, a light jacket, and a hat pulled low over her eyes. She didn't say a word as she crossed the living room to where he stood by the front door. He opened it for her. As Violet trotted down the steps, he looked back. Isaac had gone back to watching TV, but Mom's eyes were on him.

His mother was a glass half full, eternal optimist who believed that good would always prevail. She had a kind heart. He'd always thought of his mother as being somewhat naive, but as their eyes met, he realized the rose-colored glasses were missing and she looked... disturbed. Unlike Isaac, Mom wasn't blind. She may love him more than life itself, but she also loved Violet with the same ferocity and, unlike Isaac, she would believe Violet in a heartbeat. He flashed her what he hoped was a reassuring smile before he turned away, his stomach in knots.

It wasn't until he unlocked the truck that it struck him. He stared through the window at Violet, who stood on the opposite side. They hadn't ridden in this vehicle since that day. They couldn't switch to the SUV because he needed the truck bed for the paint cans and lumber he had to pick up. He blew out a breath before he pulled the door open. Automatically, his eyes scanned the interior, even though he'd thoroughly cleaned it. He turned the key in the ignition and waited.

It took Violet several minutes to open the door, and a few more before she actually got in. As she settled beside him, he sensed her reluctance, resentment, and the smallest trace of fear. He didn't blame her. He hadn't known he was capable of what he'd done in that field.

They rode in absolute silence. Despite Dad's decree that they sort this out, Violet didn't try. Both of them knew nothing could fix this.

He slumped in his seat and tilted his head back while keeping his eyes on the road. Violet was right beside him, but her presence was so faint, it was almost like she wasn't there at all. She'd become a wraith, drifting through life, lost in her head. Even though she loathed him, the urge to reach out and touch her, to bridge the distance between them, was a gnawing, dragging compulsion that made him tighten his hold on the steering wheel.

He hadn't touched her since the day they visited the bluebonnet field. Not even a stray brush of his fingers while passing her a plate at dinner. He knew if he did, he wouldn't be able to stop himself from taking more, and he'd taken enough.

You think if it felt so good, if we were meant to be, that I would spend an hour scrubbing my body every time you touch me and still never feel clean?

The memory of her voice, filled with venom and revulsion, tore through him like shrapnel, reopening wounds that hadn't even begun to heal. He wholeheartedly believed Violet loved him and, at some point, would surrender to what was between them. It never occurred to him that their bond could fracture beyond repair or that, one day, she would look through him as if he wasn't there.

How had he misjudged her feelings for him so badly? Had he imagined her eyes following him months before she gave herself to him? Had he convinced himself she desired him when she didn't? He straightened and raked his hand through his hair as he shifted restlessly in his seat. No. It hadn't been all in his head. *She* kissed *him*, which tipped their relationship into the physical realm. And before the reality of their circumstances tainted what they had, Violet had given herself freely, eager to experience any and everything he could offer her. The memories of her initiation and the handful of days where they experimented to their heart's content reassured him that it wasn't all in his mind, even as it tormented him with what was forever out of his reach.

When their bodies writhed together and the crap from the outside world faded away, what bloomed between them was so special, he vowed he would do whatever it took to keep it. So, he'd ignored her struggles, denials, and breakdowns. Ignored her babbling about all the reasons why they couldn't be together. He tried to give her time and space to come to terms with what was between them, but the more he had of her, the more his appetite increased. The fact that her body wept for him, and she clung so tight in the throes, yet repeatedly rejected him, drove him insane. He assumed the constant imprinting on her body would overcome her reservations. He'd believed that in the end, love would conquer all.

How wrong he'd been.

I feel nothing for you at all.

Black spots marred his vision as rage engulfed him. He squinted at the road as he tried to think past the bloodlust. He lost his mind when she said that. When he realized she would never love him back. He built his life around her, and she wanted nothing to do with him.

She called him a monster, and he proved her right by giving his demon free rein. He punished her for not loving him back, for annihilating his dreams, and ruining the man he could have been. He mauled her like an animal, and she fought back with an aggression that, even now, made his dick hard. They had been stripped of all civilization, which resulted in a transcendent experience that unequivocally proved she was his equal. That field of wildflowers would always be his version of Eden and Violet, whether she wanted to be or not, was his wicked, savage temptress, Eve.

He glanced at her. She stared straight ahead, one hand loosely clutching the seatbelt resting on her chest. If she truly hated him, why hadn't she reported him? She'd been given many opportunities to expose him, but she hadn't. She claimed she didn't want to break Mom's heart, but Mom had nothing to do with how she let him tend to her when they came home that day or how she took what she needed from his body.

He took a deep breath and let it out slowly, ignoring the surge of adrenaline and the way his muscles flexed as his mind replayed her riding him. The only time Violet gave into their chemistry is when he roused her to a fever pitch, or she was too emotionally shattered to care about her scruples. Only then did she allow herself to indulge in their bond and allow it to soothe her.

The day after their violent clash, he visited the recruiter's office to complete the enlistment process to join the Air Force. He'd put off making a final decision in hopes that Violet would come to her senses, but he was running out of time. Mom and Dad assumed he was going to a local college. He stopped talking about the military because it had upset Mom so much, but he hadn't changed his mind. Joining the Air Force was a promise he made to his father that he always intended to keep. He had never second guessed his decision until Violet. If he went into the military, his life wouldn't be his own. He drove to that secluded location, intending to lay himself at her feet and have her decide his future, only to be told in no uncertain terms that she wanted nothing to do with him.

Any man who had been as brutally rejected as he had, should have been instantly cured of his infatuation. To have the love of his life encourage him to have sex with other females and to label their relationship as poisonous and rotten should have made moving on a piece of cake. He ran a hand down his face, disgusted with himself. If he believed in witchcraft, he may have believed she cast a spell on him because he still yearned for her. She was a part of him, imbedded bone deep. There was no getting her out. He'd tried. There were countless girls who would have him, but the one he'd kill for hated his guts. He still loved her and a part of him suspected that he always would. His life was a cruel joke.

He pulled into the empty church parking lot and reversed the truck to make it easier to load the supplies. He sorted through the keys Pastor Sonny had given him as he approached the chapel and lifted his head when he heard a door slam. He paused as Violet rounded the truck and passed him to jog up the steps. He couldn't resist staring at her ass and had a vivid image of her on all fours with the red outline of his hand on her right cheek along with a bite mark that had long since faded.

Need slammed into him with the force of a baseball bat. He'd taken great pains to steer clear of her. He'd been grateful that she caught rides with friends to and from school and had spent as much time as she could at their homes. It helped him wean himself off of her, to exercise self-control, but he was starkly aware that they were alone with no one around for miles on a late, quiet Friday afternoon.

His demon salivated and flashed erotic images in his mind, snapshots of their last, devastating encounter. Depraved desires snaked through his mind, edging out the pain of her rejection. He hesitated at the bottom of the steps. The reformed part of him wanted to order her to stay in the truck or, better yet, call their parents to pick her up. She wasn't safe with him.

But he didn't say a word. Instead, he made his way toward her, fingers tingling, heart racing. He knew what he was going to do. Maybe a part of him had known the moment she got in the truck with him. It was always going to end this way. If he was presented with the opportunity to have her, he didn't have the will to resist. Even if it jeopardized his freedom. Even if it wrecked their family. Nothing compared to the absolute bliss of possessing her. He would pay any price to have her. To be buried inside of her where he belonged.

It didn't matter if they ran the risk of being caught. He would take her anytime, anywhere. He didn't give a fuck if it was in God's house. If sex was all he could have of her, he would take as much as he could until she reported him, or someone put a bullet in his head. He was an addicted maniac. There was something terribly wrong with him for wanting someone who despised him. But he didn't care. He'd take her hatred and disdain. He'd take her fighting. He'd take whatever she gave him as long as he got *her*.

He kept his eyes downcast, maintaining the role of chastened stepbrother. If Violet looked into his eyes, she'd know what was coming. There was a fine tremor in the hand that inserted the key in the lock and turned it. He pushed open the door and Violet stepped through. He watched her walk down the aisle between the pews. Cast in the light that came through the massive stained-glass windows, she looked ethereal, untouchable. No matter how many times he claimed her, she remained maddeningly out of reach.

Hands on hips, Violet surveyed the empty stage. What was she thinking? He gave the church a cursory glance. This is where their parents married and where they'd come nearly every Sunday for four years. He spent countless hours here praying, worshipping, volunteering. He spent a significant portion of his summer renovating this church... For what? To have God laugh in his face and take from him the only thing he'd ever wanted?

Fury heated his blood. He'd been a good son, taking care of his mother when his father died. He studied diligently for good grades, worked hard to attain his skills as an athlete and earned his money through manual labor. He didn't cheat or steal. He had one dream. One weakness. One thing he desired above all else. He thought God placed Violet in his life because she was meant to be his, only for God to be one of the reasons Violet was convinced they couldn't be together.

Violet had quoted every scripture about how God judged the sexually immoral, and how sex outside of marriage went against God's design. He would have let Mom and Dad catch them in the act if he thought they'd force her to marry him. But he suspected their parent's remedy would be to bury their indiscretion instead of trying to rectify it. They would be relieved to ship him off to the military and ensure they had no future contact with each other, which left him with no leverage to bind Violet to him.

God and Violet had been major pillars in his life. They guided and shaped him. He gave them his all only to walk away empty-handed and heartbroken, with his best friend and soul mate lost to him for all time. God had played him for a fool, tormenting him with false visions and hopes that would never come true. Didn't God know what happened to faithful men who weren't rewarded? They stopped praying and took matters into their own hands. If being the good guy didn't get him what he wanted, what was the point of restraining himself?

He drew in a deep breath, taking in Violet's powdery scent mixing with the smell of old Bibles, furniture polish, and wood pews. He didn't have it in him to be gentle, loving, or patient any longer. He was desperate, deprived, and starving. With graduation just two months away and his ship date for the military pending, he had mere weeks left with her. He wasn't going to abstain. He was going to gorge, knowing, no matter how much he indulged, it would never be enough.

As if Violet caught the tail end of his thought, her head whipped around. The moment their eyes collided, hers flared in instant recognition.

"You promised."

Her voice was nearly soundless even in the hushed, quiet sanctuary.

"I've done my best." His voice was gruff with lust. "I've never been able to keep my promises where you're concerned. I can't be around you and not…" He swallowed hard and extended his hand, palm out. "It won't be like last time. I can be gentle."

When she recoiled, his hand balled into a fist and dropped to his side.

"Don't run," he ordered, knowing it would trigger primitive instincts that he was trying to stifle. She deserved gentle. She deserved sweet. If she came to him, if she allowed him to touch without fighting, he could control his rampaging demon, but if she… His control vanished as Violet bolted down the aisle.

If the back door had been unlocked, Violet would have escaped. Instead, she wasted precious seconds fumbling with the lock and had to dash away before he could get his hands on her.

She leapt up the stairs, intending to cross the stage, to reach a door on the other side of the sanctuary, but she didn't make it. He flattened her on the steps.

"You can't do this here!" she hissed fiercely.

He was pleased her warrior spirit was back. That meant he didn't have to rein himself in. He could indulge his demon's appetite and give them an experience that would be etched into their memories for all time.

"Why not here? God already knows what we've done," he said as he flipped her onto her back and unceremoniously yanked her pants down.

She engaged in a furious tug of war with him while simultaneously trying to keep an eye on multiple entrances. When he yanked hard enough to pull her down a step, she tried to kick him in the head, which allowed him to free one leg from her pants. That was all he needed. He ripped her maroon lace underwear off, forced her legs wide, and clamped his mouth on her pussy. Her breath whooshed out of her and her body went taut as a bow.

It had been weeks since he tasted her. Weeks since he'd been inside her. The moment his tongue sank inside her, he knew he was lost. He'd gone back to taking her underwear to get him off, but that paled in comparison to this. To drinking from her. To feeling her thigh muscles quiver as she strained to get away. To the honey that spilled from her against her will. Those tormented, helpless sounds she made were music to his ears. His awareness of their surroundings vanished. He didn't care where they were or who tried to interrupt them. He wasn't stopping unless someone physically hauled him off her.

He slid his finger inside her to coax her to spill a little more for him.

"Please, stop," she begged as she hauled her quivering body up a step.

He followed, keeping his mouth on her while he felt around for her G-spot. He knew he found it when she let out a wanton moan that echoed around the sanctuary before she muffled it with her arm.

He lifted his head, eager for proof that she still needed this from him. She let out a stifled sob as he pushed her arm aside. She glared at him, eyes shining with self-loathing, lust, and hatred. She'd never looked more beautiful to him.

"You," she began gutturally, but her voice cut out when he cupped her.

Her thighs snapped together, trapping his hand, which he didn't mind in the least. As his fingers expertly stroked, her legs tossed back and forth.

"You've been missing me, Vi. Admit it," he rasped.

"You're a heartless..." She bared her teeth as she pulled herself up another step. "Evil."

She collapsed on the stage and turned on her side in the fetal position. Mouth watering at the feast before him, he took his hand from her to undo his jeans. Violet shot up and tried to make a break for it, but he was on her in a flash. She didn't gain more than three steps before he wrapped his arms around her and got her down on all fours. He put her in a chokehold as he blanketed her body with his.

"Nuh-uh, baby. You're not getting away. I've gone too long without you."

"Please don't do this," she pleaded.

"You want this so bad, you're soaking my jeans," he hissed as he rocked against her.

"We're in *church*!"

She sounded scandalized.

He pressed his cheek to hers as they stared at the rows of empty pews. "It doesn't matter where we are. I'll always want you."

He gripped her throat with one hand while the other undid his jeans and shoved them down.

"You know you want this," he panted as he dragged his dick up and down her weeping slit. "Your body still craves me. Still wants me to fuck you senseless." He nuzzled her as she let out a choked sob. "That's exactly what you want me to do, isn't it? Tell me that's what you want, Violet."

"You have no shame," she croaked.

"You have enough for the both of us," he mocked as he lapped up a stray tear. "How we feel about each other is nothing to be ashamed of. It's supposed to be something we rejoice in."

"The devil will say anything to make a sin seem like a gift," she said bitterly.

So now he was the devil on top of being a monster. All because he loved her and wasn't willing to lie about his feelings or hide how she made him feel.

"If the way of the righteous means I can't have this..."

He gently thrust. It was so quiet, they both heard the sloppy sounds her body made. She whimpered in shame and tried to hang her head, but he wouldn't let her, forcing her to face their invisible jury.

"Then I'll be a sinner," he said through clenched teeth and tried to hold back his beast, which wanted to slake his lust savagely, ensuring her submission and repentance. "I wish everyone could see you, dripping all over the stage, taking every inch of me. *Loving* every fucking moment of this. Whenever you come through those doors, and look at this stage, you're going to think of this, of us."

"No!"

She made a desperate lunge for the edge of the stage, but he held her in place. She wasn't going anywhere.

"Pray for divine intervention," he taunted as her vagina clutched at his invading cock. "If this is wrong, God will save you. He wouldn't let His faithful daughter be defiled in His own house, would he?"

She reached back and gripped his thigh, fingernails raking his skin. "Stop! You can't..."

He was so fucking tired of hearing her say that. He cut her off as he abruptly slammed himself inside of her, making her release a shrill scream that echoed around the chapel.

"I can't what?" he whispered, fingers tightening around her throat as his demon howled in triumph. "I can't fuck you in a church? I can't make you want me?"

"I hate you!"

Her words skewered his heart. Despair and lust tangled in a devastating mix that decimated his control and his desire to be gentle. He abruptly straightened and gripped her hips.

"You better hope someone walks through that door and saves you," he growled as he began to move in hard, brutal strokes that caused her whole body to jolt. "And puts us both out of our misery."

He took what he wanted, what he needed, or he'd go insane. He didn't hold back, couldn't. Not after being so long without her. He dared God to take her from him, to deny him this after everything he'd sacrificed. He made Violet beg, cry, scream, and moan. He was certain this form of worship had never been practiced here, but he ensured if God was watching, it was memorable.

He wasn't ready to come, but when she rippled around him, he almost went over the edge with her. He ground his teeth, fighting his response as she impaled herself on him, taking what she needed and shuddering in relief as he met her needs.

Unable to withstand another second, he flipped her on her back. He straddled her chest, knees pinning her arms on either side of her even though she was no longer fighting, but he wasn't taking any chances. He gripped her cheeks and forced her mouth open. His jubilant shout echoed through the church as he spilled, as he defiled a place he'd once considered sacred, and accepted the fact that he was going to hell.

Violet stared up at him with glazed eyes. Needing to prolong the moment, he slid his dick in her mouth and released her cheeks. He was tense, waiting for her to bite, but he relaxed and stroked her hair when she sucked and let her tongue feather over the sensitive head.

"Good girl," he husked.

That broke the spell. She went rigid beneath him and tipped her head to the side to expel his dick. She coughed and retched, but she'd already swallowed most of him, which is all he cared about. She began to buck and kick beneath him. He admired her for a few seconds before he rolled off her and collapsed behind Pastor Sonny's wood podium.

Violet stumbled to her feet and wove drunkenly toward her clothes strewn on the steps, swiping at her face as she hastily dressed. He listened to her run out of the church and the loud bang as the heavy door slammed shut behind her.

He waited to be clobbered by those incipient emotions that had dogged him since he jacked off at church camp—shame, guilt, regret, remorse, fear, disgust. All he felt was warm satisfaction. Anyone could have come in and discovered them, but God hadn't intervened. Maybe God hadn't abandoned him after all.

His climax left him drowsy, but he had work to do. He forced himself to his feet and dragged his jeans up and fastened them. He made his way to a closet with cleaning supplies and grabbed a spray bottle and washcloth. He wiped up all signs of debauchery before he began to execute the task Pastor Sonny had entrusted to him.

When he made his way out to the truck with four paint cans, he saw Violet huddled in the front seat. She hadn't been able to take off since he had the keys in his pocket and there was no one in the vicinity that she could ask for a ride. He propped the front door open as he loaded up lumber and the other building material they hadn't used during the renovation. Tomorrow, they would be working on the McMillan's house, members of the church who had a house in dire need of repair.

It took thirty minutes to load everything. By the time he joined Violet in the truck, the sun was beginning to set. He wasn't surprised when Violet angled her body away from him. If she had allowed it, he would have drawn her against his chest and held her. He wanted to tell her he loved her, that it didn't have to be this way, but he knew she wouldn't listen.

He knew she was hating herself, hating him. That was her default whenever they came together. It didn't matter how pleasurable and gratifying. She would always turn it into something amoral and twisted. She couldn't admit that a part of her reveled in what they'd done.

As they made their way home, he wondered what Violet would say to their parents. Had fucking in church pushed her over the edge? Was that the final straw? He felt a burble of unease, but it couldn't morph into true fear because of the overwhelming contentment that canceled out all else. His mind was empty, his inner turmoil gone. Possessing her in any capacity made him feel right, centered, whole. He refused to believe she didn't feel the same. It wasn't possible for such a connection to be one-sided. Their chemistry had been ordained by God. If she had loved him a fraction of how much he loved her, they could have conquered anything. Instead, she doomed them to lives where neither would ever be truly fulfilled.

When he pulled into the driveway, he glanced at Violet and waited to see if she had any last words for him before she decided his fate. She kept her face averted as she pushed open the door and hopped out. He ambled in her wake, hands in pockets.

As he expected, their parents hung around. Mom was still in the kitchen and Dad was in the living room. Both turned when they walked through the front door. Violet stopped in her tracks, clearly not anticipating this. He waited several seconds before he moved her inside so he could close the door.

"So?" Isaac prompted.

Mom came out of the kitchen, wiping her hands on a dish towel, her face still pinched with worry.

Violet was so rigid, she was trembling. He glanced down at her and saw her mouth open and eyes fill with tears.

"Violet?" Mom asked.

He curbed his arm around Violet's shoulders and turned her into him a second before she burst into tears. His hand sank into her hair and kept her face pressed to his chest as he said, "She forgave me, but she's still hurt and angry."

Violet's hand fisted in his shirt.

Mom's expression eased slightly. "Forgiveness doesn't take away the hurt, but it'll pass." Mom came up to them and rubbed Violet's back. "Are you okay, honey? Want to talk about it?"

His hand dropped to Violet's nape and squeezed. A second later, Violet shook her head.

"Violet helped me load up the truck. We're a little dirty," he said.

Mom nodded and stepped back. "Dinner will be ready in a half hour."

He glanced at Isaac and got a curt, approving nod. Isaac was satisfied with his explanation and wouldn't push Violet any further, for which he was grateful. He used his body to shield Violet from their scrutiny and ushered her down the hallway. He entered his bedroom since it was closer and directed her into the bathroom. Intending to get her in the shower, he started to lift her shirt without registering the fire in her eyes until it was too late. Her slap snapped his head to the side.

"You got what you wanted from me," she seethed. "Now, get out."

He ignored his throbbing face and reached for her. "It's not like that. I wanted..."

She wrenched away, grabbed her hairbrush, and held it like a knife. "I know what you wanted! It's the only thing you care about!"

"Vi."

"I swear to God," she choked. "If you touch me one more time, I'm going to lose it."

He held up his hands. "Okay, I'm going."

He backed into his bedroom. She closed the bathroom door and a second later, locked it. He stood there, face smarting, and heard the shower switch on to drown out the sound of her sobbing.

He leaned back against the door and closed his eyes. Those feelings he thought he bested came back with a vengeance, clobbering him over the head, drowning him in self-loathing. His chest swelled with the need to roar, but he swallowed it and staggered to his bed.

Even though he regretted the pain he caused, he knew that wouldn't stop him from partaking in the future. If he had a shred of decency, he would put Violet out of her misery and turn himself in, but he wasn't the self-sacrificing hero. Thanks to her, he'd finally embraced what he was. He wasn't the knight in shining armor. He was the villain. What self-respecting monster willingly walked into a cage? If Violet wanted him out of her life, she had to declare what he was to the world. Until then, he was going to take his fill.

At some point, she would find the strength to turn him in. He wasn't sure if that would be this evening over dinner or a month from now, but she would. If he wanted a chance at a future that wasn't behind bars, he had to get the hell away from her. Having the military dictate his life was the best thing for him since he had no control where she was concerned. It was best that he leave before they destroyed one another.

249

CHAPTER 18
VIOLET

1 MONTH LATER

"How was work, honey?" Mom asked as she set a pile of steaming bread rolls in the middle of the table.

"Funny you should ask," Dad drawled with a lopsided grin as he reached for one and broke it in half. "It was an eventful day."

Mom held up a hand. "You didn't deal with any dead bodies, did you?"

"Not today," Dad said as he bit into his roll.

Mom relaxed. "Okay. So, what happened?"

"The first call we got was from a woman who got her toe stuck in a faucet."

Violet came out of her reverie and frowned at her father. "What kind of faucet?"

"A tub faucet."

Violet's brows bunched together. "Why would she do that?"

"I stopped asking questions like that my first year on the job," Dad said as he forked up chicken and green beans.

"You didn't have to amputate anything, did you?" Mom asked.

"Ew, Mom!" Violet waved her hand to dissipate the images in her mind.

"No amputation necessary. Just some lubricant." Dad snickered. "She seemed thrilled to have an audience and carried on drinking her wine and eating chocolates long after the bubbles were gone." Dad bobbed his eyebrows at Mom, who gasped and smacked his arm. "I covered her in a bath towel, which she kept trying to take off while asking if any of us were single. She was entertaining, to say the least."

"Was she?" Mom said testily.

Violet's lips quirked. Automatically, her gaze flicked to Jesse to see his reaction to their parents' playful bickering. Her amusement faded. Jesse stared pensively down at his food, oblivious to their conversation. She noticed he'd been preoccupied lately. She could hear him pacing in his room in the wee hours of the morning. He'd also been coming home late from school, even when he didn't have practice.

Whatever was bothering him hadn't affected his sex drive, however. He was more ravenous than ever. Ever since they had sex at church, it was like he *wanted* to get caught. He was becoming alarmingly brazen. She didn't know who he was anymore. When he looked at her, she didn't see her brother at all, but a stranger.

At lunch today, Brody nudged her and jerked his chin across the cafeteria, where Jesse sat with an odd mix of people.

"What's going on there?" Brody asked.

"No idea," she'd said, but her gaze was on the stunning redhead who had her hand on Jesse's arm.

Georgia had pressed against her back to whisper excitedly, "Ooh. Are they dating?"

She'd turned away with a shrug while Brody said, "Jesse and Faye? He hasn't said anything about her, but it sure looks like she's willing."

While the guys joked around, Georgia said, "They make a

striking couple. Jesse hasn't dated anyone this year, has he? What's the deal?"

When Violet bit into her sandwich to avoid answering, Georgia poked her in her side.

"You're his sister. You should be able to give us the inside scoop. I can't believe he doesn't tell you anything. You guys are always together."

"Jesse's a gentleman," Marie interjected. "He doesn't kiss and tell. He's the only guy I know who's stayed friends with all his exes. None of them has a bad thing to say about him, except for the fact that he broke up with them. He gave them princess treatment for a few weeks—opening their door, pulling out their chairs, buying them flowers, and then *bam*." Marie clapped her hands. "He says they're done. No warning, no explanation other than it wasn't working out. None of them can make sense of it. They'd take him back in a heartbeat if he asked."

"I think Madyson took it the hardest. I heard Trent broke up with her because Jesse's all she talked about." Georgia looked around before she added, "It's been, like, a year. You'd think she'd be over him by now."

"Can you really blame her? Jesse's everything any girl could want in a boyfriend."

Violet tuned out her friends and fantasized about her senior year when she wouldn't have to listen to her friends gush about what a gentleman Jesse was. If they only knew what he'd done to her on the way to school that morning...

Jesse's gaze abruptly rose and speared hers. Her stomach clenched. She switched her attention back to Dad and forced herself to eat, even though she wasn't hungry. She hoped Jesse dated Faye and transferred all his kinky, erotic fantasies to the gorgeous redhead instead of her. He was a sex fanatic. Perverted, twisted. He never missed an opportunity to have his way with her. The only time she was free of his advances was when she turned in for the night and locked the bedroom and bathroom door. The next day, the battle to avoid him began anew.

Jesse was still staring at her. She resolutely ignored him and focused on Dad, who laughed as he told a story about his coworker who had to defend himself against a guy wielding an umbrella like a sword while high on some psychedelic drug.

"And then, Derrick leaps at him and says..." Dad chortled.

"I joined the Air Force."

Jesse's statement was said so casually that Violet ignored it. It wasn't until silence fell, and she registered that Mom and Dad were both gawking at Jesse, that she processed what he said.

Shock made her fingers fumble her fork, which clattered loudly as it dropped on her plate. She assumed Jesse would go to college, but if he went into the military, that would be even better! Her lips curved in what felt like the first genuine smile she'd had all year.

"You did *what*?"

Lynne's hoarse voice snapped Violet out of her giddy delight. Registering the tension in the air, she bowed her head to hide her joy, but at Jesse's silence, she glanced at him and found him watching her through narrowed eyes.

"Jesse?"

Lynne's tone was part plea, part demand. Slowly, Jesse transferred his attention to his mother who sat across the table from him.

"I enlisted," Jesse said calmly.

"H-how? You didn't ask for my consent. I didn't sign anything allowing you to—"

"I'm eighteen, Mom."

Lynne's expression went from horror to outrage as she shouted, "You haven't talked about the military for years!"

Jesse didn't bat an eye at his mother's outburst. "Because it upset you, not because I changed my mind."

"You saw what losing your father did to me, and you're volunteering to put yourself in the same position?"

"I made a promise," Jesse said quietly.

Lynne slammed her fist on the table. "Do you think your father would ask you to honor that promise if he knew he would die at thirty?"

"He died with honor."

"He *died* instead of having a life with us. He *died* instead of getting out when I begged him to." Lynne's eyes glistened with tears. "Have you sworn in?" When Jesse hesitated, Lynne shot to her feet. "I forbid it, Jesse. Quit now before it's too late."

"Mom."

"I'm serious. I can't go through that again." Lynne ran her hands through her hair. "I can't believe you'd even consider…"

Violet jolted when Lynne abruptly turned on her.

"You didn't try to talk him out of it?"

Taken aback, Violet opened and closed her mouth, unsure what to say. She knew Lynne had a temper, but she had never been on the receiving end of it until now. Her glee vanished in the face of Lynne's wild despair.

"Violet didn't know. I did this on my own," Jesse interjected.

"Lynne," Dad said in a consoling tone. "Let's talk about this."

"Talk?" Lynne scoffed as she paced with her arms wrapped around herself. "Apparently, talking isn't something we do in this house anymore. People just make major life decisions without telling anyone."

"Mom, this is my dream."

Lynne planted her hands on the table and leaned toward her son. "You idolize your father, but his choices don't have to be yours. You don't have to walk the same path as him. There are better paths. You could be somebody, Jesse. You're talented in so many areas. Why let them decide what to do with your life? Why submit yourself to that harsh environment? You should enjoy your freedom." A tear slid down her cheek. "Why do you want to leave us?"

Jesse swallowed, displaying his first sign of discomfort.

"I don't want to leave you."

"So, don't! Don't go!"

Jesse lowered his gaze to his plate. "I have to do this."

"Why?" Lynne cried.

Violet's heart thudded in her ears as silence fell. Jesse was usually so careful and considerate of his mother. It was painful to see them at odds. Lynne looked distraught, but Jesse was standing his ground. Even though she'd initially been ecstatic at the news, Lynne's devastation was contagious and made her own eyes water.

A crack of thunder made her flinch as the heavens opened and rain began to lash the windows.

"Vi," Dad said quietly.

She was relieved to be excused from the table and the highly charged environment. No one said a word as she left her half-eaten dinner and made her way to her bedroom. She closed the door and winced when she heard Lynne explode. Her shouting was accompanied by another deafening boom of thunder that shook the house. She put on her headphones and let her punk rock music drown out the unexpected storms that had appeared out of nowhere.

Conflicting emotions sloshed around inside of her. On one hand, she was thrilled. If Jesse went into the Air Force, she'd be free. As Mom said, *they* would decide Jesse's life. He wouldn't be able to come home whenever he felt like it, like he would if he attended college and had holidays and school breaks. Once he signed, he had to fulfill his commitment, which was a minimum of four years for Active Duty.

It never crossed her mind that Jesse would join the military. Like Lynne, she used to get upset when he brought it up. That was when she actually cared about what he did with his life. Now, she wanted him gone. Out of her life, out of the state, out of the country, if possible. She bit her lip. She despised him, but she didn't want him dead. Lynne was acting like Jesse would be sent to the front lines. Surely, Mom was overreacting?

Is this what he wanted to talk about when he drove her out to see the bluebonnets? She assumed he wanted to talk about which college he should attend. He hadn't talked about the military in years. If Jesse had given her a choice of him going to college or the military, what would she have said? She tossed her hair, not willing to entertain such thoughts. Jesse's future wasn't her business. It was his, and he made the decision to enlist, which she was happy about —ecstatic, in fact.

Her life had become an endless tunnel with no light, no detours, no one to hold her hand. Jesse would jump her in the dark and corner and coerce her to get what he wanted before he disappeared, leaving her to piece herself back together and carry on, hand outstretched, as she tried to find her way in the pitch-black abyss. Sometimes, when she was too broken to walk, she crawled. She kept going, believing there had to be something up ahead. Jesse's announcement caused a pinprick of light to cut through the dark, giving her a vision of a near future where there would be no tunnel, no filth, no more structuring her life around ways to avoid him. There was an end to her misery and despite Lynne's fear, all Violet felt was overwhelming relief.

She tried to distract herself with homework, but her attention strayed. She tugged aside the headphones periodically to check if the coast was clear. The arguing went on for hours. Most of the time, it was Lynne who was shouting, but there was also the low murmur of Dad's voice in what sounded like a conciliatory tone.

She'd decided to turn in for the night and had just brushed her teeth and locked the bathroom door behind her when her bedroom door opened. When Mom poked her head in, Violet tugged off her headphones and held them in one hand as she took in Lynne's red, puffy eyes. Her anxiety spiked as she waited for the verdict. Had Mom talked Jesse out of joining the Air Force?

"Mom?"

When Lynne's face crumpled, she rushed forward, partly because it looked like Lynne was going to collapse and partly because she didn't want Lynne to see her jubilation. Comforting Lynne while she inwardly did cartwheels made her feel like a bad person, but she couldn't help it. No one knew who Jesse truly was. This was best for all of them, Lynne just didn't know it. As Lynne wept, that tiny bead of light in her tunnel began to expand and brighten, so she could practically feel its warmth.

Lynne pulled back and braced her hands on her shoulders. "Please talk to him. He hasn't sworn in. There's still a chance for him to get out of his commitment."

Alarm cut through Violet's contentment. "I... I don't think anything I say will make a difference. His mind is made up and..." She looked away from Lynne's heartbroken eyes. "He didn't tell me what he was going to do. It seems like he didn't want anyone to dissuade him."

Lynne squeezed her arms. "You're his best friend. You two are closer than blood siblings. If you tell him you want him to stay, that you need him here, he might do it for you."

Her throat began to close as anxiety ripped through her. "We've grown apart."

"You still mean the world to him. You can save him from making a huge mistake."

"I..."

"Just try. Please."

An invisible object obstructed her throat so she couldn't breathe, making her eyes tear. Lynne cupped her cheek, expression softening, assuming they were on the same wavelength when nothing could be further from the truth.

Lynne kissed her cheek. "Sleep. Hopefully, we'll wake up and this will all just be a horrible dream."

After Mom left, she waited a few minutes to see if Dad was going to pop in. When he didn't, she locked that door, too, and climbed into bed. She stared at the ceiling as she listened to the rain hammer down on the roof. A tree branch Dad had been meaning to cut scraped the side of the house as the wind picked up.

Is that what Jesse had been doing after school? Getting his paperwork and tests done to qualify and enlist? Even though Jesse hadn't sworn in (whatever that meant), hopefully he was too far along in the process to back out without consequences. She would do almost anything for Lynne, but begging Jesse to stay wasn't one of them. She pounded her pillow as she turned on her side. Jesse would be fine in the military. There was no need for Lynne to worry about him. This was a dream come true.

———

She woke when a hand clamped over her mouth. Her eyes flew open as a man sat on top of her. She panicked and thrashed as his weight sank her into the mattress. She let out a scream that was significantly muffled by his hand and the storm, which was still raging.

A head ducked down, and a nose brushed against hers before she heard, "Happy I'm joining the military, baby?"

Her heart stuttered at Jesse's furious hiss.

"If I hadn't promised my dad I would follow in his footsteps, I wouldn't be going anywhere," he growled as he took his hand away.

Fear made her strike out. She heard a satisfying crack as her palm hit his cheek. He cursed and a second later, his mouth landed on hers. The taste of spearmint mouthwash overwhelmed her as his tongue invaded. She raked her nails over him and realized he was naked. He hissed, back arching as she tried to draw blood. His mouth left hers and coasted down to where her neck flowed into her shoulder. He sank his teeth into her as he grabbed her wrists and pinned them to the mattress. She kicked her feet as he bit to punish. When she whimpered, he eased the pressure and then kissed her throbbing flesh as if he hadn't used brute force to make her submit like they were part of the animal kingdom.

"You want to fight, baby? I'm in an obliging mood," he said against her skin. "Mom used everything she could to make me quit." His tongue slid over her racing pulse. "I assume she asked you to beg me to stay?"

She clenched her teeth.

He nipped her jaw. "Answer me."

"Yes," she said sullenly.

He lifted his head to look down at her. With her nightlight at the foot of her bed, his face was in shadow, but she still felt the intensity of his stare.

"So? What are you going to do, Violet?" He pressed his lips to hers. "What are you willing to sacrifice to make Mom happy?"

"I love her."

He stilled.

"But not enough to ask you to stay."

He was silent for a beat before he said, "So be it."

He parted her legs with his knee and nestled his erection between her legs. Her flimsy pajama shorts were poor protection from his scorching heat and his hard dick, which she knew would be inside of her very soon. She yanked at her imprisoned wrists, which only made him tighten his grip. She wished she had the balls to scream her head off and have Mom and Dad catch him in the act. But she would rather endure whatever Jesse had planned than witness the look on Dad's face when he discovered she was no longer pure.

"You can't do this here!" she said desperately. "Mom and Dad are right down the hall!"

"Then we better be quiet."

As he brushed kisses over her face, she considered head-butting him. What was with this affectionate bullshit? They rarely kissed. All he usually cared about was getting off. Foreplay was minimal. That's how she preferred it. She just wanted to get this over with. Why...? She stiffened as it finally hit her.

"How did you get in here? I locked both doors!"

"I broke the lock on the bathroom door."

"You—"

"Ask Dad to repair it, I'll break it again."

He slid off her onto his side and hauled her up in bed, so she was propped on her pillows. Before she could roll away, he yanked her camisole down and latched onto her breast while his hand slid into her pants.

"You want me out of your life, fine, but that means I get full access," he growled as he parted her.

His middle finger slid in with embarrassing ease.

Ashamed by her body's response, she snapped, "Can't you get this from Faye instead of me?"

"Faye?" he muttered around her nipple.

She gritted her teeth. "Yes, the redhead hanging on your arm at lunch."

His dick jerked against her thigh. "Jealous?"

She smacked his shoulder as his thumb began to tease her clit. "No! I want you to find someone else to fulfill your sick fantasies instead of me!"

"There's little chance of that happening," he said distractedly as he worked her. "Faye's brother just joined the Air Force, so I've been talking to him about his experience and what to expect. I've been connecting with others who are joining other branches, and Faye decided to tag along. She's nice, but..."

He rubbed himself against her.

"She isn't you." He kissed the base of her throat. "Touch me, Vi."

Her hand balled into a fist. Quick as lightning, the hand in her pants disappeared, and his wet finger was shoved into her mouth. She gripped his wrist with both hands to stop him from shoving his finger down her throat.

"I swear to God if you don't put your hand on me, I'll..." He let out a breath when her hand closed around him. "Good. Now, stroke me the way I taught you."

She obeyed, simultaneously sucking on the finger he hadn't withdrawn from her mouth. He hissed through his teeth and arched into her touch.

"Slow down," he ground out.

Fuck you, she thought, tightening her grip to make him blow.

She sensed his control snap a second before he yanked her hand off him.

"I warned you I wasn't in the mood," he hissed.

When he sat up and reached for her, she lost her temper. Screw him! She didn't care about his mood or what he wanted. He wasn't supposed to do this kind of shit when Mom and Dad were present. What the hell was wrong with him?

They tussled. Her stuffed animals and pillows went flying. Jesse leapt off the bed, yanked her onto her back and dragged her, so her head was hanging off the mattress. Before she could figure out why he'd positioned her so bizarrely, Jesse cupped her jaw, forcing her head back. She had a split second of warning before his dick slid into her mouth and Jesse planted himself in her throat.

She panicked, hands and legs wheeling through the air as she choked. Jesse withdrew enough for her to breathe. She coughed and tried to turn her head aside, but he collared her throat and ordered, "Be still."

She moaned in protest and pushed at him, but she was trapped by his iron thighs and the rock-hard dick impaling her mouth. In this position, she was completely helpless and at his mercy.

"You didn't listen to me, so now we're going to do this my way." He let his hand wander from her throat to her breasts. "You're gonna suck me until I tell you to stop. You fight me and try to make me come before I'm ready, you'll regret it."

Slowly, he pushed forward. She screwed her eyes shut and made a concentrated effort not to fight him and control her gag reflex. She heard him expel his breath and knew he was pleased when he gripped her breast.

"Yes, just like that," he groaned.

She gripped the backs of his corded thighs and obeyed every husky command. She was rewarded for her good behavior when he yanked off her bottoms, spread her thighs, and put his mouth between her legs. As all the blood rushed to her head, she felt a euphoric rush. Jesse knew her body well and used everything in his arsenal to rouse her to a fever pitch. She got so lost in what they were doing that she grabbed his ass to yank him toward her so she could take every inch of him.

She felt more than heard his guttural groan before he yanked out of her mouth as if it were an electrical socket. As she lay there, panting, he cupped the back of her head and lifted it to give her a deep, wet, upside-down kiss.

"That's my girl," he husked before he pulled her into a sitting position.

She didn't have time to get her bearings because he pulled her off the bed and promptly bent her over it. She buried her face in her tangled sheets, which was convenient because a second later, she screamed when he slammed inside of her. He froze with his body blanketing hers, but she was too far gone to care. She bounced under him and wrapped her hand around the back of his neck, urging him on. He dropped his head on her shoulder, panting as he grappled for control.

"You're killing me, Vi."

"Hurry," she whispered.

Outside, the storm seemed to be picking up, thunder crashing like cymbals, gearing up so they could have this moment.

He nuzzled her cheek. "Tell me you want me."

She bared her teeth. He wasn't satisfied that he controlled her body, he always pushed for more. He was such an asshole.

"Vi, you need this, same as me. You can't deny it." When she didn't answer, his hand fisted in her hair. "Why can't you admit it?"

Because she would rather die than give in completely. He may rule her in these moments, but there was still a part of her he hadn't conquered. Would *never* conquer. It was what gave her the strength to resist and soldier through every day, even though sometimes she considered giving up. She would never surrender that piece of her identity to him. If she did, she would be lost.

He capitulated with a ragged, "Fuck," before he began to move.

With nature colluding with them to disguise their forbidden

tryst, she let herself go. She let herself enjoy the pleasures of the flesh she normally denied herself in the light of day and made demands he gave into, leading to an orgasm that made her gnaw her sheets.

"Tell me," Jesse pleaded. "Just this one time. Please."

She ignored him and lay like a limp, wrecked doll. She knew what to expect and wasn't disappointed when he went berserk. Jesse took his frustrations out on her body. When she began to make too much noise, he clapped a hand over her mouth. When that didn't work, he shoved her face in the mattress and put a pillow over her head. He ended up using it himself when he came, folding over her and shouting her name into the stuffing.

Even as he spilled inside of her, he shoved the pillow away and hissed, "Deny all you want, but we both know the truth. You love what's between us, you're just too much of a coward to admit it."

He pulled out of her, spilling down the back of her thighs. By the time her quivering legs collapsed, and she landed on her knees beside the bed, he was already gone.

CHAPTER 19
VIOLET

2 MONTHS LATER

Despite the warm July evening, there was a healthy fire crackling in the fire pit. The backyard, house, and garage were filled to capacity for Jesse's farewell party. Firefighters mingled with Jesse's coaches, teammates, and their church friends. It seemed that half the neighborhood had decided to attend. Mom's friends, mostly teachers, went around patting cheeks and catching up with students they hadn't seen since elementary school.

Violet couldn't believe this day had finally come. Jesse was leaving tomorrow. A part of her kept expecting something to go wrong—for his paperwork to fall through or there to be some mix up that would eject him from the military before he could be shipped off, but everything had gone smoothly. Mom tried to talk Jesse out of his decision until he swore in, and there was no turning back. This week had been rough on Mom. She'd excused herself multiple times from the party to have a crying session.

A commotion in the house caught Violet's attention. She started forward as Dad emerged, carrying a massive cake. People clapped

Jesse on the back and ushered him toward the table where Dad set it down. The cake had a pair of combat boots, a fighter jet, and the Air Force logo with, "We will miss you, Jesse," written on it.

At everyone's urgings, Jesse posed with his cake. Violet felt obliged to take pictures. Not for herself, but for Lynne. Even with everyone calling out for Jesse to look in their direction, he looked directly at her. She hastily took the photo and then fiddled with her phone until Dad began to address the crowd with his hand on Jesse's shoulder.

"I'm happy you all could join us to celebrate Jesse before he sets out on his journey," Dad said in a voice that carried clearly across the backyard. "I couldn't ask for a better son. Lynne and I are so proud of you. We know you're going to do great things in the world."

Everyone whistled and cheered as Dad and Jesse gave each other manly claps on the back. Lynne walked up to Jesse, dabbing her eyes with her handkerchief. Clearly too emotional to speak, Lynne kissed Jesse on the cheek and gave him a hug.

As people turned to Violet with expectant faces, she felt a flash of panic. No one told her she'd have to say a few words and give Jesse a public farewell.

"Come, Vi," Dad said, beckoning to her. "Let's take a family photo before we cut the cake."

She pasted a smile on her face as she made her way over. She and Lynne stood side by side, while Dad and Jesse stood behind them. As everyone playfully jostled for the best position to take their photo, pride swelled in her chest. She knew what the photos would capture. Dad and Jesse with their impressive, fit figures towering over her and Mom, who wore matching floral dresses, hers in pink and Mom's in yellow. Dad and Jesse wore matching white button up shirts for precisely this reason. Mom had known there would be a ton of photos taken and wanted them to be ready. Their family had its issues, but at that moment, Violet didn't want to be anywhere else. This is where she belonged.

Blinding flashes came from every direction. Their heads whipped back and forth, trying to give everyone the opportunity to get the perfect shot, but it was so chaotic that everyone began to laugh. Grinning, Violet stepped forward, only to be stopped by a pair of arms that pulled her back against a toned frame. Jesse wrapped his arms around her, pressed his cheek to hers, and rocked her from side to side. A series of "aww's" came from the women who thought Jesse's gesture was sweet. She kept her lips curved as her nails sank warningly into the back of his hand.

"Violet! Jesse! Look here!"

She looked in the direction of the voice and saw her friend Allison holding up her phone to take their photo. She endured Jesse's touch for a few more seconds before she tried to move away. Jesse hesitated for a split second before he released her.

"This cake is something else," Violet said enthusiastically as she stepped up to Mom's side.

"And it's supposed to taste even better than it looks," Mom said as she handed Jesse the first slice, which was a shocking bright blue.

"It's blueberry?" Jesse asked, eyeing the cake warily.

Mom laughed. "No, that's just dye. It's chocolate."

Everyone laughed at Jesse's obvious relief. As Dad went to fetch ice cream, Violet arranged slices of cake on a tray and began to circulate through the crowd.

She was waylaid often. It had been a while since she'd seen her uncles—a mix of firefighters, paramedics, and police officers who had known her since she was born. They wanted to know if she was going to follow in Dad's footsteps, as she'd said she would when she was five. They guffawed when she gave an adamant, "Nope!"

After a series of hugs, she moved on and found herself face to face with Pastor Sonny. "Hey!"

"Hey, yourself," he said and eyed the last plate on her tray. "Is that spoken for?"

"No! It's all yours."

She handed it to him and prepared to run when he tapped her shoulder.

"I've been meaning to talk to you, Violet."

Her heart dropped to her toes as she turned back to him. "You have?"

She avoided him just as much as Jesse, if not more so. If anyone could discern what was happening, it would be Pastor Sonny. He was a kind man, but his gaze was piercing and stern, and she felt like he could see straight through people to their rotten core. She dreaded going to church. It seemed his sermons were tailor-made to rip her conscience to shreds every week.

"Yes. I was wondering if you were interested in becoming a mentor for the youth."

"Mentor?" She cleared her throat. "That's... wow."

His eyes tracked over her face and fractionally narrowed. "You're not interested."

It wasn't a question.

She tucked the empty tray under her arm and glanced around the room instead of meeting his eyes. "I've never considered being a mentor."

"That's why I think you should do it. I notice you prefer being in the background, assisting rather than taking a leadership role, but I think you have a lot to offer. I've known you since you were a little girl. You have wisdom to share with the young ones who need guidance for this next stage in life."

As she struggled to think of something to say, he lightly touched her arm.

"Think about it and let me know."

She watched him walk away before she gave herself a shake and hurried out to the backyard to do exactly what he said she liked to do —assist. Assisting meant she didn't have to take the fall if something went awry. Assisting meant there was always work to be done. Keeping busy kept her from pondering too much. He thought she had wisdom to share? She was the last person anyone should come to for advice. She'd made a mess of her life.

When she tried to load her tray again, Mom gave her a little push.

"You've been on your feet all day. If people want cake, they'll come looking. Enjoy the party. Go hang out with Jesse and your friends."

Mom jerked her chin at the fire pit where most of the teenagers had congregated. She didn't want to talk to anybody, but she could see Mom wasn't going to let her continue to bustle around.

She accepted the cake slice Mom placed in her hands and wandered over to her peers. Allison hopped up from the lounge chair where she and her boyfriend, Jesse's classmate, Blaine, were relaxing.

"This picture of you and Jesse is so *cute*," Allison exclaimed as she tapped her phone screen. "I already posted it and everyone is dying."

Allison held up her phone, so Violet could see the photo of her and Jesse. She wasn't expecting much, considering how far away Allison had been, but the edited results were devastating. She and Jesse beamed at the camera, faces pressed together, his arms wrapped around her. There was no trace of unease, anger, or bitterness on her face. She looked like she didn't want to be anywhere else but in his arms. They looked happy. How the hell was that possible?

"Violet?" Allison lowered the phone and steadied her plate, which was shaking. "Are you okay?"

She pulled herself together. "Yes, of course."

Allison rubbed her arm. "I can't imagine how you feel. You two are inseparable. It's going to be so weird seeing you without him."

"He's following his dream."

Allison nodded. "I had no idea he wanted to go into the military. Most thought he would go into the NFL. I heard some scouts were interested in him, and that's why Coach Rick was so upset when he quit football."

Violet's stomach flipped. "I never heard that."

Allison gestured to her boyfriend. "That's what Blaine said."

"And what's Blaine's plans now that he's graduated?" Violet asked, blatantly changing the subject.

Allison lit up. "He's staying here."

"That's great. But didn't he get into Dartmouth?"

Allison looked over her shoulder at Blaine before she turned back and whispered, "He decided to stay for me. He was worried we wouldn't be able to do long distance, so he'll wait another year before we decide where we want to go."

"Aww, you guys are so in *love*," Violet teased.

Allison practically glowed. "Yes, we are. I think he's it for me." Allison gripped her arm and whispered, "He proposed."

"What?"

"He didn't get me a ring yet, but we've talked about getting married after I graduate next year." Allison gave a little squeal. "Can you imagine me married exactly a year from now?"

"No."

"Well, if we do, just know you're going to be a bridesmaid." Allison giggled when Violet made a face. "Come on. Who doesn't love a wedding? Is it crazy that I want to be the first friend to get married and have kids?"

"Yes," Violet said emphatically.

Allison pouted. "Can't you be happy for me? Isn't he a great guy?"

Violet swallowed hard. "He's the best."

"How lucky am I to have found *the one* in high school? What are the chances?"

Their mindsets couldn't be more different. Allison was thinking of settling down and getting married and having kids, while Violet felt like her life hadn't begun. She wanted freedom and to get away from everyone and everything she'd ever known. Commitment was the last thing on her mind.

Instead of voicing her negative, cynical thoughts, Violet smiled and offered Allison a piece of her cake.

Two hours later, the crowd had significantly thinned as people began to take their leave. The mood had shifted as well, becoming more somber as people said their official goodbyes. Everyone kept giving her sympathetic pats or squeezes, assuming she was taking Jesse's departure as bad as Lynne when she felt nothing at all. Her stoic demeanor had been getting her some odd, sidelong looks. Shouldn't people be happy she wasn't imitating a human water faucet?

She escaped down the hallway for a break from the intense scrutiny and entered Jesse's bedroom. His door had been left ajar, so guests could use their bathroom if the other was in use. She was relieved to discover it empty. She turned to close the door, which abruptly began to swing open again.

"Oh, I'm sorry," she began with a laugh, intending to say the bathroom was occupied, but her voice died when Jesse pushed his way in. "What are you...?"

She didn't get to finish her question because his head swooped down, and his mouth settled on hers. He clasped her face and kissed her like the world was about to end. She was momentarily stunned, but the sound of someone cheering in the distance reminded her that they had a house full of guests. What the hell was he *doing*?

She wrenched her mouth away. "Have you lost your mind?"

"This should be the happiest night of my life," he said gruffly. "Everyone I care about is gathered in one place to see me off. I'm about to set out on my lifelong dream and make my father proud. I should be over the fucking moon, so why do I feel so miserable?"

Had one of his friends slipped him alcohol, even with cops and a pastor present? Sucking in an annoyed breath, she looked up, intending to snap him back to reality, but the sight of his spiky lashes and blue eyes shimmering with tears made her mind go blank.

"How did I fuck this up so badly?" he said thickly.

She averted her gaze. "Everyone will be looking for you. You should go back to the party."

"I can't leave tomorrow with things like this between us," he said, resting his forehead against hers. "Tell me there's a chance we can still be together in the future."

"This isn't the time for this!" Her voice was terse with stress.

"We're out of time, Violet. This is it." He massaged her nape to encourage her to look at him. "Tell me I didn't lose the most important person in the world to me."

She braced her hand on his chest and strained away from him. "The door isn't locked. Anyone could come in. All these people are here for you. You should be focused on them, not—"

"Look at me!"

His raised voice made her stiffen in alarm.

"Are you crazy? What the hell are you trying to do?" she hissed.

His face flushed with anger as he gripped her shoulders and gave her a shake. "I'm trying to get through to you. I need you to stop looking through me and actually hear what I'm saying."

Of course, he was forcing this confrontation the night before he left, when everyone they'd ever known was just a few rooms away.

She jutted out her chin. "What *are* you saying?"

His hands flexed on her shoulders. "I'm saying that I know what I did was wrong, and you have every right to hate me. I promised to protect you and couldn't protect you from myself."

His expression was a mix of frustration and desperation.

"I know I need to work on myself and that it's best for both of us if I leave. I told myself I wouldn't pressure you, but I need to know." He brushed her hair back with trembling fingers. "Give me some hope. Tell me there's a part of you that still feels something for me."

She held his gaze and deliberately let seconds that felt like hours tick by. She felt no remorse as his face contorted with pain.

He swallowed hard, making his Adam's apple bob. "Can you forgive me?"

Months ago, she forgave him without thinking, naively believing what Dad said—that no act was unforgivable. But what Jesse had done to her, what he stole over and over again... it wasn't forgivable. As if he heard her thoughts, a tear slid down his cheek.

"Vi," he whispered, but whatever he was going to say was interrupted by someone calling his name.

Fear gave her the strength to shove him hard enough that he rocked back.

"They need you. Go!" she ordered.

His anguish was plain to see. Hopefully, everyone would attribute his distress to nerves over leaving home for the great unknown.

"Violet."

"Go, now!" she said harshly.

He swiped his sleeve over his dripping eyes before he turned and walked out of the bathroom. She stood there for a minute, staring at the place where he'd been standing, before she glanced in the mirror and saw her pale, blank face. Abruptly, she pushed on the door that led to her bedroom. The drawers she'd pushed in front of it, so no guests would wander into her bedroom by accident, gave way. Once she was in, she repositioned her makeshift barricade and locked her other door as well. She sent a quick text to Mom, letting her know she had a migraine and needed to lay down, and got a heart emoji in response.

She kicked off her shoes and, without bothering to change, lay on the bed in her dress. She stared at the ceiling with her hands folded neatly over her middle and tried to relax. Jesse's behavior and mood swings over the last few weeks had swung from one extreme to the next. Some days he was cold and remote. On others, he was cruel. The worst days were when he was affectionate and kind. She didn't know which Jesse she would get day to day, so she kept her guard up and didn't trust any version of him she encountered.

Including this one.

Can you forgive me?

Her hands balled into fists. How dare he ask her that after everything he put her through? He'd hijacked not just her junior year, which was one big blur, he'd taken over her *life*. He segregated her from everyone, making her an outcast not just amongst their friends, but in their family as well. Because no one believed he was capable of such dastardly deeds, she had no one to confide in or turn to.

To have her brother, who she trusted implicitly, turn into her worst enemy was a betrayal of such epic proportions that she still couldn't wrap her mind around it. She hadn't just lost her sense of self—she lost her best friend and confidant. The person she used to run to for comfort, advice, and support disappeared. In his place was a monster who looked like him and sounded like him but did the most horrific things to her. He weaponized all her faults and weaknesses against her.

Jesse stopped seeing her as a person. She became an obsession, an object to be conquered and claimed. Sex whittled their relationship down to nothing. Their verbal communication and emotional connection ceased to exist, leaving them with no foundation to rebuild upon. He irreparably damaged her trust, not just in him, but herself. How could she trust her judgment when she'd been so easily duped by his sincere, good brother act? How could she not have sensed the evil lurking behind his guileless smile? Her confidence and self-esteem had taken so many blows, she didn't feel like a whole person anymore. She no longer knew how to make a simple decision without examining it from every angle and listing every possible repercussion and consequence.

Lately, Jesse's fixation had gone into overdrive. It was like he was trying to fuse them together. He was insatiable, possessed. To preserve her sanity against his brutal onslaught, she wrapped herself in a cocoon that insulated her from his destructive wrath. The more erratic and out of control Jesse became, the calmer and more detached she was. She could see that infuriated him, but she didn't care. Self-preservation was all that mattered. All she had to do was hang on just a little longer.

She'd been counting down the months, weeks, and now, hours.

She glanced at the clock and felt her heart soar. Twelve hours until he was gone. Until she got her freedom back. Until everything went back to normal. All she had to do was close her eyes. When she woke, they would have a few hours together, and then she could close the book on this chapter of her life and move on.

CHAPTER 20
VIOLET

Violet lurched up in bed before her eyes were fully open. Sunlight filtered through her blinds. She sprang up, energized, even though she'd only gotten a few hours of sleep. She tossed and turned past midnight, listening to the constant hum of voices drift down the hallway. She worried that she may have to deal with Jesse on his final night, but thankfully, he'd been otherwise occupied.

She muscled aside the drawers to gain access to the bathroom and hastily locked the door that led to Jesse's bedroom before she washed her face and brushed her teeth. There was no sound coming from Jesse's bedroom. Either he'd gotten even less sleep than her and was already up, or he was sleeping soundly. She hoped it was the latter so she wouldn't have to deal with him until he was ready to leave.

As she pulled her hair into a ponytail, she met her eyes in the mirror. Although her body buzzed with excitement, it didn't reflect in her dull eyes or stony expression. Keeping their secret had taken its toll.

Once Jesse was gone, she could actually sleep through the night —what a concept! She could enjoy life again. This was her last full summer in Texas. She should enjoy it because after she graduated, she was going to get as far from here as Mom and Dad would allow. Jesse hadn't even left yet, and she was already dreading him coming home for a visit. She needed a place where she felt safe. As long as he was allowed to walk through the front door, that would never be here. She wanted to forget everything that had happened between them and bury the sinful desires he provoked within her.

Tell me I didn't lose the most important person in the world to me.

If that were true, he would have respected her boundaries. He wouldn't have gone as far as he had. He had moments of remorse that never lasted long. Several times, he had the gall to suggest the things he did were an act of love. He was so manipulative and controlling. He would say anything to justify his behavior. His acting skills would serve him well in the future. It had gotten him this far without being caught.

She unlocked Jesse's door before she escaped back into her bedroom and hastily changed out of her pajamas. She walked down the hallway to the dining room but paused when she heard Mom sniffling and Dad's consoling tone.

"I don't want him to go," Lynne cried.

"You knew this day would come. Jesse's smart and strong. He's going to do well in the military. It's what he's always wanted," Dad said.

"He's just liked his father. He's too willing to lay his life on the line and too loyal to let anyone down. He'll give his life to them when there are so many opportunities outside of the military. He could have done anything! I was hoping he would change his mind and take after you."

There was a pause before Dad said, "It's not like my job doesn't come without risks."

"But at least we get to see you throughout the week. I can't believe he didn't stay for Violet. They were so close. What happened between them?"

Violet retreated to her bedroom. Mom had been convinced she

could make Jesse change his mind and had badgered her more than Jesse. Every day, she had to lie through her teeth about pleading with Jesse to stay and being repeatedly turned down. Lynne's disappointment made her feel awful. Trying to act as if she were upset about Jesse's choice when it couldn't be further from the truth drained her. She couldn't wait for him to leave. The strain of keeping up this act was killing her. Once he left, Mom would learn how to cope without Jesse being within arm's reach, and they could build a new life without him.

She pushed her bedroom door open and stopped on the threshold when she saw Jesse standing beside her bed.

"Morning," he said.

"Morning," she echoed and stayed where she was.

He wore shorts and a white tee with his gold cross on display. His eyes were bloodshot and puffy from lack of sleep. She hoped, for his sake, his training didn't begin the moment he stepped foot on base. Actually, on second thought, she hoped there was a drill sergeant ready to stomp his ass the moment he arrived.

"You look..."

He ran his hand through his hair. "I didn't sleep."

"What time did everyone leave?"

"Brody left an hour ago." He rubbed the back of his neck. "I can't believe I'm leaving today."

"I think it's best."

He winced but nodded. An awkward silence fell.

"You should rest while you can," she said.

"No. I can always catch up on sleep. I don't want to waste the time I have left."

His eyes moved over her with such naked hunger that she tensed.

"Vi..."

"Mom's crying," she interrupted. "You should go to her."

"She has Dad."

"But she wants you."

"She's going to have to get used to me not being around." He extended his hand, palm up. "Please."

She hastily drew back. *"No."*

"Not that. I just want to hold you, I swear. I..." His expression morphed into one of abject torment. "I need you, Violet."

Ignoring his beseeching tone, she turned on her heel and marched down the hallway. When she entered the dining room, she was grateful to see Mom's episode had passed, and she was cooking in the kitchen while Dad sat at the table, drinking coffee and reading his Bible.

"You're up early, Vi," Dad observed.

"Couldn't sleep," she said and tried to look sad. She must have done a good job because Dad held out his arm. Since he wasn't one to offer hugs, she seized the opportunity and let him wrap her up tight. A second later, his hold loosened.

"Jesse," Dad greeted, ruining their moment.

She didn't turn to look at him but walked away to help Mom. She took over cooking, so Mom could sit with Jesse. Pastor Sonny's words slipped through her mind as she served breakfast and hopped up every time someone needed something. For some reason, she couldn't stay still.

Her hands fidgeted on her lap as Dad shared the passage he'd been reading in his Bible and wove the scriptures into Jesse's new beginning. Mom and Dad said fervent prayers over Jesse to protect and guide him. When silence fell, an opening for her to add her two cents, she was saved by a knock at the door. The general contractor Jesse had been working with hadn't been able to make it to the party last night, so he stopped by to see Jesse before he left. Even as Jesse stepped outside to chat with him, several cars pulled up.

Grateful for the interruption, Violet began to tidy up. She paced around the backyard, picking up stray napkins and plastic utensils that didn't make it into the trash, before she attacked the pile of dishes. Her gaze kept flicking to the large clock on the wall. Why were these last hours dragging? When the dish rack was full, she moved onto the half bath their guests had used and gave it a thorough scrub down.

When she emerged, yanking off her rubber gloves, she saw Dad's perplexed expression. She raised her brows in inquiry.

"Are you okay?" he asked.

"Yes. Why?"

"Don't you think you should be...?" He held up a hand. "Never mind."

She jutted out her hip. "What?"

"Nothing," he muttered. "Just thought you'd rather be doing something other than cleaning toilets right now."

She supposed he thought she would be clinging to Jesse's side to soak up every last second with him. A glance out the front window showed that even more people had come to say last-minute farewells. Jesse was surrounded by a small crowd. There was no need for her to fawn over him. He had enough admirers.

As she plugged in the vacuum, she saw Mom and Dad exchange concerned looks. They seemed unnerved by her calm, practical demeanor. She almost wished she could give them the over-the-top emotional reaction they expected so they would stop looking at her like she was a freak. She was *fine*. A little anxious because she hated goodbyes in general. She had no idea how she was going to handle Jesse's farewell with their parent's present, but she would deal with it when the time came.

She'd vacuumed all the bedrooms and hallway and had made her way to the living room when Dad strode to the front door with Jesse's duffel. Her head whipped toward the clock. Jesse had to leave in less than fifteen minutes. The blast of excitement was so potent that she went lightheaded and dropped to her hands and knees. She was so happy, her eyes welled up. He was really leaving. The vacuum roared beside her, concealing the sound of her weak giggling, which escalated into joyous laughter. She wasn't sure how long she stayed that way, but she snapped out of her delirium when the vacuum switched off.

"Violet?"

Mom's hand smoothed over her hair before it rested between her shoulder blades.

"Did you fall? Are you okay?"

She nodded and opened her mouth to reassure Mom that she was fine, but there was an invisible obstruction in her throat.

Mom rubbed her back in a circle. "Honey, what's wrong?"

Lynne's concerned tone punctured a hole in Violet's cocoon. The rush of euphoria was overpowered by a vicious flood of emotion that grabbed her by the throat, strangling her so she couldn't breathe.

"Isaac, come! Something's wrong with Violet. She's shaking like she's having a seizure or something. I—"

A horrible sound ripped through the room. It was the bone-chilling, tortured scream of a wounded animal. It went on and on. Violet tried to raise her head to see what was going on, but for some reason, she couldn't move. Why wasn't anyone helping the poor thing? It sounded like it was being gutted. Someone had to make it stop.

There was a flurry of activity around her, and then she was lifted into the air. Strong arms wrapped around her and her face was pressed against an all too familiar chest. In a distant part of her mind, she realized the awful sound had stopped. She didn't want Jesse touching her, but she wasn't in control of her faculties. She was trembling, covered in cold sweat and... sobbing? When had that happened?

"Oh, Vi," Mom choked. "What should we...?"

"Give us a moment," Jesse rasped.

He moved swiftly. Violet's ponytail swished from side to side as he carried her somewhere. He cupped the back of her head as he spoke to her, but she couldn't hear a word when she was drowning in a churning sea of emotions she'd suppressed for far too long. They were back with a vengeance, ambushing her at the worst possible moment.

Her wailing had turned into pitiful whimpering by the time a door closed.

"Thank you, God," Jesse murmured fervently as he lowered her onto something soft.

Mortification, confusion, and despair sloshed around inside of her as she tried to wipe her eyes, which was difficult since Jesse was trying to cover every inch of her face in kisses. She realized they were in her bedroom, and he'd settled her on the edge of her bed.

"I... I don't know what's wrong with me," she said raggedly.

"Say it," he pleaded. "I need to hear you admit it just once."

"Say what?" she said fretfully as she swiped at her dripping nose.

"Tell me you love me."

"*What?*"

She jerked back and raised her hand to slap him, but he anticipated that and seized her wrist.

"Don't fight. We don't have time," he said urgently.

"How dare you say that to me?"

Even in the midst of her fury, she kept her voice down, aware Mom and Dad were probably hovering at the end of the hallway.

"You're crying for me," he pointed out, staring at the tears that continued to trickle down her cheeks.

"I'm crying *because* of you, not *for* you, jackass."

His fingers flexed around her wrist. "You screamed like someone plunged a dagger in your heart, Vi."

A part of her had suspected that she was responsible for that bloodcurdling, banshee shriek, but she hadn't wanted to admit it to herself. She scraped her mind for a plausible explanation for her breakdown. Ten minutes ago, she could have gone jogging and now, she felt like she had the flu. She was feverish, shaky, nauseated, and her body ached like she'd been beaten with a bat.

Jesse cupped her clammy cheek. "You care for me, Violet. As much as you want to deny it, as much as you wish you didn't, you do."

Her free hand twisted in his damp shirt as she bared her teeth at him. "How could I possibly love someone who's hurt me as much as you have?"

His mouth twisted in a bittersweet smile. "Because when you love, you do it with your whole heart. You give so completely, there's no taking it back."

Even as his words speared her heart, she held his gaze as she enunciated in a voice that trembled, "I do *not* love you."

"Okay," he said gently.

"I hate you," she spat.

His fingers brushed through her waterfall of tears. "I know."

She desperately tried to get a hold of herself as her emotions ravaged her insides. "I need you to go."

"Is that what you really want?"

"Yes!"

He looked down at the hand she didn't realize was still twisted in his shirt. She was horrified to see that, contrary to what her mouth was saying, she was tugging him toward her. She released him as if he burned her and shot to her feet. She snatched tissues from her nightstand and frantically mopped up her face. What the hell was wrong with her? Why couldn't she stop crying?

"Violet."

She whirled with a snarl. "Why are you still here? Go! *Leave!*"

His eyes were a little wild as he stared at her. "I would have stayed if you asked me to, but it's too late."

Her heart skipped. "I didn't ask you to." That fiery volcano inside of her spewing lava added, "Why would I ask you to stay? I'm thrilled you're leaving! This is a dream come true. I've been counting down the days!"

"You're going to deny it to the bitter end," he said with a shake of his head.

"There's nothing to deny! I hate your guts!"

His eyes narrowed a second before he lunged at her. He clapped a hand over her mouth before she could utter a sound and drove her backward into the wall.

"You don't know when to quit," he bit out through clenched teeth. "If I had more time, I'd prove what a fucking lie that is."

He buried his face in her hair, inhaled, and groaned before he slumped against her.

"How am I going to live without you? I miss you already, and you're right here." His hand fisted in her hair. "I'm going for both our sakes, to give us time and space to regain some sanity."

He tugged on her hair, forcing her head back to look at him. His shadowed gaze, full of aggravated yearning, moved over her face.

"Hopefully, while I'm gone, you'll come to your senses."

She yanked his hand off her mouth to hiss, "I have come to my senses! I never want to see you again!"

A muscle ticked in his jaw. "You're so fucking stubborn."

She pushed at his chest. "You have to go."

"Kiss me goodbye."

She went rigid. "No!"

"Please. Just this once," he said raggedly and brushed his lips back and forth across hers, tempting her to engage. "One last kiss."

Why did her heart feel like it was breaking? Why was her entire body trembling with grief and sorrow? This is what she wanted. What she'd prayed for. She reached the end of the tunnel but hadn't stepped into the sunshine. For some reason, she hesitated in the shadows and wasn't making a break for freedom. What the hell was wrong with her? Why had one of her hands twisted in his shirt, once again holding him to her, instead of shoving him away as he deserved?

As if he knew her tumultuous thoughts, his mouth curved in a shaky, agonizing smile. His bloodshot eyes were suspiciously bright.

"You're beautiful on the inside and out, pitying a monster, even though you try not to. I can see you're fighting it, but God did say to love your enemy."

Even as she hauled in a breath to verbally rip him to shreds, he disarmed her when he brushed the tip of his nose against hers, a gesture of affection he hadn't done since they were kids. Her mind flooded with memories of a happier time. A time she hadn't allowed herself to think about because it hurt too much to remember how much they'd lost. How had this all gone so wrong? Her mouth trembled as a tear slipped down her face.

"I'm sorry, Violet. For everything. If you can't forgive me, have mercy on me."

She wasn't sure why that plea made her stomach drop but combined with the sound of an invisible clock ticking, she felt a mounting sense of dread and urgency. This was it. He wasn't going away for a weekend or even a week or two like he did when he went to sports camps. He was *leaving*. They didn't know when they would see each other again. His life wouldn't be his own once he walked out the door. The military would dictate everything from here on out. She despised him, but if something happened to him, and she denied him this, could she ever forgive herself?

Shutting down all rational thought, she clasped the back of his neck and set her mouth on his. Anger was her driving emotion. She funneled the tornado of her destructive emotions into him. She was the aggressor, the one who nipped and bit and wanted him to hurt. He let her do what she wanted to him and when she gave him an opening, he returned her aggression with tenderness. He kissed her in a way that left her feeling raw, shaken, and heartbroken.

When her legs gave out, he held her in the crook of one arm and cradled her face as he cherished her and repented for all the wrong he'd done. Attuned to him as she was, she sensed his desire, but it was tainted by the sharp tang of fear. Realizing he wasn't as confident as he appeared, she couldn't stop herself from trying to console him. Her fingers bunched in his hair as she kissed him back, comforting and reassuring him in the only form of communicating they had left.

"Jesse?"

Mom's call seemed to come from a million miles away.

Jesse reluctantly disengaged and cleared his throat before he called out, "I'll be out in a minute."

Eyes awash with regret moved over Violet's face as if he were trying to memorize it.

"Thank you," he said gruffly, and tried to ease away from her, but her arms locked around him. "Violet?"

She was struck with sudden terror over a future without him in it. He had been the only constant in her life for almost five years. He was her tormentor, but also her protector. A part of her knew he would always have her back, and now she would have no one. She was going to be alone again.

"Vi, I have to go."

"Jesse."

She heard the inadvertent plea in her voice. Pain ripped across his features as he closed his eyes, shedding a tear that he transferred to her when he gave her a hard kiss.

"I'll come back," he said fiercely, before he ripped himself away from her.

She took a step after him, hand outstretched to grab hold of him, but he was too quick. He didn't look back as he strode out of her bedroom. She listened to his swift, heavy footfalls go down the hall.

"Is Violet okay?" Mom asked.

"No," Jesse said curtly. "She isn't going to see me off. We have to get going."

There was a flurry of movement and then the sound of the front door closing, the rev of an engine, and then silence.

Violet dropped to the carpet and finally let loose the scream that had been bottled up inside of her. Now that she was alone, everything she had crammed down for over nine months spilled out. She raged, pounding the carpet with her fists until they were numb. She cried until she retched and, when she collapsed on the bathroom floor, wondered why she felt like she'd just lost her best friend.

Violet tossed and turned. She moved around so much, her fitted sheet came undone, forcing her to remake her bed.

By the time Mom and Dad had returned home, she was semi-presentable, though her eyes that were nearly swollen shut let them know what she'd done in the interim. Strangely, her volatile emotional state seemed to have cured Lynne of hers. Mom spent the rest of the day treating her like she was sick—swaddling her with blankets even though it was hot as hell outside, making her soup, and coddling her.

Violet pummeled her pillow before she flopped on her side and stared at the bathroom door that she'd closed out of habit. Now, she could leave it open if she wanted to. She had to remember to ask Dad to fix the lock. She was so tired, she felt ill, but she couldn't sleep. She should be dead to the world, getting the best sleep of her life. Instead, she was staring at the door, willing it to open.

With a low growl, she rolled out of bed, yanked the door open and marched into Jesse's bedroom. She surveyed his tidy, empty room, illuminated by streetlights, with bitter, glistening eyes.

She ruined the taut sheets when she crawled over it. She breathed deep. The scent of his musk imbedded in the sheets comforted, even as it infuriated her.

She rolled onto her back and, under the gaze of his favorite football player, sank her hand into her pajama bottoms. She was soaking wet. Depraved memories played through her mind, making her writhe and pant and when she came, she hated that she moaned his name.

She stared at the ceiling as she came down from her high. She thought she was reclaiming her sexuality by masturbating in his room, the place where he initiated and corrupted her. She should have felt victorious, but as always, she felt empty. She couldn't believe he was really gone.

She turned onto her belly and, in the darkness, sobbed her heart out.

"Violet?"

She opened her eyes and was confused by the orientation of the room until she realized she was in Jesse's. Mom stood in the doorway with bleary eyes and messy hair.

She opened her mouth to say something, but before she could, the tears started again. Mom's expression softened as she came forward. Violet held up a hand, not wanting to be touched, but Mom ignored that and hauled her into her arms.

"I know, honey. I miss him too," Mom murmured.

Violet fisted her hand in Mom's robe. Her body still yearned for him and her emotions were still entangled, despite her best efforts to block him out. It would take time to break the ties between them, but once she did, she would never let him back in.

CHAPTER 21
VIOLET

2 MONTHS LATER

"Happy birthday to you. Happy birthday to you. Happy birthday, dear Violet," Mom and Dad sang. "Happy birthday to you!"

Violet couldn't help but laugh as Lynne clapped, hopped, and sang at the top of her voice. The kindergarten teacher in her had never been more evident than at this moment.

"Now close your eyes and make a wish!" Lynne encouraged and held up a finger. "And know that all your dreams are within reach!"

Violet dutifully closed her eyes for show and waited an appropriate amount of time before she blew out the candles.

"Woo-hoo!" Lynne cheered and turned on the dining room lights to reveal the smoking candles. "Eighteen," Lynne marveled and wrapped her arms around Violet. "I can't believe it. You're all grown up."

Violet allowed herself to lean into Lynne. Dad watched them with a fond smile.

Lynne kissed the top of her head. "You're the best daughter. We're so happy to have you here with us."

Violet lowered her gaze and ignored the sudden lump in her throat. Lynne gave her a squeeze and went into the kitchen to fetch bowls and ice cream.

"Did you have a good day at school?" Dad asked.

Violet nodded and, to avoid eye contact, reached out to stroke the velvet petals of a rose in a vase in the middle of the table. "Everyone remembers my birthday since it's back-to-back with us starting school. My friends got me enough balloons to make my backpack float," she joked.

"Are you sure you don't want a party? This is the first time you haven't had one, and eighteen's such a special year," Lynne said as she cut into the strawberry cake.

"I don't need a party. I'm happy with this," Violet said, gesturing between the three of them. "And you paid for us to go to that concert. We'll celebrate then."

"Here you go." Mom placed a generous slice of strawberry cake and two scoops of ice cream in front of her. "For the sweetest birthday girl."

They had followed the same ritual for her birthday that Lynne established five years ago. She woke to one dozen pink roses and red velvet pancakes for breakfast, followed by her favorite meal for dinner and now strawberry cake and ice cream. Usually, she had a party on the weekend after her birthday, but this year she asked to skip it. The concert tickets Mom and Dad had bought for her and her friends were more than enough. Everything was as it should be. Better, actually. So, why wasn't she happy? Why didn't she feel anything?

She refused to look to her left, where Jesse used to sit. Even though he wasn't there, she felt the heaviness of his presence. He was everywhere and yet, nowhere. It had been almost two months since he left. She assumed once he was gone that she would magically revert to who she'd been, only to realize that part of her was gone forever.

Her grand plans of enjoying the rest of her summer never came to fruition. After Jesse left, she shut down. She had a hard time getting out of bed and struggled to do basic daily functions. The thing that snapped her out of her zombie state was Mom suggesting she speak to Pastor Sonny or one of the other church leaders. Fear of being questioned galvanized her into action.

She thought she would no longer have to act, but she was putting on the performance of her life. All eyes had always been on Jesse. Without him to deflect everyone's attention from her, she now had to work three times as hard to appear normal. She did what was required of her. She did her chores, went to church, and had recently returned to school for her senior year. She responded when spoken to and smiled on command, but she felt absolutely nothing. When she was alone and no longer had to pretend that she was like everyone else, she plummeted into a mental space so bleak that she worried about her sanity.

Although she'd been half expecting it, her heart stopped when Mom's phone rang. Mom dropped her bowl with a clatter and sprinted to the counter, where the phone was charging. From her delighted expression, Violet knew who the caller was before Mom announced, "It's Jesse!"

As her body went numb, she asked Dad, "How's Uncle Perry?"

Dad took his gaze from Mom and focused on her. "He's still in the hospital." Dad shook his head. "He dropped two stories with that toddler in his arms. The kid didn't have a scratch. Perry's lucky he just broke his leg and not his—"

"Violet?"

She turned her head and saw Mom holding out her cell phone.

"Jesse wants to wish you a happy birthday."

Even as dread weighted down her limbs, making her stumble as she rose from her chair, Violet tried to look eager rather than sick to her stomach.

Mom gave her a puzzled look as she handed over the phone. "Jesse said he's been trying to get in touch with you all day."

Violet pressed the mute button before she said, "Really? Huh. I don't know why I didn't see his messages." She put the phone to her ear and said a bright, "Hello?"

"Violet?"

The sound of Jesse's voice unleashed a torrent of emotion that made her knees buckle. She braced her hand on the table as she bowed her head and closed her eyes to get a handle on herself.

"Thank you," she said, as if Jesse had wished her a happy birthday and tried to inject some warmth and enthusiasm into her voice as she asked, "How are you doing?"

She hadn't heard his voice since the day he left. She blocked his number so he wouldn't be able to contact her, and managed to avoid speaking to him whenever he called their parents by making herself scarce or saying she would call him back on her phone and never doing so. She considered having a party just to have more people around so she would have an excuse to skirt this phone call. Stupidly, she'd hoped Jesse would forget or be too busy to call. Now she had no choice but to carry on a fake conversation in front of her parents. She would leave it up to Jesse to explain why he was unable to hear anything on his end. He was good at making up lies.

"I'm sorry, I didn't get your messages. Maybe I need to get my phone checked out," she said.

"Mom, are you there?" Jesse asked impatiently.

Her nails sank into her palms. Memories swarmed over her, reviving needs she was desperately trying to forget. She opened her eyes and saw Mom watching her intently. Violet flashed a megawatt smile as she said, "We just finished dinner. We're eating cake and ice cream." She let out a false laugh and said, "No. Not German chocolate cake, but we did have buttermilk pie recently. Dad got two pies all to himself."

"That's what you get when you go to the military! No home cooked meals!" Dad said loudly and took a swat on the arm from Mom before he carried his bowl into the living room to finish eating in front of the TV.

"Mom? Violet?" Jesse called.

Violet moved into the kitchen as Mom began to clear the table and asked, "What have you been up to? Are they treating you good?"

"Mom," Jesse bit out.

Violet's stomach churned. He sounded different. Harder, colder. Even his voice had deepened.

"Mom? What the hell?" Jesse snapped and hung up.

Violet blew out a breath. "Uh-huh," she said, nodding. "That doesn't sound too bad." She wiped down the counters as she chattered for show. "School's been good. At first, I loved driving myself everywhere, but now I miss being a passenger princess. Can you believe that? Oh my gosh. You know who I saw recently? I…"

She yanked the phone away from her ear when it began to ring loudly. Why hadn't she thought to turn off the volume? Damn! When Mom frowned, Violet widened her eyes. "I didn't even know we got disconnected."

She answered the phone and immediately pressed the mute button again.

"How long was I talking to myself?" Violet asked ruefully.

"Mom?" Jesse called in a clipped tone.

"That long?" Violet chuckled before she flicked her hand. "I was just talking about school and wishing you could chauffeur me around like the good old days."

When Mom turned away with a smile and went to join Dad in the living room, Violet's tense shoulders dropped.

Jesse's voice abruptly hardened. "Damn it, Vi. I know you're there. Answer me."

Her hand tightened on the phone. "You're almost done with basic training, right?"

"It's been two months," he rasped. "Let me hear your voice."

Fuck him. She wouldn't give him anything he wanted ever again, even if it was just the sound of her voice.

"Oh, really?" she asked, trying to sound interested.

"If you don't talk to me, I'm going to tell Mom," Jesse said.

Outrage seared her throat. She should be the one threatening him, not the other way around! She wanted to slam the phone on the counter until it came apart in pieces. Instead, she held her smile, though it was now more of a sneer as she unmuted the call. Thankfully, Mom and Dad were watching the news and not paying attention to her.

"You're an asshole," she said quietly.

He exhaled before he said grimly, "This is the only way I can get you to talk to me since you blocked me."

"You're blocked for a reason."

He ignored that and asked, "How... how have you been?"

He sounded nervous and awkward.

She glanced at Mom and Dad before she hurried down the hallway to her bedroom. If she had to speak to him, she wanted privacy to say what she needed to.

"I was okay until I had to talk to you," she retorted as she closed her bedroom door and punched one of the balloons a friend had given her.

"I wanted to tell you happy birthday."

"Thank you," she said ungraciously. "Is that it?"

"No, I..."

"You what?" she demanded. "What do you want from me?"

She hated the warble in her voice. She'd hoped the next time they interacted that she would be stone-cold, but clearly, not enough time had passed. His voice whipped her emotions into a frenzy. She hated that he had such power over her, but she hated even more her body's response. The neglected space between her legs throbbed, begging to be possessed. What the hell was wrong with her? What kind of sicko missed the fucked-up things he used to do to her?

A filthy slut, that's who, her inner critic jeered. She bit her lip hard enough to make it bleed to disrupt the scathing litany and focused in time to hear Jesse say, "I want what I've always wanted. You."

Her hand whistled as it slashed through the air. "You can't have me! You'll never have me. I want nothing to do with you. Why can't you understand that?"

"I didn't call to upset you," he said wearily

"Then you should have left me alone! You know I don't want to talk to you. Why force me?"

His voice shredded as he said with a little heat of his own, "Because I miss you! Not seeing you, not being able to talk to you has been hell. We've never been apart this long. I'm going crazy. Don't you miss me at all?"

She swallowed the lump in her throat. The worst part was, she did miss him, and she hated herself for it.

Her prolonged silence made him sigh. She couldn't see him, but she imagined him running his hands through his hair.

"I thought..." He hesitated and then said in a rush, "The day I left, you held on to me. You didn't want me to go. Damn it, you kissed me back, Vi!"

She flinched as her stomach churned, threatening to expel her favorite cake. That day haunted her because it demonstrated how weak she was when it came to him. It didn't matter what he did to her. Her defenses would never be as strong as they needed to be where he was concerned. She had to keep him at a distance, which was possible now that he was in the military. She thought she'd built up some resistance to him, but this phone call proved her shields were as sturdy as wet napkins.

"You can't hold what I did that day against me. I didn't know what I was doing! I was messed up—I'm *still* messed up because of you. I don't know if I'll ever be..."

She pressed the back of her hand to her mouth to smother a rogue sob without success. She shut her eyes, utterly humiliated. She hadn't even been talking to him for two minutes, and she was spiraling out of control.

"Don't cry," he said gruffly. "Or so help me God, I'm going to show up."

"I'm not crying," she lied defiantly. "And you can't 'show up'. They decide what you do now."

"That's why I wanted to talk to you. I'm almost done with basic training, and I have the opportunity to come home before I—"

"What?" she quietly shrieked.

"I may be able to stay for a week or two before I ship off to Alaska."

"D-did you mention this to M-mom or Dad?" She was so rattled, her words tripped over one another.

"No. I wanted to talk to you first. It was supposed to be a surprise for your birthday."

"No!"

"I need to see you," he said desperately. "I'm dying without you."

"You can't shove me back into your twisted game again! I can't do it!"

"I won't," he began earnestly, but she cut him off.

"Don't make promises we both know you can't keep!"

The thought of seeing him again threw her into a panic. She thought she would have six months or more to prepare before facing him. The thought of seeing him any sooner was horrifying.

"You don't know what you did to me," she said in a strangled voice. "I am not okay. I'm just starting to feel human again, and you want to come back and break me all over again."

"I don't—"

"You've done it countless times! That's all you know how to do! I don't know how you can live with yourself when I don't want to live with myself. How do you do it?"

"Violet."

His voice cracked like a whip, but she didn't want to hear what he had to say. He had to stay away. Her sanity depended on it. She was barely hanging on. If he came back, it would destroy her. She couldn't take another round of him, not when she had finally adjusted to his absence. In the past, she did her best to keep him from seeing how much damage he inflicted, but she would reveal all if it would keep him at bay.

"I thought once you were gone, I would feel better, but..." She shuddered as the ever-present shame rose up to choke her. "Every time I get in the car, I think of all the things you've done to me in it. I go to church, and I think of what you did to me on that stage. I go to school, and I think of all the places you took me, the things you forced me to do..." Her hands brushed at the invisible sludge she could feel on her body, but could never remove, no matter how hard she scrubbed.

"Baby."

She stomped her foot. "Don't call me that! Don't call me anything. Don't talk to me!" she said wildly as she mentally unraveled.

"Violet."

"Do you know what I did today?" She clutched the phone in a death grip as her eyes filled with tears. "My friends wanted to treat me to lunch, but instead of going with them, I drove to that park where you broke me the first time. The place where you showed me the real you. I sat there and thought about ending it all."

There was no sound on the other end of the line. She wasn't sure if the call dropped, but she kept talking. Now that she'd confessed the dark path her mind had taken to the one person who would understand why, she couldn't stop.

"I am barely hanging on," she said hoarsely as tears poured down her face. "All the secrets and lies... I can't do it anymore. I can't live like this."

As the pain mounted to an unbearable degree, her eyes flicked around the room for something to inflict damage on her person before she closed her eyes, willing away the violent, compulsive urges brought on by the self-loathing she couldn't shirk.

"If you ever felt anything for me, you'd stay away."

Silence.

"I'll never ask anything of you ever again," she pleaded. "Just don't come home, at least while I'm here. After I graduate, you can see Mom and Dad whenever you want."

"Is that what you really want?" he asked in a stifled tone.

"Yes."

There was a brief pause and then, "If that's what you need."

Relief made her legs weak. She collapsed on the edge of her bed and dropped her face in her hand. "Thank you."

"Violet, I... I never meant to hurt you."

She knew he heard her whimpering because his voice broke.

"I swear I can fix this if you give me a chance."

"You can't f-fix something that's shattered into a m-million pieces," she said raggedly.

"I'll spend the rest of my life finding every piece and putting it back where it belongs," he said fervently.

"I used to think you were heaven sent," she said in a hollow voice. "I loved you more than I loved myself. I made so many excuses for you because I didn't want to believe the truth." Her breath hitched before she finished, "You're the worst thing that ever happened to me. I don't ever want to see you again."

The call ended. She wasn't sure if they got disconnected or if he hung up. Either way, she was grateful because she reached the end of her rope. The phone tumbled across the carpet after it fell from her nerveless fingers.

She had officially severed their bond. She felt the disconnect as acutely as if she severed a limb. Internally, she was screaming that same bloodcurdling cry she had the day he left. It was the grief-stricken wail of a woman who had lost someone she didn't think she could live without, but she had no choice. Cutting him out of her life was the only way she could cope. She had the misfortune to give her heart to a monster who damaged her so severely, she would never be the same. It was the right thing to do, so why did she feel like she was back in that dark tunnel without light or hope?

She wrapped her arms around herself and folded at the waist.

Fat, salty tears rained down on her pink heart socks. Her agony was so profound she couldn't make a sound.

She lost countless battles, but she just won the war. Jesse would honor his promise. She would never see him again. She should have been elated and relieved. Instead, she mourned. Jesse was right. When she loved, she did it completely, which meant she would never be whole again.

Author's Note

I HOPE YOU ENJOYED THIS INSTALLMENT OF JESSE AND VIOLET'S STORY. THIS prequel was written almost 6 years after I wrote Corrupt Idol. I never intended to write a prequel, but when I read Corrupt Idol during a break from another series, my brain started turning over some ideas.

Piecing their history together through details I carelessly dropped in Corrupt Idol was an interesting challenge. I hadn't planned for this book to be dual POV, but was pleasantly surprised when Jesse stepped up to the plate in chapter 1. I don't know if any book has surprised me as much as this one has. I felt like every chapter held a twist or revelation I was clueless about until Jesse or Violet decided to share it. This book was an emotional rollercoaster that challenged me personally and professionally. I stepped back and let the characters tell the story at their pace. I think the results are heartbreakingly, uniquely theirs.

I do plan to write a sequel to Corrupt Idol, but I have contracts and other projects I need to fulfill as dark romance writer, Mia Knight. I will post an update when I am back in Violet and Jesse's world! If you'd like to read the raw draft of Corrupt Obsession or deleted scenes, you can join Ream.

Thank you for coming on this journey with me. If you have a chance, please leave a review and recommend my books to other readers. This helps me out so much, especially since my stories are banned from most retailers.

Thank you for your support. I couldn't do this without you.

SINCERELY,
Dinah

Acknowledgments

I wanted to thank all of my supporters on Patreon & Ream! I wouldn't be able to do this without you. Your support grants me the time needed to bring this story to life and I'm so incredibly grateful for each and every one of you!

Special thanks to my amazing Super Patrons/Baddies:

- A. Jay
- Alexandria
- Bibiana
- Carrie Cross
- Pooja
- Sam Sodi
- Sami Bullock

CORRUPT IDOL

CONTENT WARNING

This is an erotic novel that depicts a toxic relationship between step-siblings. This book has been banned from numerous retailers so read at your own discretion.

For a full list of triggers, you can visit my website:

https://www.dinahharper.com/corrupt-idol-content-warning

CHAPTER 1

"W HY DIDN'T YOU TELL ME?" V IOLET WHISPERED.

"We didn't want to worry you."

"Worry me?" She jabbed her finger at the hospital room door. "My stepmom has *cancer,* and you didn't think I should know?"

Dad ran a hand down his face. "We did what we thought was best."

"I don't know how I'm supposed to take this. She... she only has a few weeks left?"

Dad nodded as he sank onto a chair and stared down at his interlocked fingers. "Lynne's tired, Vi."

She hadn't seen her father in two years and in that time, he had aged significantly. The grooves in his face were more pronounced, he had put on weight, and his once gray hair was now snow-white. Taking care of Lynne had clearly taken its toll.

She took the seat beside him and tried to take it all in. She landed in Texas two hours ago, unaware that Lynne had been diagnosed with cancer and was losing the battle, which is why they called her home. She stared at the far wall and shook her head. "I don't know what to say."

"Lynne wants us to spend as much time together as possible before she goes."

"Of course," Violet said, blinking rapidly as her eyes burned with tears.

"That goes for Jesse too."

Her head whipped in his direction. "Jesse?"

Dad held up a hand. "Don't start, Vi."

"I haven't said anything!"

"You don't have to. The few times he's come home, you made excuses why you couldn't visit. Not this time. I don't care what happened between you two. You're going to sort it out, and we're gonna be one big happy family like the good old days."

A cold wave swept over her as memories of the 'good old days' skipped through her mind. Before he turned into a monster, Jesse Sampson was her best friend, protector, hero. And then one day, everything changed. She managed to avoid him for five years. It wasn't nearly long enough.

"Ten years, Vi."

The warble in Dad's voice captured her attention immediately. Her father wasn't an emotional man. He was hard-working, religious, conservative and raised her by himself until Lynne came into the picture. Lynne made their house into a home and filled their lives with light and joy. Lynne had softened her father considerably. Violet had never seen him so happy. Watching him struggle to keep his emotions in check made her heart feel as if it were being shredded.

"I had ten amazing years with her. Next year she was supposed to retire, and we were going to Hawaii for a month before we bought an RV and went on the road." He spread his hands in a gesture that conveyed his helplessness. "We had so many plans and now..."

She gripped his hand and squeezed. "I'm sorry, Dad."

He cleared his throat. "I'm glad you're here, kiddo."

She couldn't stop herself from grumbling, "You should have told me from the beginning."

"It was Lynne's decision to keep this quiet." He patted the back of her hand. "All that doesn't matter now. Whatever time we have left will have to do. You're here. Jesse's coming in. We're gonna enjoy the time we have left."

She hesitated before she asked, "Does he know?"

"Yes, he had to know how serious her condition was to request leave." Dad glanced at his watch. "Can you pick him up?"

She jolted. *"Jesse?"*

He gave her a stern look. "I have to stay with Lynne."

"But—"

"Don't argue. Pick him up and sort out your issues before you bring him here. Lynne doesn't need you two arguing at her bedside." He got to his feet and dropped his keys in her lap. "He's coming in on United. Flight 243, arrives at 4:15."

When she opened her mouth, he leaned down and cupped her chin.

"Please, Violet, I'm having a hard time as it is. I need you to do this for me."

She took in his weary, defeated expression and swallowed her arguments. He saw her acquiescence in her expression and gave her a wan smile.

"That's my girl." Her eyes watered as he pressed a kiss on the top of her head. "It's going to be all right."

When he went into Lynne's hospital room, she didn't move. She sat there with his keys on her lap, pondering how quickly her world flipped upside down. She wasn't prepared for this. *None* of it. This morning, her biggest concern was asking if she could move home and confessing what a mess she'd made of her life in Utah. The moment Dad picked her up, she launched into her speech. She was too deep in her feelings to notice that he was unusually subdued. He didn't ask questions. He said yes before she finished her explanation and didn't give her the lecture she deserved. Before relief could set in, he told her about Lynne, and her already gloomy world darkened considerably.

Slowly, she got to her feet and stood in the doorway of Lynne's hospital room. Dad spoke to a nurse while Lynne lay in bed, a mere shadow of the woman she remembered. Her father nodded as the nurse handed him a list and went over it with him. Protests bubbled up in her throat as everything in her revolted against Dad's simple request.

Lynne let out a moan. Dad and the nurse immediately broke off their conversation.

"Jesse?" Lynne's voice was laced with pain.

Her father's eyes moved to the doorway and speared her. "Violet's picking him up. He should be here soon."

"Oh, that's good," Lynne said hoarsely.

There were things she wanted to say, but like all the other times she felt compelled to speak, nothing left her lips. Six years she had kept a filthy secret locked inside of her and even though she ached to let it out, she knew she couldn't. One utter of the truth would destroy their family. This wasn't the time. She had to acknowledge there would *never* be a right time. She would have to keep it locked inside of her, even if it continued to rot her from the inside out. She had to deal with her inner demons as she always had—alone.

She walked through the busy halls on legs that felt as if they were made of lead. The sun blasted her the moment she stepped out of the hospital. She slipped on her shades and climbed into her parent's SUV. The stifling heat forced her to roll down the windows. She glanced at the clock and felt her stomach lurch. Jesse would be landing in twenty minutes. Since they lived on the other side of town, she didn't have time to dawdle, but she made no move to put the vehicle in gear. She sat there, staring through the windshield as memories careened into her.

Visiting Texas was bad enough—it brought back everything she strived to forget, and now she had to face *him*. It had been five years since she saw her stepbrother. Even though she made vows to avoid him for the rest of her life, a part of her had known this day would come. She just hadn't expected it to be so soon. The day Jesse left for basic military training was the best day of her life. He was a year older, which allowed her to finish most of her senior year in peace before she moved to Utah to attend college and start over.

Her phone pinged. She glanced at the text and ground her teeth as she put the car in gear. Dad messaged her Jesse's flight info so she couldn't claim she'd forgotten the details. She exited the parking lot and merged onto the freeway. She calculated the time. Jesse would have to wait. Hopefully, he would get impatient and get his own transportation, and she could put off this fucking reunion for another hour or so.

She blasted the radio as she navigated through traffic. She tapped the wheel in time with the beat to convince herself that this was no big deal even though dread lay like a ten-pound weight on her chest. She kept the windows down, even though the wind whipped her hair in her face. She tried to combat her panic by taking in the familiar sights. She had grown up in Austin and after being in the desert, the sight of the rich, green countryside comforted her. The air smelled sweet, or was that just her imagination?

Five years ago, she chose the furthest college from Texas that her parents would allow her to attend, the University of Utah. She moved to Salt Lake City and got the fresh start she needed. After two years of floundering in college, she dropped out and went from shit job to shit job. Nothing lasted long, and she had been living paycheck to paycheck for a while now. She hadn't been too worried until her roommates announced that they were moving out of the house they had been living in for four years. To make matters worse, she had been fired from her latest job for being tardy one too many times. She couldn't afford to live on her own and didn't want to move in with strangers, which left her stranded. She was swimming in debt and had been playing around with the idea of moving home so she could sort out her finances when Dad asked her to visit. She took that as a sign and had been totally unprepared for the news that Lynne had only weeks to live.

Her life had been going downhill for a while now, but this was the cherry on top. Her stepmom, who she loved dearly, had terminal cancer, and she had to face her stepbrother after avoiding him like the plague. Life was fucking cruel.

Too soon, she turned into the Austin-Bergstrom International Airport.

Her heart thudded in her ears. If Lynne wasn't dying, she would be on the next fight out of here. This couldn't be happening. The thought of seeing Jesse made her lightheaded with panic. This had to be a bad dream.

Her palms began to sweat as she rode the middle lane and eyed the crowd on the sidewalk. She'd rather pick up a damn stranger than Jesse. Her hands flexed on the wheel as she reminded herself that she was older and more mature. She wasn't the naive teen she'd been, and he couldn't be the fucker she remembered. He had been in the Air Force for five years. The military probably beat the shit out of him, which he deserved. She was freaking out over nothing. They were both here under dire circumstances. Jesse was here for his mom, nothing else. She took a fortifying breath as traffic inched along. She was twenty-three, not seventeen. She could handle this.

At first, she didn't see him and her heart soared as she convinced herself that he had missed his flight or, better yet, Dad was mistaken, and Jesse couldn't come at all. Before she could sail past the pick-up area, she spotted a lone figure at the end of the terminal in a military uniform. Her heart slammed so hard against her ribs, she thought she might be having a heart attack. He was covered head to toe in traditional camouflage. He wore dark sunglasses, combat boots, and had a large pack slung over one shoulder. She was too far away to know for certain, but her body recognized him. Jesse Sampson, her stepbrother, tormentor, and object of her nightmares.

As she cruised toward him, she considered stomping on the gas and telling Dad she hadn't seen him, but Jesse wouldn't play into her lie. He would say she left his ass, which would stress out Dad and Lynne even more. She couldn't do that. She straightened her shoulders and pulled into the next lane as her body broke out in goosebumps. This wouldn't be a replay of the past. She wouldn't let it. He had changed and so had she. This was her opportunity to show him he didn't rule her any longer.

It took every ounce of courage she possessed to pull up in front of him. She turned her head and felt her insides quiver as he stared at her through the window for a long minute. She caught a glimpse of his smile before he headed to the back of the car. He pulled on the lever and paused, eyeing her through the tinted glass. She swallowed hard as she pressed the unlock button, allowing the devil into her safe place. Her stomach rocked, making her feel ill. He tossed his heavy bag into the trunk and came around to the passenger door. She stared straight ahead as he folded his large frame into the seat.

"Vi."

She didn't acknowledge him. She looked to the left to see if she could merge into traffic and tried to control the fine trembling in her fingers.

"No, hello?" he asked.

She didn't answer. She couldn't. Her mind was a complete blank. The years in between made no difference. The sight of him, the sound of his voice, flooded her with memories.

She slammed her foot on the gas, causing the SUV to buck forward. She gripped the wheel with white knuckles as she navigated out of the airport.

"Want me to drive?"

She shook her head and silently willed him to shut the hell up. She was rattled and desperately trying to find her footing.

"It's been a long time."

She wanted to get back to the hospital as quickly as possible. Unfortunately, rush hour was in full swing, which meant she would have to take back roads that would prolong their time together. Hell.

"You're going to have to talk to me some time," he said.

She planned to show him how little he mattered to her and how much she had changed, but the moment she saw him, her voice deserted her. He made her feel small, vulnerable, insecure. She thought years on her own would magically fix her, but in his presence, she reverted to her teenage self and hated herself for it.

"Have you seen her?"

The question snapped her out of her inner turmoil. An image of Lynne passed through her mind, wiping away the past and putting her solidly in the present. "Yes."

Her voice was small, but steady, and could be heard over the wind whistling through the cab.

"How does she look?"

Her eyes burned. "Not good."

"How long are you staying?"

Her lips compressed. She didn't want him to know, but Dad would tell him anyway. "I'm moving back."

When she didn't receive a response, she glanced at him and wished she hadn't. He had taken off his cap, revealing slicked back hair that was now in disarray. He was cleanly shaven with a strong jaw, generous lips, and straight nose. She hoped he'd be covered in scars or had his nose broken at some point. No such luck. Unfortunately, he appeared unmarred. He had always been a big guy, but now he was larger than life. He was so broad, his shoulders branched across the console and nearly touched hers.

Her friends had drooled over him. He was a great athlete and particularly talented at football. Many had pegged him as a future NFL player. He shocked everyone by going into the Air Force instead. Lynne begged him not to, but nothing would sway him. He was determined to follow in his late father's footsteps. She counted her lucky stars the day he announced his decision at the dinner table. She hadn't been quick enough to conceal her joy. He made her pay for it later that evening.

"What about college?" he asked.

She returned her attention to the road. "I dropped out."

"Why?"

She was surprised the steering wheel didn't bend under the force she was exerting. She had a death grip on the damn thing. "I couldn't figure out what I wanted to do, and I was wasting time and money."

"And now?"

"I still don't know."

"So, you're moving home."

She nodded and waited for more questions, but he didn't voice any. She should have been grateful that he didn't push, but the silence was worse. The radio was still going, but it didn't cut the tension in the car. They passed cows and horses in pastures as far as the eye could see. She should feel safe and comforted by the familiar scenery. Instead, she felt as if an invisible clock was ticking. Being near him made her feel claustrophobic, as if she could step on a landmine at any second. Minutes passed, and she pressed more heavily on the gas pedal while she diligently searched for cops who liked to hide along this long stretch of highway.

"Pull over."

She whipped her head in his direction. "What?"

"Pull over," he said again.

She stared at him for a heartbeat. She couldn't read his eyes since they were covered by sunglasses, but she didn't need to. His tone had changed and despite the years they had been apart, she knew what he wanted.

"No." When he reached for the wheel, she slapped his hand. *"No, Jesse."*

Her smack didn't deter him. He took hold of the wheel and started to steer her toward the side of the road.

"Stop!" she shrieked.

"Get your foot off the gas before we crash," he rapped out.

"You're going to kill us!"

"You will if you don't do what I say."

"You can't do this to me!" she wailed.

"Fuck," he said through clenched teeth and reached for her leg to lift it off the gas, but she had already done so.

"Jesse…"

He kept one hand on the steering wheel while the other went to her neck and massaged the tense muscles. "Good girl."

"Don't," she seethed.

"Shh. Turn here. Come on, you know where to go."

She was so rattled she could barely think. "T-think about Mom. We have to—"

"I'll see her after I see to you."

He had taken her down many deserted roads during her junior year of high school. They spent more time than she cared to remember at every rest stop or park along the way to their house.

She dragged his hand from her neck and thrust it away from her as she stopped under the shade of a familiar tree. "You can't—"

Two large hands gripped her face and hauled her over the console, dislodging her shades. His lips covered hers and when she tried to scream, his tongue thrust in, and she choked on it. Her body flushed with biting cold and then a searing heat that felt as if she was being nipped by thousands of fire ants. She gripped handfuls of his hair and tried to yank his head back, but it had no effect on him whatsoever. One hand clasped her nape to keep her still while the other quested down her body. He gripped her breast through her thin shirt. She bucked and raked her nails down his cheek.

When he reared back, she felt a burst of relief until he unsnapped her seat belt.

"Jesse, you can't do this anymore!"

His response was to drag her out of her seat and onto his lap. She let out an enraged bellow and slapped him, knocking his glasses off his face to reveal sky-blue eyes clouded with lust and fury. If she'd seen his eyes when she pulled up to the curb, she never would have let him in the car.

"Jesse," she whispered, but he ignored her and shoved his door open.

She looked around as he stepped out with her in his arms. When she was younger, she'd been too ashamed to ask for help, but times had changed. This time, she was desperate enough to get someone's attention, but there was no one in the empty parking lot to come to her rescue. If she had known he would revert to old habits, she would have taken a different route.

"Jesse, you can't—"

He ignored her struggles as he opened the back door, folded the back seats by pulling on a lever, and tossed her in.

She lunged between the front seats to get to her phone, but he pushed her aside as he climbed in, using his body to force her into the trunk. She knew from experience there was no way to open the back door from the inside. Her mind glazed with nightmares as he boxed her in.

"Five years," he bit out as he crawled toward where she huddled in the furthest corner.

She held her hands up to ward him off. "Jesse, you can't do this. It's rape! You have no *right*—"

Her voice was cut off as he grabbed her and swung her to the floor. He shoved his pack to the side as he crouched over her.

"Rape?"

His voice was curiously soft as he hovered over her like a massive lion. His eyes moved over her as his hand splayed over her quivering stomach.

"You want me, you just won't admit it."

She levered herself up to get in his face. "I *don't* want you! I never did! You forced me!"

He eased closer, so their lips were a breath apart. "You want me to fight you for it."

"You conceited mother*fuck*—"

His mouth collided with hers. When she dropped to disengage their lips, a hand cradled the back of her head to keep her in place. When he moaned, her nipples grew hard. She clawed him, but his uniform protected him from harm. His hand went between them and undid her shorts. She bucked and fought, but he yanked them down with brute force.

"Stop!" she sobbed.

"No fucking way."

He tossed her shorts and underwear and grabbed her shirt. When it ripped, she hit him again, which caused him to pin her arms over her head. He leaned down and bit her breast.

"Behave," he said around her nipple.

"I hate you!"

He moved to the other breast and sucked until she screamed and pleaded for him to stop. He gentled and flicked her nipple with his tongue. She stared at the ceiling and prayed this was a nightmare, but the feel of his coarse uniform brushing over her bare skin was too fucking real to be a figment of her imagination. This was happening and there was nothing she could do to stop it.

He dragged her shirt off and then balled it beneath her head as a makeshift pillow. He forced her legs apart and slid a finger inside her. Her body bowed and her toes curled. She gripped his wrist.

"Please stop."

"You know I can't."

Eyes wet with tears met his fevered ones. "You mean you won't."

He focused on his hand moving between her thighs. "No, I can't. This..." He shook his head and gripped his dick through his uniform and began to stroke. "I can't help myself. You're wet, but it's not enough. What do you need?"

"I need you to leave me alone!"

"Not gonna happen."

He scooted her up so he could stretch out on his belly. She tried to roll away, but he spread her legs and put his mouth on her. She screamed. He lifted her thighs as he stabbed deep. She tried to suffocate him, but his groans told her he was far from dead. No matter how hard she fought, she couldn't win. She tried to ignore his caresses as he played her body, but he knew what got her off. It didn't take long for him to make her come.

When she lay limp and defeated beneath him, he lifted his face, which was smeared with her. He jerked her under him and fumbled with his pants as he settled between her quaking thighs. He kissed her, forcing her to taste herself as he slid inside her. He shuddered and broke the kiss to pant, "Fuck!"

She felt as if she was floating out of her body as her pussy yielded to him. He yanked on her hair until she looked at him.

"You know how long I've been waiting for this?" He pulled out and then slipped back in. "You know how many times I've jacked off, imagining you beneath me, smelling your hair, having you look at me..." He quivered above her. The tendons in his neck stood out as he struggled for control. "Fuck, I can't wait. I need you."

That was the only warning he got before he fucked her. No finesse, no technique, just animal lust. He pounded her into the hard floor and within minutes, climaxed. She got rug burn and bruises in the process, but she didn't make a sound. When it was over, he braced himself over her, his hot breath fanning her face. Slowly, he pulled out of her. She followed his gaze and watched him drip over her. He had a thing for his cum. Sure enough, his hand played with his semen in her pussy before he smoothed it over her stomach. His eyes bored into hers as he leaned down and kissed her. This time, she didn't fight it.

"No more running, Vi."

CHAPTER 2

Violet stayed in the trunk since he destroyed her shirt. She wasn't about to sit in the passenger seat in her bra. She tipped from side to side as he finished the drive home. Her pussy throbbed, and her senses were elevated, while her spirit was heavy. It happened again. Five years didn't mean shit. He hadn't changed and neither had she since she'd just been thoroughly fucked.

She didn't move when he parked. When the garage door came down, they were encased in darkness. The interior light came on as he stepped out of the car. She told herself to grab her shorts and bolt before he could do anything else, but she lay there like a dead thing. The trunk door rose. She sensed him standing there, examining her. He reached in and shouldered his bag before he grabbed her ankle and dragged her toward him.

"Ow!" she snapped and tried to kick him.

He pinned her ass on the tailgate and kissed her pussy before he hauled her into his arms. He managed to grab her ruined shirt and shorts and juggled them all as he carried her into the house.

"Let me go!" she hissed as she tried to get free.

"In a minute."

He walked into his bedroom and dropped his pack on the floor before he walked into their Jack and Jill bathroom.

"We aren't showering together!" she spat.

He set her in the tub and eyed her as he dropped her ruined clothes on the floor and stripped off his uniform. Her mouth went dry as she took him in. When she was seventeen, he forced her to learn every inch of his body. His years in the military had changed his physique beyond recognition. Every inch of him was solid muscle. She held up her hands as he stepped in with her.

"Please don't," she whispered.

"I'm not going to hurt you."

She punched him in the stomach. "Then what was that in the car? You hurt me all the time! No matter how many times I beg you to stop, you *never*—"

He kissed her, putting a stop to her escalating voice and emotions. He picked her up and pressed her against the wall. His last load helped ease his entry this time. He fucked her nice and slow, the enclosed space amplifying the sound of her panting and hitched breaths. He covered her face with kisses and when he came again, he whispered, "There's no one like you."

"I hate you."

He bathed her, blocking any escape with his big body. He detached the shower nozzle to clean his cum from her and asked casually, "Are you on anything?"

She went rigid. "What?"

His eyes were steady on hers, eyelashes spiked with water as he waited for an answer. She renewed her struggles to get away from him.

"I'm... I'm..." Her mind was blank with fear.

"You aren't on anything?"

"I-I didn't pick up my pills after I broke up with my last boyfriend."

His eyes darkened. "What the fuck did you say?"

"Jesse."

He gripped her face. "You know how I feel about you with other guys."

"You don't own me."

"You think not?"

Two fingers slid into her pussy. He pinned her against the wet tiles as his hand worked her. She was swollen and throbbing and when he scraped his fingers against her G spot, she nearly brained herself when her head kicked back.

"You know what I did to Tucker. We don't want any more accidents, do we?"

She clawed his arm. "Jesse, *stop*!"

He applied pressure, making her cramp. She screamed and gripped his wrist with both hands, trying to pull those marauding, brutal fingers out of her. A hand wrapped around her throat and squeezed, forcing her eyes to his. He pressed his wet forehead against hers.

"Tell me how many you've been with, so I know how to punish you."

"Fuck you!"

He did something that made her womb weep. She hunched over as he kissed her temple.

"Tell me," he ordered.

She glared at him. "Too many to count," she panted with relish.

He wrenched her head back and kissed her hard. "You're gonna regret that."

He finished washing her before allowing her to stumble out of the shower. She wrapped herself in a fluffy towel and fled to her room where she locked both doors—the one that connected to the bathroom and the other that led into the hallway. She stood in the middle of the room, mind awhirl with fragmented thoughts. She couldn't stay here, not with Jesse around. It didn't take more than thirty minutes for him to get her on her back. He wouldn't stop. She knew that from experience. He would take what he wanted anytime, anywhere and leave her wasted and empty again. She clamped her trembling thighs together. She would tell Dad and Lynne that she had to go back to Utah to pack up her life there. Hopefully, by the time she came back, Jesse's leave would be up, and she could focus on Mom without that fucker ruining everything.

She dropped to her knees beside her open suitcase and pulled on jeans and a new top. She stood in front of the floor length mirror and brushed her hair while her mind buzzed with static. Her reflection had changed little in the intervening years and the fact that her bedroom remained untouched gave her an odd sense of déjà vu. The hydrangea bedspread was the same, as were the matching curtains. Everything was bright and colorful, but it was a sham. Unspeakable depravity clung to the walls of this place. The few times she came home for a visit, she slept on the couch. Dad thought this was a weird quirk of hers. He didn't realize that she couldn't be in this room without remembering the hell Jesse put her through. Seeing that soft cotton candy shade of blue or pink sent her spiraling into the past. She nixed those colors from her life and preferred black and gray instead.

She pressed her ear against the door that led into the bathroom. No sound. Cautiously, she unlocked it and found the bathroom empty. The door leading to his room was open. Quick and silent, she swung it closed and didn't breathe until it was locked. She kicked her shorts and ripped shirt into the corner and pulled out the blow-dryer. When she flipped it on, her eyes went to his door. She expected him to try to break the door down or shout at her, but nothing happened.

She did her best to dry her wavy, long black hair as her hands shook. She focused on her task and refused to dwell on what happened. She would blank it from her mind, as she had done all the other incidents. Her goal was to get back to the hospital where their parents were. There was safety in numbers. She would bring Dad home and then escape back to Utah, where she would bide her time until Jesse left.

Her hazel eyes looked green in the bright light. People often mentioned her eyes changed color with her moods. She hadn't seen her eyes this particular shade in years. Her lips were a little swollen and her body was throbbing, but nothing showed on the surface. He had always been careful not to mark her too much. She shuddered.

When she walked into her bedroom, she stopped short when she found Jesse sitting on her bed. Her eyes flicked to the door she had locked before she met his inscrutable gaze.

"Ready?" he asked.

He was going to act like nothing happened. Of course, he was. His moods were as quick-changing as the Texas weather. As a teen, his abrupt personality switches gave her whiplash. He was so good at playing a role while she floundered and struggled to conceal her emotions. Five years later, nothing had changed. Jesse taught her a lot about men. Men only wanted one thing, and once they got it, she ceased to exist for them. She tried to go lesbian even though she knew it would give her religious father a heart attack, but unfortunately, women didn't do anything for her sexually. She indulged in a long string of lovers that didn't add up to much and only reinforced the fact that most men sucked.

"Ready." She was proud her voice sounded even and cool when she felt as sturdy as tissue paper.

He got to his feet, and she noticed for the first time that he was in jeans and a white shirt. His casual attire reminded her so much of the past that she went dizzy for a moment.

"Vi?"

She shook herself and marched toward the door. "Let's go."

She led the way to the garage and hesitated before she slipped into the front passenger seat. Sitting in the back would only start an argument, and she didn't want to give him a reason to put his hands on her again. Now that he got what he wanted, he would behave for a while. She had to keep him on an even keel. All she had to do was sit here until they made it to the hospital. She could handle that, right?

He slipped into the driver's side. When he backed out of the garage, he turned toward her and draped his arm around the back of her seat. She shied away from him. He caught the small movement and stared at her for a few beats before he put the car in drive.

She leaned against the window and examined the neighborhood, which hadn't changed much. A neighbor recognized the car and waved. Out of the corner of her eye, she saw Jesse lift his hand in acknowledgment. Jesse, the golden boy with impeccable manners. No one would believe what had been going on under everyone's noses for years.

She clamped her legs together as her pussy pulsed. She climaxed. What the fuck? He turned her body against her, as he had when they were teens. How she felt about him didn't matter. He could manipulate her body and took great pleasure in doing so. Once, she had loved him with every fiber of her being, but things started to change when she turned sixteen. She woke several times in the middle of the night to find him in her room. At the time, she refused to believe what was happening and came up with a ton of excuses for him, but when she was seventeen, they hit the point of no return. The veil of denial was ripped to shreds when he fucked her. And when it continued, she had no choice but to conclude the stepbrother she had once idolized was a depraved psychopath. The strain of pretending that everything was normal while Jesse forced her compliance broke her. Her threats, hate, or silence made no impact on him. He stole everything from her... and he was still doing it. He was heartless.

She pictured their reunion many times over the years. In some fantasies, she kneed him in the balls. In others, she smacked him across the face and in her favorite, she was able to skewer him with a look, and he fell to his knees and begged for forgiveness. Her insides writhed with shame. None of those came true. She put up a fight, but it didn't matter. He still won. He *always* won.

Neither of them said a word during the ride. The moment he parked, she was out the door. Although she hurried ahead, he easily caught up with her. She was five foot six, but Jesse was a freaking giant at six foot three. As they entered the hospital, her mind switched from her issues with Jesse to the larger one—Lynne's impending death.

She glanced at him as he paced beside her. He looked unruffled, relaxed, and unaffected by his surroundings. How could he be so calm when his mom had only weeks to live? Wasn't he terrified? Dreading the end? If he felt anything, it didn't show on the surface.

Sensing her regard, he turned his head and speared her with those eyes that haunted her dreams. She looked away and noticed he was attracting quite a bit of attention. That was no surprise. Women had been throwing themselves at him for as long as she had known him. He never lacked female attention, so why had he fixated on her? Why risk so much to fuck his stepsister? Was it because it was taboo? Because she was the only female who didn't want him? Or was she just convenient and he enjoyed controlling her? Whatever his reasons, he was a sick bastard.

The door to Lynne's room was open, so she walked in with Jesse following in her wake. Dad sat beside the bed with Lynne's hand pressed against his mouth as they talked. Her heart clenched when Dad turned his head, revealing glistening eyes. He looked down to compose himself as Jesse rounded the bed to greet his mother.

"Jesse, you're home!" Lynne cried.

Violet went to her father's side. "Dad, are you okay?"

"I'm good," he said with a pained smile.

He clearly wasn't, but she didn't want to embarrass him further, so she switched her attention to the mother and son reunion taking place. Lynne looked even smaller in comparison to her son's bulky frame. Jesse reached out and cupped his mother's face. Something twisted in Violet's stomach as they smiled at one another. Lynne stared at Jesse with luminous eyes. It was clear she adored her son, and it wasn't one-sided. Jesse pressed his forehead against his mother's and whispered to her as tears trickled down her cheek.

"I'm so happy you're here," Lynne said.

"Nowhere else I'd rather be," Jesse murmured.

Violet turned away and pressed a hand against her mouth as her stomach rocked with nausea. How could he be the monster who forced himself on her and the loving, doting son not even twenty minutes later? He was doing it again—making her doubt her sanity by transitioning seamlessly between his multiple personalities.

"What are these marks on your cheek?" Lynne asked.

Violet stopped breathing.

"I was helping a woman get her luggage from the overhead bin and a buckle scratched my face," Jesse answered.

Violet swiped at the cold sweat on her brow. He said it so easily, so effortlessly. She would have believed him if she hadn't put the scratches there herself. How did he lie so effortlessly?

"I'm so glad you're here, son," Dad said.

She heard the manly clap on the back they gave each other and then Jesse's, "It's good to be home."

Her father loved Jesse. He had no reason not to. Jesse was well-liked by their parents and everyone in the community. To everyone else he was well-mannered, courteous, and a hard worker. No one would dream that there was something wrong with him. It was only when she and Jesse were alone that he morphed into an entirely different person.

She listened, dumbfounded, as Jesse talked to her father about fishing. He was so composed, so damn smooth, she wanted to pull her hair out. She didn't know what to say or how to act. He made her feel isolated, lonely, bereft. The only way she knew how to cope was to ignore Jesse and stuff her emotions into the dark corners until she was alone. She had been in Austin for only a few hours and was already on the brink of a breakdown.

"Vi."

She turned to see Lynne holding out her hand. She ignored the men and went to her mother's side. Lynne wore a pretty silk scarf wrapped around her bald head. She had thinned and was alarmingly pale, but her smile never wavered. Lynne grasped her hand in a surprisingly firm grip.

"I'm so happy to see you two together," Lynne gushed. "You had time to talk and settle your differences?"

Dad and Jesse were on the other side of the bed. They were talking, but Jesse was turned toward her. She could feel his gaze on her. Was he worried she would tell the truth? There was a tiny voice in the back of her mind that urged her to spill, but she wouldn't, and he knew it. Lynne was waiting for an answer. She looked so goddamn hopeful that Violet didn't have the heart to disappoint her. She nodded because she couldn't speak.

"I'm so glad." Lynne kissed the back of her hand. "You two used to be so close. Once Dad and I are gone, you're all each other has."

"Stop talking like that. I can't..." Violet shook her head as her throat closed.

"I'm sorry I kept this from you. I know you've had your struggles in Utah. I didn't want to add to that."

"But..." Violet's eyes filled with tears. "I wish I'd known. I could have been here for you."

Lynne cupped her cheek with an ice-cold hand. "My sweet girl. This isn't something you should be around. It's been a long journey of tests, bad news, and dashed hopes. You have your whole life ahead of you. If I told you, you would be as tired as your father. This way, you're focused on the here and now. We know the verdict and we have time. That's all that matters."

Violet brushed away a tear. "What happens now?"

"I'm coming home tomorrow."

She stiffened. "You're refusing treatment?"

"There's nothing more they can do, and I want to be home."

"But what if—"

"It's all set, Vi."

"This can't be all they can do for you!"

"It is." Lynne's smile stretched even wider as a tear slid down her cheek. "We've done everything possible, but it wasn't good enough. My time's up, but I have some requests before I kick the bucket."

"Mom!"

Lynne slumped against the pillows and laughed. Violet didn't know how to handle Lynne's cavalier attitude about her mortality. She had never found anything less humorous in her life. When Lynne saw her expression, she sobered.

"I'm sorry, honey. I know this is hitting you all at once, but dying is a part of life. We're not promised tomorrow. At least you know I'm about to die instead of getting a phone call from Dad saying I was killed in a car accident or something."

True, but *still*. "I'm... I can't think right now."

"Both of you must be exhausted. You should get some rest. Dad and I will be home tomorrow."

Alarm bells went off in her mind. She looked at Dad as he rounded the bed. "You aren't coming home?"

"No, I'm spending the night here with Mom."

Violet's gaze flicked to Jesse. "Maybe I should stay, too."

"Absolutely not," Lynne said firmly. "Staying in hospitals isn't fun. You two go out to dinner. Isaac, give them some money."

When Dad reached into his pocket, Jesse shook his head.

"We're good. I have money."

"So, do I," Violet said, even though she'd have to charge a meal to her credit card.

Lynne waved her hands. "Go eat out. Talk and get a good night's rest. We'll be home bright and early, and then we can talk about my bucket list."

"But I—"

Dad leaned down to whisper in her ear, "She's holding it together for you two, but she needs to rest. We'll be home tomorrow, okay?"

When she nodded, he kissed her temple.

"I'm glad you're home, kiddo."

Violet kissed Lynne's cheek and retreated to the door as Jesse said his goodbyes as well. Once she was in the hallway, she leaned against the wall and closed her eyes. A mixture of dread, sorrow, and worry sloshed around inside of her.

"Are you good?"

She opened her eyes as Jesse reached for her. She straightened and slapped his hand away. "No."

He wasn't allowed to be a monster one moment and her brother the next. She stalked away with her arms wrapped around herself.

The sun began its descent as they walked through the parking lot. Neither of them said a word as they got in the car. Once more, she leaned against the window and prayed she would wake from this nightmare.

"Are you hungry?" Jesse asked.

"No." There was no way she could eat after a day like today.

When he pulled out of the lot, she said, "We should stop at the store."

"For what?"

"Groceries. I doubt they have any."

"I'm beat. We can go tomorrow."

She wanted to argue, but she didn't have the energy. Not a word was said during the mercifully short drive back to the house. As he pulled into the driveway, she said, "You don't have to park. I'm going to run to the store."

"We'll go in the morning," he said as he pulled into the garage.

"I want to do it now." She needed the morning after pill.

"Tomorrow," he said as he shut off the engine and pocketed the keys.

"What the hell, Jesse? I don't need you to come with me," she said as he got out of the car.

"You're dead on your ass. Get in the house."

"Don't tell me—" she began but stopped abruptly when his body language changed. She eyed him through the windshield. Her finger hovered over the lock button, but it would do no good. He had the damn keys.

"Get out of the car, Vi."

Her mind raced as she tried to think of her options, but she didn't have any. She shoved the door open, slammed it, and marched up to him.

"Now what?" she challenged, ready to spit in his face and knee him in the balls if he touched her.

His mouth quirked. "You've changed."

She hadn't changed where it counted. He was more mellow than he'd been when she picked him up from the airport. Was it because they fucked or had seeing Lynne put a damper on his libido? Either way, he wasn't Jesse the psycho, he was Jesse the nice guy, but she didn't trust him. It would only take a second for him to switch into someone else.

"You *haven't* changed," she retorted.

He said nothing. He just stared at her. She couldn't decipher what was going on behind those blue eyes and was too fucking tired to try. When she walked past him, his hand brushed over her hair. She recoiled and raced to her room. She locked the bedroom and bathroom doors and listened. She couldn't hear him coming after her, which meant he stayed in the living area. Hopefully, he would watch TV, leave her the hell alone, and pass out on the couch.

She was thirsty, but not about to go to the kitchen for water. Drinking from the bathroom sink would have to do. Hastily, she washed her face and drank from the faucet before she barricaded the entrances into her room. She wedged her desk chair beneath the doorknob that led to the bathroom and pushed her drawers in front of the other door before she changed into pajama shorts and a college tee. She climbed into bed and collapsed on the plethora of pillows. She took a deep breath and was pleased by the scent of fresh sheets.

She reached for her phone and dialed Reese's number. "Hey."

"Hey." Reese's voice was soft and subdued. "I'm sorry about your mom. Are you okay?"

She blinked rapidly to stop the tears. "No."

"I'm so sorry, Vi. Is there anything I can do?"

She swallowed hard and shook her head before she got out another shaky, "No."

"Me and Meg were talking," Reese said slowly. "We sprung this move on you out of the blue and now this thing with your mom... Meg and I can stay longer to give you time to figure everything out, so you don't have to worry about moving on top of everything else. We know money's tight, so we'll pay your share of the rent this month. Don't worry about it."

Her heart swelled. "You guys are the best, but you don't have to do that. I'm moving home."

Reese's voice changed. "Home? To Texas?"

"Yes."

"Do you want to? Or do you feel you have to because of your mom?"

"I was thinking about it before I found out she has cancer. Now that I know, I want to be here." She sighed. "I dropped out of college years ago and haven't been able to find my feet. I don't want to go into more debt, and I should be here after..." After Lynne was gone. She still couldn't say it out loud.

"How soon are you going to move?"

She rubbed the space between her brows as she tried to think. "I'll be back within a couple of days. Right now, she's stable, so I want to do this before she declines even more." Her chest ached. "And I know you guys are trying to move out and everything."

"Meg and I can get your stuff sorted."

"That would be wonderful. Thank you."

"Of course."

"I'll keep you posted."

"Please let us know if we can do anything for you."

"Thanks. You guys are the best."

"We love you, Vi."

"Love you too. I'll be in touch."

"Okay. Bye."

She hung up and stared at the ceiling as tears leaked out of the corner of her eyes. When her breath hitched, she flipped onto her stomach and wrapped her arms around a pillow. Her hands fisted as she fought for control, but in the end, she couldn't hold back the tide. She wasn't sure if she was sobbing because of what happened in the SUV and shower or because of the impending death of the only mother she'd ever known.

A part of her registered the smell of cooking sausage, but she ignored it in favor of a much-needed crying spell. When the storm passed and her head felt as if it was going to explode, the doorknob rattled.

"Vi?"

She tensed.

The knob jiggled as Jesse turned it again. "I made dinner."

As if she would eat anything he made for her. "I'm good," she called in a stuffy voice.

"You should eat."

She scowled. Now he was Jesse the nursemaid. He could kiss her ass. "I'm going to sleep."

"I'll save some for you."

Whatever. She exchanged the damp pillow for a dry one and blew her nose as she hugged a blush-colored pillow to her chest and curled into a ball. She'd been so sure she could handle Jesse. She thought she had the balls to stop him from taking advantage and that she would laugh in his face. She wasn't laughing now. He had taken her over so easily.

The way he talked to Dad and Lynne, as if nothing was out of the ordinary, sent a chill down her spine. How did he do that? How could he act as if nothing happened? Why was she curled in a ball in her bedroom while he was eating and probably watching sports on TV? Was there something wrong with her? Why couldn't she shrug off everything like him? Why couldn't she be cool and detached? She hated that he could dissolve her into a blubbering mess. She wasn't a teenager anymore, but she still felt like one. She hadn't changed one damn bit.

MASON, HER EX-BOYFRIEND, WAS MAKING LOVE TO HER. HE BRUSHED KISSES over her face as he did something with his hips that made her arch her back. Whoever he had been with since they broke up had taught him some things. He was showing more technique and finesse than he had when they were together.

Something about that niggled at the back of her mind, but she couldn't focus, not when he was working her just right. Her body hummed as zips of pleasure nipped at her heels. *Yes.* She rarely got off during vaginal sex. She always had to take care of herself later, but Mason was nailing it tonight. He was hitting all the right points while biting her breasts and sucking on her neck. Damn. He upped his game big time. He tilted her hips, going even deeper, and she moaned.

"You forgot the window."

It took a moment for the words to register. Shouldn't he be whispering hot, dirty shit in her ear? What the hell did *'You forgot the window'* mean? Whoever Mason learned these moves from needed to give him lessons in dirty talk.

"You were made for me."

Something wasn't right. Mason's voice wasn't that deep and on second thought, the hands moving over her were rough, calloused. Mason worked at a movie theater. He didn't have the hands of a construction worker.

"That's my good girl."

Good girl. Her eyes flew open. It took several seconds for her mind to clear and her vision to adjust to the light. It wasn't Mason fucking her slow and sweet. It was Jesse riding her as if he had every right to. There was a bedside lamp on, and he was as naked as she was.

She braced her hands on his shoulders. "Stop!"

"I told you to spread and even in sleep, you listened to me. You know my voice, my touch. You know *me*, Vi."

"I *don't* know you!"

"Yet your body clutches at mine." He planted himself deep, making her squirm as he pulsed inside her. "God, you're fucking soaked for me. You think locked doors can keep you from me?"

"You're a monster," she whispered.

He switched his rhythm from fucking to hip rolling. His fingers came into play, and she stiffened. Rough, she could handle. Gentleness hurt her in places she couldn't describe. She clawed his back, provoking him so he would go back to the cruel asshole he'd been earlier today. He didn't take the bait. He covered her face with light, teasing kisses that made her lash out. She scored his neck before he pinned her wrist to the mattress.

"Didn't you miss me even a little?" he breathed in her ear.

"No!"

"I missed you. I missed *this*."

His low, earthy groan made her wetter. Fucking hell! He tucked his face beside hers as he lifted her knees so he could go deeper.

"If I hadn't made a move, we never would have made it here."

She gripped his hair and yanked savagely. "You had no right!"

How many times had her mind replayed a scenario like this? Her pinned to the bed with Jesse over her and her childhood bedroom as the backdrop? But this time he was stronger, she was angrier, and there was no one here to save her.

"I claimed the right," he said against her lips. "And I don't regret it. I still don't."

She bit him, but before she could split his lip, he gripped her jaw, forcing her to release him.

"Bad girl. If you're hungry, I'll give you something to eat."

He slid out of her and crawled up her body. She panicked as his heavy thighs pinned her arms, and he settled on her chest. He stroked himself over her mouth, which was forced open by his hand squeezing her cheeks. She spewed hate from her eyes. He didn't seem bothered. It seemed to arouse him even more. His fist pumped, and she heard him groan a moment before warm cum splattered her mouth and face.

"Fuck yes."

Her limbs jerked as she fought with all her might, but it was no use. He was like a boulder sitting on top of her. She was helpless and at his mercy. He eased his grip on her jaw, allowing her to swallow.

"This brings back memories."

"You're a sick fucker."

He used her pajamas to clean her face. She bared her teeth.

"Will you stop ruining my clothes?"

His teeth gleamed as he stretched out on top of her and tucked his head beneath her chin. "It feels good to be home."

"Get off me!"

His hand moved down her body and slipped inside her. "I almost forgot."

"Don't!"

"If you hadn't pushed me, we both would have got off at the same time," he chided.

"I don't want this!"

"You do."

She fought him, but she fought herself harder. She didn't want to give him this. He didn't deserve it. He was watching her, calculating every flicker of emotion that crossed her face. At first, she tried to play dead. Then, she got physical. She fought with every ounce of strength she had. He rose to the challenge and became hard enough to slip inside her again.

"Why fight this?" he murmured.

"I have to!"

"Why?"

"This is wrong!"

He applied pressure on her G spot, and she moaned.

"Does this feel wrong?"

"Please, please stop," she pleaded.

When he pumped his hips, she let out a choked cry. He fucked her until she was flung into a climax that forced her mouth to open and close like a fish out of water. Her vision flashed white as she came down from the excruciating high.

"That's my girl. Give into me," he praised.

Tears seeped out of her eyes as he continued to fuck her, reviving their dirty past before he came again, planting himself deep and holding himself there. His eyelids were heavy and his breathing ragged as he slumped over her. His hand stroked over her hair as he whispered, "No one compares to you."

CHAPTER 3

"Get up, Vi."

She opened her eyes. She was on her side, curled into a ball, without a stitch of clothing on. Sunlight streamed through the blinds, revealing Jesse, who stood beside the bed dressed in jeans and a tee. She sat up and reached for the comforter, only to find that it had been tossed on the floor. She hugged a pillow to her chest and glared at him as she brushed her hair out of her eyes. She had a vague recollection of being spoon fucked at some unholy hour this morning.

"Mom and Dad are on their way," he said as he headed to the door.

She stared after him for a minute before her eyes tracked around the room. The dresser had been put back in its place, and the chair she wedged under the doorknob was back at her desk. Her head whipped toward the window. Is that how he came in? Why had the window been unlocked? She shook her head as she tried to clear the cobwebs from her mind. She hobbled to the bathroom and washed herself thoroughly before she stripped the bed and threw her sheets in the wash, desperate to erase any sign of what happened last night.

When she walked into the living room, she found Jesse in the kitchen flipping pancakes. He looked up from the stove.

"Are you hungry?" he asked.

Her hands balled into fists as she stalked toward him. *"Hungry?"*

"You didn't eat last night."

She pounded her fist on the counter. "How do you *do* that?"

"Do what?"

"Act like nothing happened! You..." She jabbed her finger at him, at a loss for words. Her eyes burned with tears, but she refused to let them fall. Her tears and pleas had no effect on him. "You *fucked* me!"

His eyes moved over her. "Yes."

Her mouth dropped open. "Yes? That's all you have to say?"

"What do you want me to say?"

Her hands opened and closed as she tried to articulate what she wanted from him. She had never confronted him or talked about his assaults in the light of day. She had taken her cue from him and never said a word, always acting like nothing was going on, but things were different now. *She* was different. She wanted to fight. "What the fuck is wrong with you?"

"You swear a lot," he said mildly.

She smacked the counter so hard, her hand tingled. "Stop treating me like a kid and answer me!"

"What's the question?"

She was so pissed, she was shaking. She went toe to toe with him. "What kind of person does what you do to me?"

His eyes moved over her face. "I told you yesterday."

"Told me what?"

His finger trailed down her throat. "I can't stop."

She stepped back and clutched her neck to banish the effect his touch had on her. "You have to."

He said nothing, he just watched her.

"Is... is this your thing?"

"Thing?" he echoed as he slid a hot pancake onto a growing stack.

She was miffed to see they were all perfectly round and golden.

"You force women? That's your thing?"

He visibly stiffened. "I don't force women."

"You force *me*, jackass."

He turned from her. "You're different."

Butter sizzled as he whipped pancake batter and poured it in the pan. Her stomach rumbled, but she wasn't going to be distracted by food.

"How am I different?" she challenged.

He didn't answer.

"I think you have multiple personality disorder," she announced.

"You think so?"

His lack of reaction enraged her.

"Yes! There's something wrong with you, Jesse! You need help! I also think you have a taboo fetish."

He paused in the middle of buttering pancakes. "Fetish?"

"Yes. That's why you're fixated on me." She waved her hand as she tried to find the right words. "You get off on our relation to one another. It has nothing to do with me. If I wasn't your stepsister, I'd be nothing to you."

His eyes narrowed, but the words were finally coming, so she didn't stop. She had to get this out.

"You like the risk of being caught. That's why you did it in the car yesterday and why in the light of day." She gestured to the sunlight streaming through the windows. "You can act perfectly normal. You—"

It happened so fast; she didn't have time to run. One second, he was standing beside the stove and the next, he was on her. He gripped her face before he kissed her. She screamed and beat her fists against his chest as he backed her against the fridge. The cool metal was a shocking contrast to her feverish skin.

"I fucked you in the SUV because I couldn't wait another second to have you again." His hand fisted in her hair and pulled, bearing her throat to him. "And I can act normal right now because I've had you enough times that I can think straight. But, if you want more, I'm ready."

When he arched against her, she went rigid. He was rock hard. How was that possible?

"We could go to a foreign country where no one knows us and get a hotel room for a month. I'd fuck you so many times, you'd forget your name." He bit her jaw and then licked away the sting. "It has nothing to do with a fetish and everything to do with you. The compulsion I have to get you on your back doesn't care that our parents are down the hall or that someone could discover us in a parking lot, a field, or at church."

When his hand went to her jeans, she gripped his wrist.

"Don't."

"I don't want you because you're my stepsister. I want you because you're you. I wanted you from the start, but you refused to see."

He undid the button and shoved his hand into her jeans, despite her attempts to stop him.

"So, I forced you," he said against her ear as his fingers slipped inside her. Tension eased from him, as if he had stuck his cock in her. He sighed and rubbed his face in her hair. "I should feel bad, but I don't. You make me feel too damn good to regret what I've done."

She shuddered as he worked her roughly. "Jesse."

"You like that? You like what I do to you?"

"Stop!"

He glared at her, face carved with lust, anger, and determination.

"Five years, Vi. Five years you stayed away. You want to diagnose me? Paint me as a monster? I can take it. I'll take anything as long as I get this."

As he rubbed her clit, she hissed through her teeth. He groaned and withdrew his fingers. In seconds, he had his pants undone and was sliding into her wet heat.

"Years, I've dreamed of this. No one came close."

His tongue stroked hers and when she tried to turn her face away, he braced a hand against her cheek.

"How can you deny what's between us?" he asked hoarsely.

The fridge began to move as he hammered into her, so he transferred his grip to the metal box to hold it steady. The sound of the garage door opening made her stiffen.

"Jesse! They're back!"

His eyes gleamed with maniacal recklessness. "You want to tell them, Vi?"

"No!" She shoved at him, but he wouldn't budge. "We have to stop!"

"Make me."

She stared at him, absolutely horrified.

"You could have stopped me anytime. All you had to do was tell them what I was doing to you. Why didn't you?"

"I... You—" She heard the garage door close and wailed, "Jesse!"

"Your choice, Violet."

She squirmed in panic before she yanked his mouth to hers and kissed him. He stiffened, shocked for a moment, before he moaned. She sucked on his tongue as she gripped his ass and pulled him closer. She milked him desperately. He punched the fridge as he came.

"Fuck!"

The moment he was finished, she shoved him. When he staggered back, she pulled up her pants and slipped past him. She started toward the garage, but turned when she didn't hear him move. He had both hands braced on the fridge and his pants were around his ankles.

"Jesse!"

She dashed back to him and pulled up his pants and zipped and buttoned them.

"You're such a fucker," she spat as she turned off the stove and ran to the garage just as the door opened.

"Morning!" Lynne called as she entered, leaning heavily on her father.

"Hi," Violet said hoarsely as she smoothed a hand over her hair and then her neck, which was damp from Jesse's saliva. "How are you feeling?"

"Better with you two here," Lynne chirped.

"Mom." Jesse brushed against Violet as he leaned over to kiss Lynne's cheek. "Hungry?"

"Bags in the car?" Violet asked Dad, who nodded.

She escaped to the garage. When the door swung shut, she slumped against the wall. She was shaking. How the hell did that confrontation backfire so badly?

"Jesse, you made pancakes. My favorite!" Lynne crowed.

Violet shook her head as she retrieved the bags from the trunk.

BREAKFAST PASSED WITHOUT A HITCH UNTIL THE WASHER BEEPED TO announce her load was done.

"Someone's washing clothes?" Lynne asked.

"I tossed in my sheets," Violet said as casually as possible.

Lynne frowned. "You're washing your sheets? I changed them right before you came."

She willed herself to stay calm as she said, "I spilled soda in bed last night." She refused to look at Jesse, even though she sensed his amusement. Fucking asshole.

"Oh no! I hoped they didn't stain. You always loved that comforter."

She made a noncommittal noise. On second thought, she should have stained those damn sheets long ago so she could get new ones. Once she moved home, she would repaint the walls and change out everything, so there were no reminders of Jesse and the past.

Despite Lynne gushing about how tasty breakfast was, she ate only five bites before she needed to lay down. Violet helped Dad get

Lynne settled and hung her bedsheets on the clothesline to dry while she tossed her parent's things in the wash and started a new load. She cleaned up the kitchen and saw Jesse standing on the driveway, greeting friends who stopped by to welcome him home. Nothing had changed.

You could have stopped me anytime. All you had to do was tell them what I was doing to you. Why didn't you?

He knew damn well why she hadn't told anyone. Why did he make it sound as if she encouraged his advances, as if she *wanted* him? She tossed the dishes in the sink with more force than was necessary and was instantly contrite when Dad appeared in the hallway with a frown.

"Sorry," she mouthed.

Dad shook his head before he disappeared back into the bedroom. Violet washed the dishes, put away the food, and grabbed the car keys. She tiptoed to her parent's door. Dad was reading in bed with Mom's head on his lap. The scene tugged at her heartstrings. He peered at her over his glasses.

"I'm going out," Violet whispered.

"Where?" he asked in a low voice.

"I'm going to run to the store. Do you need anything?"

"No. Do you need money?"

She did, but she wasn't going to take any from him. "No, I'm good. I'll see you in a bit."

As she walked out of the hallway, Jesse came through the front door with a friend.

"Violet!"

She smiled as Blaine wrapped her in a hug. She caught a glimpse of Jesse's narrowed eyes before she pulled away.

"I see you even less than Jesse," Blaine said as he stepped back to take her in. "How've you been?"

"Good. And you?"

He puffed out his chest. "Four kids."

She blinked. "How is that possible?"

Jesse snickered as Blaine said, "Two sets of twins."

"Oh my God!"

Blaine shrugged. "They're a blast. You should come over. Allison hasn't seen you since high school."

"Maybe I will," she said, even though she wouldn't. "It's good to see you."

"Likewise."

Violet used her thumb to point to the garage. "I'm heading out. We'll catch up later?"

"Sure."

As she made her escape, she saw Jesse point Blaine toward the living room before he started after her. She tried to slam the door in his face, but he stuck his combat boot in the opening and shoved his way in.

"What?" Violet snapped when he loomed over her.

"Where are you going?"

"To the store. Is that against the law?"

"For what?"

She bared her teeth at him. "None of your business."

He grasped her chin. "You should know by now, everything you do is my business."

She slapped his hand away. "I can take care of myself."

"Don't do anything stupid," he warned before he brushed a kiss over her parted lips and headed back in the house.

She didn't move for a full minute. He never touched or kissed her unless he intended to fuck her, so what was that? She let out an aggravated growl and slammed the car door when she got in. She couldn't take a full breath until she put a few miles between herself and the house.

What game was he playing? What happened in the kitchen filled her with cold terror. He couldn't want to be discovered. It would destroy their family. Their parents were devout Christians who didn't believe in premarital sex, much less a sexual relationship between two kids they had raised as siblings. It was blasphemous and yet in less than 24 hours of being home, they were closer to being discovered than they had ever been in high school. What the fuck was he thinking? He would ruin their lives, and their family would never be the same. Why court such stupid risks?

She walked into Planned Parenthood, accepted a clipboard with a questionnaire, and took a seat. Was she sexually active? *Yes.* (But not by choice.) Was there a chance she could have an STD? *Yes.* (Who knew what the hell he did on base?). What was she here for? *Test for STDs, morning after pill, and birth control.*

The waiting room wasn't full, which was a good sign. She pulled out her phone and went through the group text with Meg and Reese, who took pictures of her belongings and asked if she wanted to keep, sell, or toss. She met Reese and Meg in Algebra in her freshmen year of college. They moved out of the dorms and rented a house, where they'd been for four years. Reese and Meg had recently graduated and were both happy in their careers.

Out of their trio, she was the screw-up. Her friends encouraged her to go back to school, recommended better jobs, and urged her toward good, upstanding men, but nothing good lasted long. Meg and Reese tried their best, but they couldn't make her better. She had short spurts of motivation that put her on the straight and narrow, but it was only a matter of time before she reverted to bad habits that kept her from advancing in life. It was no wonder they were moving out. She was holding them back. Reese was engaged, and Meg had been with the same guy for two years. They were going to marry, have kids, and excel in their careers while she moved home and watched her mother die.

"Violet Carr?"

She pocketed her phone and approached the nurse, who waved her to the back with an impatient look. The nurse repeated questions she had already answered on her paperwork before she was weighed and directed to a room where she was ordered to strip and wait for a doctor.

While she waited, she continued to answer Reese and Meg about what to do with her things. God, by the time she got back, they would have it all sorted. She checked the flights and winced when she saw the price. There weren't affordable flights to Salt Lake City this week. She checked her credit card statement to see what wiggle room she had. The ticket would max out one of her credit cards, leaving an alarmingly small margin on the others. She needed a job ASAP.

An unfamiliar number popped up on the screen. She ignored it and frowned when the number reappeared a minute later. It wasn't a Utah or Texas number, so she rejected it again. She shivered and clamped her thighs together beneath the thin paper sheet draped over her lap. Why did they make these rooms so cold?

When Dad's number appeared on the screen, she eyed the closed door before she answered.

"Hey, Dad."

"Where are you?"

She jerked. "Jesse?"

"I called you twice."

How the hell was she supposed to know his number? And why the hell would she answer his call? "What do you want?"

"You've been gone over an hour. Where are you?"

"Does Dad need me?"

"Where are you?"

The door opened, and a doctor came in with a clipboard and a smile. "Violet Carr?"

She hung up. "Yes. Hi."

"How are you feeling?" the doctor asked.

"Good," she said, and switched the phone to silent when it began to ring. "Sorry."

She tossed the phone in her purse and tried to shrug off her irritation. Here she was, trying to take care of business, and he was trying to track her down. Why did he care where she was? Did he think she was going to jump off a bridge? She smothered her temper and focused on the doctor, who wanted more details about her sex life.

AS SHE APPROACHED THE HOUSE, SHE SAW A CROWD GATHERED ON THE driveway. Mr. Popular was holding court. Everyone moved aside so she could park in the garage. She waved as she passed, taking in the familiar faces. Her heart sank as she turned off the car. She knew they would expect her to chat with them, but she had never felt less like socializing. Nevertheless, appearances needed to be kept up.

She mentally braced as she walked out of the garage. She was immediately engulfed in a round of hugs and kisses. She and Jesse being only one year apart meant they knew each other's friends, even though they ran with different crowds. Jesse played every sport he could, while she was pulled into student government by her friends and ended up becoming heavily involved in the school newspaper. She wasn't an introvert or an extrovert, but somewhere in between. She didn't seek the spotlight and preferred to stay behind the scenes organizing. All of that changed in her junior year. When Jesse ruined their relationship, she withdrew from everyone. He effectively isolated her in a world of her own where she had no one, and she would never forgive him for it.

"God, Vi, you're looking *good*," Brody drawled.

She looked him up and down. "You're not looking so bad yourself."

He tossed an arm over her shoulder and drew her against his side. "Dinner?"

Jesse stood across from them. She couldn't read his expression since he wore dark sunglasses, but she got the distinct impression that he didn't like what was happening. Good. Anything that pissed him off made her happy. He had always been an overprotective older brother, even before their sexual relationship began. In her junior year, he went ballistic when he caught her with her boyfriend, Tucker. That was the day everything changed.

She gave Brody an apologetic smile. "Can I take a rain check? I need to spend time with my mom."

"Right." Brody sobered and jerked his head at the house. "My mom heard you two were back. She sent me over here with a casserole."

"Aw, that's so sweet."

"How long are you here for?"

She focused on Marissa, the girl at Jesse's side. Marissa was his middle school girlfriend who had never gotten over him.

"I'm not sure," she said.

"Jesse says you're moving back," Marissa persisted.

Violet eyed Jesse, who had the military stance down pat. "Yes, I am."

"You looking for a job? My mom's shop needs a sales associate."

"I might take you up on that."

Hours passed as they stood on the driveway, catching up on life. She had dodged these people, convinced they would be able to sense what was happening if she spent too much time with them. She was surprised to hear herself laugh and banter with them. They treated her like one of the pack, even though she had cut herself off from them long ago. They brought up happy memories that had been overshadowed by the filth Jesse wrought in her life. Her hopes and dreams died when Jesse painted her world in shades of gray. He made her an outcast. She struggled to make true connections with people because she couldn't let anyone know her secret.

As Marissa caught her up on all their friends' marriages, she constructed a mental flowchart that would come in handy since she was moving back. The easy camaraderie between all of them banished her anxieties and made her feel almost normal. People came and went, and she made plans to get together with all of them and by God, she was going to keep her promise. Jesse may have fucked up her teenage years, but she couldn't let him ruin her future as well. She was going to start over. She had people rooting for her, people who wanted to help and reconnect with her. None of them thought it was embarrassing that she was moving home. They were excited to have her back. By the time the last person left, the sun had set, and she and Jesse were left standing beneath the orange streetlights.

"Where did you go today?" he asked.

She walked away from him.

"Vi."

She rounded the SUV and heard the garage door coming down. As she reached the steps that led into the house, Jesse spun her around to face him.

"What?"

"Where did you go?" he demanded.

"I told you I was going to the store."

He glanced in the car. "Where's your bags?"

"What do you care?"

"Where," he enunciated slowly and deliberately as he hauled her close, "did you go?"

She lifted her chin. "Planned Parenthood."

He stiffened. "For what?"

"Are you serious?" She wrenched away from him. "I got an STD test and the morning after pill, jackass."

"STD test?"

"I don't know what the hell you do at your base!"

He scowled. "I'm not fucking anyone else."

"Fuck you," she snapped as she marched into the house and tried to slam the door in his face.

She poked her head in her parent's bedroom and heard the shower going. She decided to do the same and locked both doors before she stripped and stepped under the spray. She had been in Texas for two days, but it felt like two weeks. Her mind bounced from one thing to the next. She had so much to do. She had to wrap up her life in Utah, spend as much time as possible with Lynne, steer clear of Jesse's bullying ass, and get a job. By going to Utah, she could accomplish two of her goals—tie up a loose end and dodge Jesse. Avoiding him was paramount in her mind.

After she dressed, she went to her parent's room again to find Jesse sitting beside Mom. They were talking in low tones and Lynne's face was drawn with worry. She left to give them privacy and found that someone had brought her sheets in from the line and hung the second load. She made her bed before going into the dining room to find Dad eating at the table.

"Okay?" she asked.

"Yeah." He ran a hand down his face. "Nice to see your friends come by."

"They're Jesse's friends."

"And yours."

She couldn't refute that, not after what she experienced today. She braced her arms on the back of a chair. "Marissa says she can hook me up with a job at her mom's shop."

Dad frowned. "You don't need to work."

"I do," she mumbled.

"Violet."

She held up both hands. "I told you, I got myself in trouble."

"How much do you need?"

"No, Dad."

"Tell me."

"I don't want you paying my bills."

"I don't want you working right now. Lynne needs us here." She grimaced.

"Tell me how much."

She waved a hand. "I don't need it right now."

"Then let me know when you have a figure."

She took the seat beside him and grabbed a fork to dig into the dish in front of him. "Brody's mom's casserole?"

"Yep."

"She's an angel."

"Brody's a good guy."

She paused in mid munch and raised her brows. "What?"

"Brody." Dad looked a tad uncomfortable as he speared a broccoli. "He has a good job and took care of his mom and siblings after his dad died."

"Dad," she said repressively.

"Just saying."

She shook her head. "Wow."

When Jesse appeared and took the chair on Dad's other side, she left the table. She headed down the hallway and was relieved to see Lynne sitting up in bed.

"Mom?"

Lynne gave her a welcoming smile. "Hi, honey."

Violet sat beside her and examined her closely. "How are you feeling?"

Lynne ignored her questions and patted her knee. "Dad tells me you're moving home?"

"Yes."

"It's not working out in Utah?" Lynne asked sympathetically.

She shook her head.

"I can't deny I'm relieved you're coming home. Dad's going to need company after I'm gone."

She flinched. "Please don't talk like that. I haven't even begun to process all of this yet."

"You'll be fine."

Her eyes burned with tears. "How can you say that?"

Lynne cupped her chin. "Because I know you. You're a sensible girl with a good heart. You know when to throw in the towel and come home. You're the rock your father needs."

She wanted to believe in Lynne's view of her, but knew it was false. How could she be a rock for her father when she couldn't stand up for herself? And the good heart Lynne believed she possessed had been corrupted by Jesse long ago.

"Do you have a lot to do in Utah?"

She nodded. "I think I should go back and get it all sorted. Is that okay?"

"Of course. It'll give us all peace of mind and when you come back, we can go to Florida!"

"Florida?"

"Yes, remember that trip? It was the best! I think about it all the time. I want to swim in the ocean and get some sun. That's second on my bucket list, right behind you and Jesse being home. What do you think?"

"Going to Florida sounds wonderful."

Lynne beamed. "As soon as you get back, we'll plan. The faster you wrap up everything in Utah, the sooner we can go."

"Great."

"How long do you think you'll be?"

"I'm not sure, but my friends are already helping me get my things together."

Lynne's brows drew together. "How are you getting your car here? Or are you going to sell it?"

"I'll pack it up and drive it here."

"That's too far, Violet."

"It'll just take a day or two," she said with a shrug.

She was looking forward to the long drive. She needed some alone time to get her head straight and come to terms with everything.

"Jesse should go with you," Lynne said.

She jolted. "No! I got this."

"Violet," Lynne said, sounding much more like the mother she remembered. "I don't want you doing this all by yourself."

"I'm twenty-three!"

"So?"

As she scrambled to come up with more excuses, she heard, "When do you want to leave?"

She turned to see Jesse leaning against the doorjamb. He looked as if he had been there for some time.

"I'm fine," she said in a flat tone that told him to butt out.

"Did you book your flight already?" he asked.

"No, I—"

"I'll do it."

When he disappeared down the hallway, she shot up from the bed. "Hey!"

Lynne chuckled. "You two," she said fondly. "Always bickering."

She would have taken exception to that, but there were more urgent matters to see to. She charged into Jesse's room and found him sitting on the edge of the bed with his phone in hand. He looked up as she came in.

"Do you want to leave first thing in the morning?" he asked.

She was lightheaded with rage. "You're not coming with me."

"Mom doesn't want you driving all that way by yourself. Dad won't let you, either."

"I'm grown!"

"I want to sleep in a bit. How about a ten o'clock flight?"

"You aren't coming with me," she said through clenched teeth.

"I think we should leave mid-morning," he said absently as he scrolled.

"Jesse!"

He looked up. "We don't have much time. Mom wants to go to Florida, and the only thing stopping her is you. We'll get your shit and drive back. We'll be gone three days max."

"You don't know what I need to do there!" He was taking over and ruining her plans, as usual.

"We'll handle it when we get there."

She snatched his phone and hid it behind her back. "There's no *we*. I'm doing this by myself."

He rose. "You aren't. Give me my phone."

She felt a modicum of safety since their parents were present. She took a step toward the door as she said, "Mom needs you here."

"Mom needs us both here. She isn't going to be able to relax if she's worrying about you. The sooner we leave, the sooner we can come back and enjoy ourselves."

"Enjoy?" she choked.

His eyes narrowed. "You're stalling."

Hell yes, she was stalling. She was trying to get away from him, not have him invade more of her life than he already had. "You aren't—"

He shoved her against the wall and pinned her there with his body.

"Back up," she hissed.

"I'm going with you," he said, voice equally low. "You can throw a tantrum, but Mom and Dad will back me up. You're not doing that long drive by yourself."

"You're trying to take over!"

His eyes moved over her face and then focused on her lips. "You can give in, or we can fight. Either way, I'll win."

Motherfucker. No matter how she resisted, he always triumphed. Circumstances hemmed her in, but he couldn't win every battle. Eventually, he had to leave, and she would move on with her life. She held his gaze as she tossed his phone. He didn't move a muscle as they listened to it tumble across the carpet. She lost this fight, but she didn't intend to lose more if she could help it.

"If you insist," she drawled.

"I do," he said, eyes still on her mouth.

"Suit yourself." If he wanted to book the tickets, he could pay for them, and she could give her credit card a breather.

"Mid-morning?" he asked, voice low and gravelly.

"Yes. Now, back off."

For a moment, he didn't move. She could hear the TV in the living room and the faint sound of Lynne's snores. She couldn't read Jesse's expression, but she felt his erection between them. She silently dared him to make a move. She would castrate him if he touched her with their parent's present.

He reached out and fingered her hair. "Your STD test will come back negative. I wouldn't put you at risk like that."

Before she could digest that, he turned from her to retrieve his phone.

"I'll book the tickets."

She slipped out of his room, went into her own, and locked the door. She leaned against it, put her hands over her face, and stifled a scream.

CHAPTER 4

"THIS MUST BE A NICE BREAK FROM THE COLD," DAD SAID. "TWO YEARS IN Alaska? I don't know if I could do that."

"It wasn't too bad," Jesse said. "But I'm glad to be home."

They were on their way to the airport and despite the early hour, Dad and Jesse were way too fucking chipper. She woke with a headache that was getting worse by the second.

"I'm glad you're here to help Violet with her move," Dad continued. "I would have gone with her if I could."

"No problem. I don't mind," Jesse said easily.

She glared at the back of his seat. Jesse was always winning brownie points, while she came off looking ungrateful and churlish. Mom and Dad were clearly relieved that Jesse was accompanying her on this trip. She'd been hoping to regroup in Utah, and now her plan was in ruins. She spent most of the night examining her situation from all sides, trying to find a way out, but there was none. She half-expected Jesse to sneak into her room. Their parent's presence hadn't stopped him in the past, but wonder of wonders, he hadn't intruded. Couldn't he give her a heads-up so she could get a decent night of sleep? She tried to doze, but the sound of Jesse's voice kept her alert.

When Dad pulled up to the curb, she stepped out and slammed the door with more force than was necessary, not that anyone noticed. Dad gave her a one-armed hug.

"Wrap it up and hurry home." She gave his waist a squeeze and was about to step away when he added, "And don't give Jesse any hassles."

Her head snapped up. She opened her mouth to argue, but Dad had already turned to Jesse and clapped him on the back.

"Thanks for doing this. Keep an eye on her," Dad said.

"Of course."

She stalked away from them and headed to the check-in kiosk. She tapped the screen before she realized she didn't have the itinerary details. As she stood there, a big hand reached past her and began to type. She gritted her teeth and stepped aside as Jesse claimed their tickets and surrendered her duffel and his backpack. When he headed toward TSA, she trailed behind, hoping he would get impatient and go on without her. He didn't. He waited patiently and stayed by her side. As soon as she got through security, she made a beeline for the nearest coffee shop. When she finished ordering, Jesse added his drink and two breakfast sandwiches as well. She glared at him until he handed over his credit card. She didn't thank him as she went to the end of the counter to wait for the coffee that would make her feel better.

As she stared intently at the barista's, Jesse shuffled her to the side so some man could grab his coffee.

"He was behind us," she grouched.

"He ordered black coffee," Jesse explained.

She glanced up to find him smiling at her. She scowled. "What's so funny?"

"You are." He brushed her hair back. "You're still not a morning person."

As she shied away from his touch, she bumped into a table. As she apologized to the startled couple, Jesse swept her under his arm and drew her against him.

"You need someone to keep you out of trouble."

She elbowed his hard abs. "*You're* trouble. I've been fine on my own!"

"That's debatable, baby."

"Don't call me—"

"Iced caramel coffee for Violet!" the barista called.

She broke off to fetch her drink. She stabbed her straw in and took a sip. Everything else faded away. She was about to skip out of the shop when Jesse grabbed her arm.

"We stay together," he said.

"I'm not a kid," she mumbled around her straw.

"Sometimes you act like one."

"Speak for yourself," she retorted, but it wasn't said with enough heat since she was distracted by her drink. She closed her eyes as coffee raced through her veins and awakened her senses. She was deaf and dumb until she got her morning joe.

Once Jesse collected his drink and food, he led the way to their gate. They had less than thirty minutes until boarding time. She chose a seat five down from him and gave him a disgruntled look when he got up and took the seat beside her. Seriously. He was beyond annoying. She did what she did best and ignored him as she savored her coffee and people watched.

There were quite a few interesting characters to examine. A woman in head-to-toe designer labels strutted past. Even though it was summer, she wore a coat, scarves, and a hat. She must be heading to Antarctica. A few people wearing pajamas and looking as tired as she felt ambled by. A group of hippies wearing androgynous clothing floated past with contented smiles.

Austin hosted an eclectic mix of people who were committed to the city slogan: *Keep Austin Weird.* Austin was the Music Capital of the World and home to many creatives and techies. The vibe in Austin was laidback and open with an undercurrent of Southern hospitality, tradition, and old school values.

A group of girls passed, laughing loudly enough to capture

Violet's attention. Their eyes were on Jesse. She glanced at him and inwardly snorted. He was too busy eating to notice the teenagers eyeing him as if he were on a menu. His strong, classic features had always attracted females. Yeah, he was good-looking, but his heart was fucking black. If people only knew... Her mind conjured up an image of Marissa doing everything in her power to get his attention yesterday. Jesse dated his fair share of girls during school, but he hadn't dated anyone his senior year.

She didn't want to talk to him, but curiosity got the better of her. "Does Marissa come around every time you come home?"

When he turned to her, she realized he was too damn close. She scooted as far as her chair would allow, which wasn't more than an inch. Stupid, small, uncomfortable airport seats.

"Marissa and I are friends. You know that," he said.

"She doesn't see you that way."

He gave her an odd look. "Are you jealous?"

She blinked. "Jealous?"

"Why are you asking about her?"

"I think you two would make a great couple." She paused and then added, "And if you got some, you'd leave me the hell alone."

When he leaned toward her, she tensed.

"No one holds any appeal in comparison to you."

"You're sick."

He moved even closer. Her hand itched to slap him.

"You're sick with me," he said as his eyes tracked over her face. "You can't deny it, not when I make you come so hard, you can't even scream."

Her pussy spasmed even as her heart withered in shame. Arousal and anger warred inside her. His mouth curved as if he knew the response he elicited from her body. She considered splashing his cocky face with coffee, but she wasn't sure it was worth the sacrifice. In the end, she looked away from him.

"I hate you."

"You don't," he said as he took the lid off his steaming cup of coffee. "You want to, but you can't."

"Don't tell me I don't when I do," she hissed.

"Want me to prove you wrong?"

"Touch me and I'll kill you." The aroma of his black coffee made her grimace. "How can you drink hot coffee when it's so warm?" It could be snowing, and she'd still order iced coffee.

"When you're in Alaska, you learn to treasure heat in any form. I'm going to drink hot coffee for the rest of my life. I can still feel the cold."

"Too bad you weren't eaten by a polar bear," she mumbled.

"If I was eaten by a polar bear, who would eat you?"

She squeezed her plastic cup, which caused her lid to pop off. "Shut up!"

His eyes laughed at her over the rim of his cup. "So touchy," he taunted.

She leaned in close and was pleased when he tensed. She wanted to wipe that fucking smirk off his face. She made her eyes heavy-lidded as she purred, "I've met a lot of men who know what they're doing in the bedroom. Don't give yourself so much credit."

She put her hand on the arm of the chair in preparation to stand, but the hand that clamped on her thigh stopped her.

"You're brave in public, baby," he said in a flat tone that warned her he was at the end of his rope.

She didn't give a damn how close he was to losing it. Hundreds of people were around. He couldn't do shit to her. "Get your hand off me."

His fingers flexed. "That reminds me. I heard what Dad said about Brody." His eyes bored into hers. "Don't."

The silky warning made her tense. "Don't what?"

"You know," he said mildly as he set his cup on the ground, scanned the crowd, and then looked back at her. "Don't test me."

"You're a fucking psycho!"

He shrugged. "Maybe."

"There's no maybe about it. You can't tell me what to do. I'll date Brody if I want to!"

She wasn't prepared for him to grip her hair. As she opened her mouth to protest, his lips collided with hers. His other hand spread across her cheek, concealing from passersby that she was resisting. He went deep, shoving foreign flavors in her mouth, effectively canceling the taste of caramel that lingered on her tongue.

"I can give you what you need," he said against her mouth and bit her lower lip. "No one comes between us."

Her hand hit his chest, nails digging in when he refused to let her go. "There is no *us*."

"There's always been an us, you're just too fucking stubborn to see."

"Let me go."

"For now," he whispered and brushed a kiss over her cheek before he released her.

Immediately, she leapt to her feet. As she strode away, she heard, "Coward."

That stopped her in her tracks, but she didn't turn around. She stalked to the bathroom with her hands clenched into fists. She slammed herself into a stall, sat, and buried her face in her hands. How the fuck was he always getting the better of her? She was supposed to be cutting him down to size, making him squirm, and feel remorse for everything he'd done. Instead, he was still pulling the strings and needling the fuck out of her. How was that possible? She was rattled, there was no denying it. She had shut down tons of assholes. What made him different from the others?

To start, no one dared what he did. Jesse was unpredictable and had a huge, unfair advantage. He had known her since she was thirteen and used everything he had learned over the years against her. Motherfucker. Everything was happening too fast for her to plan an attack. He was doing what he did best—keeping her unbalanced and playing defense. Bastard.

She wasn't sure how long she stayed in the bathroom, but by the time she emerged, most of the seats in their section had been emptied as everyone boarded the plane. She didn't look at Jesse as she grabbed her bag. She texted Abel, Reese's fiancé, who would be picking them up at the airport and got an immediate reply as she waited in line. She was very aware of Jesse standing beside her, cool as a cucumber. She wanted to rake her nails down his face.

The wait to get on the plane seemed to take forever. When she reached her row, she was miffed to see it wasn't a three-seater. She'd been hoping to negotiate with a stranger to sit between them. No luck. She needed a damn break from Jesse, but once again, there was no escape. She collapsed in the window seat while he took the seat beside her. She was on a plane for the second time in three days with her stepbrother beside her. Never in her wildest dreams had she pictured this scenario.

Change entered her life with the force of a freight train. She was in the boxing ring trying to duck the worst of the blows, but she was bruised and bloody and struggling to stay on her feet. How much time did Lynne have? What would happen to her father after Lynne passed? He retired a few years ago and had spent most of his time fixing up the house, biding his time until Lynne retired from teaching second grade. They had pins on the map of future road trips they planned and now... Now, everything had changed in such a way that she still had trouble accepting it.

Lynne was the only mother she'd ever known. She had a vague recollection of her biological mother who left in the middle of the night when she was two. No note, no warning. Just, here today, gone the next. Dad never said a word about her leaving. She took her cue from him and acted as if she had never existed. Since her father was a firefighter, he relied heavily on the church community to look after her when he was working. She hopped from home to home until Lynne came into their lives.

Before Lynne, she had no idea how to be a girl. Dad raised her the best he could, but he was clueless where females were concerned. He had no advice for her. She'd been a wild tomboy and not popular by any means. Lynne taught her how to dress and showered her with love and affection, which she couldn't get enough of. Jesse mirrored his mother. It was natural for him to put his arm around her or cuddle with her on the couch while watching a movie. He used to play with her hair so much that Lynne taught him how to braid it, which he used to do before school.

She glanced at Jesse, who was watching a man trying to stuff the already full overhead bin with one more bag. His features were so heartbreakingly familiar. He was her best friend before he became her enemy. It hurt to look at him.

The first three years with Jesse and Lynne were magical. The four of them fit together as if they had always been. They went on trips and since she and Jesse were only a year apart, she had someone to look out for her in school. Everything seemed idyllic. Lynne was the best stepmom she could ask for, and Jesse was the best big brother... until he wasn't.

He turned his head and speared her with those sky-blue eyes that made her feel as if she were being dissected. She sat back and closed her eyes as the flight attendants launched into their safety demonstration and the plane began to move.

Her eyes burned with tears as the past played behind her closed eyelids. They used to spend every waking hour together. His charisma guaranteed that he was popular in school. He brought her under his wing and made her feel like she belonged for the first time in her life. They did everything together—school, camping, church, family trips, and everything in between. His friends were her friends and vice versa. He was her everything, and before he flipped the script on her, she thought he loved her just as much as she did him. How wrong she'd been.

He was her boogie man, the monster under the bed, and yet here he was in broad daylight. He had been so cruel and heartless, ignoring her wants for his own gratification. He turned her bright future into ash and cast dark shadows over everything she did. She had no drive or ambition, couldn't hold down a job, and had a hard time connecting with people. She didn't do commitment and found it hard to trust anyone. How could she after what she experienced with Jesse? She hadn't been able to shrug off the past and move on as he had.

Her knee bounced as she tried to control her emotions. When a large hand landed on her thigh, she froze. Her eyes popped open. She swiped at her brimming eyes and smacked his offending hand.

"Don't touch me."

"What's wrong?"

"What's right?" she sassed back.

"You're worried about your move?"

She clenched her teeth as the plane left the ground, making her tummy flip. "That's the least of my problems." She brushed away an errant tear. "How long have you known Mom has cancer?"

"Six months."

She jolted. "Six months? Why didn't you tell me?"

He held her furious gaze. "You wouldn't have answered my call."

"That's not the point."

"What is the point?"

Her hands balled into fists. "I should have been told."

"Why?"

"So, I would have time to wrap my mind around all this. So, I would know everything's going to change and spend more time with her..." Her voice broke off as emotion got the better of her. She swallowed hard and looked out the window so he wouldn't see her face. "I should have been told at the same time as you."

When he took her hand and twined their fingers together, she tried to jerk away, but his hold was solid. "What the hell are you doing?"

"Relax."

"I am relaxed!" she snapped.

He gave her a steady look that made her feel as if she were being childish. He was acting like the supportive older brother she needed but couldn't trust. He was switching personalities again, jockeying for the position that would aid his cause, which was what? She wanted him to be consistently vile or nice. She couldn't handle him playing both sides.

"I don't want you touching me."

He sat back and closed his eyes. She dug her nails into the back of his hand, but he didn't move.

"Jesse."

He appeared to be asleep. She gave her hand another experimental tug, but only got their hands moved from his lap to hers. She stared at their interlocked fingers and felt something inside of her tear.

Past and present clashed, leaving her emotionally shattered. She didn't have time to fortify her walls or regain her composure. She was stripped and stranded in the middle of a storm. All she could do was buckle down and hope she didn't break before it was over.

By the time they arrived in Salt Lake City, she felt worse than ever. She hadn't been able to get a wink of sleep, not when her mind was racing a million miles a minute. Thankfully, Jesse slept the whole way and only woke once they touched down.

She led the way to the baggage claim and bought another coffee as soon as she could. She didn't argue when Jesse shouldered his pack and her duffel. She pulled out her phone to text Abel as they exited through the double doors into the sunshine.

It was warm, but Utah didn't have the blanket of humidity that Texas did. She stood at the curb and searched the lineup of cars for Abel's as she sipped her second iced coffee of the day.

"Why Salt Lake City?"

She ignored his question until he tugged on her hair. "What's your problem?"

"Why Salt Lake?" he asked again.

"Why not Salt Lake?"

"What's here that isn't in Texas?"

She held his gaze as she said, "It's about what *isn't* here."

His eyes narrowed. "Meaning?"

"I wanted away from you, away from anyone who knows you." She tipped her face up to the sun. "The fact that I fell in love with the city was a bonus."

"Did running away work?"

Temper canceled out exhaustion. She stepped toward him, so close she could smell him. He didn't wear cologne, but she never forgot the smell of his musk. Before, his scent had been familiar and comforting before she began to associate it with nightmares.

"I did what I had to," she said through clenched teeth. "You don't get to judge me for that."

"Violet?"

She had been too focused on Jesse to notice Abel had pulled up to the curb. He had his windows down and was watching them intently.

"Abel," she said with false brightness and swallowed her rage. She got into the passenger seat and leaned over to kiss his cheek. "Thanks for picking me up."

"You didn't mention you were bringing anyone," Abel said as Jesse tossed their bags in the trunk.

"My stepbrother came to help."

Abel, ever courteous, turned in his seat to shake Jesse's hand. "I'm Abel."

"Jesse."

"I'm glad you're driving back to Texas with Vi. We were a little worried."

"I'm not driving to Alaska," she grumbled as she belted herself in.

"Still. You can get in trouble at a kid's birthday party," Abel said as he pulled into traffic. "It'll give us all peace of mind if you have someone to watch your back."

"What does that mean?" Jesse asked from the back seat.

She shot him a quelling look that he returned with a stoic one.

"You're her brother. You must know," Abel said with a grin. "She attracts the wrong kind of attention and always gets herself into trouble."

"Abel," she said in a repressive tone.

He laughed and patted her hand. "It's not your fault, Vi."

"No," she said with great restraint. "It isn't."

"Men won't leave her alone," Abel shared as he pulled onto the interstate. "And she tends to put them down hard. Men don't take kindly to that."

Nothing from the back seat.

"By the way, Mason stopped by," Abel said with a sidelong glance.

"What for?"

"To get you back, I suppose. Reese told him you're moving. He wants you to call him."

"If I wanted to talk to him, I would have returned his calls." But that would be a difficult feat since she blocked him. "He didn't cause any trouble, did he?"

"Nah." His voice changed. "I'm sorry about your mom."

Just the thought of losing Lynne made her feel as if she couldn't breathe. She couldn't bear to talk about it. "Thanks. I need to leave as soon as possible."

"We figured that. We're going to help as much as we can." Abel's attention went to the rearview mirror. "I didn't know Vi had a brother. Do you live in Texas?"

"I'm in the Air Force," Jesse said.

Abel brightened. "My brother's in the Army."

She tuned them out as they made their way to her home for the past four years. Even though she knew moving to Texas was the right thing to do, she felt a niggle in her gut. Salt Lake City had given her a fresh slate. She made friends here and created a new life. This city helped her grow and heal... or so she thought.

Did running away work?

A wave of heat washed over her. She didn't run; she moved on with her life. Did he think she would wait around so when he came home on leave, she would be at his disposal? She had a life to live and wasn't going to waste any more of it wallowing on the past or him.

Listening to him and Abel put her on edge. She didn't like Jesse encroaching on her life. This was hers. Here, he was nobody, and she wanted to keep it that way. Unfortunately, he and Abel seemed to be getting along swell. She strangled her seat belt as she listened to him extract information from Abel she wouldn't have provided—that she had originally dated Abel before she realized they didn't suit and introduced him to Reese. Abel filled him in on her brief college experience, some of her jobs, and was starting on her extensive dating life when she cut him off.

"That's enough," she snapped.

Abel grinned. "Don't want him to report back to your parents?"

No, she didn't want *him* to know. "You should be careful. You were at all those wild freshmen parties with me. I have a lot of ammunition for the speech I'm going to give at your wedding."

"Don't be so touchy, Vi. I'm talking to your brother, not your boyfriend."

She looked out the window. "Yeah, whatever. Let's not bore him with this shit. Have you guys set a date yet?"

"No."

When she caught the note of hesitancy in his voice, she turned to him. "What?"

He shrugged. "It might be delayed a little longer. We just put an offer on a house."

She straightened. "You did?"

"Yeah, and we got it." He shot her an uncertain look. "We've been thinking about it for a while. Reese wanted to wait, but it was too good a deal to pass up."

That explained the abrupt announcement that Reese wanted to move out, and Meg had agreed. As she had suspected, everyone was moving forward. She ignored the pang of regret in her chest and squeezed his forearm. "That's great news. I'm happy for you."

Abel shot her a quick glance. "You know, you don't have to move back to Texas if you don't want to. We can delay our move, or you can come to the new house with us. We're going to have lots of room—"

"You guys are so sweet, but I'm good," she said, even as a part of her considered the offer.

Life was still shoving her along too quickly for her to think. She had to make big, life-changing decisions on the spot. Was she in or out? It was tempting to stay when the city looked so pristine. It was a beautiful day with the mountains jutting toward the sky.

"Reese feels bad. She's going to try to convince you to stay," Abel said in a low voice. "And I know you need a job. I talked to my dad. Our receptionist is going on maternity leave, so you can see if that suits you."

"Abel." She was touched. "You know my track record and would still let me work at your family's company?"

"You're not a bad worker. You just haven't found the right job yet."

Her eyes stung with tears. Reese, Meg, and their men had become her support system. She was a fucking screw-up and forever dragging her drama along with her, but they never gave up on her. They were loyal and amazing and at that moment, she seriously reconsidered her move back to Texas. If she was here, she wouldn't have to see Jesse when he came home, but what about her father? An image of Lynne swam into focus, and her indecision died.

"I may take you up on it in the future, but right now, I need to go back. I think it's best."

Abel nodded. "Family is everything, but if it doesn't work out..."

"Yes." She rubbed his arm. "I'll be on your doorstep."

"I just want you to know you have somewhere to go," he said as he pulled up the driveway and killed the engine.

She leaned over and kissed his cheek. "Thank you."

Abel helped Jesse with the bags while she started toward the house. The door opened before she reached the front steps. Reese stood there in her business suit.

"What are you doing home? Aren't you supposed to be at work?" Violet asked as she approached.

"I got off early so I could be here." Reese gave her a tight hug. "Are you sure this is what you want, Vi?"

She returned the hug and rocked her from side to side. "Yes. Abel offered to let me live with you. You guys are the best."

Reese pulled away and searched her face. "You said no?"

"Yes, but I may come back to be your live-in nanny one day."

Reese blinked back tears. "I can't believe you're moving back to Texas."

"I know."

Reese's eyes moved past her and widened. "Hello."

Jesse put his hand on Violet's lower back. She stiffened and moved Reese over the threshold so they could all come inside.

"Well, *hiiii*," Reese drawled and gave her a pointed look. "I'm Reese, Violet's roommate."

He shook her limp hand. "Jesse."

Reese looked a bit dazed as her eyes moved over him.

"This is my stepbrother," she said, and Reese jolted. "He's here to help."

"Oh." Reese looked disappointed for a moment before she asked, "Lynne's your mom?" When he nodded, Reese's pretty face softened into sympathetic lines. "I'm so sorry."

"So am I," he said.

"Well." Reese clapped her hands together. "What do you want to do, Vi?"

"Might as well start now," Violet said and headed to her bedroom, which was the only one on the first floor.

"Let me change," Reese said and gave Abel a kiss before she headed upstairs. "Meg and Trent are coming this afternoon, and they're available tomorrow if you need them."

Violet nodded as she rounded the kitchen and approached her

lair. She should have been prepared, but she wasn't. Her bedroom looked like it had been ransacked. Meg and Reese had emptied everything out of the drawers and closet so she could see what she had to pack.

Jesse came up beside her and examined the room for a moment before he asked, "What kind of car do you have?"

"A Jeep," she said faintly.

"You won't get much in there."

"I didn't think I had this much stuff."

"We may need to rent a truck if you want to take even a quarter of this stuff home."

She scrubbed her hands over her face and resisted the urge to turn around and walk out.

"All right!" Reese slipped past Jesse and held up both hands. "Don't freak out, okay? I have a system."

"Thank God."

As Reese explained the method to her madness, Jesse left the room. She heard the rumble of male voices in the kitchen and hoped Abel didn't disclose any more information about her. The less Jesse knew about her life post high school, the better.

With Reese's help, the room began to look less like it had been hit by a tornado and more as if she really was moving. They made piles for things to donate and what she wanted to take. It was clear she would have to rent a truck. That wouldn't be too expensive, right?

The guys made several trips to the Salvation Army, but it didn't seem to be clearing up the space. She kept unearthing things from under the bed.

"Maybe I shouldn't move," Violet said as she stared at the room, which looked worse than it had when they arrived.

"Tomorrow we'll pack what you want to take and figure out what size truck you'll need," Reese said as she brushed sweaty tendrils from her eyes. "Whatever you leave behind, Meg and I will take care of."

Thankfully, Meg and Trent arrived with food. Violet gave them quick hugs before she dug into the Chinese food and retreated to the living room, which had three couches around the fireplace. Everyone grabbed their plates and joined her. Most of the focus was on Jesse, no surprise. Her friends gave her odd looks but refrained from asking why she hadn't mentioned him in the past. Jesse was doing his impression of a well-mannered Southern man and honorable soldier.

Her stomach churned as she watched her friends fall under his spell. He would have excelled as a politician or businessman. If he was looking for a career outside the military, he could take his pick. His facade of open honesty made people trust him instinctively. She had, and it cost her everything. Listening to the familiar timbre of his voice made her want to curl up in a ball and cry. When she was seventeen, she experienced a betrayal so deep, she still hadn't recovered. He violated her love and trust for him, and it had tainted every relationship since.

Her friends offered funny stories about her, which only reinforced what a fuck up she'd become—her ever-changing jobs, failed relationships, and lack of direction. She inwardly groaned when Trent revealed that they met on the job and after a week of dating, she had introduced him to Meg. Even though she wanted to tell them all to shut up, the atmosphere was light and teasing, and they wouldn't understand why she wanted to keep this from Jesse. To them, this was harmless information, but for Jesse, it revealed how much he changed her. The cold, unaffected facade she wanted to project was in tatters. She felt the weight of his gaze but refused to look at him. She didn't want him here with her friends—good people who loved and supported her when she had no one. She wanted to hide beneath their protective wings, but it wasn't their job to care for her. She had wasted enough time, and Lynne was reminding her how short life truly was. She had to learn to stand on her own two feet and move forward.

"Is he for real?" Meg asked out of the side of her mouth.

"Really," Reese breathed and elbowed Violet, who was slouched between them. "Tell me there's something wrong with him."

She had a vivid memory of him pinning her down in the back of the SUV. "There's a lot wrong with him."

"Really?" Reese sounded intrigued.

Her heart sank. "Really."

"He's not married," Meg said, still speaking out of the corner of her mouth as Trent and Abel quizzed Jesse about the military.

"He must have a string of women at his beck and call," Reese said in low undertones. "Who wouldn't want him?"

Violet shot to her feet. "I'm going to shower."

"Of course," Meg said and leaned toward Reese. "He would have been perfect for Janelle."

"Yes, oh my God, you're so right!"

Violet stalked into her demolished bedroom and dug through her duffel for clothes before she headed to the bathroom. She filled the tub and tossed in all the bath salts she had been saving for a special occasion and lit the ocean breeze candle that had been sitting on her toilet tank for two years. The clash of aromas soothed her. She swished her foot in the water to dissolve the last of the salts before she submerged herself. Heat penetrated her bones and melted her tension.

Tomorrow they would pack and rent a truck. That possibility hadn't crossed her mind, but maybe that was a good thing. Jesse could drive the truck, and she would follow in her Jeep. That way, she could still get her alone time and converse with him only when they had to refuel. How much would that cost? Her hands flexed beneath the water as she tried to suppress her financial worries. These were her last expenses. Once she moved home, everything would be okay.

The sound of laughter drifting from the living room made her blood pressure rise. She didn't want them to like Jesse, but it was obvious they did. No one would believe what he was capable of. Even though she was the victim of his sick fantasies, a part of her still wanted to believe it was all some misunderstanding, but she knew better. He really fucked her. Fucked her so many times that she couldn't keep count. He forced himself on her every chance he got. He never showed any remorse for his actions, either. Even now... *Did running away work?* She slapped the surface of the water, sending a mini wave sloshing out of the tub. He was such a fucker!

She raised both hands and made Zen fingers—pointer and thumb creating a circle with her palms up. She listened to her candle sputter for a second before it quieted. She closed her eyes and tried to zone out. More laughter rang out. Her breathing quickened. She forced it to even out. She tried to blank her mind, but flashbacks rose to choke her. She erupted from the tub, unable to stay still or gain any semblance of tranquility.

By the time she emerged from the bathroom, the house was quiet. She tiptoed toward the living room and saw Jesse sitting on the couch with his phone. His face, illuminated by his screen, lifted when she stopped.

"I'll get you some pillows," she said.

"Reese brought me some."

Of course, she did. She lifted her hand in a stiff, awkward wave. "See you tomorrow."

She walked into her bedroom and locked the door as she dialed Lynne's phone. "Hey, Mom. How are you?"

"Great! Jesse just called and said your friends are so nice."

She gave the room a tight smile. "Yes, they're the best."

"He said you'll probably head out the day after tomorrow."

That's what she had planned, but she didn't like that he was calling the shots. This was *her* move, not his.

"I can't wait for y'all to come back. Dad and I went out today. I bought a new bathing suit. It's yellow, my favorite color! I got you one too. It's this lovely fuchsia that will look great on you. I'm looking forward to lying on the beach."

"Me too," she said as she sank onto the edge of the bed.

"Dad's happy you're moving home," Lynne said quietly. "He's missed you, and you didn't visit that much."

"Well, I'm about to make up for my absence."

"You're a good girl, dropping everything to come home."

She blinked hastily. "You're my family. I'd do anything..." Her voice broke, and she clapped a hand over her mouth, but it was too late.

"Vi," Lynne cooed, which made Violet keel over as something twisted in her chest. "Don't cry. This is the beginning of something great, a new beginning for all of us."

She shook her head with her hand over her mouth to hold back her sobs. She didn't want anything to change. She needed everything to stay just like this.

"We have to accept God's will for our lives."

Violet immediately rejected that sentiment. God had abandoned her long ago. "Everything is happening too fast," she rasped.

"That's when you know God is taking over and carving out the right path for you."

Both of her parents were devout Christians. She had no idea how they would handle the truth about Jesse. Would they sweep it under the rug? Pray for him and think that would cure him? Would they call her a liar? She shook those thoughts away. "I'm beat."

"I'm sure you are. It's been a rough week for you. Get some rest and I want to hear your progress tomorrow."

"Will do. I love you."

"I love you more. God bless."

Violet dropped back on the bed, crossed her arms over her chest, and wept.

CHAPTER 5

"Ma'am, your card's been declined."

Violet's fingers tingled with cold panic. "Are you sure?"

"I tried twice. Is there another card we can use?"

She fumbled in her wallet as her mind raced. "Can we divide the total between three cards?"

"Here." Jesse extended his card. "Put it on this."

She closed her eyes as mortification consumed her. "Thank you," she said hoarsely.

"No problem," he said easily.

"You have a stand-up guy," the man across the counter said with a wink. "I think you better keep this one."

She opened her mouth to say something, but nothing came out.

"Add the trailer too," Jesse said.

When she glanced at him, she found him watching her.

"We don't want to get separated," he said.

"Of course, you don't," the worker said jovially and added the trailer she had nixed to their total. "So, we're doing a twenty-foot moving truck with a trailer to transport your car. Nice."

Jesse took over as she sat frozen in her seat. The men went over the contract and in short order, Jesse had a set of keys in hand. When he and the employee went outside to look over the truck and trailer, she ambled in their wake, arms crossed over her chest.

The day had been progressing nicely. She woke early and with Meg, Trent, and Jesse's help, they were able to get everything sorted and packed. She was taking more shit home than she had ever dreamed, but she told herself it was worth it until she heard how much it would cost to rent the truck. She was indebted to Jesse, the last person on the planet she wanted to feel gratitude toward.

When Jesse waved her over, she climbed into the passenger seat. He made some minor adjustments to his seat before he drove off the lot.

"Thank you," she said again, staring straight ahead.

"Don't worry about it."

"I'll pay you back."

"I said, don't worry about it."

She clasped her hands in her lap. "I think I can still drive even with a trailer on the back. It shouldn't be too hard, right? I mean, especially on the long stretches. I think we should take turns. I don't want you to—"

"You're rambling."

She glanced at him as he navigated the city with ease, thanks to his GPS. He looked so competent, while her image of a mature adult was in tatters. He got a front-row ticket to the mess she had made of her life while he was still standing tall. She was so frustrated, she wanted to cry, but she'd be damned if she showed any more weakness.

"You want to talk about it?" he asked.

"No," she said through clenched teeth.

The cab was uncomfortably intimate. Knowing they would spend almost twenty-four hours in the small space made her palms sweat.

When they pulled up to the house, Trent came outside to help disconnect the trailer so they could load the truck. When they finished, Trent drove her Jeep onto the trailer. As the sun set, Jesse parked the loaded moving truck on the street so they could leave bright and early tomorrow. Reese pulled up as Jesse hopped out of the cab. Reese looked from the truck to Violet and fanned her face as her eyes filled with tears.

"I can't believe you're leaving!"

"I know. I can't believe it myself."

They walked into the house with their arms around each other.

"You know you have to visit regularly," Reese said.

"I will."

Reese pushed her toward the bathroom. "Get dressed. We're going out."

They piled into Abel's SUV and headed to her favorite Mexican restaurant. Trent took his car since Meg was spending the night at his place. As soon as they were seated, she ordered a margarita. Meg and Reese ordered sangria's while the guys ordered beers. The girls didn't need to look at the menu. They got a variety of dishes they were going to share. This restaurant was their go-to for celebrations, breakups, and pick-me-ups. After the week she'd had, she was looking forward to good food and company... Minus Jesse.

She spent most of the meal ignoring him and trying to cram in as much quality time with her friends as possible. The more drinks they slugged back, the more emotional they became until Jesse put a stop to it.

"She's done," he told the waiter.

"He's a kill joy," Violet said in a loud whisper to her friends.

"You're going to feel like shit on the road tomorrow."

She scowled at him. "I can handle it."

"I don't feel like stopping so you can throw up on the side of the road."

"He's right," Reese said and slid a glass of water in front of her. "You have a long drive ahead of you."

Which is why she wanted to be shit-faced. That long ass drive in a confined space with him? Hell no. Despite Jesse's interference, she was feeling pleasantly fuzzy as she said a tearful goodbye to Meg and Trent. Apparently, Jesse hadn't been watching Abel as closely as he'd been watching her. Abel and Reese were tipsy and leaning on each other for support when they left, which made him the designated driver.

She must have fallen asleep during the drive because she woke draped over Jesse's shoulder. She thumped his buns of steel.

"Can walk," she groaned and began to giggle. Everything looked so weird upside down.

Her world spun as he settled her on the bed. She clutched the covers because her head was spinning.

"Oh, God."

"You're plastered," he said as he slipped off her shoes.

She grunted and closed her eyes. She felt like she was on a rocking ship, which was quite pleasant. She was about to drift off when her body jerked.

"What the—?"

"You need your jeans off."

"Why?" she grouched.

He didn't answer. He pulled them off and then unbuttoned her wrinkled blouse.

"What doing?" she huffed and batted at him.

He rubbed her belly with a calloused hand. She smiled and lazily kicked her feet, which dangled over the side of the bed.

"Feel good?" he murmured.

"Umm hmm."

"I'll make you feel even better."

He brushed sweet kisses over her face. She didn't fight. She lay there with her arms spread wide as he soothed her with comforting strokes over her bare skin. She felt a whoosh of air as he sank to his knees beside the bed and pulled on her heavy body until her butt rested on the edge. He kissed her knees before he parted them.

"Tickles," she mumbled.

When he did it again, her toes bumped against his abs. What

happened to his clothes? He braced her feet on his stomach and massaged her calves, kneading the tense muscles. She moaned. Ooh, that felt nice. When his lips brushed over her inner thighs, her toes curled.

"Who am I?"

His voice seemed to bounce off the walls. She jolted.

"Why are you yelling?"

"I'm not yelling. I need to know you're with me, Vi. Who am I?"

"Fucking boogieman," she said as she plucked at the quilt beneath her.

"What?"

"Mr. Perfect. No one knows the real you."

He rose over her and planted his hands on either side of her head. The streetlights coming in through the blinds gave him strange orange stripes. He looked evil, dark, otherworldly.

"Monster," she said and placed a hand on his bare chest.

He gripped her chin. "My name, Vi." When she stared at him, he pressed a kiss to her parted lips. "Foolish girl. Drinking leaves you defenseless." His finger traced her jaw and then the line of her throat. "You should take better care."

He nibbled on her lips while his hands shaped her body. He pressed his groin against hers and let out a soft groan.

"I jerked off with the underwear you left in the bathroom last night. I didn't want to do that tonight, and you gave me the perfect opening."

His next kiss was so deep, he stole her breath. She clutched at him as he ground himself against her. When she arched, he broke the kiss.

"I'm gonna come on your fucking leg," he hissed as he gripped her hair and pulled. "Say my fucking name."

"Jesse."

He pressed his forehead to hers. "Yes. Jesse. That's the only name that should be on your lips."

His hand played with the waistband of her underwear before

slipping beneath. Thick fingers parted her folds and then slipped inside her. She closed her eyes and hummed as she enjoyed the fire heating her blood.

"Beautiful," he breathed as he kissed her collarbone. "You were made for me."

His weight and heat disappeared. Her eyelids fluttered as firm hands folded her legs up and pinned her knees to her chest. This position wasn't comfortable. She was trying to gather the energy to move when she felt something part her folds. It took less than five seconds for her to be okay with her legs being pressed to her abdomen. Nothing mattered except that tongue dancing over her. Her blood fizzled in her veins. As pleasure built, her hands moved restlessly over the covers, herself, and then found anchor by gripping handfuls of sweat soaked hair. Her breath hitched as that talented mouth worked her into a frenzy. She trembled like a plucked string.

"Jesse."

The mouth disappeared. Before she could cry out in disappointment, a large body covered hers. A thick penis intruded, stretching her unbearably. She grunted, and a mouth covered hers as he began to thrust, fucking her on the edge of the bed where it was firmer so he could go deeper. When she orgasmed, she screamed into his mouth. He gave her his groan as he shoved deep and came.

CHAPTER 6

Her rage was ice-cold. It didn't matter that her head was pounding, her mouth was dry, and despite drinking water and coffee, she could still taste tequila on her tongue. The cloudy day matched her dark mood. Jesse woke her at the crack of dawn. He was dressed and ready to go while she was naked, hungover, and dirty. There was a moment of disorientation as she stared at him, a hand wrapped in his shirt as she tried to think.

"A shower will help," he said as he brushed her hair back from her face.

She grimaced and ran a hand over her aching body. "What?" She had a fuzzy recollection of their drunken fuck. She stiffened. "Did you...?"

"We," he confirmed as he brushed a kiss over her lips. "Come on, let's go."

She erupted from the bed and shoved him. "Damn it, Jesse! How could you?"

"Easily," he said without a shade of remorse. "Shower, get dressed. We leave in twenty minutes. We have a long day ahead of us."

He left her standing in the middle of the empty room, staring after him.

She didn't understand him. He knew she hated him for it, yet he continued to push and use her for sex every chance he got. Was he a sex addict? A sociopath? A rapist who got off on her resistance? One moment he was helpful, generous, caring. The next, he was intent on sating himself no matter the cost. Lynne's impending death hadn't affected his libido. He was as forceful and ravenous as he had been five years ago, maybe even more so.

Why?

She woke Reese and Abel to say her goodbye and was pissed when Jesse made an appearance and thanked them for their hospitality. His ability to fool everyone infuriated her. She was incredulous when Abel extended an invitation to Jesse to attend their wedding. She hoped Abel was just being nice and not serious. These were *her* friends, not his. If Abel and Reese hadn't been drunk and gone upstairs, would he have made a move? Who was she kidding? Even if their rooms were side by side, Jesse dared. What the fuck was wrong with him?

Not one word was said between them as they headed out of Salt Lake City. The only sound in the cab came from the robotic female voice on the GPS giving them directions and the radio playing classic country tunes.

She should sleep, since she couldn't have gotten more than a few hours, but she was too angry. Hazy images from last night kept slipping through her mind. He had been gentle with her. He aroused her with petting and sweet kisses before he took her. To her, this was worse than the other times because it was a complete farce. He took advantage of her inebriated state to bend her to his will. Her blood curdled with resentment and shame.

Hours passed. Jesse didn't seem bothered by the silence. On the contrary, he acted as if she wasn't present, which pissed her off even more. He hummed along with the radio and drove hour after hour without complaint. He acted as if road trips weren't out of the ordinary for him. To her knowledge, this was the first time he had ever done such a thing. Once again, he was showing his adaptability while she scrambled to keep up.

She updated her friends and parents on their progress through text and during their first rest stop, received a voicemail from Planned Parenthood who said the STD test was negative. That was one small piece of good news. Every time they stopped for fuel, she used the facilities and took the time to stretch her legs. He didn't ask her to pay, so she didn't offer to. She didn't feel like she owed him anymore. Apparently, he thought her body was his to use whenever he felt like it, so if he wanted to pick up the tab for this move, she would let him. She waited until the last possible second before she reluctantly climbed back into the truck with him.

They crossed into Colorado and then New Mexico. By one in the afternoon, she was over it. Traveling on the road had a very similar feel to flying in an airplane. She was dehydrated, exhausted, and felt dirty even though she had done nothing more strenuous than sit. She had seriously underestimated how taxing this move would be financially, emotionally, and physically. She tried to sleep, but it was impossible with every fiber of her being focused on the devil sitting within touching distance.

He was too close for comfort. The cab had two captain's chairs with a space in between where they had their bags and a small cooler. Directly behind their chairs was a wall. Thankfully, the windshield was massive and gave the illusion of space, but the confines were stifling. He was slightly slouched in his seat, completely relaxed, with one hand on the steering wheel. He was in his customary jeans, white shirt, and boots. It annoyed her that no matter the setting, he looked as if he belonged there. Asshole.

She couldn't take in the landscape, not when memories she thought she erased rose to taunt her. For years, she had kept everything bottled up, but he roused everything to a fever pitch. When she moved to Utah, she kept busy with school, partying, men, shopping—anything to keep herself from dwelling on what happened between them. Time had done it's work and made the memories easier to bear, but his reappearance brought them back to the fore. She wanted to weep, rage, attack. Instead, she sat there with her hands in her lap, staring straight ahead, while everything in her revolted to being in his presence.

"You're lucky you found such good friends in Salt Lake City."

His voice, so unexpected after hours of silence, made her jump. She shot him a lethal glare before she returned her attention to the road. She knew she was fortunate. She didn't need him to tell her that.

"You've been busy."

Something about his casual tone made her tense.

"Lots of jobs," he said as he tapped a finger on the steering wheel.

His attempt at making conversation was fucking lousy.

"Lots of men, too."

She sucked in a breath, but the sound was drowned out by traffic and the truck as it rattled down the interstate.

"Did it work?" he asked.

"Work?" The word left her mouth before she could stop herself.

He glanced at her, but she couldn't see his eyes since they were covered by dark shades.

"You fucked them to forget about me. Did it work?"

Her mouth dropped open. "You conceited son of a bitch!"

"Mom would be hurt if she heard you say that," he said mildly.

"You're the biggest narcissist I've ever met!"

"If I have nothing to do with your body count, then what's your explanation for the man parade your friends talked about?"

She leaned toward him so far, her seat belt locked. "I wanted, so I took. That should sound familiar to you!"

He didn't look at her as he continued in that placid tone that made her want to hit him.

"Seems no one measured up. None of them lasted longer than a few months."

"I have high standards!"

"Doesn't sound like it. I heard one of the guys you dated a few months ago worked at a video game store."

"Justin was sweet!"

"It's *Dustin*, actually," he said coolly. "Seems he wasn't sweet enough for you to remember his name."

"His name *is* Justin!" It was, right?

He shrugged. "You should know."

"Yes, I *do* know. What I do and who I do it with is none of your fucking business!"

He shook his head. "We've been over this before."

Everything you do is my business.

"I'm a big girl. I can take care of myself."

"Debatable. It sounds like your friends have been carrying you for a while now."

She felt as if she had been kicked in the gut. "You don't know anything about my life."

"You dropped out of school, can't keep a job, and bang anyone who catches your eye. Am I missing anything?"

He had turned into Mr. Hyde again. Now that they were alone, he had morphed back into the monster she brought out in him with little effort. His succinct and brutal summary of her life made her flush.

"You haven't changed. You're still dating losers because you don't want it to go anywhere, and you want to be in control. The few times you ran into good guys, you gave them to your friends or walked away. You took what you wanted before you got bored and moved onto the next schmuck."

"Stop," she said faintly.

"Empty fucks." The tendons in his arm flexed as he gripped the steering wheel. "I know exactly how that feels. I took every woman who offered."

He was no longer slouched in his seat. He was sitting up straight, body radiating with tension. He was driving a little faster than he'd been a minute ago. The unruffled veneer he had maintained throughout the day was beginning to shred.

"Did sleeping with all those men help you forget about me, or did it make you realize nothing comes close to what's between us?" he challenged.

"Shut up!"

"Last night, you gave yourself to me."

"I was *drunk*! You took advantage of that."

"When your guard is down, you show your true feelings."

"True feelings?" she echoed in a strangled voice. "My true feeling is that I hate you! *Loathe* you. If I never saw you again, I—"

"You begged me to never leave you."

He conjured up memories too painful to revisit. "Stop."

"You said we were a unit."

She shrank in her seat and stared straight ahead. "That was a long time ago."

"Feels like yesterday to me."

"That was before..."

"Before I caught Tucker with his hand in your shorts?"

"We're not talking about that!"

Her hands were clammy with panic. He was bringing it all back —her worst memories and the moment everything changed. She searched for an exit, but there was none. She was locked in this suffocating cab with a man intent on emotionally stripping her.

She could still remember Tucker being ripped away from her and the look on Jesse's face as he pinned Tucker to the pavement and beat the shit out of him. It sent a chill down her spine. He could have killed him. If she hadn't thrown herself at Jesse, who knew how far he would have gone? Jesse drove her home, and... She shut her eyes against the memories bombarding her. That was the day her world turned gray.

"You haven't changed. You're still throwing yourself away on men who will never satisfy you."

"You think you're the only one who can get me off? You're

delusional. You're lucky I remember your name. You're just another dick to me. Nothing special."

He turned his head and stared at her for so long that she reached for the wheel.

"Jesse!"

When he returned his gaze to the road, the cab was once again enfolded in silence, but this time the tension was so thick she couldn't breathe. She watched him out of the corner of her eye, waiting for him to lash out or explode. He did neither. He slowed his speed to match the other cars, sat back, and resumed the journey as if nothing had happened. The fact that he could swallow up his emotions like that unnerved her.

She tried to mimic his unruffled poise. It took every ounce of control she had not to rail at him as he deserved. He got her worked up and then switched off again while she was at the boiling point. Who was he to judge her choices? She turned her face away so he wouldn't see her furious tears.

By the time they covered another hundred miles, most of her rage had seeped out of her, leaving her drained and wishing this was over. Crazy ideas passed through her head of catching a flight home, but they were in the middle of nowhere and their parents would know something was wrong. Mom assumed they were having quality bonding time. If she only knew... Lynne sent a steady stream of images from the Florida resort they would be staying at. Knowing every minute brought them closer to Austin kept Violet sane. She could handle this. Just another thirteen hours...

She had sunken into a glum daze when Jesse cursed and lurched forward. She jolted and watched as he messed with his phone. She glanced at him, the road, and back.

"What's going on?" she asked warily, ready to make another grab for the wheel.

"I should have stopped at the last gas station. I thought we'd make it to the next town, but I don't think we can. I need to refuel quick."

"Here." She held out her hand and was relieved when he handed the phone to her. It took her a few seconds to figure out how to find the nearest gas station. "In ten miles, take the exit."

She held his phone and fed him directions. She couldn't see the gas gauge from where she was sitting, but if he was worried, it must be alarmingly low. Because they were towing the trailer, the truck needed to be fueled frequently. Every time they filled the tank, it cost around one hundred and fifty dollars. She wouldn't have been able to make it halfway home before her credit card maxed out.

They were the only vehicle to take the exit. They were in the middle of nowhere. There were no signs for a town, just a lone service station that couldn't be seen from the interstate. It was late in the afternoon and her non-existent energy was at an all-time low. She hoped this gas station had a store with sugary goodies in it. That hope died quickly when she saw not one vehicle at the four available pumps.

"Is this place abandoned?" she asked.

"I hope not. We're not going to make it far if it is."

As he hopped out, she set his phone in the cradle and paused when she saw a message flash across the screen.

Tanya: I miss you.

She felt an odd dipping sensation in her stomach. He told her he wasn't fucking anyone else, but he was a compulsive liar. She couldn't believe a damn thing he said. But at least he didn't have any STDs. He could play with whomever he wanted. Maybe she would push Marissa on him once they got home. He could fuck her for the duration of his leave.

As she slid out of the truck, she raised a hand to block her eyes from the hot breeze that blew sand and dirt everywhere. She watched as he stuck his card in the machine and was relieved when the screen lit up and beeped.

"I'm gonna check it out," she said without meeting his eyes.

She spotted bathrooms off to the left but walked into the tiny store first. There was no one behind the counter and all they had to offer was one case of assorted sodas, a smattering of candy bars that were faded with age, and corned nuts. She exited as quickly as she came in. She wasn't looking forward to the state of the restrooms, but she had to take what she could get. Who knew when they'd stop again?

There were old beer bottles and trash scattered around, and some trucks parked in the distance. Presumably, the drivers were taking a nap. Odd place to stop.

Despite how small the station was, there were separate male and female bathrooms and when she pushed the door open to the women's side, she found two stalls. They were covered in graffiti and there was no light aside from the sun streaming through the wooden louvers high up on the wall. Only one of the stalls had a door, but there was no lock. Of course, it didn't. She was relieved to see toilet paper and vowed that on her next road trip she was going to bring several rolls with her. She squatted over the toilet, sure her ass would break out in a rash if she made contact with that nasty seat. This place was hella creepy. She wanted to get the hell out of here as soon as possible.

She had just finished washing her hands when the door opened behind her. In the cracked, dingy mirror, she saw Jesse standing there. She whirled around with dripping hands.

"What's wrong?" she asked, ready to run, sure he was about to tell her some crazy shit was going down outside.

She blinked when he stepped in, letting the door swing shut, once again enclosing her in semi-darkness.

"What—?" she began, but her voice died when she heard the snick of the lock being turned.

He stood in the shadows, not saying a thing. Her heartbeat accelerated. She took a step back and bumped into the sink.

"Jesse?"

He erupted from the darkness. Hard hands gripped her shoulders and shoved her against the grimy tiles. Her scream was cut off by a large hand clamping over her mouth.

"Don't." His voice shook with rage. "You think you can say I'm just another dick, and I'll let that pass?"

She moaned into his hand. Oh, God. He had been stewing over this for the past hour?

He unbuttoned her jeans and shoved his hand in her pants, easily bypassing her silky underwear and sinking his blunt middle finger into her. She gasped, jumped, and thumped his chest with her fists, but he was an immovable brick wall in front of her. Outside, the wind picked up, making the louvers sing.

"You want me to be just another dick to you, but I'm not. You're in my blood, just as I'm in yours. Those men you threw yourself away on didn't last long because they weren't me."

She went on her tiptoes as he slipped another finger in her and applied pressure on her G spot. She shrieked and shoved at him, but he leaned into her, making anything she did with her hands ineffective. She was at his mercy. He smelled of sweat and himself. It was so familiar, a smell she associated with her childhood and the good old days before he tainted those memories with debauchery.

"I claimed you at seventeen," he said harshly. "I took your virginity and imprinted myself on you. You'll never be free of me."

She tried to shake her head, but she couldn't with his hand pinning her to the tiles. She wasn't sure if it was fear or her body reacting instinctively to his intrusion, but her body secreted, coating his fingers in natural lube. He dropped his face into her hair and groaned.

"You feel that, baby? Your body yearns for mine. How can you deny what's between us? You were made for me, Violet. Why won't you admit it?"

"Noph!"

Her denial came out garbled, but he apparently understood because he tensed. He lifted his head and examined her face, illuminated by slivers of sunlight, while his was cast in shadow.

"You fight me, but you fight yourself harder," he murmured.

His fingers began to caress. Fear morphed into pleasure. She clawed his wrist, but he didn't let up.

"You're so worried about what people will say that you would deprive us both."

He did something with his fingers that made her whimper.

"I'm not so self-sacrificing. I suffered, Vi. Five years without you. I can't do it anymore. I'm taking my fill."

He scissored his fingers, making her jerk like a puppet on a string.

"You're trying to be a good Christian girl, but you like it rough and dirty. How can anything that feels so good be a sin? Feel me. Yes. You like that, don't you? I remember everything that makes you tick. I taught you to crave me."

She gripped his wrist with both hands and rocked her hips before she caught herself and stilled. She saw the glint of white as he smiled.

"That's my girl."

Abruptly, his hand disappeared from between her legs. He pressed a hand against her chest to brace her against the wall as he dragged her pants down. She widened her stance to stop him from pulling them off completely. He tipped her off balance and roughly yanked her jeans off one ankle before he turned and shuffled her toward the sink.

"Jesse!"

Her voice echoed loudly around the restroom and traveled easily now that the wind had died down, but that didn't stop him. She heard the hiss of his zipper before he bent her over with a hand on her back, flattening her against the sink. She gripped both sides of the grimy porcelain and opened her mouth to shout, but she wasn't paying attention to what he was doing. He slammed into her with such force, she nearly crashed into the mirror. She yelped and slapped a hand on the dusty surface as he let loose.

She didn't have the breath to call for help, not when he was fucking her so hard, she could barely think straight. It was no holds barred. He gripped her hair and yanked her head to the side as he scraped his teeth on her shoulder and then bit down. His other hand coasted down her front before he grabbed her breast and pinched her nipple. She screamed and bucked as he lapped at his bite and then moved to her ear lobe and bit again.

"Stop!"

The hand on her breast went to her mouth and squeezed so hard, she panicked and clawed at him. His grip eased enough for her to breathe. One hand splayed on the mirror as he fucked her. Their reflection was alarming—a large, clothed man demanding submission from a smaller form. Her nipples stood at attention while her shirt rode up because of the veined arm wrapped around her middle, holding her in place. Her gaze collided with his. He was watching her. His eyes seemed to glow with manic, animal lust. She closed her eyes and tried to shut off her mind and distance herself from what was happening. Her eyes flew open as he pulled out, spun her, and pushed her back against the wall. He hefted her up and slid into her as she tried to get her bearings.

She wasn't prepared for his tongue to steal into her mouth. He tasted of the grape Gatorade he had been nursing from their last pit stop. He let out a low groan as he rocked against her. She could feel him vibrating against her, trying to hold himself back. For what?

He kissed her cheek, the bite on her shoulder, and sucked on her neck before he came back to her parted lips. She couldn't comprehend what was happening, so she lay there pliant, body throbbing, mind in shambles.

"I need you with me," he whispered.

She tried to turn her face away, but his hand held her still as he assaulted her mouth. He stole her breath and gave her his. It was carnal and tinged with desperation. He stirred up emotions she didn't understand or want to feel. Her nails sank into his chest as his other slid down and touched her clit. Oh, shit. She let out a mewl of angry pleasure and felt his lips curve against hers. When she fought him, he focused on keeping her mouth busy, a double assault that short-circuited her brain. The orgasm caught her off guard. One moment she was fine and the next, she exploded, bucking forward, nearly unseating him. He growled as he fought her back against the tiles and thrust, making her orgasm painfully pleasurable. As she spasmed, he buried his face in her hair and roared, pounding her ass into the wall as he came.

Her ears rang as she came down from the high. She was aware of his hot breath fanning her cheek and the wind that began to pick up again. Her legs, which had wrapped around his waist at some point, dropped heavily to the ground. His hand skated over her throbbing ass and gripped, pulling her more firmly against him. When she moaned, he hummed contentedly. His calloused hand stroked her hip as he pulled out of her. She sucked in a breath as his hand slid inside her, bathing his fingers in his cum and spreading it over her belly as he rested his forehead against hers.

"I'm capable of anything when it comes to you," he said in a low, gravelly voice. "But you already know that. Don't push me."

She stared at him. She didn't know what to say or how to feel. He must not have liked her expression because the hand coated in cum came to her face. His stained fingers drifted over her lips. When she opened her mouth to protest, he slipped them in her mouth.

"Taste us," he ordered.

Her mouth watered as his fingers stroked her tongue.

"Suck."

She had no choice but to swallow or let her saliva dribble out of her mouth. When his hand threatened to sink deeper, she gripped his wrist and dutifully suckled.

"As the years passed, I convinced myself that you couldn't be what I remembered," he said hoarsely. "That what you roused in me was a mad adolescent obsession, and I'd be over it by now."

He retracted his fingers from her mouth and held her still as he sampled her lips and sent his tongue into her moist cavern. His tongue explored with aching slowness. Her breathing was ragged when he pulled away. He stared at her for a long minute. She waited.

"I never got over it," he said quietly.

She shivered as his fingers traveled down to her breast and cupped her with a tenderness he hadn't shown a minute ago. She braced her hand on his chest.

"Stop," she whispered. She didn't want him petting to make up for what just happened between them.

His hand massaged as his head dipped down. He latched their lips together, even as she pushed for space and tried to sidle away. A hand on her hip kept her where he wanted her. He kissed her with such absorption, she started trembling. He made a noise in the back of his throat and stroked her back as he gentled the kiss.

"Maybe I deserve to burn in hell for what I've done," he said against her lips, "but it'll be worth it."

When he stepped back, her legs nearly gave out. He steadied her before he moved to the stall without a door. She slumped against the tiles and stared at the windows and the flickering light as clouds passed overhead. The wind was raging again. Dust drifted over her bare legs. She stumbled to the sink and washed her face, pieces of her hair, and scooped what she could of him out of her. She used her underwear to pat herself dry since there were no paper towels and pulled up her jeans.

Jesse came up to the sink beside her. She turned away and strode for the door. She unlocked it and burst through, desperate for air and precious seconds without his stifling presence.

Out of the corner of her eye, she saw an old man sitting in front of the store smoking a pipe. He hadn't been there earlier. She skidded to a stop and stared at him before she felt a hand on her lower back.

"Let's get out of here," Jesse said.

She smacked his hand away and marched toward the truck. "Don't touch me."

She stood outside the passenger door as he climbed in from the opposite side. The truck rumbled when he turned the key. She waited until the last possible second before she climbed in. He didn't say a word as they pulled away from the service station. She glanced at the GPS and felt her eyes burn with tears. They had eight hundred miles to go, which would take another twelve hours. Their estimated time of arrival in Austin was four in the morning. She wanted to give up already. Fuck all her stuff. Leave it in the middle of the desert. Nothing was worth this.

Her head throbbed with an oncoming migraine. Not a surprise when she was stressed, had no sleep, and was being physically and emotionally fucked by her stepbrother. She fumbled through her purse and said a silent prayer of thanks when she found aspirin. It would take the edge off. She shook out two pills and gulped down water before she huddled against the door and prayed that God would save her from this hell.

She couldn't wrap her mind around what happened in that restroom. Or last night. Or the other times he forced her since he had come home. She felt just as lost, dazed, and shell-shocked as she had when he turned the tables on her when she was seventeen. One day, he was her brother and the next he was a stranger. There were long stretches of time when everything seemed normal. So much so, she wondered if she was going crazy and doubted her sanity until it happened again. And again. And again. Her junior year of high school, she felt like she was walking on a tightrope. One misstep and her world would crumble. It was happening all over again. No matter how much time passed, no matter how much she fortified her walls, he would lay siege. And he would win. He didn't recognize any barriers, which made him dangerous and terrifying.

A tear trickled out of the corner of her eye. She didn't understand him or what drove him to do the things he did, but he had dragged her under with him and she couldn't see the light. He forced her to partake in his salacious fantasies, and she would never be the same. He was right. She liked it rough and dirty. None of the men she dated could give her what she needed. None of them came close and when she nudged them towards the dark pool she wanted them to swim in, they backed away after dipping a toe in the water.

Jesse changed her, and she hated the person she had become. She was afraid to let anyone close because she didn't want them to see who she really was. Ever since him, she hadn't felt right. Nothing assuaged the restlessness within her. She wanted routine and stability yet continually acted on rash impulses. She wanted to be around her friends and yet, when she was in a crowd, perversely wished she were alone. She was never satisfied and constantly craving something she couldn't define.

Her vision blurred as she stared out the window at the passing scenery. She was in line with the vent that blew out icy air and turned her face numb. Good. If only the air conditioning had the same effect on her emotions. She would rather feel nothing than have her insides churn and riot. There was only one escape open to her, so she took it. She closed her eyes and tried to take refuge in sleep.

CHAPTER 7

SHE KNOCKED ON THE DOOR LEADING INTO JESSE'S ROOM FROM THE bathroom. She cracked it open and saw him sitting up in bed with a book. He frowned at her, but she ignored that and hopped onto his bed.

"They're fighting again," she said miserably.

"I noticed."

"I hate it."

"It'll blow over."

She leaned into him as the shouting got louder. "What if they break up?"

"They won't."

Jesse didn't sound concerned in the least.

"How can you be so sure?"

"My parents used to fight all the time."

"But don't they love each other?" She twisted the ends of her shirt, a habit Lynne hated because it stretched out all her clothes.

"People who love each other can still fight."

"*We* don't fight!"

His brows shot up. "Didn't we fight two days ago at the movie theater?"

She scowled. "You wanted to watch a war movie, and we don't fight like *that*."

She jabbed her finger at the door. Even though their parent's room was down the hall, and the door was closed, she could hear every word being said. It wasn't pretty. They were arguing about money. Lynne and Dad rarely fought, but when they did, it felt like World War III.

Jesse shrugged. "Fighting isn't bad. It gets your feelings out."

She shuddered. "I hate it."

"It'll pass."

"It's been going on for half an hour." She flinched when she heard something crash. "Why does she *do* that?"

"She wants a reaction out of him," Jesse said mildly as he turned the page.

Desperate for a distraction, she peeked at his book. "What are you reading?"

"It's about a sniper."

She made a face. "You aren't really going into the military, are you?"

His eyes moved from the book to her. "You know, I promised my dad I would enlist."

"What about *me*?"

"What about you?"

Her eyes bugged. "You're going to leave me?"

"Mom and Dad are here."

"But we do everything together. What am I going to do without you?"

His eyes moved over her upturned face. She didn't know what he was thinking, but he put his arm around her and tucked her close. She closed her eyes and breathed in his scent. He always smelled nice. Her friends thought he was a hottie. She liked his face, but she didn't allow herself to look deeper than that. Jesse was Jesse.

The fight continued, but she found she could handle it now that she was weathering the storm with her brother. He played with her hair as he read, which had a drugging effect on her. When she slumped against him, he told her to stretch out. She did so and tucked her face against his thigh. His hand returned to her hair, and she fell asleep, knowing that everything was going to be okay.

She roused slightly when she heard, "Jesse?"

"Shh, she's asleep."

Soft footsteps and then, "Why's she in here?"

"You know she freaks out when you two fight."

"Sorry. Here, let me take her."

"She's fine."

"Are you sure?"

"Yeah."

She heard Lynne kiss his cheek. "You're such a good big brother."

"Did you two settle your issues?" Jesse asked.

"Yes. I'm sorry you had to hear that."

"I'm fine, but next time, give me a heads-up, so I can take her out before you start breaking things."

"I'll do that. Isaac's the opposite of your father. He doesn't tell me how he feels and shuts down instead of talking to me. It takes drastic measures to make him open up."

"I hope you didn't break anything valuable."

"No, I stopped at Goodwill a week ago to buy things for this showdown. Everything's fine now. Good night, son. Don't stay up too late."

Lynne left the room and closed the door behind her. Violet listened to the sound of pages being turned and was on the verge of sleep when she heard the soft thump of the book being put on the nightstand. Jesse stretched out beside her and gathered her against his chest. Her body hummed with contentment as he buried his face in her hair and took a deep breath.

"Jesse?"

He stiffened. "Yeah?"

"Promise you won't leave me."

He sighed into her hair. "Vi."

She twisted her hand in his shirt. "We need to stick together."

"I don't—"

She tilted her head back, so she could see his shadowed face. "You love me, don't you?"

He stared at her, eyes unreadable in the dim light.

She thumped his chest. "Hello!"

"Yeah," he said as he ran a hand down her spine.

"Yeah, *what*?"

He sighed. "I love you."

"And I love you." She pressed as close as possible. "We need to stay together. We're a unit that nothing can tear apart. You know I have abandonment issues."

"Go to sleep, Vi," he said, voice thick with amusement.

"Don't laugh at my abandonment issues!"

"I'm not."

"You are! You're not taking me seriously!"

His thumb brushed over her lips. "Hush."

"You better not leave me to shoot guns in the military," she growled.

"Sleep," he murmured.

His fingers tunneled through her hair and massaged, easing her into sweet, dreamless slumber.

CHAPTER 8

She woke in mid-fall. She let out a stifled shriek and flailed before she collided with something hard and unyielding.

"I got you."

She blinked up at Jesse as he toted her across a badly lit parking lot. "Wus happening?" she slurred as she tried to get her bearings.

"Got a room."

She started. "What?"

"It's midnight. We'll crash here for a couple of hours and finish the drive tomorrow."

"I can drive," she offered and tried to clear the cobwebs from her cloudy mind.

"No, you can't," he said as he shouldered through a door and dumped her on the bed. "I'm going to get our bags."

"But I can—"

He slammed the door behind him. She sat there, dizzy and exhausted, despite her catnaps. Throughout the day, she slipped in and out of consciousness. It was awful to wake every hour and realize they were still on the road. She glanced around the room, which seemed worn, but clean. As she stared dazedly at the blank TV, the door opened, and Jesse came in with his pack and her duffel. He set both on the floor before he locked the door and fell face down on the bed.

"Are you okay?" she asked belatedly.

He grunted. "Falling asleep at the wheel. Lots of animals on the road. Not worth it. Need sleep."

Resting for the night was logical, but it extended their time together. She eyed his unmoving form for a minute before she heard deep, even breathing. He was clearly exhausted, and no wonder. They left Salt Lake City around six in the morning. He had been driving for eighteen hours. She grabbed her phone and sat in a chair by the window. According to her phone, they were in Texas, about five hours from home. That wasn't too bad. She messaged her friends and parents and sent them their location, even though they were probably asleep. Tomorrow, it would be over. They would be around friends and family, and she would do her best to avoid Jesse and his psychotic episodes.

She grabbed her duffel and went into the bathroom. She showered, brushed her teeth, and smeared lotion over her dry skin. She leaned toward the mirror and examined the bite on her neck. He hadn't broken the skin, but it was red and swollen. What the fuck was wrong with him? Her ear was fine, but there was a dark smudge on her breast from his rough handling, and she was sore and achy. Her eyes were bloodshot, hair a frizzy mess, and she was trembling. It could be because she had been eating junk food all day. Or maybe it was stress and the emotional overload. Realistically, it was probably all those things combined.

It was one in the morning, which made six days since she had come home to Austin and discovered Lynne's diagnosis and come face to face with Jesse. A week ago, her biggest worry was a job and where she would live. That seemed like a piece of cake compared to what she was dealing with now.

She stared at her reflection, eyes glassy, jaw set. On the outside, she looked unhappy, and a touch pissed. Beneath the surface, she was spiraling. If she was a different kind of person, she would have shot Jesse with one of the guns her father kept in the safe. If she was a different kind of person, she could have overcome her nightmarish teenage years and made something of herself—become a guidance counselor and helped others with their trauma and replaced the bad with good. Instead, she was this...

You dropped out of school, can't keep a job, and bang anyone who catches your eye.

She looked away from her reflection as her eyes stung with tears. Fuck. Against her will, her mind began to replay their encounter today in excruciating detail. Even now, she could feel the imprint of the tiles against her back and Jesse's strength as he effortlessly held her in place while he fucked her. She screwed her eyes shut and bit back a moan as her pussy spasmed. Self-loathing cascaded through her. She sank to her knees with her hands over her head. She climaxed. Every. Fucking. Time. It was no wonder he didn't stop. Her mouth said one thing while her body did another. She was fucked up. She wasn't supposed to respond to him, but she did.

When the urge to vomit had passed, she rose, using the counter to brace herself. She felt sick and had sea legs. She popped vitamins and guzzled water before she emerged from the bathroom. She paused at the foot of the king-sized bed and listened to his heavy breathing. Out like a light, just the way she liked him. Another annoying thing about Jesse—he could sleep anytime, anywhere. He dropped off easily, while she spent hours trying to shut her mind off. His lack of conscience probably helped him a lot in that department. Fucker.

There was no way in hell she was going to sleep in that bed with him. Her only choices were the chairs by the window or the discolored carpet. She could imagine how filthy the floor was. She turned both chairs towards each other so she could prop her legs up and make an awkward nest. It was extremely uncomfortable, but it was only one night. Tomorrow, she would be home. She repeated that to herself as she shifted restlessly, trying to find a position that didn't hurt.

She listened to the cars coming and going and pulled back the curtain to look outside. She spotted their massive moving truck on the far side of the parking lot with her Jeep still on the trailer. Although she would never admit it to him, she knew there was no way in hell she could have done this on her own. She resented that he barged in uninvited, but he treated her move as if it were his and footed the bill for the airline tickets, rental truck, fuel, and now a motel room. Her feelings for him were a complicated mix of begrudging gratitude, fury, resentment, and embarrassment. Her eyes moved to him. He hadn't bothered to take off his boots. She intended to drive part of the way, but between the size of the truck and trailer and that pit stop fuck, she decided to let him handle it, and he had without complaint.

Her mind swung from one thing to the next, keeping her awake when she desperately needed sleep. In between light dozes, she kept looking out the window, expecting to see the first hint of sunlight through the curtains.

She woke in mid-lift. "Wha—?"

"You're a pain in the ass," Jesse growled as he carried her to the bed.

She struck out and hit something. He cursed and dropped her on the mattress, which wasn't as soft as it looked. She lost her breath and tried to roll away, but she wasn't fully awake and ended up in the middle of the bed.

"You hit my fucking ear," he growled before he launched himself at her.

"Jesse, *no!*"

Her hands were knocked to the side as he pinned her beneath his bulk. His hairy leg slid over her smooth ones and the fog cleared enough for her to realize that he had removed almost all his clothes aside from his briefs.

"Jesse—"

"Hush," he said roughly as he pulled her more securely against him and buried his face in the pillow beside her. "I need sleep."

"I don't want to sleep with you!"

"Too bad."

She slapped his side, but that didn't get a reaction from him. She stared at the ceiling. It was still dark out. The only source of light came from the bathroom, which he must have used before he noticed she was sleeping on the chair.

"Get off me," she said.

His hand stroked down her side. "Go to sleep."

"I *was*!"

"We'll sleep better like this."

"How many times do I have to tell you, I don't want you touching me?" she hissed.

"Relax."

His words were slurred from fatigue. Clearly, he wasn't in any state to do anything sexual.

"Can you move over? Why are you on top of me?"

"Like it," he said and inhaled deep. "You smell like home."

"What?"

His even breathing told her he'd drifted off to sleep again. Even as she tried to figure a way out of this, her eyelids drooped. His weight had a drugging effect on her. Even as she fought it, her mind began to power down, convinced she was safe enough to get some rest.

SHE WOKE ON A MOAN. HER EYES OPENED. SHE WAS ON HER SIDE FACING THE window. She knew where she was, with whom, and that her body was on fire. There was an arm banded across her chest, keeping her in place as Jesse rocked in and out of her.

She had always been a sucker for this position with past lovers. Intimate, but since she was facing away, she didn't have to maintain eye contact. If the guy knew what he was doing, it was a great position to hit her G spot. Her cheek was flush to the mattress, one hand twisted in the sheets as her body moved with his. His gentle thrusts were driving her crazy. A distant part of her mind screeched, *What the hell are you doing? Run! Fight!* Instead, she lay there, boneless, wanton, swimming in sleep and sex.

"You with me?" he murmured in her hair.

She shut her eyes against the sunlight seeping through the curtains. Another day, another fuck. When he dropped her in bed last night, she knew this was how she would wake up. He never failed to take advantage. Her body felt as if it had been doused in peppermint. She was tingling all over as he kept her right on the edge. She was too far gone to put up a fight. His hand brushed over her breasts before it came to the base of her throat.

"Violet."

She clenched her teeth. Why did he have to talk? He never used to. Why didn't he just fuck her and get it over with?

"Violet."

"What?"

He tipped her on her back while he stayed on his side and draped her thighs over his. His hair was tousled, eyes bloodshot, and he was in desperate need of a shave. His thumb brushed over the apple of her cheek. She didn't want to see him as he fucked her. While he was behind her, she could suspend reality, but this... She turned her face away.

"Look at me."

"No."

He gripped her jaw, forcing her to face him. "I told you how I feel about that word."

She lashed out, but he was ready. He grabbed her wrist and pinned it to the mattress.

"Let me in, Vi," he growled against her sweaty temple.

"Never!"

He planted himself so deep, she grunted.

"You want me to force you so you can hate me, but deep down you know this is where you want to be."

"You're wrong!"

"Am I? Then why are you soaking wet? If you hate this, why are you squeezing me so goddamn tight?"

"Finish it," she said through clenched teeth.

"I'm not in a hurry," he said lazily as he changed his rhythm, making her body arch. "I want this to last."

"I don't."

"You don't always get what you want out of life," he chided as he kissed the side of her face. "Let me make you feel good."

His hand coasted down her body and slid between her legs. Her eyes collided with his as he rubbed her clit. He was watching every fleeting expression that crossed her face. He was analyzing and cataloguing so he would have more ammunition against her. She bared her teeth and clawed his arm, but he didn't budge.

"Stop messing with me." He made her into his plaything, and she resented it with every fiber of her being. "I'm a person, not a fuck doll."

He frowned. "I don't think of you like that."

"Then why are you doing this?"

"Because you're lying to yourself. Your mouth spits lies, but your body speaks the truth. Forget everything and just feel, Violet."

When he applied pressure to the right spot, she tossed her head back and forth. His thrusts became more forceful. Her head spun as he kissed her, applying layer after layer of sensation until she forgot to hate him.

"Tell me you want me."

His voice came from a long way off. She didn't focus on it. She was almost there... He gripped her face and gave it a sharp shake.

"Look at me," he ordered.

It took considerable effort to obey his dictate when her body was ready for take-off. When she focused on him, his grip gentled and he stroked her cheek.

"Tell me, Violet."

"What?" She sent her hand down her body to finish the job, but he captured it and twined their fingers together.

"No touching yourself. That's my job."

"You're not doing it!" she spat.

He gave her a pained grin. "Frustrated, Vi?"

"I hate you!"

He kissed the corner of her mouth. "You need to stop saying that."

"You need to stop torturing me," she panted and lifted her leg to change the way he was fucking her. "Uh, *yes*."

"You know it isn't like this with anyone else." His breath hitched as she moved on him. He gripped her waist to stop her, but then he groaned and buried his face in her hair. "Fuck me. This is how it's supposed to be between us."

When he increased the tempo, tears leaked out of the corner of her eyes.

He glared at her with stormy eyes. "You feel that, Vi? This is bliss. There's nothing else like it on the planet. No one comes close for either of us. Admit it."

Her head thrashed as the crescendo built.

"Please," she begged.

"Please what?"

She let out an enraged bellow and threw herself at him. The only reason she got him on his back was because he wasn't expecting it. He clamped his hands on her to stop her from getting away, but that wasn't her goal. She straddled him and braced her hands on his chest. She tipped her head back and mindlessly rode him for her pleasure. She was too lost to care what she looked like with her hair loose, mouth open as she gasped and moaned. When lightning struck, she screamed. He yanked her down and covered her mouth with his. He gripped her ass to hold her in place as he began to thrust. When her orgasm hit, she pounded her fist into the mattress while he let out a loud, guttural groan and said her name.

She slumped over him in a state of satiated shock. It had never been this good.

"Okay?" he murmured.

As she shifted away, his hands smoothed down her back.

"Wait."

"We need to get going."

He kissed her neck. "We're close to home. We have time," he said in a lazy voice.

His hand sifted through her hair, reminding her of all the times he had played with it or braided it. Her eyes stung as past and present clashed. She missed this part of him. The gentle, affectionate Jesse who made her feel loved and protected. It had been so long since someone touched her like this. She didn't allow anyone close enough to coddle her. Even as she longed for her innocent past, she was aware of his dick still throbbing inside her and the smell of sex permeating the air. There was no going back.

"What's wrong?" he rumbled.

"Everything," she whispered.

She grunted as he rolled her beneath him. He braced himself over her and smoothed her tangled hair back from her face.

"Don't cry," he ordered roughly as he kissed away her tears.

She placed her hand on his chest. "We can't keep doing this."

He sat up. She moaned as he withdrew from her. He knelt between her spread thighs. She wasn't surprised when his hand slid inside her.

"I want to be a good man. In every aspect of my life, I'm a model citizen." His eyes flicked up to hers. "Except when it comes to you."

She tried to scoot away, but he gripped her hip, warning her to stay still.

"I've broken laws, vows, and my own code to have you. I thought I had it under control, that I would see you after all this time and feel nothing." He shook his head as he looked down at his fingers sunk inside her. "But it doesn't matter how much time's passed. I had to touch, taste. I'd pay any price to possess you." He pressed his face against her belly. "I *need*, Violet."

As his fingers stroked, her toes curled.

"Mom's days are numbered and all I can think about is losing myself in you." His voice was so low, she could barely understand him. "Love me back, Vi."

An invisible pick pierced her chest and sank deep. "What?"

He lifted his head, blue eyes spearing hers. "I've been in love with you since I was fourteen."

Her body reacted before her mind could process his words. Her foot landed on his shoulder and sent him reeling back. She rolled off the bed and faced him with her hands clenched into fists.

"How dare you say that to me? You don't know the meaning of that word!"

"I know exactly what it means."

"You don't love me! If you did, you wouldn't have done all this!" She jabbed her finger at the bed. "This is sex, not love. It's lust, greedy, sinful..."

"You see it the way you want to."

She stomped her foot. "I see it the way it *is*! You took what you had no right to take! And you're *still* taking! You stole everything from me and have the nerve to say you love me?"

He shrugged. "Love can make monsters out of men when it's not returned."

Her mind went blank. There was no sound in the room aside from her ragged breathing, but inside, she was in the eye of an emotional storm. Before her mind could bolt, she held up a hand. "No."

"No?"

He was a master manipulator and pathological liar. She wasn't going to play into his hands. He was toying with her. He wasn't satisfied with owning her body, he wanted her mind too. Fuck that.

"I'm going to shower," she announced. "And then we're leaving."

She averted her face as she headed to the bathroom. She locked the door, climbed into the shower, and stared at the yellowed walls as water beat down on her head.

After everything he had done to her, he *dared* utter that word? Did he think that word absolved him of his crimes? Justified his actions? No. Love had no place in their relationship, and she'd be damned if she trusted anything that came out of his mouth.

She stepped out of the tub and wrapped a towel around her hair and then her body. She glanced at the door. She didn't want to go out there. He was making an already bad situation even worse. They had five hours left until they reached Austin, but even ten more minutes in his presence was too long. She had dreaded facing him and convinced herself that it couldn't be as bad as she imagined, but it was worse. He was determined to bring up a past she buried long ago. Her jaw ached from clenching her teeth. He thought she was stupid enough to believe he had feelings for her. She wasn't naive. He stole her innocence years ago.

She took a deep breath and put her shoulders back. Five more hours. She could do this. She had to. She got through the worst of the trip yesterday. They were so close to home. Lynne and Dad were waiting on them. She could withstand anything he wanted to throw at her, and then it would be over.

She yanked open the door with a defiant scowl, but her bravado was for nothing. He was sitting on the bed talking to Lynne on his cell phone.

"We needed some rest, so we got a room for the night," Jesse said.

His voice was lighthearted and back to its normal cadence. He was a class act.

"I'm glad you two are being so responsible and doing this trip safely," Lynne said while on speaker.

"Safe is my middle name."

Violet cast him a disgusted look as she knelt beside her duffel. He pulled on jeans, but didn't bother to button them. She couldn't resist giving his body a once over. Yes, she'd fucked him numerous times since she picked him up from the airport, but she had always been focused more on fighting than taking in his body. He was ripped. He'd always had a nice body since he was an athlete. Before he'd been broad and lean, and now he was just... huge. He had defined abs, and the veins stood out on his arms. There wasn't an ounce of fat on him. He could be Captain America's body double.

If she took a picture of him right now, it would be the perfect ad for a male gigolo. His jeans rode low on his hips, hair tousled, and the wrecked bed told its own story. Women would pay well for one night with him. If he wore his uniform, he could make even more money. Another career path if he decided to leave the military.

"We're going to grab breakfast before we head out and be home by late afternoon," Jesse said.

His tone warm and easy. He was back to being the good son while her body still throbbed from his attention. Seriously? She wanted to hurl her shoe at his head.

"Knowing you're there with Violet makes us feel so much better. Have you two been having fun?" Lynne asked.

"Yes."

Violet ground her teeth as he told what whopping lie.

"We've been taking in the sights and talking about the past."

At that, Violet whipped her head around. Their eyes locked.

"I'm so glad we have this time together," Jesse said and winked at her.

"Fuck you," she mouthed, and he smiled.

"Here, talk to Vi. I need to take a shower and feed her. She's grumpy."

Jesse tossed the phone on her duffel before he strode to the bathroom.

"Violet?"

Lightheaded with rage, she tried to gentle her voice as she said, "Hey, Mom. How are you?"

"I'm good. I've been worried about you two but knowing you're in Texas makes me feel better. You haven't been taking many pictures."

She cleared her throat. "Yeah, no. Sorry. It's been super hectic."

"I'm sure. You two got everything wrapped up so quickly. I'm so glad. Just a little further and then you'll be home."

"Right," she said as she got dressed.

"I'm not trying to be pushy, but what are your thoughts on heading to Florida the day after tomorrow? Is that too soon? Do you need more time to get settled or—"

"No, that sounds perfect. Let's head to the beach." She needed as much activity as possible.

"Yay! We're on the same wavelength."

Her anger was tempered by Lynne's excitement and good cheer. Just hearing Mom's voice made her feel better. Lynne was an anchor in her otherwise messed up world. All she wanted to do was curl up beside Lynne and just be. It was fucked up that she was seeking comfort from her mom when she should be giving it, but she felt so fucking lost and needed her more than ever.

"I can't wait to get home," she said.

"Me either. Having both of my babies' here..." Lynne's voice hitched suspiciously.

She walked to the window as she heard the shower cut off in the bathroom.

"Don't, Mom," she begged.

"I know, I'm sorry. I'm just so happy. You two are my world."

She swallowed hard. "And you're mine."

"Well, you'll be here soon enough. Take pictures, have fun, and be safe."

"I love you."

"I love you more," Lynne said with a sniffle. "I'll see you soon."

As she hung up, she saw that Jesse had over fifty unread text messages. She, in comparison, had no messages aside from the group texts with her parents and Reese and Meg. Hopefully, after she moved home, she would get reacquainted with classmates and beef up her social life. No more living in the past, no more isolating herself because of Jesse. No. She was going to live, and that started now.

CHAPTER 9

Jesse came out of the bathroom as she repacked her duffel. "There's a diner next door."

"I'm not hungry."

"You're eating."

She swung around to yell at him and immediately turned away. He was buck naked. The view from the back was just as good as the front. Contoured thighs, ass, back. She had never been one to goggle at men's bodies, but his was phenomenal. There was a saying, "Never trust a pretty face." Usually, it was applied to women, but in her case, her stepbrother was the epitome of pretty outside, ugly insides.

She was miffed that by the time she had zipped her bag, he was dressed and ready to go with his pack on his shoulder. He held the door open for her. As she passed, she averted her face, before she marched across the mostly empty parking lot. It was a sunny day without a cloud in the sky. When she tried to climb in the cab, he grabbed the waistband of her pants and yanked her back out.

"Eat," he said.

She smacked his hand. "I told you—"

She ground her teeth as he tossed her duffel and his pack in and locked the truck.

"We don't have time for this," she snapped.

"We do, and I'm hungry," he said as he pushed her toward the diner.

She had no choice but to go with him.

The diner was hopping. The moment she stepped through the door, the smell of bacon and maple syrup made her stomach rumble. She and Jesse waited while a frazzled waitress searched for an open table.

"We can sit at the counter," Jesse offered.

"All right. Make yourselves at home," the waitress said.

Jesse's hand landed on Violet's lower back. She quickly stepped away and gave him a withering look before she navigated through the cramped, packed diner. The counter was occupied mostly by trucker's and old men chatting over their morning coffee. They found a spot between two sets of men, who did double takes when she took a seat. She grabbed the menu and perused it before she glanced at the old man beside her, who was staring openly.

"Morning," she said.

"It's turning out to be a good one," he said with a wink.

She relaxed and tapped the menu. "What's good?"

"Depends on what you got a hankering for," he drawled.

"I want something sweet and salty."

He grinned. "You're my kind of gal. You should get French toast with some meat on the side."

"That sounds great."

When she opened the menu, he pointed out her options.

"Thanks," she said as the waitress stepped up.

"What'll you have?"

When she gave her order, the old man gave her a thumbs up before he turned back to his friend, who was reading a newspaper and munching on toast.

"You military?"

She glanced to the right to see the burly trucker beside Jesse looking him up and down.

"Yeah. Air Force," Jesse said.

The man tipped his hat. "Thank you for your service."

She was surprised, pleased, and then annoyed when they launched into military talk. Jesse couldn't go anywhere without being acknowledged, honored, and admired. The surrounding men were all listening and nodding as he explained where he had been stationed and his last two years in remote Alaska. She didn't want to listen, but it was impossible not to when he was sitting right beside her. She was intrigued despite herself as he told stories about the men in his unit, the friends he'd lost, and that he was heading to Japan next.

"Is this your lady?" one of the truckers asked.

She whipped her head around, mouth full of French toast. Jesse's eyes crinkled at the corners when he saw her dilemma.

"Yeah," he said as he rubbed her back. "This is Violet."

"You got a good man here, miss. Not many guys still have old-fashioned values nowadays. You better hang onto him."

The trucker shook Jesse's hand and left with his buddies.

She swallowed and glared at Jesse as he ate his omelet. "Really?"

He stabbed a piece of French toast and ate it before she could stop him. "These are good."

"You're such an ass," she hissed.

He examined her for a moment. "You didn't get your coffee. That's why you're cranky."

Her mouth sagged. He used the L word, fucked her *again*, told strangers she was his, and didn't think she had grounds to be upset? "You're a goddamn psycho."

He glanced at his watch. "Finish your food. I want to be on the road within the hour."

She hopped off her stool and held out her hand. "Give me the keys. I'll wait in the truck."

"It's hot," he said.

"I don't care!"

He dropped the keys in her hand. She stalked out of the diner and realized halfway across the parking lot that he had picked up another tab for her. Oh, well. She climbed into the cab, rolled down the windows, and waited. He was right. It was hot, uncomfortably so. If she didn't give a damn, she would have run the air conditioner, but she didn't want to waste fuel. Apparently, she still had a conscience, unlike him.

She texted her friends to let them know she would be in Austin in a few hours and watched the morning traffic ebb and flow. She was sweating and starting to wonder if he was making her wait on purpose when she saw him striding toward her. Relieved, she started up the truck and leaned toward the vents to cool down.

"Here."

She glanced at him and blinked when she saw that he was holding an iced coffee. She took the cup and gave it a wary sniff.

"What?"

"You wouldn't put anything in this, would you?"

He buckled his seat belt. "What would I need to drug you for?"

Right. He got everything he wanted from her.

He pulled out of the parking lot and navigated through the small town before he found his way onto the interstate. She took a tentative sip and let her eyes flutter shut. It was an excellent white mocha. She bit back a moan.

"Good?"

She opened her eyes and saw he was watching her.

"Yes," she said grudgingly, and then waved a hand. "Eyes on the road!"

He grinned as he obeyed her order. She sat back and despite what occurred in the motel room, her spirits began to lift. She was almost home. Soon, they would be with Lynne and her father and Jesse would be heading off to Japan. She would settle in Texas and set about recovering financially, emotionally, mentally. Then, she would figure out what to do with her life.

One good thing came out of facing Jesse again. He wasn't the bogeyman under her bed any longer. He was a psycho, but one she could handle. She faced him and lived to tell the tale. For now, she would play nice for their parent's sake. Neither of them would rock the boat on that front, but in the future, she would go back to avoiding him at all costs.

Would Jesse come back to Texas if Lynne was no longer around? A surge of ambivalent emotions swept through her. Lynne was the only family he had. After she was gone, he would have no one. Well, he would have Dad. She glanced at Jesse out of the corner of her eye. Today, he added a trucker's hat to his ensemble, but everything else was the same. He hadn't shaved, which gave him a five o'clock shadow. On the surface he seemed content, but the tales he shared in the diner told a different story. He had lost many friends and people he respected since he had joined the military, and although he had glossed over the details, she could read between the lines. His five years in the military thus far hadn't been a picnic.

She wrestled with herself. She didn't want to engage him in conversation or show empathy because he would get the wrong idea, but... "I'm sorry about your friend."

Out of the corner of her eye, she saw his head turn in her direction.

"What?"

She waved her hand. "You were talking about him in the diner. Eric."

He nodded. "Yeah."

When he said nothing more, she added, "Jeremy too."

"That was a tough one."

She pursed her lips. "Is... is your job dangerous?"

He shrugged. "There's always risk."

"A *lot* of risk?"

"Worried about me, Vi? I thought you hated me."

She bristled. "I do."

"Then what's with the sudden concern?"

"Dad would be upset," she quipped. "Why have so many of your friends passed?"

"Shit happens."

"How can you sound so casual about death?"

"Death's been a constant presence in my life from when I was very young. When I was six, both of my grandfather's died within weeks of each other and my grandmothers went a couple of years later. Then there was my dad." He shook his head. "Death's inevitable."

"So, you're *okay* with Lynne going?"

He frowned. "Of course not. Just because you know it's coming doesn't make it any easier."

"Then, how—?"

"I know there's nothing I can do, so I accept it, and focus on spending as much time as possible with her."

"We're heading to Florida the day after tomorrow."

"Good."

She stared out the window. The mountains and desert had given way to flat lands as far as the eye could see. They passed fields of crops, oil rigs, and green pastures. The atmosphere in the cab wasn't as hostile as it had been yesterday. It should be worse today, especially after what transpired in the motel room, but she chose to blank it from her mind.

It was easier to act like it never happened than to ponder his motives. That pastime would drive her insane. She thought she knew Jesse better than anyone else until he started acting out of character.

It bothered her that despite everything he had put her through, there was an easiness between them that carried over from their childhood. Their familial bond hadn't been severed despite their tumultuous relationship. They knew each other's preferences and habits and may have spent half a decade apart, but their core was still the same, which gave them common ground. When they were kids, she thought they could read each other's minds. That was before he ruined their relationship with sex.

I want to be a good man.

He could be. He just had to stop his horny, manic episodes. When he was with her, he was a completely different person. With everyone else, he was courteous, patient, helpful. That's the boy she had grown up with, the one she loved. She would do anything for him... and had for a while, even though she knew it was wrong. Maybe that's what she hated most. Her desire to please him trumped rational thought, her self-respect, and propriety. She let it go on too long before she came to her senses and started fighting back.

Her mood began to dip. She tried to ignore the heaviness in her chest and the dark wave that swept over her, obliterating the burst of optimism she got while drinking her white mocha. Her moods were like the tides—high, low. Sometimes tsunamis swept in, and she didn't come up for air for days. That feeling of excitement and homecoming turned to ash as her spirit sank like a stone.

As if he sensed the change, Jesse said her name.

"Don't," she sighed.

"Don't what?"

She shook her head. "I just want to get through this in one piece."

"Get through what?"

Lynne's death and whatever else occurred before his departure.

Silence enfolded the cab. She leaned her head against the window and stared at the landscape, but she wasn't taking it in. Memories floated to the surface—good, bad, and ugly.

"When my dad died, I thought my life was over," Jesse said.

She tensed.

"He was my world, my hero. Mom did her best to fill the gap, but it wasn't the same. She dated a couple of guys. None of them lasted long."

They passed a grove of trees with a river running through it before they came upon open, untouched land with a lone farmhouse in the distance.

"Isaac didn't cater to me or try to make me like him. I didn't know how to take that. He was a firefighter, which was cool, but not as cool as my dad being in the military. When Mom mentioned he had a daughter, I told her that wouldn't do. I didn't want anything to do with a prissy girl. And then we met at the park. You weren't what I expected."

She remembered that day. Dad had never introduced her to a girlfriend before. She'd been ecstatic. She had been trying to set Dad up with one of the ladies from church for years. She was tired of being shuffled from family to family when he had to work. When she met Lynne, she instinctively knew she was perfect for her father.

"You were dressed like a boy in a striped, green shirt and khaki shorts," Jesse continued. "Your hair was messy and tangled and when we played soccer, you kicked me in the shin to get the ball. You were aggressive, competitive—the complete opposite to every girl I knew. You got in my face and challenged me. You called me names and taunted me when I refused to play as rough as you."

The images he evoked caused a strange flurry in her chest. "I don't want to talk about this."

"You welcomed us in, wanted us around all the time, and cried when we left. You clung to me, made me feel needed, and looked up to me."

Her stomach lurched. "Stop."

"I fell in love with you the day we met and never snapped out of it."

She rolled the window down to drown out his voice.

"Every year it got worse until I couldn't take it anymore—"

"Pull over!"

"You didn't see—Fuck, Violet, *don't*!"

Even as she shoved her door open, she felt a hand twist in her shirt, hauling her backward. The truck swerved and Jesse cursed.

"Pull the fuck over!" she bellowed.

He pulled off the state highway beside a field of flowers. She hopped out of the truck and marched through the high grass, uncaring about the stains she was getting on her jeans or the fact that she could step on snakes and God knew what else. She didn't care. She stopped and braced her hands on her knees as she tried to catch her breath.

"Vi."

He was right behind her. Of course, he was. He couldn't give her a fucking moment.

"You need to back off," she warned.

"I gave you five years."

She whirled around to face him. "You didn't *give* me five years. You went into the Air Force, and I made you promise to stay away!"

"And I did, until now."

He was breathing hard, chest pumping beneath his gray shirt as he faced off with her.

"The only reason I went into the Air Force is because I realized how out of control I was and the effect it was having on you. I hoped after all this time, I'd be able to restrain myself, but you make me go haywire."

"You don't *want* to help yourself! You get off on dominating me, *forcing* me—"

"I don't want to dominate you. I want *you*. Any way I can have you, I'll take you."

"You're sick."

"Maybe."

"There's no maybe about it. Anyone who's done what you have should be locked up."

He pulled off his shades so he could pierce her with eyes that reflected the unreal blue sky. The bill of his cap cast a shadow over his face, but that didn't take away from the intensity of his stare.

"You could have made that happen. Why didn't you?"

When she tried to walk away, he blocked her path.

"No, answer me. If you wanted me to stop, if you hated me so much, why didn't you tell someone?"

"Who would believe me? Even *I* couldn't believe what was happening and you were doing it to *me*! Who would believe perfect Jesse Sampson was fucking his sister? You're the best actor I've ever met. You're able to turn it on and off like *that*." She snapped her fingers in his face. "You did me dirty and then carried on with your day as if nothing happened. You *still* do that!" She rubbed the place where her punctured heart thudded. "And Mom and Dad would die if they knew. You know that."

A warm breeze tugged her hair as the sun beamed down on them. Volatile emotions tumbled around inside her. She dimly noted that she had traveled further from the truck than she intended. Jesse stood between her and freedom, a silent declaration that she wasn't going anywhere until he allowed it.

"What do you want from me?" she demanded.

"I want you."

"You've had me!"

His hand slashed through the air. "Your body isn't enough. I want *you*."

"That's never going to happen."

Her heart slammed against her ribs as he invaded her space, making her feel trapped even though they stood in an empty field with miles of open land around them.

"I fell for you before Mom taught you how to dress or what it meant to be a woman. You bloomed right in front of me and started attracting and picking the worst guys to date. You made my life a fucking hell."

"And that's my fault? How was I supposed to know?"

There was a minute shift in his expression that made her stomach clench.

"You knew how I felt about you," he growled. "You woke up that night, you looked right at me."

Her heart careened into her throat. She backed away. "We aren't doing this!"

He grabbed her shoulders, halting her escape.

"We are," he gritted.

"You're fucked up!" She beat her fists against his chest. "You were sneaking into my room at night and jerking off on me! Why—what —who *does* that?"

"A desperate, horny teenager," he said in a flat, unapologetic tone. "I was obsessed. I stole your underwear at first, but that wasn't enough."

Her mouth watered as panic spread through her. She looked around, even though she knew they were alone. This was their fucked-up history, the beginning of the deterioration of their relationship. These were things she had wiped from her memory, that were so taboo she vowed never to tell a soul, and here he was, laying it out in broad daylight.

"You were turned on by it, Vi. I saw your hand moving beneath the covers. You were touching yourself while I—"

"Stop!" she screamed and ripped out of his hold so she could pace, hands swiping at the cold sweat that covered her skin.

"You're so deep in denial, I don't know how to reach you," he said as he dogged her steps. "You want to act like none of this happened, but it did and it's still happening. You want me, but you put on this act because you're afraid of what others will say."

She swung around to face him head on. "I don't want you!"

He didn't stop until their chests touched. He wasn't Jesse, but he wasn't the monster either. He was someone else, a stripped-down version of himself she had never met before. His eyes glittered with wrath that didn't bode well for her. She mentally braced as his hand gripped her throat.

"You're lying to me, but what's worse is you're lying to yourself. You're so locked in your head that you don't know what's real and what isn't."

"You're my brother," she said through clenched teeth.

"Legally, not biologically, and I never saw you as a sister. I did everything in my power to let you know I saw you as more. Some part of you knew it, too."

She clawed at his hand. "Let me go!"

His hand flexed on her and she stilled. His eyes bored into hers as he leaned down, so his lips were a hair's breadth away from hers.

"You love me and not as a brother either. I could feel your eyes on me during games, in school, at church. You wanted to be with me all the time. We were so in sync with each other, we didn't even have to talk. I thought we had an understanding until you started dating."

Something dangerous flared in his eyes. His eyes moved over her face as his finger stroked her hammering pulse.

"Not only did you date other men in front of me. You picked losers. The only thing that kept me sane was believing you weren't going too far with them." His tone roughened. "And then I caught Tucker touching you and lost it."

He cocked his head as the hand on her neck went to her chin and angled it so she couldn't avoid his gaze.

"I let my body do the talking, assuming you would understand all the things I couldn't say."

She jerked her chin out of his grasp. "I can't do this."

"You have to. There's nowhere for you to run and no one to interfere. Talk to me, Vi."

"I have nothing to say to you!"

He gave her a small shake. "We can't move on if we don't settle our shit."

"I don't care if we move on. You ruined everything for sex!"

"I told you, it's not just sex."

"Love?" she spat as she tried to get away from him and failed. "I don't believe you. Love is *patient*, love is *kind*—"

"Love is cruel," he snarled. "Love is selfish. Love makes good people do terrible things. People think love is this soft, fluffy emotion that magically makes everything better. It isn't. It can fuck you up so bad, you'll never be the same."

"You can't use that word to justify what you've done!"

"It's all I have."

She shook her head. "This never should have happened between us. I want it to go back to the way it used to be. I want my brother back."

He brushed loose tendrils of hair away from her face. "You can't get back what you never had. I was your friend before I became your lover."

"You mean enemy."

"I never wanted to be your enemy. I meant to be your champion, your man, *yours*. You let me touch you, let me teach and pleasure you. It was only after that you started fighting—"

She shoved away from him. "I gave into you because I didn't know what to do. You were my first. You were showing me what it meant to be a woman, and it was *you*! I loved you and... I didn't know what I was doing, Jesse! You can't use that against me."

"I can. It's been between us from the moment we met and once I had you under me, you gave into it for a while before we almost got caught and you panicked. Since then, you've refused to give an inch because everyone sees us as siblings. We're not, Violet."

"Mom and Dad see us that way! They'd have a heart attack!"

"If we stand together, eventually they'll have to accept—"

She stomped her foot. "What the hell are you talking about? *We're* nothing!"

He flushed with rage. "Because you won't let us be! We belong together."

She gaped at him. He was a madman. "You think you can say you love me, and it makes everything better? You have no idea what you did to me. I haven't been the same since you. I can't focus, can't breathe, can't *dream* anymore. I loved you more than I loved myself. You were my hero, my life. I idolized you. I would have done anything for you and you... You destroyed me."

"Vi."

"No!" She held up her hands as her eyes filled with hot tears.

"You made me feel dirty, used, alone. You never addressed what was happening between us, and you stopped talking to me. All you wanted was sex. You made me feel like a thing rather than a person. You made me your dirty secret. That doesn't sound like love to me —" A sob interrupted her tirade.

Tears blinded her to the fact that he had moved in. When his fingers brushed over her face, she jerked back, but he wrapped her against him.

"Let me go, you son of a—"

"I'm sorry."

She stopped breathing. He cradled the back of her head and rocked her from side to side as she began to shake.

"I never meant to hurt you," he said against her temple. "I never meant to make you feel used or alone. I meant to worship you."

His hand smoothed over her quivering back as she sobbed against his chest.

"I'm sorry I didn't take more care with you. I'm sorry I didn't have enough patience. What I feel for you isn't gentle or sweet. It's this dark, insatiable craving and even after years of training and discipline in the military, I still don't know how to handle it. I'm sorry I'm not stronger."

"You can stop," she said raggedly.

His hand fisted in her hair. "You know I can't."

She punched his shoulder. "What's the point of apologizing if you aren't going to change?"

"I can't be around you and not have you."

"You can!"

"Every time I take you, it gets worse. I should stop. I should let you go. I should feel like a piece of shit for pushing you, but I need you."

As close as they were, she could see the conflicting emotions in his eyes—lust clashed with pity. She could feel him vibrating against her and didn't move for fear of pushing him over the edge. He was capable of anything.

"What we have, I've never felt with anyone else. Tell me you've felt like this with one of those assholes you used. I dare you."

Tears slid down her face. "You hurt me."

He kissed the tears away. "I know. I'm sorry. I can make it up to you. I'll give you anything you want, Vi."

She strained to get away from him. "We're both here for Mom. We should focus on her."

He clasped her face between trembling hands. "Tell me you love me."

She closed her eyes against the sight of him. "We need to go."

"I won't believe you if you say you don't."

Her hands fluttered between them. "I can't do this."

"Say it!"

"I... I did love you, but—"

He gave her a sharp shake. "No buts. You love me."

She shoved at him, but he didn't budge. "I'm not doing this with you."

"Give me something," he said harshly.

She stared at him through a haze of wet. "I already have."

"I need more."

"I don't have anything else to give you."

She jerked out of his hold and marched back to the truck. Her chest was so tight, she couldn't take a full breath. She wasn't sure if he was going to follow, but she had to get away. She would hitchhike if she had to. His words made her feel as if she had razor-thin cuts all over her body. She couldn't take another verbal blow. She was barely holding herself together.

She swiped at her eyes as she stomped through the grass and climbed back into her seat. She glanced at the GPS. Two more hours. They were so fucking close to home. She had just belted herself in when his door opened. She kept her face turned toward the window but felt his searing gaze move over her. She held her breath as silence filled the cab. Her hand went to the door handle, but she relaxed when he fired up the engine. When he pulled onto the highway, she slumped in her seat and closed her eyes.

She wasn't sure what he hoped to accomplish with this confrontation, but they were still at an impasse. They hadn't reached any agreements or compromises. Neither of them would budge. She didn't know what to think of his declarations. He claimed he loved her, but she refused to believe him. Going down that road would only lead to more pain and heartache. She wanted a clean, happy life away from him and his lies and sexual barrages.

"I told myself this time around, I'd try to give you the words, even if you didn't accept them," he said.

She wanted to clamp her hands on her ears and sing at the top of her lungs, but that wouldn't stop him. Nothing would.

"I'm sorry, Violet."

Her eyes slid shut on a fresh flood of tears. She received the apology she had always longed for, but it was an empty one since he wasn't going to stop. Where did that leave them?

"I'm sorry that I loved you too much."

THE MOMENT JESSE PULLED UP TO THE HOUSE, SHE HOPPED OUT AND RACED up the driveway. The last two hours felt like an eternity. She had to sit there in a silent, emotional hell. She felt as if he released a hornet's nest inside of her. Thousands of angry insects ricocheted inside of her, demanding to be set free. She needed a distraction, people, anything that would drown out the words she refused to ponder.

She burst through the front door and saw Dad coming toward her. She gave him a quick hug. "Hey."

He patted her on the head. "You made it."

"Yes." She looked up. "Where's Mom?"

"Out back."

She gave him another squeeze before she headed toward the

back door while he went out front to help Jesse. She found Mom sitting on the porch swing. Despite the warm day, Lynne was dressed in a jacket and long pants. She started when the door banged shut.

"Sorry. I didn't mean to startle you," Violet said as she walked forward and kissed Mom's cheek.

"You're here! Everything went okay?"

"Yes." Violet dropped onto the seat beside her. "How are you feeling?"

Lynne gave her a wan smile. "Tired, but happy. Where's Jesse?"

"He's taking care of the truck. Dad's with him."

She felt raw, confused, and in desperate need of a safe place. She rested her cheek on Lynne's bony shoulder. The comforting smell of lavender and vanilla soothed her as nothing else could.

"You and Jesse patched things up?" Lynne asked.

She tensed but covered up the telling motion by pushing off the ground to make the swing sway. "Yeah."

Lynne draped an arm around her and patted her side. "I'm glad. It hurt me to see you two drift apart. You were so close, closer than most blood siblings."

She said nothing.

Lynne sighed and rested her cheek on Violet's head. "We're family. We fight, but we should never let so much time pass without settling our differences. Life is too short for that."

Violet grunted.

"I know you don't need the lecture, but I feel the need to impart as much wisdom as I can," Lynne said in a tone filled with wry humor. "You're going to carry a heavy load when I'm gone."

Violet straightened and surveyed her. Lynne had dark circles under her eyes and, in just the few days they had been gone, seemed to have lost more weight. Seeing this strong, larger than life woman morph into a frail caricature of herself made her lightheaded with rage. Life was so unfair.

"What are you talking about?" Violet asked.

"I'm worried about them—Jesse and your father. Women are the glue that hold families together." Lynne cupped her cheek. "I need you to promise me you'll keep the family intact."

Her heart leapt into her throat. "I don't—"

"You and Isaac are all Jesse has. He's strong. He always has been, but don't let that fool you into thinking he doesn't need anyone. He's changed since he went into the military. I knew he would. Promise me you'll look out for him."

She escaped from one emotional skirmish only to run headlong into another.

"Your father is so angry. I don't know how he's going to be after I'm gone. I've been talking to Pastor Sonny about it. We're glad you're coming home, so your dad will have company."

She shut her eyes against the flood of tears.

"I'm sorry, Violet. You've had the shortest amount of time to digest this and will have the biggest responsibility after I'm gone. They need you." Lynne held her tight as a tear coursed down her cheek. "I know you can do this."

Violet swallowed hard. "I need a moment."

"We have that."

A slight breeze ruffled the leaves of the forty-foot Texas Ash trees that lined the backyard. Beyond the trees were rolling hills that went on forever. It was a tranquil, peaceful scene, but that had no effect on Violet's inner turmoil.

"I thought I had so much time," Lynne mused. "Before I found out I was sick, I was worried about paying off the mortgage and buying a new car. Now, I'm grateful for soft socks, beautiful days like this, and everyone around me."

Violet's heart tore.

"A lot of my students have stopped by. I love listening to their stories and hearing how far they've come." Lynne let out a heavy sigh. "I wish I could see where you and Jesse will end up."

"Mom."

Lynne gave her a watery smile. "You two are so young." She

stoked her cheek. "Promise me you won't take anything for granted and you'll live life to the fullest. No regrets."

"I will," she promised.

Lynne's eyes tracked over her face and brushed back her tangled hair. "I couldn't ask for a better daughter."

"And I couldn't ask for a better mom," she whispered.

"I'm so glad you're here. Help me inside, honey. I want to stretch out on the couch."

Violet immediately got to her feet and put her arm around Mom's slim waist as she led her to the living room. She was taken aback by how weak Lynne was.

"Are you okay?" she asked as Lynne grabbed a blanket and huddled in on herself.

"Of course, dear. Are you excited to head to the beach?"

"Yes. I can't wait."

"We're going to have so much fun! Now, tell me all about your road trip."

She did her best to weave an interesting story but was saved by a group of Lynne's friends who stopped by for a visit. A glance out the window showed that there was a small crowd gathered around the moving truck and trailer. Dad and Jesse were talking to the neighbors, who wanted the latest scoop on their lives. Violet sighed. She would have to get used to being part of a small community again.

She busied herself by starting dinner and noted Lynne's smile of approval. When the guys finally came in, she had a pot of chili and coleslaw ready. They sat at the dining table like they had so many times in the past. She made a concentrated effort to keep a smile on her face and the mood light as she told her parents about her friends in Utah. Jesse stepped in when her energy flagged and went into great detail about the road trip. Mom took one bite of food and pushed her plate away. Violet was alarmed, but tried not to let it show. When Dad assisted Mom to their bedroom, she started to clean the kitchen. She was so tired, she felt faint.

"I got it," Jesse said.

"It's okay," she said without turning around.

When he gripped her hip, she stiffened.

"You're dead on your feet. Get some rest," he said firmly.

She wasn't going to argue with him. She walked away without a backward glance. Taking a shower was almost beyond her, but she did so, turning Mom's words over in her mind as she washed her hair and scrubbed the grime from her body.

She fell face-first into bed, hair wet, with no underwear beneath her nightgown. She was beyond caring about anything. She needed sleep before she took on tomorrow.

CHAPTER 10

A warm, comforting weight stroked her stomach while someone nuzzled her cheek. "Wake up, baby."

She moaned as she tried to come up from the murky depths.

"I made breakfast."

She could smell something tantalizing that awakened her taste buds. That was a good reason to get up, right? She struggled to get a hold of her faculties.

"We're going to unpack the truck and then return it."

Her brows came together. Truck? Unpack?

"Come on, Vi. Wake up."

Hard lips covered hers and a tongue sank into her mouth. The taste of coffee and sausage hit her a second before she remembered where she was. Her eyes opened as she shoved at the shoulder of the man crouched over her.

"What the hell are you *doing*?" she hissed and prepared to roll away when she realized her nightgown was hiked up to her waist. "What the fuck, Jesse?"

He stole another kiss before he tugged her nightgown down. "Tempting, baby, but we have work to do."

She sat up and glared at him. "What the hell are you doing in my room?"

"Would you rather Dad came to wake you and found you like this?"

She flushed. "Get out!"

"Get dressed. We have to unpack your things and return the truck. Some guys are coming over to help, and you need to decide where you want everything. Dad cleared a section of the garage if you want to put stuff in there until we come back from Florida."

With that, he walked through the bathroom to his bedroom. Hell. She rolled out of bed and heard the chatter of multiple voices coming from the dining room. She had overslept. How the hell was Jesse up? He should be in worse shape than her.

She brushed her teeth and glared at her reflection. If she had to choose between her father and Jesse finding her like that, she'd have to choose Jesse. If she hadn't been so tired, she never would have gone to bed like that. Now that she was living at home, she'd have to make sure she was always presentable, so she wouldn't give her poor father a heart attack. Her father was a man's man. It pained him to see her in anything too feminine or revealing.

When she came into the dining room, she found everyone gathered at the table. The sight of Lynne laughing with her father warmed her heart. She felt Jesse's eyes on her, but she ignored him as she made herself a plate of food and listened to their flight arrangements for tomorrow morning. She was just finishing her breakfast when some cars pulled up. She shoveled the last of the food into her mouth as Dad and Jesse went outside while a bunch of Lynne's friends swept through the door. She said her hellos and made hurried small talk before she walked out the front door.

The group of assembled men gave her pause. Brody and several other classmates had come to help, along with her father's friends—retired firefighters, police officers, and paramedics that she considered uncles. One of them caught sight of her and put a hand to his chest and staggered back.

"That can't be my baby girl," he shouted.

She laughed and ran toward him. He caught her up in his arms as if she were still a girl instead of a grown woman. She laughed as he spun her around and then gave her a bone cracking hug. She was passed from man to man and kissed bearded cheeks and even got some head noogies from the more reserved men.

They talked for an hour before they began to unload the moving truck. Thanks to Reese's organizational skills, she knew exactly what she wanted in her bedroom and what could be left in the garage to be sorted later. With so much help, it took less than an hour. Jesse and a friend returned the truck and trailer while she chatted with her uncle's and eventually broke off from the others with Brody, who had stayed by her side.

"How have you been holding up?" he asked as they settled on the rock wall under a tree.

"Okay," she said in a subdued tone.

He nodded. "Your life's been turned upside down. It's a big deal, you moving home."

"I wasn't doing that great in Utah, so it wasn't a big deal to make the leap."

"Still. You had a life there, and it's not easy to pick up and go."

She touched his arm. "I'm sorry about your dad."

He looked away. "Yeah."

Her heart turned over. His pain was a preview of what she would soon be experiencing. "You're taking care of your siblings and your mom. That's a heavy load, Brody."

He shrugged. "That's what you're supposed to do."

"Not everybody thinks that way."

He looked back at her. Her heart skipped as his eyes moved over her face in a way that wasn't merely friendly.

"I'm glad you're back, Violet."

It was her turn to look away. Her dad leaned against one of the trucks, smiling and talking to his friends about the good old days.

Same stories, but they never tired of rehashing them. "Me too. I haven't seen these people in years."

"Tragedies have a way of bringing people together."

She wasn't prepared for Brody to cup her chin and turn her face back to his. This was a bold move, considering her father was within hollering distance and there were a bunch of people around. Her eyes bugged as she stared at him.

He grinned. "Why do you look so shocked?"

"You..." Out of the corner of her eye, she saw her father looking in their direction. "My dad..."

"He likes me."

She jerked out of his hold. "I don't know if he likes you *that* much," she lied. Dad had already given his blessing where Brody was concerned, but she wasn't about to tell him that.

"He isn't going in the house for his guns. I think I'm safe."

"I wouldn't chance it," she said with mock severity.

His eyes held hers. "You're worth the risk."

"Brody..."

He held up a hand. "I'm not asking for anything. I'm just letting you know I'm available."

"Available?" she echoed warily.

He jerked his head at the house. "I know you're here to support your family, but if you need someone to talk to, I'm here."

She relaxed a little. "Thanks," she said, touched by his offer.

"I wanted to state my intentions this time around."

"Intentions?"

A grin tugged at his lips. "I like you. I always have."

"As a friend."

"As more, but you didn't see me that way. Now you do."

"Says who?" she demanded.

He gave her a cocky smile. "Let's just say I can tell the difference. We did everything we could to get your attention, but you made it clear you weren't interested." He shook his head. "You have bad taste in men, honey. You chose the worst guys when you could have had your pick of the best."

She threw up her hands. "Why do people keep *saying* that?"

"Because it's true. You dated the bad boys, the loners, the freaks. You put Jesse through hell. It's no wonder he beat the crap out of Tucker after those rumors went around."

"What rumors?"

Brody's brows shot up. "You don't know?"

"No! What rumors?"

He grimaced and rubbed the back of his neck. "I thought you knew. I don't know if it's my place to—"

"Brody!"

"Tucker said he popped your cherry, and he was sharing you with his bandmates."

She shot to her feet. "He said *what*?"

Brody held up a placating hand as he rose. "It was a long time ago."

"I don't care how long ago it was! I can't believe he said that!"

"The day that rumor started circulating was the day Jesse beat the hell out of Tucker. How could you not know that?"

Because Jesse took her virginity after that confrontation with Tucker and everything else ceased to exist for her. She had no idea Tucker started such a filthy rumor. What the hell?

"I never even slept with him!" she burst out and immediately glanced at her dad.

Dad wasn't paying her any mind, and that was a good thing, since sex wasn't discussed so openly here in Texas. That was another thing she would have to remember now that she was home. Dad would go apoplectic if he heard her using such language.

"I'm glad to hear that," Brody said as he slid an arm over her shoulder and gave her a light squeeze. "He was an asshole."

"Does he still live here?" she growled.

He chuckled. "No. I think he moved to Los Angeles with his band. Never heard anything about him after that."

"What a jerk," she fumed, and suddenly wished she hadn't stopped Jesse from beating the crap out of him.

"I think your taste in men is about to improve."

She glanced up at him. "You think so?"

He had an extremely satisfied look on his face. "Apparently, I have your father's blessing. He just gave me the nod."

His eyes flicked to the left. She followed his line of sight to see Jesse hopping out of his friends' truck.

"Jesse on the other hand…" Brody's smile widened. "He's always been protective of you, and no wonder with the guys you choose. I'll have to show him my paycheck and health benefits before he lets me take you out."

She elbowed him. "Cut it out."

"Maybe your dad can vouch for me. I have honorable intentions."

"You're ridiculous," she said as Jesse and Anton came to a stop in front of them. "Hey, bro."

She was baiting the tiger, but with her dad in sight and Brody's arm around her, she was feeling safe and daring.

Jesse's eyes flicked from her to his friend. "What's this?"

He sounded calm, but she knew better.

"Vi and I are getting reacquainted," Brody said.

"Man, I called dibs!" Anton said.

Brody tucked her into his side and kissed her temple. "Vi and I have a connection."

She smacked his stomach and noticed distractedly that it was just as hard as Jesse's.

"She's here for our mom, not for all you hounds to move in on her," Jesse said.

"I know," Brody said. "I'm just letting her know who to call if she needs anything. You're not always going to be here."

Jesse focused on her. "You have to pack for our trip, don't you?"

She gave him a long look before she went on tiptoes and planted a kiss on Brody's jaw. "I'll call you if I need you."

"What about me?" Anton demanded. "My shoulder's free to cry on!"

She laughed as she went to him and gave him a hug. "You guys are crazy. Thanks for your help today."

"Of course," Anton said. "You're one of us."

That put a hitch in her step, but she smiled at them before she went inside. She did need to pack, and her room was a freaking disaster. The need to organize and nest was riding her hard. She wanted to do as much as she could before they left tomorrow, but she was waylaid by Mom's friends, who jumped on her the moment she walked through the door.

"It's so good to see you!"

"Did you get your college degree?"

"You're such a good girl, moving home to be with your parents during this time."

"Jesse's such a sweetheart for helping with your move!"

By the time the interrogation was over, she didn't have the energy to do anything. She plopped on the sofa beside Lynne and moaned.

"They mean well," Lynne said.

"I forgot what it's like to have people questioning you about your life." Violet spread her hands. "I don't have any plans, and I don't know what I'm doing."

"You don't need a plan. God will guide you," Lynne said.

She looked away, uncomfortable with the casual reference to God when she held such dirty secrets in her heart. How would Lynne feel about the sinful relationship she and Jesse had maintained throughout the years? Was that God's plan as well?

"I'll make dinner," she said and got up from the couch.

She was moving a piece of butter over the top of the cornbread she had pulled out of the oven when Dad and Jesse walked in.

Dad clapped Jesse on the shoulder. "I'm proud of you, son. You're doing great things in the world."

Her stomach clenched as melted butter seeped into the top layer of the cornbread. It was clear that Mom and Dad were proud of Jesse serving in the military and his many accomplishments. They loved and adored him. If her parents knew what occurred between them, would that change their opinion of him?

Jesse looked at her from across the room. She held his gaze for a moment and heard the echo of the words he uttered in the motel room.

Love can make monsters out of men when it's not returned.

She shook her head and looked down as she continued to prepare dinner.

CHAPTER 11

"Here."

She took the iced coffee Jesse handed her with a grunt and took a seat amongst her family and the other passengers waiting for the flight. It was early and once again, she hadn't gotten much sleep. There were a myriad of reasons why she couldn't settle, but for some reason, that tidbit Brody dropped about Tucker circled round and round in her mind.

How could a rumor she hadn't even known about bother her six years later? She knew Tucker had a reputation as a bad boy, but he'd been so sweet when they were dating. She also resented the fact that Jesse and Brody had commented on her bad taste in men. It was an ongoing joke with Reese and Meg, but she had never paid much attention to it until now. It wasn't like she went out of her way to find shitty guys. Apparently, they flocked to her. And she didn't always attract losers. She hooked her friends up with Abel and Travis. Apparently, she gave the good guys to other people and kept the freaks for herself.

When they started to board the plane, Mom and Dad went first since Lynne was in a wheelchair to preserve her strength. Like they had the first time, she and Jesse waited while everyone rushed to get on, even though they had assigned seats.

"Thank you for helping me with my move," Violet said, staring straight ahead. It galled her to say it, but she owed him. She wouldn't have been able to do it without him.

"You're welcome."

She got up and dumped her cup before she came back and shouldered her oversized purse. The lines had gone down, so she and Jesse made their way over to the ticket agent. She pursed her lips before she rounded on him.

"Did Tucker really say he shared me with his band?" she asked in a rush.

His eyes narrowed. "Who told you that?"

"Brody brought it up yesterday."

"Brody talks too much," he said and ushered her forward with a hand on her lower back.

She dug her heels in. "Is it true?"

"Yeah."

She stiffened. "But, why would Tucker say that? I never even…"

Jesse's eyes moved over her flushed face. "He knew you were too good for him and that everyone was wondering why you were with him. He wanted to ruin your reputation so no one else would want you."

She huffed and handed her ticket over to be scanned before she walked down the short tunnel to the plane. Again, she had to wait and again, she felt the heat of him at her back. She whirled to face him.

"You believed that rumor?" When he hesitated, she demanded, "You thought I'd sleep with all those—?"

"Of course not," he snapped. "I didn't believe any of it until I caught you with him."

With his hands in her pants. That was the furthest she had ever gone with a boyfriend. She probably would have given Tucker her virginity if Jesse hadn't claimed it for himself. "Did you beat him up because of the rumor or because you caught us?"

"Both." He pushed her forward. "You shouldn't have been with him in the first place."

"Why didn't I hear about this?"

"Because I put a stop to it."

"How?"

His eyes seared hers. "I told the truth—that you had never slept with him."

She entered the plane and shuffled down the narrow aisle. She grinned at Mom and Dad before making her way to their row, which was toward the back. They hadn't been able to reserve seats together since they booked their tickets last minute. She'd been hoping she and Jesse were sitting apart, but no luck. She took the window seat while he took the aisle. She shoved her purse under the seat in front and buckled herself in.

"About Brody."

She had been expecting this. She mentally braced before she looked at him. "Yes?"

His eyes speared hers. "You shouldn't mess with the guys."

"*Mess* with them?"

"Don't encourage them."

"Like Brody said, you aren't always going to be around. I'm going to do whatever." She paused for emphasis, "Or *who*ever I want."

He grasped her chin. "You're mine."

She grasped his wrist and tugged. She dimly noted she couldn't wrap her fingers around the width of it. Everything about him was supersized. "I'm not."

"You've been mine since you were thirteen." His knuckles skimmed down her throat. "It started so innocently. Enjoying each other's company, building memories. We spent every waking moment together." His thumb brushed over her sprinting pulse. "I remember when it changed. We were camping at the lake with church friends, and you wanted to play chicken. Malcolm lifted you on his shoulders. Your legs were draped around his neck. He was holding your thighs, touching you…" His eyes darkened as his fingers left her pulse and slid between her cleavage before she jerked back. "He tried to get you to ride the jet ski with him."

She remembered that. "You made me ride with you instead."

His eyes glinted as the flight attendant launched into her safety speech in case of an emergency.

"I got to feel your arms around me, your breasts against my back," he said in a low, gravelly voice. "And I told Malcolm to keep his goddamn hands to himself."

"You're insane."

"Maybe."

"No, you *are*," she retorted.

She rolled her shoulders to brush off the effect his voice had on her. When he gripped her thigh, she tensed.

"Let Brody off easy. Anton, too."

She glared at him and smacked his hand, which didn't budge. "They're nice guys."

"I don't care."

"You have no claim on me."

"I told you how I feel about you," he said in a low voice as his fingers glided up her bare thigh. "And even though you threw my feelings back in my face, that doesn't mean I'm going to let you go off with some other guy."

She clamped her thighs together when he tried to slip beneath her shorts.

"Are you crazy?" she hissed.

"Did you hear what I said?"

"I heard you. Will you stop touching me?"

"No."

She peeked over the seats in front of them to locate their parents. Her dad was reading a book while Lynne rested her head on his shoulder.

"We're here for Mom," she reminded him in a low undertone.

"I know," he said as the plane lurched into motion.

"Remember that and focus on her, not me. This trip is about making sure she has the time of her life."

"She will."

Violet made a clearing motion with her hands. "And that's it."

When he didn't reply, she glanced at him and wished she hadn't.

"I can't be your brother, but I'll try to be your friend," he said as his eyes moved over her face. "And make you want more."

"That'll never happen," she said and sucked in a breath as the plane lifted off the ground.

"We'll see."

He traced distracting patterns over her skin.

"You want to join the mile-high club?" he asked several minutes later.

"Only if that means I push you out of the plane, and you fall to your death."

His mouth twitched. "No, it means I fuck your brains out in a stall where any moment there could be turbulence, and we die before we get back to our seats."

"I'll pass."

"Next time," he said lazily.

She shoved his hand away. "Never! And keep your hands to yourself. I'm not here to entertain you."

SHE EXAMINED HERSELF IN THE MIRROR. THE FUCHSIA BIKINI LYNNE BOUGHT her fit perfectly, but it was more revealing than anything she would have chosen. She was a t-shirt and jeans kind of girl and if she wore a bathing suit, it was a one piece. The bright color complimented her pale skin, but she felt very exposed even after tying a white sarong around her waist. Oh, well. Wearing it would make Lynne happy, and it fit well, even if it wasn't her style.

She walked out of the bathroom and surveyed their room, which was decorated like a beach cottage rather than a hotel room. Vintage pictures hung on the walls, while weathered-looking wood furniture graced the room. They had a connecting room with their parents. She and Jesse were sharing, of course, but she wasn't too worried. He was playing the good son, waiting on Lynne hand and foot. Even though the sight of him doting on Lynne warmed her heart, she reminded herself to be on her guard.

Despite everything that happened on the road trip, there was no trace of anger or resentment in his attitude toward her. He constantly had an arm slung over her shoulders. Neither of their parents thought anything of it. To them, everything was back to normal when it was anything but. Her attempts to avoid him were ignored. She fell asleep on the flight and woke to find she was using his shoulder as a pillow. When she glared at him, he laughed. Her grumpy mood lasted until they pulled up to the hotel, and she saw the sparkling blue water.

She walked toward the glass sliding door and pulled it open. She could hear the ocean from here. They were on the first floor, right on the beach. She was as giddy as a child. She wanted to sprint across the sand and dive into the water, but the sound of Lynne's voice kept her from racing outside. She turned to see what the holdup was and found Jesse staring at her. He had changed into red surf shorts, a t-shirt, and cap. She couldn't see his eyes since he wore sunglasses, but she knew what he was thinking.

"Don't even think about it," she warned before she sailed into their parents' room.

Lynne wore a sheer cover up with palm trees over her sunny bathing suit and a massive straw hat. When she saw Violet, she clapped her hands together.

"It looks great on you!" Lynne exclaimed.

When Dad saw her, his brows drew together, a predictable reaction to her wearing something so revealing. Inwardly, she shrugged. Lynne bought her suit, so if he had problems, he had to take it up with her.

"Are you ready?" she asked.

"Yep!" Lynne handed her beach bag to Dad and linked their arms together. "Let's go!"

People were milling around, but it wasn't crowded. They bypassed the pool and headed straight to the ocean. They found two loungers with an umbrella for shade and set their things on it.

"Isn't it just like you remember?" Lynne gushed as she held on to her hat, so the sea breeze wouldn't take it.

"It's even better," Violet said as she unwound the sarong and started toward the water.

"Hey."

Two fingers slipped beneath the string holding her top together. She glanced back at Jesse, who held up a tube of sunscreen.

"Yes, you better lather up. You don't want to get burned on the first day," Lynne said as she slathered white paste over her arms.

Violet held out her hand. Jesse's mouth curved as he squeezed sunscreen on her palm. Impatiently, she rubbed it over herself and knew she wasn't doing a good job, but her eyes were on the figures gliding through the aqua water.

"Turn around. Let me do your back."

She gave Jesse a long look before she turned. Rough hands slid over her. He didn't do anything inappropriate and when he was through, he was by her side as she headed to the water. The first step in was a shock. It was colder than she expected, but that didn't stop her. She dove into a gentle swell and screamed underwater before she came up laughing.

Jesse surfaced beside her. She splashed him before she caught sight of Mom and Dad wading in after them. She cheered and put her arms in the air and danced in pure joy.

"Doesn't it feel great?" she crowed.

Lynne's smile was as bright as her bathing suit. "This is exactly what I needed."

They bobbed in the water, talking and taking in the sights. Lynne tired quickly. When she had to make her way back to shore, Jesse helped his mother to the lounger and stayed with her while she and Dad swam and chatted about her road trip.

Too soon, the sun began to set. They went to their rooms to change before making the short walk to the hotel restaurant, which looked like a massive tiki hut. There was live music and good food. When she ordered a cocktail with a slice of pineapple in it, she got a disapproving look from Dad, but he didn't comment. Lynne didn't eat at all, though she seemed happy and relaxed. When Violet fell into bed several hours later, head swimming, stomach full, and lips curled up in a smile, she knew she was going to make every moment of this vacation count.

CHAPTER 12

DAYS PASSED IN A BUSY BLUR. NAPS IN HAMMOCKS, SWIMMING TO HER heart's content, bike riding through town, and quality time with her parents lifted the weight she had been carrying for years. She felt like the sea and sun were cleansing her, giving her a fresh start. The past didn't exist, just the here and now.

Jesse was the only blip on her horizon, but she didn't have time to worry about him when there was Lynne to tend to. She and Jesse had an unspoken agreement that one of them would always be with Lynne to give Dad time to rest as well. They catered to Lynne's every whim, not that she had many. Although Lynne's optimistic attitude never wavered, it was clear that every day was more taxing than the last.

On their last day in Florida, they watched the sun set. She and Dad lay in one hammock, while Lynne and Jesse lounged in another.

"You guys are awesome," Dad said, and placed his hand on Violet's wet, tangled hair. "I couldn't ask for better kids."

"I guess you raised us right."

He gave her a lopsided smile. "I guess so, but I can't take as much credit as I would like. I know I wasn't around as much as I should have been. Thank God for Lynne."

Violet glanced at the neighboring hammock. Lynne had the biggest smile on her face as she listened to Jesse. "Yes."

"I'm glad you aren't like your mom."

Violet's attention snapped back to her father. "I'm sorry?"

His skin had a pink hue from the sunset. His eyes were unfocused and lost in thought as he stared at the ocean. "Your mom was a selfish person. I thought she would change once she became a mother, but it only made things worse. All she wanted to do was party."

Violet could count on one hand the number of times Dad had talked about her mother, and none of them had been about her personality or the issues in their relationship.

"She wanted more out of life than to be a mom or housewife. She wanted to be famous. I thought she was joking, but one day I woke up, and she was gone." He let out a long sigh. "I went to church because I was lost and angry and needed help. The church helped me get on my feet and gave you a solid foundation. I know you were raised by a lot of people, maybe more than you wanted to be, but I did my best."

"You're a great dad."

He wrapped a burly arm around her head and kissed her brow. "You're a good girl. Sweeter than I deserve. I know I'm not good at talking about all this stuff, but I'm glad you moved home."

"Of course," she said and tried to keep her voice level, so she wouldn't ruin the moment.

"Sometimes I feel like God turned his back on me. Your mom left, and I had to raise you on my own. I had to ask others for help, which I hated doing, but I didn't have a choice. Then Lynne came along, and everything fell into place. I thought we'd grow old together, and now..."

"Dad," she whispered and squeezed his hand.

When he glanced at her, her heart tore when she saw his eyes were full of tears. "But I still have you, don't I?"

"Yes, you do."

He sighed. "One day at a time, right?"

"Right."

Once the sun sank beneath the horizon, they headed back to their rooms to shower before they ate. Halfway through dinner, Lynne said she didn't feel good. When they tried to wave down a server to take care of the bill, Lynne told them, "You two stay and enjoy your meal. I think I just need to lie down."

They watched Dad practically carry Lynne out of the restaurant. When Jesse looked at her, she saw the same worry and fear in his eyes. They ignored what Mom said and settled the bill and made their way back to the room, only to hear Lynne being violently ill. As she and Jesse rushed into the connecting room, Jesse hurried to the bathroom to help Dad support Lynne, who was so weak, she couldn't hold her head up. The toilet was covered in vomit so dark it was nearly black. When Dad tried to call an ambulance, Lynne threw a tantrum until he agreed not to.

Violet sat on the edge of her parent's bed and listened to the sound of Lynne sobbing as Dad bathed her. Violet dropped her face in her hands and fought tears.

"She's going to be okay," Jesse said.

She looked up at him. "You know she isn't."

His face was grave as he amended, "As good as she's going to be."

When Dad carried Lynne to bed, Violet rose to help. Lynne apologized profusely for interrupting dinner and ruining the mood.

"Don't, Mom," Violet said as she turned back the covers.

While Dad went to clean himself up, she slid into bed with Lynne and curled up against her.

"Are you having a good time, honey?" Lynne asked in a raspy voice.

She flinched. Lynne was ignoring her bouts of sickness and

focusing on them instead. It was easier than facing her mortality. Lynne needed to know they were having a good time above all else.

"Of course. This place is spectacular," she said with as much enthusiasm as she could muster.

Lynne patted her arm. "Promise me you'll come back here someday."

She would promise anything to ease her pain. "I promise," she said instantly.

"Good. What should we watch?" Lynne asked as she reached for the remote.

"Anything."

Lynne turned on *The Three Stooges*. When Mom chuckled, she tried to join in, but knew she fell short. Her heart was lodged in her throat. Before Dad emerged from the bathroom, Lynne fell into a restless sleep. Violet listened to the sound of her rattling breaths and hugged Lynne's slight body to hers and willed life into her mother. Her tears soaked the covers as she prayed over Mom, reaching out to the God who had abandoned her long ago.

"Violet."

She raised her head and looked at Dad, who stood on the other side of the bed. Her lower lip trembled as she stared at his grave expression.

"I'll take her to the hospital once we get home tomorrow." He slid into bed on Lynne's other side. "Get some rest, kiddo."

She kissed Lynne's cheek before she walked into the connecting room. Jesse sat up in bed, hands behind his head as he watched some war documentary. She stared at her bed for a moment before she walked to the sliding door and opened it.

"Where are you going?" Jesse asked.

"For a walk."

"I'll come with you."

She glanced back at him. "I don't need an escort."

He was already on his feet and turning off the TV. "Let's go."

It was close to one in the morning as they walked around the pool, empty bar, and restaurant. It was quiet aside from the sound of the ocean in the distance. Once they reached the beach, she slipped off her slippers and held them in one hand as she walked to a pair of abandoned loungers, just past the circle of light cast by the resort.

A sliver of moon offered just enough light to see the waves crashing on shore. She dropped her slippers on the sand and walked along the beach. Jesse fell into step beside her. She wrapped her arms around herself and closed her eyes as a warm breeze caressed her chilled cheeks.

Lynne was dying. As pain cascaded through her, she stopped in her tracks.

"Violet?"

She shook her head as tears slid down her cheeks. She wanted to scream and rage but knew it would do no good. Lynne was suffering and there was nothing she could do. Lynne was the heart of their family. Once she was gone, it would never be the same. Lynne filled the void left by her biological mother; a void she hadn't realized existed until Lynne showed her unconditional love. Lynne would take a piece of her when she left.

Life seeped out of her every day. Lynne wasn't eating and had more sick moments than good ones. This morning, she caught a glimpse of the number of pills she was taking, and they weren't helping. There was nothing she could do to buy her mother time. All she could do was watch and shower her with as much love as possible. Grief nearly sent her to her knees.

"Hey."

Jesse gripped her arm to steady her.

She wrenched away and bellowed, "This isn't fair!"

She couldn't read his face in the dim light, but he said, "I know."

"I can't stand this," she said raggedly. "I feel like..." Like she wanted to howl at the moon and scream at the sky. Maybe God would hear her pleas and spare her mother.

"It's going to be okay," Jesse said in a flat tone that told her he didn't believe the empty platitude any more than she did.

"It's not," she said in an anguished whisper.

He was silent for a moment before he agreed, "No, it's not."

She covered her mouth to cover the sob building in her throat. "I... I can't... I don't know what..." She tugged at her hair as she turned in a circle, searching for help she knew she wouldn't find.

"Violet."

Something in her snapped. She marched toward the water until Jesse blocked her way.

"What the hell are you doing?" he demanded.

"What does it look like?" she spat as she pulled her sundress over her head and dropped it on the sand. "Get out of my way."

"If you want to swim, we can go to the pool."

"No." She wanted the taste of salt on her tongue and to fight the pull of the current. In a world where she had no control, she wanted a moment to feel free and unrestrained.

"Who knows what's in the water? This isn't smart."

"No one asked you to come with me," she retorted. A familiar recklessness was taking hold, her knee-jerk reaction to stress.

"Violet."

His voice was no longer emotionless, but she was too focused on her goal to notice.

"Get out of my way!"

"Fuck."

He lifted his shirt over his head. Before he had his pants off, she sprinted toward the black waves. She dove in and felt instant relief the moment she was engulfed in the chilly water. The underwater white noise drowned out her agony. She broke the surface in time to see Jesse wading toward her. The twinkle of resort lights seemed miles away.

"Don't go too deep," Jesse warned.

She ignored him as she swam to get her emotions out through strenuous exercise. Jesse kept pace with her as she did laps and fought the churning water. When she had exhausted herself, she stood submerged up to her neck, panting.

"Feel better?" Jesse asked.

Her eyes stung with tears. "No."

"Let's go in," he urged.

"Not yet."

She bent her knees, so she was floating, and let her toes skim the sand as the waves moved her back and forth.

"Talk," she said.

"What?"

"Talk about something. Anything. Distract me."

"I've been doing some research on Japan. It seems like it's going to be an interesting place to be stationed."

She relaxed a little. "How long will you be there?"

"At least a year."

"You... you like being in the military?"

"Yes."

"You think you'll be a lifer?"

"Probably. I like the lifestyle, the rules, travel, and brotherhood. I like being a part of something bigger than myself."

She nodded. "You know where you belong."

"What about you? What's on your agenda?"

"I have no idea." She shivered. Now that she wasn't on the move, the cold was getting to her, but she was reluctant to leave the water and go back to the hotel room. "I don't know what life's going to be like now that I'm home... or what it'll be like without Mom." Her voice cracked. "I have no idea what I'm doing."

He tugged her into his arms. She was too sad to fight him. She rested her face on his shoulder and wrapped her legs around his waist as they allowed themselves to flow with the water.

"We'll get past this."

"How?"

"Together."

She sniffled against his chest. "But you're such a dick."

He let out a short chuckle. "But I'm being so good right now."

She thumped his shoulder. "Can't time slow down just a little bit?" she whispered. "I need more time."

"I've been saying that most of my life," he said as he stroked her back.

She sniffled. "She's your mom. This must be worse for you than it is for me."

"It's the worst pain imaginable. Even though I've done this before, it doesn't get easier. I don't know what's worse—not knowing it's going to happen or watching it happen slowly."

His desolate tone made her reach out and cup his face. "I think it would be worse if you didn't have a chance to say goodbye. At least you got to see her again and have this time with her."

She could feel the weight of his stare even in the darkness.

"Are you going to be there for me after she's gone?" When she hesitated, he rested his forehead against hers. "I need you, Violet."

Her heart felt as if it was being squeezed. "Jesse, I—"

"I'm trying to give you what you want," he said hoarsely. "I can't do this without you. I won't survive it."

Something about his miserable tone struck a chord in her. Sensing he needed comfort just as much as she did, she wrapped her arms around him. "I'm here."

"And later?"

Her soul tore. "I…"

"Promise you won't cut me out of your life again."

Even as a small voice in the back of her mind told her not to give in, her mouth said, "I promise."

Past and present collided. They were renewing promises they made to each other as children, clinging to one another, making sure they would never be alone. They were much older, but still lost and scared. She brushed her cheek against his and found it damp. Intuition told her it wasn't the ocean. His tears had gone unnoticed in the dark.

"Don't, Jesse," she whispered.

An overwhelming urge to console him made her frame his face and kiss him. When he sucked in a breath, his mouth parted, giving her an opening for her tongue to delve in. The taste of some kind of citrus made her explore him thoroughly. His hand clenched in her hair as he held her to him, but she wasn't trying to get away.

She was the aggressor. She was drowning and needed something to keep her anchored in an unfair world where nothing made sense. Something real and tangible to keep her sane. When she arched against him, he groaned.

"Violet?"

There was a question in his voice, one she didn't want to answer verbally because it would break the spell they were under. Instead, she unwrapped her legs from his waist and tugged him toward the shore. He didn't waste any time hustling them out of the water. He was focused on the distant lounge chairs, but that was too far. She dropped to her knees in several inches of water, which disappeared as the wave retracted.

Some madness came over her. She tugged down his briefs and pumped her hand down his soft shaft before she took him in her mouth.

"Holy fuck, Violet."

He sounded stunned, and rightfully so. This was the first time she had ever initiated anything sexual between them, but she was desperate for what he could provide—temporary oblivion and pleasure. This was wrong, but right now, she didn't care. In the darkness, it didn't count. There was no one to witness this coupling.

He stroked her hair as she suckled. She knew exactly what he wanted. He had taught her long ago. As she worked him, the warm breeze caressed her skin. Every wave that rolled in buried her thighs in soft, wet sand. She felt daring, defiant, and proudly brazen. Feeling him tremble from her touch made her feel powerful instead of weak and helpless.

"Fuck."

Jesse jerked away and leaned down to kiss her reverently. "I'm going to come in your mouth if you don't stop."

"I can—"

"Tell me what you need," he said in a voice rough with desire.

She positioned herself on her hands and knees, breasts smashed against the wet sand with her ass in the air. He needed no further urging. He knelt behind her, tugged her panties to the side, and sheathed himself in one brutal thrust. She braced her hands in the sand as he planted himself deep.

"Violet, I—"

"Just do it," she ordered.

He didn't argue. He fucked her hard. Her screams were drowned out by the waves and when he came, he sent her sprawling. She rested her cheek on the damp sand as he crouched over her, quivering.

"Violet," he moaned.

"Shh."

She didn't want to talk. She wanted to suspend reality for as long as possible. He gave her a few minutes before he carried her to the water to clean the sand and himself from her. He swiped up their clothes before they staggered across the beach to the lounge chair where she had dropped her slippers. She was surprised when he urged her to stretch out on the lounger and knelt between her shaking thighs. He was gentle as his tongue slid over her, tending to her swollen flesh. She stared up at the stars as she gave herself over to the moment and climaxed with her hand clenched in his hair.

He straightened and kissed her deeply, letting her taste herself on him. She gripped his neck to prolong the contact and when their lips separated, he hovered over her, searching her face.

"Better?" he asked.

She nodded.

"Let's go."

He dressed and had to help her because she didn't have the coordination to do it herself. When she stood, he picked her up in a fireman's carry. She was too tired to complain. When they entered their air-conditioned room, she tensed, but Jesse didn't tarry. He went straight to the bathroom and set her in the shower. She slumped against the wall and waited for him to leave. He didn't. Her eyes flared as he stepped in with her and slipped off his shorts and reached for her dress.

"What the hell are you doing?" she said in a muted shriek.

"The door's closed between the rooms."

"Why would they do that?" she asked, too distracted by this information to resist when he pulled off her dress.

"My guess is she's having a rough night, and they don't want to disturb us."

"Maybe I should—"

"Bathe," he said and turned on the shower, making her sputter.

He boxed her into the corner and kissed her silly. She punched him in the stomach, which made no impact on him. When he finally pulled away, she had to blink a couple of times because her head was spinning.

Not another word was said between them as he bathed her. She left the shower first and did her nighttime routine in record time before she crept into the room and spotted the closed door. Hastily, she dressed in the dark before she slipped into bed and pulled the covers up to her chin like a child.

She stared at the ceiling. She had done something stupid tonight. Monumentally idiotic. She waited for the rush of guilt and shame, but nothing happened. Instead, she closed her eyes, yawned, and fell asleep.

"Hey."

She looked up from where she was sitting on her bedroom floor, surrounded by open boxes. Jesse stood in the entrance leading into the bathroom. Her heart skipped a beat as she took in his grim look.

"Hey," she said and went back to pulling things out of a box.

As he strolled toward her, her skin prickled in alarm. This morning, they had time for a quick breakfast before they checked out of the hotel and headed to the airport. Thankfully, their seats were grouped together on the plane. She arranged Mom and Dad between her and Jesse. Once they arrived back in Texas, Dad forced Lynne to go to the hospital. She accompanied them but was left in the waiting room. When Lynne was wheeled out a few hours later, announcing that all was well, Violet noticed that Dad didn't agree with her. He was clearly concerned, but he didn't contradict Lynne. Once they reached home, Violet whipped up dinner and spent her time by Lynne's side until she fell asleep.

It was the wee hours of the morning and since she couldn't sleep, she decided to unpack. She assumed no one was awake. She should have known better.

Jesse crouched beside her. "Are you avoiding me?"

She scooped a stack of clothes out of the box and plopped it on the carpet. "Of course not."

He gripped her chin. "I'm not playing this game with you," he said in a low growl.

She blinked. "I'm not playing a game."

He cocked his head. "Aren't you?"

She batted at his hand. "No!"

"Then what happened on the beach?" When she tried to look away, he tightened his hold on her. "You gave yourself to me, Violet."

"I was sad, and I needed—"

"Me," he interjected in a steely tone. "You needed me, Violet."

"I *don't* need you!"

In a move so swift, she wasn't sure how it happened, he pinned her on the carpet and gripped her throat as he loomed over her.

"I'm hanging on by a fucking thread here," he warned. "Mom's sick and you're… I don't know what you are. You say you hate me, that you want a sexless friend, and then you come onto me. You kissed me, bent over for me, let me pleasure you."

"It was just sex."

His eyes narrowed to slits. "It's more than that. When you're feeling lost and alone, you turn to those you trust." He rested his forehead on hers. "Damn it, Vi, I thought we sorted our shit."

"Sex solves nothing!" She braced both hands on his chest and pushed. "I was having a moment. It's gone now."

His hand flexed on her throat. "Liar."

"Don't call me a liar!"

"I love you, but right now, I want to strangle you. You're making me crazy."

"Don't say that word!"

"I'm going to say it until you believe it," he said against her lips. "I've hurt you, so you want to hurt me back. I can take it, and I'll take you whenever you give me an opening, but I'm not going to let you ignore what's between us."

His hand slid over her thin top and squeezed her breast.

"I'll never forget the sight of you sucking me off on the beach. It's etched in my memory." His hand moved down her body and slid between her legs. She jerked as he unerringly found her nub and began to rub, her thin pajama shorts no detriment to his ministrations.

"Jesse, don't!"

He kissed her. She was expecting him to be rough and brutish. The gentle, coaxing kiss took her by surprise. When he deepened the caress, her eyes fluttered shut. He kissed her with such absorption that her mind wiped clean. Her hips left the ground, so his finger could penetrate her folds.

"I love you," he rumbled as his eyes tracked over her face. "And you love me too."

Her heart slammed against her ribs. "I don't."

He kissed her forehead. "Stubborn."

He rose, leaving her prone and trembling on the floor.

She stared at him. "Jesse?"

He stood over her, gripping his erection through his sweats. "You know where to find me," he said before he walked through the connecting bathroom to his room.

She stared at the dark doorway, mind and body clashing as she struggled to think past the lust he roused in her. She clamped her thighs together and threw an arm over her hot face as she cursed him.

CHAPTER 13

"Violet."

A rough shake jolted her awake. She opened her eyes and squinted at the figure beside her bed. "Jesse?"

"The paramedics are here."

She sat up and threw back the covers. "What? What happened?" she demanded and started toward the door.

He caught her arm. "They're putting Mom on the stretcher. Get dressed. We're following them to the hospital."

"What happened?" she shouted.

"Dad said she wasn't breathing right, so he called 911. Get dressed. I'll be in the living room."

He strode out of the room and closed the door behind him. She flew to her window and saw some neighbors standing on the front lawn as the ambulance pulled away. Even as panic seared her insides, she told herself Lynne was going to be fine. Just last night, they stayed up late playing Scrabble. She and Jesse had been pushing the boundaries on inappropriate words to make Lynne laugh. She glanced at the clock. It was almost two in the morning.

She splashed her face with water, brushed her teeth, and then pulled on jeans and a shirt before she rushed out of her room with her purse in hand. Jesse stood in front of the door leading to the garage. He pushed it open as she approached.

"Let's go," he said shortly.

"Dad's with her?" she asked urgently.

"Yeah."

She got in the passenger seat and buckled herself in. "What does that mean, she wasn't breathing right?"

"I don't know," he said as he backed out of the garage and turned a little too quickly, making the tires squeal as he sped down the empty road. "He said she was gasping for breath. He woke me up when the ambulance pulled up."

"Maybe she just needs an oxygen mask," she said as she twisted her hands together in her lap. When he barely tapped the brakes at a stop sign, she reached over and grabbed his arm. "Slow down, Jesse."

"I was calling her name, and she didn't respond," he said tightly.

Her fingers dug into his arm. "She's going to be okay. Just slow down. We don't want to get into an accident. We need to get to her in one piece."

It had been almost a week since their return from Florida. There was a steady stream of visitors to see Lynne. They didn't have to cook since everyone always brought a dish with them. Between cleaning, organizing her things, and caring for Lynne and her father, she was starting to feel a little ragged. Although Lynne tried to stay positive, there was no denying that she was deteriorating rapidly. Dad hovered over her night and day. She had to force him to rest when Lynne was occupied. Jesse ran interference with guests and showed them the door when Lynne pushed herself too hard. It had been a tense week, and it wasn't over yet.

She held on to Jesse's arm until he parked. They ran into the hospital and made their way to the emergency room, which was pandemonium. It took ten minutes to get answers to where Lynne had been taken. They ran into the room and were greeted by the sight of Dad kneeling beside the bed, face buried in the sheets.

"Dad?" she whispered.

When he raised his head, her legs went numb. He didn't need to say a word. It was written all over his face.

Jesse rounded the bed and took Lynne's hand. "What happened?"

"They said she had acute respiratory failure," Dad said in a lifeless voice. "She was declared dead on arrival."

"But she was fine a couple of hours ago," Violet whispered.

Dad shook his head. "I should have taken her to the hospital. I shouldn't have listened to her. She was always downplaying everything..."

When she put her arms around him, his shoulders began to shake as he broke down. Her mind disconnected from her body as she stared at Lynne, who looked as if she was sleeping. Her gaze went to Jesse, who stood on the opposite side of the bed. His eyes were glued to Lynne's face. He showed no emotion, but she saw his hand trembling as it held his mother's.

This couldn't be real life. She wasn't ready. Doctors came in. It took all of her will power to focus on what was being said. They were asking about what they wanted to do with Lynne's body, forms that needed to be signed, and other things that she couldn't hear over the buzzing in her ears. Neither she nor Dad was in any state to answer, so Jesse took over.

CHAPTER 14

The house was deathly quiet. She stared at the ceiling and watched the first hint of sunlight touch her bedroom curtains. It had been three days since Lynne passed. That wasn't enough time to wrap her mind around the fact that Mom was gone, but it *was* enough time to prepare a funeral. Everything was moving at supersonic speed. Mom's friends showed up at the hospital and took care of all the funeral arrangements, which had been planned months ago.

Two weeks ago, her biggest worry was how she was going to pay her bills. Now, she had moved back to Texas and was attending Lynne's funeral. Tears leaked out of the corner of her eyes. Life wasn't fair. Lynne should have had more time. How could she be here today and gone the next?

She, Dad, and Jesse were all handling Lynne's death in their own way. Dad had totally withdrawn. When she tried to check on him, he sent her away. She was too grief-stricken to fight him on it. Jesse seemed to be handling it the best. He dealt with the neighbors and family friends who stopped by to offer condolences. She hadn't seen him shed a tear.

She rolled out of bed and went into the bathroom. She took a shower and stared at her swollen eyes in the mirror. That wouldn't do. She walked out to the dark kitchen and put ice cubes in a towel and rested the cold compress over her eyes as she brewed coffee. After, she went into the backyard to sit on the swing. It was an overcast day with light rain falling, a fitting atmosphere for the day ahead. Her eyes stung as the conversation she had with Lynne came back to her.

Women are the glue that holds families together. I need you to promise me you'll keep the family intact.

She had done a shit job so far. She took a steadying breath and sipped her coffee. If Lynne were here, she would tell her to dress in bright colors and put a smile on her face. She held the memory of Lynne laughing in the ocean in her mind as she went inside to get ready.

She dressed in a black long sleeve top and an ankle-length skirt with bright flowers on it. Her makeup was light and easily fixable, since she was sure she was going to bawl her eyes out.

She jumped when the door to Jesse's room opened. He was in his briefs and nothing else. He looked her over before he reached out and fingered her skirt.

"Mom would have liked this," he said.

She gave him a tremulous smile. "I know." Remembering her promise, she prompted, "Are you okay?"

"No."

He stripped off his underwear and stepped into the shower. She quickly exited and went to Dad's door. She knocked. Even though there was no answer, she opened the door and peeked in. Dad sat on the edge of the bed, dressed in his suit, staring at the wall.

"Dad?"

He didn't answer. She moved forward so she could see him properly. His face was completely blank, and his eyes were staring at something she couldn't see. He looked haggard and thinner than he had been a few days ago. She settled beside him and wrapped an arm around him.

"Are you okay?" she asked, voice warbling as she tried to suppress her emotions.

"No."

Honest and blunt, just like Jesse.

"I can make breakfast," she offered.

No response.

"Do you want coffee?"

Still nothing.

"Is there anything I can do?" she asked.

"No."

That hurt, but she tried not to take it personally. She gave him one last hug before she left the room and closed the door on her way out. She felt as if there was a bowling ball on her chest, restricting her airflow. It would be better once they laid Lynne to rest, right?

To keep herself busy, she made breakfast. She was just finishing up bacon and eggs when Jesse appeared in a dress shirt that matched his eyes and black slacks. He tossed his jacket over the back of a chair and stared out the window with his hands clasped behind him, his posture military straight.

She was setting the table when Dad appeared. He said nothing to either of them but grabbed the first set of keys he came across, which happened to be the ones for her Jeep.

"Dad?" she said tentatively.

"I want to clear my head before the funeral. I'll see you two there," Dad said without making eye contact.

"Isaac," Jesse began, but Dad held up a hand and slipped into the garage.

She stood in the kitchen, twisting her hands together, not sure whether she should do anything.

"He just needs space," Jesse said.

She held up a plate of food. "Come, eat."

They sat side by side at the table, neither of them eating much as it drizzled. The house seemed empty even with both of them there. She kept looking down the hallway, expecting Lynne to appear.

When she felt the tears coming, she collected their plates and cleaned up the kitchen. All too soon, there was nothing left to do. Jesse had taken up his stance in front of the window again. She glanced at her phone and saw her messages piling up. She couldn't read the condolences. She had to conserve as much energy as possible for the funeral.

"Want to go for a drive?" he asked.

"Yes." She couldn't stay in this house that felt like an empty tomb. "Let me get my purse."

Dad took her car, which left the SUV. Jesse slid behind the driver's seat. The rain stopped as they left the house. The cloud cover gave them a break from the insufferable heat. She rested her head against the glass and tried to control her roiling emotions. Lynne was in a better place. That's all that mattered, right? She sighed heavily. Just because Lynne was no longer suffering didn't mean they wouldn't. What if Dad couldn't pull out of this? What would he do now that he didn't have Lynne to take care of? What was he going to do with the rest of his life now that he no longer had a partner by his side?

She rolled down the window as Jesse sped down the highway. Her hair was going to be a tangled mess, but she had a backup of everything in her purse and really... nothing mattered anymore. Not her bills, not what her future held, or what people thought. All that mattered was the here and now. Life was so fucking short.

When he turned off the highway, she whipped her head around. "Jesse?"

"I need a moment."

"But..." Her voice died when she noticed he was sweating profusely, and his chest was moving rapidly beneath his shirt. "Are you okay?"

"I can't breathe."

He screeched to a stop in a small park, which was deserted this early in the morning. Before he put the car in park, he had his door open. He strode away, yanking on his tie. He stopped beneath a tree and braced his hand on the trunk as he bent over. She watched him for a moment before she slipped from the car and walked across the wet grass. She pressed against his back and wrapped her arms around him.

"I'm sorry," she whispered.

She held on tight as his body shook from the force of his grief. It was hard dealing with her own emotions but listening to him struggle to contain his sorrow hurt even more. She wasn't sure how long they stayed there, but she looked up when she felt the first fat drops of oncoming rain.

"Jesse, we have to get back in the car."

She stepped around to his front and saw that he was wearing the same glazed expression Dad had. She slipped an arm around his waist and led him back to the car. She pushed him into the passenger's seat before she ran around to the driver's side just as the heavens opened, and it began to pour. Jesse sat with his head tilted back and his eyes closed. He had undone the top buttons of his shirt, baring his throat. His tie hung loose around his neck.

When she reached for the keys, he grabbed her wrist. "Not yet."

"But..."

"Give me a minute."

She glanced at the clock and saw they had over an hour to kill. Rain tapped the windshield in an odd pattern. She was thankful for the rain guards, so she could crack the windows for air. She glanced at Jesse. A muscle flexed in his jaw as he fought to control his emotions. Even as she watched him, a tear slipped out of the corner of his eye.

Her heart clenched. "Jesse."

"I knew when I came home it would end like this," he said hoarsely. "I knew what to expect, but still..."

She stroked his cheek. "I know. I'm so sorry."

He leaned into her touch before he pressed his lips to her palm. "I wish I knew how much time we had left, so I knew how to live."

"What do you mean?"

His looked at her, revealing bloodshot blue orbs swirling with emotions too complex to define. Her eyes flooded with tears as she stared at him. He was in agony, and she couldn't stand it.

"You're gonna get through this," she said as the rain fell more heavily, hitting the roof of the car with significant force.

"Am I?" he asked as a tear slid down his cheek.

"You're the strongest man I know."

His damp eyes lit with an unholy light.

"I need you."

His voice was rough, almost angry.

"I'm here," she said unsteadily, unsure what he was asking for.

"I need you." His voice vibrated with meaning.

She felt a thunderbolt of panic. "I can't."

"Please."

He carried her hand to his crotch, which was tented. He forced her fingers to close around his cock.

"You can make it all go away. Help me."

Her mouth went dry. "Jesse."

"I need you so much I can't breathe," he said through clenched teeth.

She looked at the windshield, which had turned into a mini waterfall from the downpour, and then back at Jesse. Sweat dotted his forehead and chest. He was breathing heavily, as if he was wounded and couldn't breathe past the pain. She knew how he felt.

When her fingers moved to his zipper, he moved his hands away, so she could do what she needed to. She didn't let herself think. She leaned over the console as she pulled him out of his slacks. Her tongue swirled around his tip before she closed her mouth over him. His groan was loud enough to be heard over the rain and the distant crack of thunder. He stroked her hair as she worked him.

When he cursed, she lifted her head. "Jesse?"

His thumb moved over her wet lips. "I need more."

"What?"

He had the same lust-crazed expression he'd worn when she picked him up from the airport.

"I need your pussy. I need your arms around me, your legs squeezing me so tight I can't breathe. I need it all," he said as he gripped his dick and squeezed.

"But—"

He pressed his lips against hers. "Don't fight me," he pleaded as he kissed the corner of her mouth and then her cheek, ear, and chin. "Please, give me this. I'm not going to survive if—"

"Shh," she soothed and pushed against his chest. "Let me go in the back."

For a moment, he froze, and then he whispered a fervent, "Thank you."

She climbed over the console into the back. Most of the seats were still folded to accommodate their luggage when they came back from Florida. As she pulled her shirt over her head, Jesse awkwardly shimmied his way between the narrow opening and crawled toward her.

"Let me—" she began, but she didn't get to finish.

He swung her to the ground, lifted her skirt, and thrust inside her. She screamed, but the sound was cut off when his mouth crashed onto hers. He ground into her, sinking so deep, she fought back. He yanked on her hair and devoured her mouth savagely as he pumped feverishly until he climaxed. He threw back his head and roared, pounding his fist into the ground until he collapsed on top of her.

She swallowed hard as she stared up at the familiar car ceiling. Thunder rolled overhead while the rain came down in sheets, obliterating her vision of the forest around them and turned the trees into obscure, watercolor paintings.

Jesse groaned. "I'm sorry."

"Do you feel better?"

He shifted his head, so he could kiss her cheek. "No."

Her hand slid into his sweaty hair. "I'm sorry."

When he shifted his hips, she sucked in a breath.

"I don't think I can feel okay today, but now I can breathe," he said against her ear. "Thank you."

"We should—"

He grabbed her face and turned it toward him. His lips covered hers and when she opened her mouth to protest, his tongue interrupted. Thoughts of the funeral slipped away as he paid homage—sucking on her nipples until she sobbed and fucking her so slowly that she almost ripped his shirt as she urged him on. No matter what demands she made or what she did to him, he kept his pace slow, almost reverent, and nudged her into a climax that made her shudder as if she were having a seizure.

He brushed back her tangled hair. "I love you."

She tensed beneath him.

"I'll keep saying it until you believe me," he said.

"We should go."

He made no move to get off her. On the contrary, he began to rock against her. He was hard again and clearly not going anywhere until he came. His eyes searched hers with such naked emotion that she looked away. He pressed his lips against her cheek.

"You can't hide from me, Violet."

"Hurry, we have to go!" she snapped.

He ground her against the hard floor. She punched his shoulder.

"Jesse!"

"You can choose a different path for us. You can forgive me and love me, but you reject me instead. Anything you ask of me, I'd give. You're all I want."

"I can't do this!"

"You have to," he hissed before he lifted her thighs and stabbed as deep as he could and spilled in her womb.

He pressed his forehead against hers as he tried to catch his breath.

"You know what hurts worse than laying my mother to rest today?"

Her breath stalled.

"Knowing that the one person I love more than her is still here and doesn't want to be with me."

He pressed a gentle kiss to her lips before he rolled off her. Violet lay there for a full minute as she tried to manage the pain. Minutes passed. She listened to the sound of his harsh breathing steady before she reached for her bag filled with everything she needed to make herself presentable again.

She felt his eyes on her as she redid her makeup, smoothed her hair, and cleaned herself with baby wipes and a pack of Kleenex. She didn't meet his eyes as she tended to him as well, brushing back his tangled hair and wiping away smears of lipstick.

When she tried to move away, he grabbed hold of her. "You can't forgive me?"

"We need to go," she said in a monotone.

"Violet."

She turned her face away as her eyes burned with tears. "I can't do this today, Jesse."

When she pushed, his hand dropped away. She nabbed her shirt as she crawled back into the passenger seat and slipped it on. Jesse followed and retook his spot behind the wheel. She closed her eyes as he left the park and headed to church. The short drive seemed to take an eternity. When they pulled up, she saw several cars in front, including her Jeep.

Jesse reached for his jacket and shrugged it on before he grabbed an umbrella and came around to her side. She gripped his arm as her heels sank into the soggy grass.

They walked into the church and were greeted by the funeral organizers and close friends who had arrived early to see if they could help with anything. She made small talk for a few minutes before she walked over to her father, who stood in front of the stage. There was a riot of flowers everywhere, along with a photo of mom and a collage of images from her life.

"Hey," she said.

Dad didn't acknowledge her. She wrapped an arm around his waist and squeezed.

"Dad?"

He pulled away and walked out the back of the church. Her heart thudded in her ears as he stood on the small landing, hands clasped behind his back as he stared out at the rain.

A hand squeezed her shoulder. "Don't take it personally," Pastor Sonny said.

She brushed away a tear and tried to cover up her hurt with a smile. "Right."

"He's grieving. Everyone reacts differently. I'm working with him." Pastor Sonny chucked her under the chin, something he used to do when she was a little girl. "It's good to see you, Violet. Jesse, too. I hope to see you in church in the future."

She made a noncommittal noise. As someone called his name and he moved away, she knew there was no way in hell she would step foot in this building again unless there was a wedding or funeral. She looked down the aisle and saw Jesse watching her from the opposite end. She turned away and tried to rein in her emotions. She wanted to be anywhere but here.

Too soon, people began to arrive. She and Jesse took their posts near the stage to greet everyone and accept condolences. She was very aware of her father's absence. Some of his friends went to talk to him, but no one could bring him inside. She glanced at Jesse. The tears and vulnerability he displayed earlier had disappeared. She had never felt so alone.

Pastor Sonny managed to coax Dad inside for the service. She sat between Dad and Jesse in the front row and stared straight ahead with her hands fisted on her lap. The service was mercifully short. She could barely hear the pastor over the sound of thunder cracking overhead. Neither she nor Dad got up to speak, but Jesse did. He quoted one of Lynne's favorite scriptures and spoke fondly of the woman who had made him into the man he was today. He made everyone laugh through the tears.

When the service was over, she turned to Dad. "Can I ride with you to the wake?"

He walked away as if he hadn't heard her. She watched as he strode through the rain, slid into her Jeep, and drove off without saying a word to anyone. Several people cast her sympathetic looks and patted her on the back.

"Let's go," Jesse said.

Neither of them said a word during the drive to Lynne's friend's house. The wake wasn't as bad as she thought it was going to be. It was relaxed and casual. They ate and lounged around while telling stories about Lynne. Everyone wanted to know what her plans were now that she had moved back. She had no answers and said she was going to take it a day at a time.

Dad showed his face at the wake only long enough not to be rude before he disappeared again. Jesse followed him outside and leaned on his window and spoke to him before he came back inside. When she caught his eye, he shrugged, indicating he wasn't worried.

When they pulled up to the house that evening, the Jeep was missing. She rubbed her aching temples.

"Should I call him?" she asked Jesse in a voice hoarse from crying.

"He'll be fine. He just needs to be alone."

She walked into the house and looked up at Jesse. His face was pale and drawn.

"Are you going to be okay?"

Moody eyes moved over her. "Eventually."

The darkness threatening to erupt from him made her stomach flutter. She stepped back and made her way to her bedroom. She locked her doors before she fell face first on the bed and bawled her eyes out.

CHAPTER 15

She stared at the mess she had made of her room and threw her hands in the air. It had been three days since the funeral. To keep herself busy, she unpacked, which had turned her room into a disaster area. Without Reese's organizing skills, she had somehow barricaded her closet and bathroom door shut and couldn't even make it to the bed without stepping over piles of crap. There were boxes everywhere and belongings she had no place for. She kicked a pile of clothes before she walked out. She felt as if she was coming out of her skin.

She peeked in her parent's bedroom even though she knew what she would find. Dad wasn't there, of course. He left every morning before she and Jesse woke and didn't come home until they were asleep. She was alarmed, but Jesse wasn't, so she wouldn't call for an intervention just yet. She knew losing Lynne would devastate her father and had been prepared for many things, but his flat refusal to communicate and his icy coldness wasn't one of them. She moved home to be here for him during this time, and he deserted her. She felt as if she lost both parents. She thought they would deal with this together, but Dad made it clear he wanted to be alone, leaving her with no one to turn to.

She glanced into Jesse's bedroom, which was also empty. She felt a spark of relief when she found him sitting on the couch in the living room. He sat with his hands folded in his lap, eyes closed, and head tipped back. She knew he wasn't sleeping. He was trying to escape in his head, but it wasn't working. Grief radiated from him. If Dad was here, she could focus on him, but he wasn't, so Jesse would have to do. Against her better judgment, she started forward.

"Can I get you anything?" she asked.

He opened bloodshot eyes and stared at her for a beat before he shook his head. He said little since the funeral, but he was always around. She had a feeling if she wasn't here, he would be out of the house like Dad. If she had any close friends here, she might be with them, but she hadn't reconnected with anyone enough to barf her feelings on them. So, she was stuck in the house with pent-up energy and her emotions tearing her in every direction.

She settled on the opposite end of the couch and stared blindly at the blank TV. She felt so damn lost. Crying didn't help. Keeping busy didn't work either. She slept little in the past few days and couldn't remember the last thing she ate. She wished Dad would stop avoiding her. She needed him more than ever.

"Violet."

She whipped her head toward Jesse and saw he was watching her. He lifted his arm in an unspoken invitation. She didn't hesitate. She dove at him, burying her face in his chest, and burst into tears. She cried so hard; she couldn't catch her breath. His arms came around her, giving her the hug she craved, the comfort she felt she would perish without.

"Shh, it's okay," he said as he stroked her hair.

"I m-miss her s-so much," she stammered.

"I know. Me too."

"I-I don't know what to do, and Dad... I don't know how to help him."

"Let him be, Vi."

"But he shouldn't—"

"He'll work it out on his own."

She sniffled. "How do you know?"

"Because I'm a man."

"So?"

"Men react to pain in two ways. We run or we fight. Don't get in his face. You won't like the reaction you get. Let him deal with it on his own."

"But you're here," she pointed out.

"I'm here in case you want to fight," he said.

Her lip curved in a sad smile before her face crumpled. She slumped against him. She should keep her guard up, but she needed touch more than anything in the world. She didn't know how to feel about Jesse. At times, he was her adversary, ally, lover, worst enemy, and protector. Currently, he was offering her a safe place, so she would take what he was willing to give. She didn't want to be alone right now.

She rested her cheek against his chest and listened to his steady heartbeat. Her mind swung from her worries about Dad and Jesse to seeking employment to changing her car registration and everything in between. She was spiraling. She had so many things to do, but she couldn't choose which task to do first, so she did nothing.

Jesse stroked her back. "I have to leave soon."

Panic ripped through her. She looked up, unaware her hand twisted in his shirt. "Leave?"

"I have to report for duty in Japan. I've already made my flights."

She felt as if she was going to shatter. "When?"

"I have a little over a week left here."

She leapt to her feet and faced him with her hands fisted at her sides. "You're only telling me this now?"

"You knew I'd have to leave."

"Not so soon!" she shouted and stomped her foot. "You can't go. You owe me!"

"I do?"

"Yes, you do!" she bellowed as she paced in a circle. "You changed me and then waltzed out of my life to play the honorable soldier serving his country and left me in shambles."

"You wanted me to leave."

"And now I'm telling you to stay, so what are you going to do?" she challenged.

He shook his head. "I have orders."

"Screw your orders! I need you!" She flung her arms wide. "I can't do this by myself!"

"You'll get through it."

"Don't go!"

His brows drew together. "Violet."

"You can't leave me like this!"

He grabbed her hand and drew her between his thighs. "You know I'd do almost anything for you, but I can't."

"But..." Tears slipped down her cheeks. "I'm going to be all alone."

He tugged her onto his lap, so she was straddling him. "I'll come back."

She shook her head. "You won't."

He clasped her face and brushed away her tears with his thumb. "Are you going to keep the promise you made me on the beach?"

Promise you won't cut me out of your life again.

She nodded.

"Then I'll be back." He gave her a bittersweet smile as he stroked her cheek. "Even though I want to rip my heart out because it hurts so much, just looking at you makes me feel better. You've always been my morphine."

He tipped her against him, so he could rest his face in the hollow of her throat. He let out a long breath as his hands ran up her sides. Slowly, he relaxed, as if her proximity calmed him.

"You and Isaac are all I have left," he said hoarsely. "I need you in my life."

"I'm not going anywhere," she said as she wrapped her arms around him.

"Fuck, Violet, I'm desperate for you."

She couldn't resist the forlorn plea in his tone. She grabbed a handful of his hair and yanked, so his head tipped up. She planted her lips on his and sank deep. Lust swiped its claws across her belly. She answered the call. The same madness that came over her on the beach welled up inside of her again. She wasn't concerned about right or wrong. All she cared about was numbing the pain.

She kept her mouth on his as she shifted back so she could reach down and grip him through his silky basketball shorts. He made a wheezing sound and gripped her hip as she stroked. She wanted to make him feel good and forget what they had lost and was still trickling through their fingers. His mouth hardened beneath hers. She shifted back on his iron thighs to pull him out of his shorts.

"Violet," he panted.

She slipped off his lap to whip her shirt over her head and shuck her jeans. He pumped his hand on his cock as he watched her. When she was naked, she resumed her position on his lap and held him so she could impale herself on him.

Veins stood out on his neck as he gritted, "You're killing me."

The delicious stretch of being invaded is just what she needed. She was barely wet enough to take him, so she rocked until he was balls deep in her. She needed this more than she needed to eat, more than she needed to breathe. This would make everything better and chase away her doubts and fear. Nothing mattered but this.

She clutched the back of the couch as she moved on him. She rode him the way she had always wanted to. Greedy, forceful, rough —the way she couldn't be with other men. He was her willing slave. The way he stared at her spurred her on.

"Take me," he groaned and dropped his head back and swore. "Who the fuck taught you that?"

"You," she panted in his ear and nipped.

He gripped her hair and twisted to keep her still for biting kisses. "Love me."

He began to move with her, thrusting up as she bore down.

"You want me, Violet?"

She moved faster, plastering her bare chest against his shirt as she raced to the finish line. "Give me what I need!"

"Ask nicely."

"Fuck you! You owe me!"

"I'll give you whatever you want if you tell me what I want to hear."

She glared at him. "Never."

He smiled and slammed up, nearly unseating her. "We'll see about that."

"What the hell is going on here?"

Her father's voice cut through the passionate haze more effectively than if God himself had materialized in their living room. They froze. All that beautiful lust vanished in a nanosecond. Her mind went blank with horror. Her father couldn't be here while she was naked as the day she was born, and Jesse was inside her. This had to be a nightmare.

Jesse's gaze was fixed over her shoulder. He had a strange look on his face. She couldn't move without revealing more than she already was. She was forced to stay impaled on Jesse's lap with her back to her father.

"How long has this been going on?" Dad asked.

She began to shake. Jesse reached for a quilt draped over the back of the couch and swung it around her to cover her body.

"I asked you two a question."

Oh, God. She took the coward's way out and buried her face in Jesse's shoulder. He kissed her temple and shifted her as he sat upright. He didn't seem perturbed that Dad just caught them mid-fuck. How was he still hard and pulsing inside of her?

"We've been doing this since we were in high school," Jesse said.

She jerked and would have raised her head, but the grip on her nape kept her face tucked against him. What the hell was he *doing*? He was telling the truth? Her father would kill him!

"High school."

Her father's flat tone made her shudder.

"Yes, sir," Jesse said.

"Why did you hide it?"

"We didn't think you'd approve."

Again, she tried to straighten, but Jesse kept her pinned against him.

"And you think this is better? Sneaking around all this time?"

"It's the only thing we could do," Jesse said.

"Why has she been avoiding you all these years?"

"She was mad I enlisted in the military."

This time, she managed to break his hold. She straightened and braced her hands on his chest. Her throat was bone dry, but she couldn't let him tell these lies. Jesse stared at her, as calm as could be. What the hell was wrong with him?

"Is this true, Vi?" Dad asked.

She stared at Jesse, silently willing him to tell the truth.

Jesse cupped her cheek. "Answer him, baby."

Baby? She wasn't his baby. Why was he acting like they dated? They didn't date, they just had sex—a *lot* of it.

Jesse's eyes went over her shoulder. "She's in shock. We never wanted you to find out like this."

"Did you ever want me to find out?"

Dad's disapproval was like imaginary smoke, cloying the air and making it hard to breathe.

"I wanted to tell you, but Violet didn't feel the same way."

"You're gonna do right by my daughter," Dad said.

As his words penetrated, she shoved off Jesse and fell on her ass. She clasped the quilt to her chest as she turned to find her father walking toward the front door.

"Dad!"

He turned his head as she got to her feet and immediately averted his gaze.

"This isn't what it seems," she said desperately.

Jesse gripped her shoulder. She shrugged him off and took a step toward her father, who refocused on her. His eyes were dull and lifeless. She wasn't sure if it was from grief or shock. All she knew was he had never looked at her like that before.

"I raised you better," he whispered.

She felt as if he plunged a knife in her stomach. She hunched over as pain seared her insides. She reached for him in supplication, her need to wipe that look from his face paramount, but he took a step back and shook his head.

"I can't look at you right now."

"Let me explain..."

"I won't let you become your mother," he said, voice shaking with emotion. "I don't believe in sex before marriage and since you two have been carrying on since high school, you're going to make this right. You two made your bed. Now you're going to lie in it."

"But Dad—"

He walked through the front door. When she tried to go after him, Jesse wrapped his arms around her. When she opened her mouth to call out to him, Jesse clamped a hand over her lips. She caught a glimpse of her dad walking to the SUV parked in the driveway. Why hadn't he parked in the garage? If he had, they would have had time to disengage and avoid this disaster.

Even as she struggled to comprehend what happened, Jesse lifted her off her feet. He ignored her muffled scream and carried her down the hall to his room and tossed her on the bed. He pounced on her before she could roll away and pinned her arms over her head as she raged.

"I hate you!" she shouted as tears streamed down her face.

"Did you hear what he said?"

"You screwed up everything!"

He released her wrist to cup her cheek. "It's done, baby."

She slammed her fist into his chest. "It's *not* done! He can't order me to do anything! This is a free country!"

"He wants what's best for you."

"You aren't what's best for me! You're a nightmare!"

"A nightmare you crave. Do you want to get disowned?"

She bared her teeth. "I'm not marrying you!"

"Dad just gave us his blessing."

"Because he thinks I'm a whore! He—he thinks I'm like my mother..." She turned her face to the side as she let out a sob.

"It's gonna be okay."

"It'll never be okay. I haven't been okay since you. You ruined me!"

He sat up and whipped off his shirt. When she tried to get away, he sat on her stomach and hooked his thumb in the waistband of his shorts.

"You think I'm going to let you touch me? You're out of your mind!" she shrieked as she clawed his thighs.

"I'm going to do more than touch you," he promised as he yanked his shorts off and made a space for himself between her thighs. He closed his eyes as he slid inside her, deaf to her struggles and verbal abuse. He moaned as he pressed his forehead against hers.

"I love you, Violet."

"You lied to him!" she wailed.

"I told him my truth." He stroked her cheek. "The truth you refuse to accept. You didn't want me not to leave. Now you can come with me."

"*What?*"

"We can see the world. I'll give you whatever you want."

"This will never work," she moaned.

"It will. It *is*. Don't you feel it?"

"I'm not talking about sex!" she shouted.

"Sex is how our souls speak to one another," he crooned. "No one will take better care of you than me."

She stared at him as he braced himself over her. He was flushed with desire, eyes sparkling with excitement as he ground against her. She bared her teeth and sank her nails into his back. He grinned as she drew blood.

"You want to punish me, baby?" he breathed. "Do your worst. I can take it. I can take anything now that I have you."

"I hate you!"

"I love you," he said fervently as he covered her face with kisses. "I always have. I can make you happy. We can start fresh. I'll take care of everything."

"I can't," she began and hissed when he planted himself deep.

"You will," he countered. "Dad won't let you stay here, not when he knows we've been having an affair since we were teenagers."

"I didn't..." she began hotly but was interrupted when he flipped her onto her front and slammed into her from behind. She screamed into his sheets.

"I can fuck you into forgetting that you hate me," he panted in her hair. "Whoever you need me to be, I'll be. Say you'll have me."

She buried her face in the mattress as he fucked her, balls smacking her ass as he thrust. Her body was buzzing. Ecstasy was within her grasp. A hand gripped her throat and squeezed.

"Say yes," he hissed.

She clenched her teeth as pleasure nipped at her heels.

"Fucking say it!" he roared.

"Yes," she gasped as her climax ripped through her. She moaned like a bitch in heat and screamed his name as he fucked her raw.

When she lay exhausted and limp beneath him, he brushed her hair away from her face and rested his cheek against hers.

"You won't regret this," he vowed.

AUTHOR'S NOTE

Thank you for giving this story a chance! I wrote a bonus scene of Jesse's arrival in Austin from his point of view. To read it, join my newsletter: https://www.subscribepage.com/CIbonus.

I do intend to write a sequel, but I am currently under contract for several projects as dark romance author, Mia Knight. When I have a block of time to continue the *Possessing Violet Series*, I will update my blog and social media! I'm not sure if Violet and Jesse will have one or two more books. I have some wild ideas for the continuation. We'll see how many installments it takes to wrap up their story.

You can sign up to my newsletter to stay informed about future releases. If you can, please leave a review, they help me out so much!

Sincerely,

Dinah

BOOKS BY DINAH HARPER

Possessing Violet Series:

Corrupt Obsession

Corrupt Idol

About the Author

Dinah Harper will have you squirming in your seat and looking around to make sure no one can see what you're reading. The *Possessing Violet Series* is the first of many erotic novels she has planned.

Please be patient. She is currently under contract for several projects as dark romance author, Mia Knight. When she resumes her work as Dinah Harper, she will update her blog and social media. Sign up to her newsletter (https://www.subscribepage.com/DinahHarperNews) to stay informed about future releases!

Website: https://dinahharper.com

instagram.com/authordinahharper

bookbub.com/authors/dinah-harper

goodreads.com/dinahharper

reamstories.com/miaknightwrites